THE TRAP IS SPRUNG!

As crossbow bolts flew, bringing agony and death to those around her, Talia struggled to her feet and staggered toward the stable area, trying to shut her shields down and the pain out. It seemed like an eternity between each stumbling step—yet she had hardly taken half a dozen when she heard the pounding of hooves on stone and saw a white form surging toward her.

It was Rolan—unsaddled. Hard on his heels came Tantris carrying Kris. As Companion and rider passed her, Talia leaped and Kris pulled her up in front of him. And now there was one last obstacle between them and freedom—the narrow passage between the inner and outer walls that led to the portcullis and the outer gate.

They galloped straight into a hail of arrows. Fire lanced through Talia's shoulder—just as Tantris screamed in agony, shuddered, and crashed to the ground. Talia was thrown forward, and hit the ground, stunned. But as Rolan paused in his headlong flight, Talia screamed to him with voice, heart, and mind: "Rolan—run!" For even as she felt herself drowning in an agony of pain, a single thought remained clear, *one* of them must escape—or Valdemar was lost. . . .

ARROW'S FALL

Mercedes Lackey

DAW BOOKS, INC.
DONALD A. WOLLHEIM, PUBLISHER

1633 Broadway, New York, NY 10019

DAW Book Collectors No. 732.

First Printing, January 1988

1 2 3 4 5 6 7 8 9

PRINTED IN THE U.S.A.

Dedicated to:
Andre Norton
for inspiration;
Teri Lee
for early encouragement;
     and
my husband Tony
for being understanding
about my ongoing affair
with a word processor.

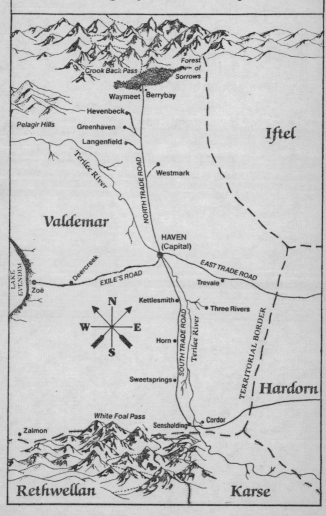

The Kingdom of Valdemar
(Reign of Queen Selenay)

Crook Back Pass

Forest of Sorrows

Waymeet · Berrybay

Hevenbeck

Pelagir Hills

Greenhaven

Langenfield

Iftel

Terilee River

Westmark

Valdemar

HAVEN
(Capital)

EAST TRADE ROAD

LAKE EVENDIM

Deercreek

EXILE'S ROAD

Trevale

Zoë

Kettlesmith

Three Rivers

N
W · E
S

Horn

Terilee River

SOUTH TRADE ROAD

TERRITORIAL BORDER

Sweetsprings

Hardorn

White Foal Pass

Zalmon

Sensholding

Cordor

Rethwellan

Karse

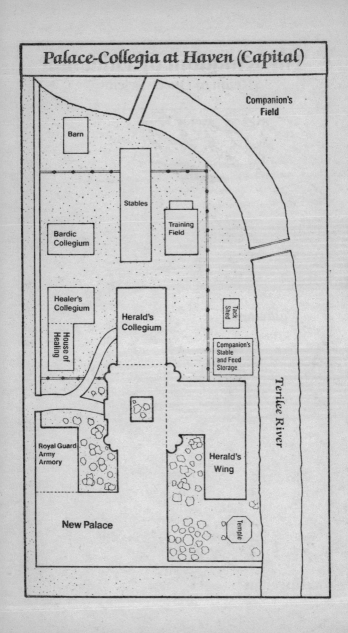

Palace-Collegia at Haven (Capital)

Companion's Field

Barn

Stables

Training Field

Bardic Collegium

Healer's Collegium

House of Healing

Herald's Collegium

Tack Shed

Companion's Stable and Feed Storage

Terilee River

Royal Guard Army Armory

Herald's Wing

Temple

New Palace

Prologue

Long ago—so long ago that the details of the conflict are lost and only the merest legends remain—the world of Velgarth was wracked by sorcerous wars. With the population decimated, the land was turned to wasteland and given over to the forest and the magically-engendered creatures those peoples had used to fight those wars, while the people that remained fled to the eastern coastline, for only in those wilderness areas could they hope to resume their shattered lives. In time, it was the eastern edge of the continent that became the site of civilization, and the heartland that in turn became the wilderness.

But humans are resilient creatures, and it was not overlong before the population once again was on the increase, moving westward, building new kingdoms out of the wilds.

One such kingdom was Valdemar. It had been founded by the once-Baron Valdemar and those of his people who had chosen exile with him rather than face the wrath of a selfish and cruel monarch. It lay on the very western-and-northernmost edge of the civilized world, bounded on the north and northwest by wilderness that still contained uncanny creatures, and on the far west by Lake Evendim, an enormous inland sea. Travel beyond Valdemar was perilous and uncertain at the very best of times, and at the worst a traveler could bring weird retribution on innocents when the creatures he encountered back-trailed him to his point of origin.

In part due to the nature of its founders, the monarchs of Valdemar welcomed fugitives and fellow exiles, and the customs and habits of its people had over the years become a polyglot patchwork. In point of fact, the one rule by which the monarchs of Valdemar governed their people was, "There *is* no 'one true way.' "

Governing such an ill-assorted lot of subjects might have been impossible—had it not been for the Heralds of Valdemar.

The Heralds had extraordinary powers, yet never abused those powers; and the reason for their forbearance—in fact for the whole system—was the existence of creatures known as "Companions."

To one who knew no better, a Companion would seem little more than an extraordinarily graceful white horse. They were *far* more than that. The first Companions had been sent by some unknown power or powers at the pleading of King Valdemar himself—three of them, at first, who had made bonds with the King, his Heir, and his most trusted friend, who was the Kingdom Herald. So it came to be that the Heralds took on a new importance in Valdemar, and a new role.

It was the Companions who chose new Heralds, forging between themselves and their Chosen a mind-to-mind bond that only death could sever. While no one knew precisely *how* intelligent they were, it was generally agreed that their capabilities were at least as high as those of their human partners. Companions could (and did) Choose irrespective of age and sex, although they tended to Choose youngsters just entering adolescence, and more boys were Chosen than girls. The one common trait among the Chosen (other than a specific personality type: patient, unselfish, responsible, and capable of heroic devotion to duty) was at least a trace of psychic ability. Contact with a Companion and continued development of the bond enhanced whatever latent paranormal capabilities lay within the Chosen. With time, as these Gifts became better understood, ways were developed to train and use them to the fullest extent of which the individual was capable. Gradually the Gifts displaced in importance whatever knowledge of "true magic" was left in Valdemar, until there was no record of how such magic had ever been learned or used.

Valdemar himself evolved the unique system of government for his land: the Monarch, advised by his Council, made the laws; the Heralds dispensed the laws and saw that they were observed. The Heralds themselves were nearly incapable of becoming corrupted or potential abusers of their temporal power. In all of the history of Valdemar, there was only one Herald who had ever succumbed to that temptation. His motive had been vengeance—he got what he wanted, but his Companion repudiated and abandoned him, and he committed suicide shortly thereafter.

The Chosen were by nature remarkably self-sacrificing—their training only reinforced this. They had to be—there was a better than even chance that a Herald would die in the line of duty. But they were human for all of that; mostly young, mostly living on the edge of danger—so, it was inevitable that outside of their duty they tended to be a bit hedonistic and anything but chaste. They seldom formed any ties beyond that of their brotherhood and the pleasures of the moment—perhaps because the bond of brotherhood was so *very* strong, and because the Herald-Companion bond left little room for any other permanent ties. For the most part, few of the common or noble folk held this against them—knowing that, no matter how wanton a Herald might be on leave, the moment he donned his snowy uniform he was another creature altogether, for a Herald in Whites was a Herald on duty, and a Herald on duty had no time for anything outside of that duty, least of all the frivolity of his own pleasures. Still, there were those who held other opinions. . . .

Laws laid down by the first King decreed that the Monarch himself must also be a Herald. This ensured that the ruler of Valdemar could never be the kind of tyrant who had caused the founders to flee their own homes.

Second in importance to the Monarch was the Herald known as the "King's (or Queen's) Own." Chosen by a special Companion—one that was always a stallion, and never seemed to age (though it was possible to kill him) —the King's Own held the special position of confidant and most trusted friend and advisor to the ruler. This

guaranteed that the Monarchs of Valdemar would always
have at least one person about them who could be trusted
and counted on at all times. This tended to make for
stable and confident rulers—and thus, a stable and de-
pendable government.

It seemed for generations that King Valdemar had
planned his government perfectly. But the best-laid plans
can still be circumvented by accident or chance.

In the reign of King Sendar, the kingdom of Karse
(that bordered Valdemar to the south-east) hired a no-
madic nation of mercenaries to attack Valdemar. In the
ensuing war, Sendar was killed, and his daughter, Selenay,
assumed the throne, herself having only recently completed her Herald's training. The Queen's Own, an aged
Herald called Talamir, was frequently confused and embarrassed by having to advise a young, headstrong, and
attractive female. As a result, Selenay made an ill-advised
marriage, one that nearly cost her both her throne and
her life.

The issue of that marriage, the Heir-presumptive, was
a female child Selenay called Elspeth. Elspeth came under the influence of a foreigner—the nurse Hulda, whom
Selenay's husband had arranged before he died to be
brought from his own land. As a result of Hulda's manip-
ulations, Elspeth became an intractable, spoiled brat. It
became obvious that if things went on as they were
tending, the girl would never be Chosen, and thus, could
never inherit. This would leave Selenay with three choices;
marry again (with the attendant risks) and attempt to
produce another, more suitable Heir, or declare someone already Chosen and with the proper bloodline to be
Heir. Or, somehow, salvage the Heir-presumptive. Talamir
had a plan—one that it seemed had a good chance of
success.

At this point Talamir was murdered, throwing the
situation into confusion again. His Companion, Rolan,
Chose a new Queen's Own—but instead of picking an
adult or someone already a full Herald, he Chose an
adolescent girl named Talia.

Talia was of Holderkin—a puritanical Border group
which did its best to discourage knowledge of outsiders.

Talia had no idea what it meant to have a Herald's Companion accost her, and then (apparently) carry her off. Among her people, females held very subordinate positions, and nonconformity was punished immediately and harshly. She was ill-prepared for the new world of the Heralds and their Collegium that she had been thrust into. But the one thing she *did* have experience in was the handling and schooling of children, for she had been the teacher to her Holding's younger members from the time she was nine.

She managed to salvage the Brat—and succeeded well enough that Elspeth was Chosen herself just before Talia was sent out on her internship assignment.

During that assignment she and Kris, the Herald picked to be her mentor, discovered something frightening and potentially fatal—not only to themselves, but to anyone who happened to be around Talia. Due to the chaos just after her initial training in her Gift, she had never *been* properly trained. And her Gift was Empathy—both receptive and projective—strong enough to use as a weapon. It wasn't until it had run completely wild that she and Kris were able to retrain her so that her control became a matter of will instead of instinct.

She still had moments of misgiving about the ethics of her Gift.

She also had moments of misgiving on another subject altogether; another Herald. Dirk was Kris' best friend and partner—and Talia, after being with him only a handful of times, none intimate, was attracted to him to the point of obsession. There *was* a precedent for such preoccupation; very rarely, Heralds formed a bond with one another as deep and enduring as the Herald-Companion bond. Such a tie was referred to as a "lifebond." Kris was certain that this was what Talia was suffering from. Talia wasn't so sure.

This was just one minor complication for an internship that included battle, plague, intrigue, wildly spreading rumors about *her,* and a Gift that was a danger to herself and others.

At last the year-and-a-half was over, and she was on her way home.

Home—to an uncertain relationship, a touchy adolescent Heir, all the intrigues of the Court—and possibly, an enemy; Lord Orthallen, who just happened to be Kris' uncle.

One

We could be brother and sister, Kris thought, glancing over at his fellow Herald. *Maybe twins—*

Talia sat Rolan with careless ease—an ease brought about by the fact that they'd spent most of their waking hours in the saddle during her internship up north. Kris' seat was just as casual, and for the same reason. After all this time they could easily have eaten, slept—yes, and possibly even made love a-saddle! The first two they *had* accomplished, and more than once. The third they'd never tried—but Kris had heard rumors of other Heralds who had. It did *not* sound like something he really was curious enough to attempt.

They figured on making the capital and the Collegium by early evening, so they were both wearing the cleanest and best of their uniforms. Heraldic Whites—those for field duty—were constructed of tough and durable leather, but after eighteen months they only had one set apiece that would pass muster, and they'd been saving them for today.

So we're presentable. Which isn't saying much, Kris mourned to himself, surveying the left knee of his breeches with regret. The surface of the leather was worn enough to be slightly nappy—which meant it was inclined to pick up dirt. And dirt *showed* on Whites—after riding all day they both were slightly gray. Maybe not to the casual eye, but *Kris* noticed.

Tantris curvetted a little, and Kris suddenly realized that he and Talia's Rolan were matching their paces.

:On purpose, two-footed brother,: came Tantris' sending, tinged with a hint of laughter. *:Since you two are so*

terribly shabby, we thought we'd take attention off you. Nobody's going to notice you when we're showing off:

:Thanks—I think.:

:By the way, you couldn't pass for twins; there's too much red in her hair, and she's too little. But sibs, yes. Although where you got those blue eyes—:

:Blue eyes run in my family,: Kris replied with feigned indignation. *:Both father and mother have them.:*

:Then if you were going to be sibs, your mother must have been keeping a Bard in the wardrobe for Talia to have hazel eyes and curly hair.: Tantris pranced and arched his neck, and one of his sapphirine eyes flashed a teasing look up at his Chosen.

Kris stole another glance at his internee, and concluded that Tantris was right. There *was* too much red in her hair, and it was too curly to have come out of the same batch as his own straight, blue-black locks. And she barely came up to his chin. But they both had fine-boned, vaguely heart-shaped faces—and more than that, they both *moved* the same way.

:Alberich's training. And Keren's.:

:Probably.:

:You're prettier than she is, though. The which you know.:

Kris was startled into a laugh, which made Talia glance over at him quizzically.

"Might one ask—?"

"Tantris," he replied, taking a deep breath of the verdant air, and chuckling. "He's twitting me on my vanity."

"I wish," she answered with more than a little wistfulness, "that just once I could Mindspeak Rolan like that."

"You ought to be glad you can't. You're saved a lot of back-talk."

"How far are we from home?"

"A little more than an hour." He took in the greening landscape with every sign of satisfaction, now and again taking deep breaths of the flower-laden air. "A silver for your thoughts."

"So much?" She chuckled, turning in her saddle to face him. "A copper would be more appropriate."

"Let me be the judge of that. After all, *I'm* the one who asked."

"So you did."

The rode in tree-shadowed silence for several leagues; Kris was minded to let her answer in her own time. The soft chime of bridle bells and their Companions' hooves on the hard surface of the Trade Road made a kind of music that was most soothing to listen to.

"Ethics," she said at last.

"Whoof—that's dry thinking!"

"I suppose it is—" She plainly let her thoughts turn inward again; her eyes grew vague, and he coughed to recapture her attention.

"You went elsewhere," he chided gently, when she jumped a little. "Now, you were saying—ethics. Ethics of what?"

"My Gift. Specifically, using it—"

"I thought you'd come to terms with that."

"In a situation of threat, yes. In a situation where there *was* no appropriate and just punishment under normal procedures."

"That—child-raper."

"Exactly." She shivered a little. "I thought I'd *never* feel clean again after touching his mind. But—what could I have done with him? Ordered his execution? That . . .wouldn't be *enough* of a punishment for what he did. Imprison him? Not appropriate at all. And much as I would have liked to pull him to bits slowly, Heralds don't go in for torture."

"What *did* you do to him? In detail, I mean. You didn't want to talk about it before."

"It was a—kind of twist on a mind-Healing technique; it depended on the fact that I'm a projective Empath. I can't remember what Devan called it, but you tie a specific thought to another thought or set of feelings that *you* construct. Then, every time the person thinks that thought, they also get what *you* want them to know. Like with Vostel—every time he would decide that *he* was to blame, he'd get what *I* put in there."

"Which was?"

She grinned. " 'So *next* time I won't be so stupid!' And when he'd be ready to give up from pain, he'd get, 'But it isn't as bad as yesterday, and it'll be better tomorrow.' Not words, actually; it was all feelings."

"Better, in that case, than words would have been," Kris mused, shooing a fly away absently.

"So Devan said. Well, I did something like that with—that *thing*. I took one of the worst sets of his stepdaughter's memories, and tied *that* in to all of his own feelings about women. And I kept point-of-view, so that it would appear to him as if he were the victim. You saw what happened."

Kris shuddered. "He went mad; he just collapsed, foaming at the mouth."

"No, he didn't go mad. He locked *himself* into an endless repetition of what I'd fed him. It's an appropriate punishment; he's getting exactly what he put his stepdaughters through. It's *just,* at least I think so, because if he ever changes his attitudes he can break free of it. Of course if he does—" she grimaced "—he *might* find himself dancing on the end of a rope for the murder of his older stepdaughter. The law prevents the execution of a madman; it *doesn't* save one who's regained his sanity. Lastly, what I did should satisfy his stepdaughter, who is, after all, the one we *really* want to come out of this thing with a whole soul."

"So where's the ethical problem?"

"That was a stress-situation, a threat-situation. But—is it ethical to—say—read people during Council sessions and act on my information?"

"Uh—" Kris was unable to think of an answer.

"You see?"

"Let's go at it from another angle. You know how to read people's faces and bodies—we've all been taught that. Would you hesitate to use that knowledge in Council?"

"Well, no." She rode silently for a few more moments. "I guess what will have to be the deciding factor is not *if* I do it but *how* I use the information."

"That sounds reasonable to me."

"Maybe too reasonable," she replied doubtfully. "It's awfully easy to rationalize what I want to do—what I have no choice about in some cases. It's not like thought-sensing; I have to actively shield to keep people out. They go around shoving their feelings up my nose on a regular basis, especially when they're wrought up."

Kris shook his head. "All I can say is, do what seems best at the time. Really, that's all any of us do."

:Verily, oh, Wise One.:

Kris ignored his Companion's taunting comment. He was going to question her further, but broke off when he caught the sound of a horse galloping full out, heading up the road toward them, the hoofbeats having the peculiar ringing of a Companion.

"That—"

"Sounds like a Companion, yes. And in full gallop." he rose in his stirrups for a better view. "Bright Lady, *now* what?"

Steed and rider came into sight as they topped the hill.

:That's Cymry—: Tantris' ears were pricked forward. *:She's slim. She must have foaled already.:*

"It's Cymry," Kris reported.

"Which means Skif—and since I'll bet she just foaled, it isn't a pleasure-ride that takes them out here."

The last time they'd seen the thief-turned-Herald had been a bit over nine months ago, when he'd met with them for their half-term briefing. Cymry had spent the time frolicking with Rolan, and both she and her Chosen had forgotten about the nearly-supernatural fertility of the Grove stallions. The result was foregone—much to Cymry's chagrin as well as Skif's.

Talia knew Skif better than Kris did; they'd been very close as students, close enough that they'd sworn blood-brotherhood. They had been close enough that Talia could read him better at a distance than Kris could.

She shaded her eyes with her hand, then nodded a little. "Well it isn't a disaster; there's something serious afoot, but it isn't an emergency."

"How can you tell at this distance?"

"Firstly, there's no emotional-surge. Secondly, if it were serious, he'd be absolutely expressionless. He looks a bit worried, but that could be for Cymry."

Skif spotted them and waved wildly, as Cymry slowed her headlong pace. They hastened theirs—to the disgruntlement of the pack-mules.

"Havens! Am I ever glad to see you two!" Skif exclaimed as they came into earshot. "Cymry swore you were close, but I was half-afraid I'd have to ride a couple of hours, and I hate to make her leave the little one for that long."

"You sound like you've been waiting for us—Skif, what's the problem?" Kris asked anxiously. "What are you doing out here?"

"Nothing for you; plenty for her. Mind you, this is strictly under the ivy bush; we don't want people to know you've been warned, Talia. I slipped out on behalf of a lady in distress."

"Who? Elspeth? Selenay? What—"

"Give me a minute, will you? I'm *trying* to tell you. Elspeth asked me to intercept you on your way in. It seems the Council is trying to marry her off, and she's not overly thrilled with the notion. She wants you to know so you'll have time to muster some good arguments for the Council meeting tomorrow."

Skif reined Cymry in beside them, and they picked up the pace. "Alessandar has made a formal offer for her for Ancar. Lots of advantages there. Virtually everybody on the Council is for it except Elcarth and Kyril—and Selenay. They've been arguing it back and forth for two months, but it's been serious for about a week, and it looks as if Selenay is gradually being worn down. That's why Elspeth sent me out to watch for you; I've been slipping out for the past three days, hoping to catch you when you came in and warn you what's up. With you to back her, Selenay's got full veto—either to table the betrothal until Elspeth's finished training, or throw the notion out altogether. Elspeth didn't want any of the more excitable Councillors to know we were warning you, or they might have put more pressure on Selenay to decide before you got here."

Talia sighed. "So nothing's been decided; good. I can deal with it easily enough. Can you get on ahead of us? Let Elspeth and Selenay both know we'll be there by dinner-bell? I can't do anything now, anyway, but tomorrow we can take care of the whole mess at Council session. If Elspeth wants to see me before then—I'm all hers; she'll probably find me in my rooms."

"Your wish is my command," Skif replied. As all three

knew, Skif knew more ways than one in and out of the capital and the Palace grounds. He'd make far better time than they could.

They held their pace to that of the mules as Skif sent Cymry off at a diagonal to the road, raising a cloud of dust behind him. They continued on as if they hadn't met him; but Kris traded a look of weary amusement with her. They weren't even officially "home" yet, and already the intrigues had begun.

"Anything else bothering you?"

"To put it bluntly," she said at last, "I'm nervous about coming back home—as nervy as a cat about to kitten."

"Whyfor? And why *now*? The worst is over. You're a full Herald—the last of your training's behind you. What's to be nervous about?"

Talia looked around her; at the fields, the distant hills, at anything but Kris. A warm spring breeze, loaded with flower-scent, teased her hair and blew a lock or two into her eyes so that she looked like a worried foal.

"I'm not sure I ought to discuss it with you," she said reluctantly.

"If not me, then who?"

She looked at him measuringly. "I don't know. . . ."

"No," Kris said, just a little hurt by her reluctance. "You know. You just aren't sure you can trust me. Even after all we've shared together."

She winced. "Disconcertingly accurate. I thought bluntness was *my* besetting sin."

Kris cast his eyes up to the heavens in an exaggerated plea for patience, squinting against the bright sunlight. "I am a Herald. You are a Herald. If there's one thing you should have learned by now, it's that you can *always* trust another Herald."

"Even when my suspicions conflict with ties of blood?"

He gave her another measuring look. "Such as?"

"Your uncle, Lord Orthallen."

He whistled through his teeth, and pursed his lips. "I thought you'd left that a year ago. Just because of that little run-in you had with him over Skif, you see him plotting conspiracy behind every bush! He's been very good to *me*, and to half a dozen others I could name you, and he's been invaluable to Selenay—as he was to her father."

"I have very good reasons to see him behind every bush!" she replied with some heat. "I think trying to get Skif in trouble was part of a long pattern, that it was just an attempt to isolate me—"

"Why? What could he possibly gain?" Kris was fed up and frustrated because this wasn't the first time he'd had to defend his uncle. More than one of his fellow Heralds had argued that Orthallen was far too power-hungry to be entirely trustworthy, and Kris had always felt honor-bound to defend him. He'd thought Talia had dismissed her suspicions as irrational months ago. He was highly annoyed to find that she hadn't.

"I don't know why—" Talia cried in frustration, clenching her fist on her reins. "I only know that I've never trusted him from the moment I first saw him. And now I'll be co-equal in Council with Kyril and Elcarth, with a full voice in decisions. That could put us in more direct conflict than we've ever been before."

Kris took three deep breaths and attempted to remain calm and rational. "Talia, you may not like him, but you've never had any problems in keeping your dislike out of the way of your decision-making that *I've* ever seen—and my uncle is very reasonable. . . ."

"But I can't read the man; I can't fathom his motives, and I can't imagine *why* he should feel antagonism toward me—but I *know* he does."

"I think you're overreacting," Kris replied, still keeping a tight rein on his temper. "I told you once before that it isn't *you* that's offended him—assuming that he really *is* offended—but because he's probably feeling like a defeated opponent. He expected to take Talamir's place as Selenay's closest advisor when Talamir was murdered."

"And cut out the role of Queen's Own?" Talia shook her head violently. "Havens, Kris; Orthallen is an intelligent man! He can't have imagined that was possible! He hasn't the Gift, for one thing. And I am *not* overreacting to him."

"Now, Talia—"

"Don't patronize me! You're the one who was telling me to trust my instincts, and now you say my instincts can't be trusted, because they're telling me something you don't want to believe?"

"Because it's childish and silly." Kris snorted.

Talia took a deep breath and closed her eyes. "Kris, I don't agree with you, but let's not fight about it."

Kris bit back what he wanted to say. At least she wasn't going to force him to stay on the defensive. "If you want."

"It—it isn't what I want. What I *want* is for you to believe and trust in my judgment. If I can't have that—well, I just don't want to fight about it."

"My uncle," he said carefully, trying to be absolutely fair to both sides, "is very fond of power. He doesn't like giving it up. That in itself is probably the reason he's been displaying antagonism toward Heralds and you in particular. Just be firm and cool and don't give an inch when you know you're in the right. He'll settle down and resign himself; as you said, he's not stupid. He knows better than to fight when he can't win. You'll never be friends, but I doubt that you need to fear him. He may be fond of power, but he has always had the best interests of the Kingdom at the forefront of his concerns."

"I wish I could feel as confident about that as you do." She sighed, then shifted in her saddle, as if trying to ease an uncomfortable position.

Kris began to make a retort, then thought better of it, and grinned. At this point a change of subject was called for. "Why don't you worry about something else—Dirk, for instance?"

"Beast." She smiled when she saw he was laughing at her.

"So I am. I'm sure he'll tell me the same. Oh, well, the best thing you can do for that little trouble is to let affairs take their natural course. Soon or late, he'll come to the point—if I have to push him myself!"

"Callous, too." She pouted mischievously at him.

"Believe it," he replied agreeably. "I'm going to enjoy teasing the life out of both of you."

Talia schooled herself to remain calm. As she had told Skif, there was nothing to be done *right now*. There were other things she wanted to find out before she took that

Council seat in the morning, too—like whether the rumors that she had "misused" her Gift to manipulate others were still active. And who was keeping them active, if they were. At this point, it was a bit too late to try and find out who had originated them.

As they approached the outer city and its swirling crowds, she was made aware of just how much more sensitive her Gift of Empathy had become. The pressure of all those emotions ahead of her was so strong she found it hard to believe that Kris could be unaware of it. She wished, not for the first time, that her Gift included Mindspeech; it would have been comforting to consult with Rolan the way Kris could with Tantris. She'd forgotten what living around so many people was like—and having had her Gift go rogue on her had made her more sensitive than she had been before she left. It wasn't going to be easy to stay tightly shielded day and night, but her enhanced perception was going to demand just that. She felt a flicker of reassurance from Rolan, and smiled faintly despite her anxiety.

They made their way down the increasingly crowded road into the outer city, outside the ancient defensive walls, which had sprung up over several generations of peace. The inner city held the shops, the better inns, and the homes of the middle class and nobility. The outer was given over to the workshops, markets, rowdier hostels and taverns, and the homes of the laborers and poor.

The crowds of the outer city were noisy and cheerful. As when she had first ridden into the capital, Talia found herself assaulted on all sides by sight, scent, and sound. The myriad odors of cookshops, inns, and food vendors vied with the less savory smells of beasts and trade.

The pressure of all the varied emotions of the people around her threatened to overwhelm her for one brief moment, until she firmed up her shields. *No,* she thought with resignation, *this is* not *going to be easy.*

The road led through a riot of color and motion, and the noise was cacaphonic, confusion without mirroring some of her own confusion within.

The leather-workers kept to a section here, outside the

North Gate, and both Talia and Kris were caught off guard by a puff of acrid, eye-burning fumes that escaped from a vat somewhere nearby.

"Whew!" Kris gasped, laughing at the tears in his eyes and Talia's, "Now I remember why Dirk and I usually backtracked around to the Haymarket Gate! Oh, well, too late now!"

The brief pause they made to clear their vision gave her a chance to finish making her shielding automatic. Back in their Sector—once she'd *gotten* her shields back—she'd tended to leave them down when it was only the two of them together. Shielding expended energy, and at that point she hadn't any to spare. Now she put in place the safeguards that would ensure that her shields stayed up even when she was unconscious—and felt a brief surge of gratitude to Kris for having re-taught her the *right* way to shield.

Kris kept a careful eye on her as they made their way through the crowds. If she were going to break, *now* would be the time, under the pressure of all these emotions.

:I wasn't worried.:

:You weren't, hm? Maybe I should ask her to favor you with one of those emotional backlashes:

:No, thank you, I had one. Remember? Rolan nearly brained me.: Tantris' sending took on a serious coloration. *:You know, you really shouldn't tease her about Dirk. Lifebonds aren't easy to bear when the pair hasn't acknowledged it.:*

Kris looked at his Companion's back-tilted ears in astonishment. *:You're sure? I mean, she certainly shows every symptom of lifebonding, but—:*

:We're sure.:

:Do you by any chance know when—?: he asked his Companion.

:Dirk was the first Herald she ever saw; Rolan thinks it might have been then.:

:That early? Lord and Lady, that would be one powerful bond. . . .: Kris continued to watch her with a little bemusement as the thought trailed away.

Tradesmen and their patrons screamed cheerfully at

one another over the din of vehicles, squalling children, and bawling animals. Yet for all that the populace seemed to ignore the presence of the two Heralds passing through their midst, a path always seemed to clear itself before them, and someone beckoned them on by a smile or a wave of a hat. The Guard at the outer gate saluted them as they passed through; the Guardfolk were no strangers to the comings and goings of Heralds. They rode through the tunnel that passed under the thick, gray-granite walls of the old city, and the din lessened for just a moment. Then they emerged into the narrower ways of the capital itself. It lacked only an hour until the evening meal and the streets were as crowded with people as Kris had ever seen them. It was not quite as noisy here in the old city, but the streets were just as full. After months of small towns and villages, Kris found himself marveling anew at the crush of people, and the closely-built, multi-storied stone houses. For many months, the chime of bells on their Companions' bridles had been the loudest sound they heard; now that sound was completely engulfed in the babble around them.

The streets had been designed in a spiral; no one could move straight to the Palace grounds—as in most older cities that had been built with an eye to defense. Kris led them on a course that wound ever inward. The din died away behind them as they left the streets of shops behind and entered the inner, residential core. The modest houses of the merchant class gradually gave way to the more impressive buildings owned by the wealthy or noble, each set apart from the street by a private wall enclosing the manse and a bit of garden. Eventually they made their way to the inner beige-brick wall surrounding the Palace and the three Collegia—Bardic, Healer's and Herald's. The silver-and-blue-clad Palace Guard stationed at the gate halted them for a moment, while she checked them off against a list of those expected to be arriving. Careful records were kept on when a Herald should come in from the field—in the case of those arriving from distant Sectors, this calculation was accurate within a stretch of two or three days; in the case of those arriving from nearby Sectors, expected arrival time was accurate to within hours. This list was posted with the Gate Guard—so when a Herald was overdue, *someone* knew it, and something could be done to find out why, quickly.

"Herald Dirk in yet?" Kris asked the swarthy Guardswoman casually when she'd finished.

"Just arrived two days ago, Herald," she replied, consulting the roster. "Guard then notes he asked about you two."

"Thank you, Guard. Pleasant watch to you." Kris grinned, urging Tantris through the gate she held open, with Rolan following closely behind.

Kris continued to watch Talia carefully, feeling a surge of gratified pride as he noted her behavior. The past few months had been living hell for her. Control of her Gift had been based entirely on instinct, rather than on proper training—and no one had ever realized this. The rumors that she had used it to manipulate—worse, that she had done so unconsciously—had pushed her off-balance. His own doubts about the truth of those rumors had been easy for her to pick up. And for someone whose Gift was based on emotions, and who was frequently prey to self-doubt, the effect was bound to be catastrophic.

It was at least that. She'd lost all control over her Gift—which unfortunately remained at full strength. She'd lost the ability to shield, and projected wildly. She'd very nearly killed them both on more than one occasion.

We were just lucky that during the worst of it, we were snowed in at that Waystation. It was just the two of us, and we were isolated long enough for her to get back in charge of herself.

And then she'd met the rumors again—this time circulating among the common folk. More than once they'd regarded her with fear and suspicion, yet she had never faltered in the performance of her duties or given any indication to an outsider that she was anything except calm, thoughtful, and controlled. She'd given a months' long series of performances a trained player couldn't equal.

It was vital that a Herald maintain emotional stability under all circumstances. This was especially true of the Queen's Own, who dealt with volatile nobles and the intrigues of the Court on a daily basis. She'd lost that stability, but after working through her trial had managed to get it back, and more.

He managed to catch her eyes, and gave her an encouraging wink; she dropped her solemn face for a moment to wrinkle her nose at him.

They passed the end of the Guard barracks and neared the black iron fence that separated the "public" grounds of the Palace from the "private" grounds and those of the three Collegia. Another Guard stood at the Gate here, but his position was mainly to intercept the newly-Chosen; he waved them on with a grin. From here the granite core of the Palace with its three great brick wings and the separate buildings of the Healer's and Bardic Collegia was at last clearly visible. Kris sighed happily. No matter where a Herald came from—*this* place, and the people in it, were his real home.

Talia felt a surge of warmth and contentment at the sight of the Collegium and the Palace—a feeling of true homecoming.

Just as they passed this last gate, she heard a joyful shout, and Dirk and Ahrodie pounded up the brick-paved pathway at a gallop to meet them. Dirk's straw-blond hair was flying every which way, like a particularly windblown bird's nest. Kris vaulted off Tantris' back as Dirk hurled himself from Ahrodie's; they met in a back-pounding, laughing, bear hug.

Talia remained in the saddle; at the sight of Dirk her heart had contracted painfully, and now it was pounding so hard she felt that it must be clearly audible. Her anxieties concerning Elspeth and the intrigues of the Court receded into the back of her mind.

She was tightly shielded; afraid to let anything leak through.

Dirk's attention was primarily on her and not on his friend and partner.

Dirk had been watching for them all day—telling himself that it was Kris whose company he had missed. He'd felt like a tight bowstring, without being willing to identify *why* he'd been so tense. His reaction on finally seeing them had been totally unplanned, giving him release for his pent-up emotion in the exuberant greeting to Kris. Though he seemed to ignore her, he was almost painfully aware of Talia's presence. She sat so quietly on her own Companion that she might have been a statue, yet he practically counted every breath she took.

He knew that he would remember how she looked right now down to the smallest hair. Every nerve seemed to tingle, and he felt almost as if he were wearing his skin inside out.

When Dirk finally let go of his shoulders, Kris said, with a grin that was bordering on malicious, "You haven't welcomed Talia, brother. She's going to think you don't remember her."

"Not remember her? Hardly!" Dirk seemed to be having a little trouble breathing. Kris hid another grin.

Talia and Rolan were less than two paces away, and Dirk freed an arm to take Talia's nearer hand in his own.

Kris thought he'd never seen a human face look so exactly like a stunned ox's.

Talia met the incredible blue of Dirk's eyes with a shock. It felt very much as if she'd been struck by lightning. She came near to trembling when their hands touched, but managed to hold to her self-control by a thin thread and smiled at him with lips that felt oddly stiff.

"Welcome home, Talia." That was all he said—which was just as well. The sound of his voice and the feeling of his eyes on her made her long to fling herself at him. She found herself staring at him, unable to respond.

She looked a great deal different than he remembered; leaner, as if she'd been fine-tempered and fine-honed. She was more controlled—certainly more mature. Was there a sadness about her that hadn't been there before? Was it some pain that had thinned her face?

When he'd taken her hand, it had seemed as if something—he wasn't sure what—had passed between them; but if she'd felt it, too, she gave no sign.

When she'd smiled at him, and her eyes had warmed with that smile, he'd thought his heart was going to stop.

The dreams he'd had of her all these months, the obsession—he'd figured they'd pop like soap bubbles when confronted with the reality. He'd been wrong. The reality only strengthened the obsession. He held her hand that trembled very slightly in his own, and longed with all his heart for Kris' silver tongue.

They stood frozen in that position for so long that Kris thought with concealed glee that they were likely to remain there forever unless he broke their concentration.

"Come on, partner." He slapped Dirk's back heartily and remounted Tantris.

Dirk jumped in startlement as if someone had blown a trumpet in his ear, then grinned sheepishly.

"If we don't get moving, we're going to miss supper—and I can't tell you how many times I dreamed of one of Mero's meals on the road!"

"Is that all you missed? Food? I might have known. Poor abused brother, did Talia make you eat your own cooking?"

"Worse—" Kris said, grinning at her, "—she made me eat *hers!*" He winked at her and punched Dirk's arm lightly.

When Kris broke the trance he was in, Dirk dropped Talia's hand as if it had burned him. When Talia turned a gaze full of gratitude on Kris, presumably for the interruption, Dirk felt a surge of something unpleasantly like jealousy at the thanks in her eyes. When Kris included her in the banter, Dirk wished that it had been *his* idea, not Kris'.

"Beast," she told Kris, making a face at him.

"Hungry beast."

"He's right though, much as I hate to agree with him," she said softly, turning to Dirk, and he suppressed a shiver—her voice had improved and deepened; it played little arpeggios on his backbone. "If we don't hurry, you *will* be too late. It doesn't matter too much to me—I'm used to sneaking bread and cheese from Mero—but it's very unkind to keep *you* standing here. Will you ride up with us?"

He laughed to cover the hesitation in his voice. "You'd have to tie me up to keep me from coming with you."

He and Kris remounted with a creak of leather, and they rode with Talia between them; that gave Dirk all the excuse he needed to rest his eyes on her. She gazed straight ahead or at Rolan's ears except when she was answering one or the other of them. Dirk wasn't sure whether he should be piqued or pleased. She wasn't favoring either of them with a jot more attention than the other, but he began to wish very strongly that she'd look at him a little more frequently than she was.

A dreadful fear was starting to creep into his heart. She had spent the past year and a half largely in Kris' company. What if—

He began scrutinizing Kris' conduct, since Talia's was giving him no clues. It seemed to confirm his fears. Kris was more at ease with Talia than he'd ever been with any other woman; they laughed and traded jokes as if their friendship had grown through years rather than months.

It was worse when they reached the Field and the tackshed, and Kris offered her an assist down with mock gallantry. She accepted the hand with a teasing haughteur, and dismounted with one fluid motion. Had Kris' hand lingered in hers a moment or two longer than had been really necessary? Dirk couldn't be sure. Their behavior wasn't really loverlike, but it was the closest he'd ever seen Kris come to it.

They unsaddled their Companions and stowed the tack safely away in the proper places after a cursory cleaning. Dirk's was pretty much clean; but Talia's and Kris' needed more work than could be taken care of in an hour—after being in the field for so long, it would all have to have an expert's touch. Dirk kept Talia in the corner of his eye while she worked, humming under her breath. Kris kept up his chatter, and Dirk made distracted, monosyllabic replies. He wished he could get her alone for just a few minutes.

He had no further chance for observation. Keren, Sherrill, and Jeri appeared like magicians out of the thinnest air, converged on her, and carried her off to her rooms, baggage and all, leaving him alone with Kris.

"Look, I don't know about you, but I am starved," Kris said, as Dirk stared mournfully after the foursome,

Talia carrying her harp "My Lady" and the rest sharing her packs. "Let's get the four-feets turned loose and get that dinner."

"Well?" Keren asked, her rough voice full of arch significance, when the three women had gotten Talia and her belongings safely into the privacy of her room.

"Well, what?" Talia replied, glancing at the graying Riding Instructor from under demure lashes while she unpacked in her bedroom.

"What? *What!* Oh, come *on,* Talia—" Sherrill laughed, "—you know exactly what we mean! How did it go? Your letters weren't exactly very long *or* very informative."

Talia suppressed a smile, and turned her innocent gaze on Keren's lifemate. "Personal or professional?"

Jeri fingered the hilt of her belt-knife significantly. "Talia," she warned, "If you don't stop trying our patience, Rolan just *may* have to find a new Queen's Own tonight."

"Oh, well, if you're going to be *that* way about it—" Talia backed away, laughing, as Sherrill, hazel eyes narrowed in mock ferocity, curled her long fingers into claws and lunged at her. She dodged aside at the last moment, and the tall brunette landed on her bed instead. "—all right, I yield, I yield! What do you want to know first?"

Sherrill rolled to her feet, laughing. "What do you think? Skif hinted that you and Kris were getting cozy, but he wouldn't do more than hint."

"Quite cozy, yes, but nothing much more. Yes, we were sharing blankets, and no, there isn't anything more between us than a very comfortable friendship."

"Pity," Jeri replied merrily, throwing herself onto Talia's couch in the outer room, then twining a lock of her chestnut hair around one finger. "We were hoping for a passionate romance."

"Sorry to disappoint you," she replied, not sounding sorry at all, "Though if you're thinking of trying in that direction—"

"Hm?" Jeri did her best not to look *too* eager, but didn't succeed very well.

"Well, once he's managed to shake Nessa loose—"

"Ha!"

"Don't laugh, we think we know a way. Well, once she's no longer hot on the hunt, he's going to be *quite* unpartnered, and he's just as—um—pleasant a companion as Varianis claims. Jeri, don't lick your whiskers so damned obviously, he's not a bowl of cream!"

Jeri looked chagrined and blushed as scarlet as the couch cushions, as Sherrill and Keren chuckled at her discomfiture. "I wasn't that bad, was I?"

"You most certainly were. Keep your predatory thoughts to yourself if you don't want to frighten him off the way Nessa has," Keren admonished with a wry grin. "As for you, little centaur, he seems to have cured your man-shyness rather handily. I guess I owe Kyril and Elcarth an apology. I thought assigning him to you was insanity. Well, now that our prurience has been satisfied, how did the work go?"

"It's a very long story, and before I go into it, have you three eaten?"

Three affirmatives caused her to nod. "Well *I* haven't yet. You have a choice; you can either wait until I'm done with dinner for the rest of the gossip—"

They groaned in mock-anguish.

"Or you can check me in and bring me something from the kitchen. If Selenay or Elspeth need me, they'll send a page for me."

"I'll check her in." Jeri shot out the door and down the spiral staircase.

"I'll go fetch you a young feast. You look like you've lost *pounds,* and when Mero finds out it's for you, he'll probably ransack the entire pantry." Sherrill vanished after Jeri.

Keren stood away from the wall she'd been leaning against. "Give me a proper greeting, you maddening child." She smiled, holding out her arms.

"Oh, Keren—" Talia embraced the woman who had been friend, surrogate-mother and sister to her—and more—with heartfelt fervor. "Gods, how I've missed you!"

"And I, you. You've changed, and for the better." Keren held her closely, then put her at arm's length, surveying her with intense scrutiny. "It isn't often I get to see my hopes fulfilled with such exactitude."

"Don't be so silly." Talia blushed. "You're seeing what isn't there."

"Oh, I think not." Keren smiled. "The gods know *you* are the world's worst judge when it comes to evaluating yourself. Dearling, you've become all I hoped you'd be. But—you didn't have the easy time we thought you would, did you?"

"I—no, I didn't." Talia sighed. "I—Keren, my Gift went rogue on me. At full power."

"Great good gods!" She examined Talia even more carefully, gray eyes boring into Talia's. "How the hell did that happen? I thought we'd trained—"

"So did everyone."

"Wait a moment; let me put this together for myself. You finished Ylsa's class; now let me remember . . ." Keren's brow creased in thought. "It *does* seem to me that she mentioned something about wanting to send you to the Healers for some special training, that she didn't feel altogether happy about handling an Empath when her own expertise was Thought-sensing."

Keren turned away from Talia and began pacing, a habit the younger woman was long familiar with, for Keren claimed she couldn't think unless she was moving.

"Now—*I'd* assumed she'd taken care of that because you spent so much time with the Healers. But she hadn't, had she? And then she was murdered—"

"As far as Kris and I could figure, the Heralds assumed that the Healers were giving me Empath training, and the *Healers* assumed the *Heralds* had already done so because I *seemed* to be in full control. But I wasn't; it was all instinct and guess. And when control went—"

"Gods!" Keren stopped pacing and put both of her hands on Talia's shoulders. "Little one, are you *sure* you're all right now?"

Talia remembered only too vividly the hours of practice Kris had put her through; the painful sessions with the two Companions literally attacking her mentally. "I'm sure. Kris *is* a Gift-teacher, after all. He took me all the way through the basics, and Rolan and Tantris helped."

"Oh, really? Well, well—*that's* an interesting twist!"

Keren raised an eloquent eyebrow. "Companions don't intervene that directly as a rule."

"I don't think they saw any other choice. The first month we were all snowed in at that Waystation—then we found out that those damned rumors had made it up to our Sector and we didn't *dare* look for outside help. It would have just confirmed the rumors."

"True—true. If I were on the Circle, I think I would be inclined to keep all this under the ivy bush. Letting the world know that we blundered that badly with you won't do a smidgin of good, and would probably do a *lot* of harm. Selected people, yes; and this should *certainly* go down in the annals so that we don't repeat the mistake with the next Empath—but—no, I don't think this should be generally known."

"That was basically Kris' thinking, and I agree. You're the first person to know besides the two of us. We'll both be telling Kyril and Elcarth, and I think that's all."

"Ye-es," Keren said slowly. "Yes. Let *those* two worry about who else should know. Well, what ends well *is* well, as they say."

"I *am* fine," Talia repeated emphatically. "I have absolute control now, control not even Rolan can shake. In a way, I'm glad it happened; I learned a lot—and it's made me think about things I never did before."

"Right, then. Now, let's take these rags of yours down to the laundry chute—yes, all of them; not even one outfit for tomorrow. After being in the field, they'll all need refurbishing. Here—" she dug into Talia's wooden wardrobe, and emerged with a soft, comfortable lounging robe. "Put that on. You won't be going anywhere tonight, and in the morning Gaytha will have left a pile of new ones at your doorstep—though from the look of you, they'll be a bit loose, since she'll have had them made up from the old measurements. We've all got a lot of news to catch up on. Oh, and I've got a message from Elspeth; 'Thank the Lady, and I'll see you in the morning.' "

"Well, my old and rare, we have got a *lot* of news to catch up on."

Dirk nodded, his mind so fully occupied with things

other than his dinner that he never noticed that he was munching his way through a heap of ustil greens, a vegetable he despised with passion.

Kris noticed, and had a difficult time in keeping a straight face. Fortunately the usual chaos of the Collegium common room at dinner gave him plenty of opportunity to look in other directions when the urge to break into a howl of laughter became too great. It was the height of the dinner hour, and every wooden bench was full of students in Grays and instructors in full Heraldic Whites, all shouting amiably at one another over the din.

"So, how did *your* stint go? We greatly appreciated that music, by the way, both of us. We've got a goodly portion of it memorized by now."

"Sh—you did? You do? That's—" Dirk suddenly realized he was beginning to babble, and ended lamely, "—that's very nice. I'm glad you liked it."

"Oh, yes; Talia especially. I think she values your present more than anything anyone else sent her. She certainly has been taking very good care of it—but that's like her. I'm giving her highest marks; she is one *damn* fine Herald."

Now Dirk took advantage of the noise and clatter at the tables all about them to cover his own confusion. "Well," he replied when he finally managed to clear his head a bit of the daze he seemed to be in, "It sounds like you had a more entertaining trainee than I did. And a more interesting round. Mine was so dull and normal Ahrodie and I sleepwalked through most of it."

"Lord of Lights—I wish I could claim that! Don't forget, 'May your life be interesting' happens to be a very potent curse! Besides, I seem to remember you claiming that young Skif had you worn to a frazzle before the circuit was over."

"I guess I did," Dirk chuckled. "Did you know his Cymry dropped a foal, and he blames it all on you two?"

"No doubt, since neither of them have an ounce of shame to spare between them." Kris ducked as a student burdened with a stack of dirty dishes taller than he was inched past them. "Lord, I hope that youngling's got one of the Fetching Gifts, or he's going to lose that whole stack in a minute—yes, Skif and Cymry deserve what they got. Poor Talia would have been ready to skin both of them given the chance. . . ."

"Oh?"

Kris was more and more pleased by Dirk's reactions. He needed no further urging, and related the tale with relish, stopping short of the fight—which had been *caused*, in an obscure sort of way, by Dirk—and the swimming match that followed. He insisted then that they ought to take themselves out of the way of those students assigned to clearing tables.

"Fine; my room or yours?" Dirk was doing his damnedest to keep his feelings from showing. Unfortunately, Kris knew him too well; that deadpan dicing face he was putting on only proved he was considerably on edge.

"Good gods, not yours—we'd be lost in there for a week! Mine; and I still have some of that Ehrris-wine, I think. . . ."

The tales continued over the wine and a small fire, both of them lounging at full length in Kris' old, worn green chairs. And every other sentence Kris spoke seemed to have something to do with Talia. Dirk tried his best to seem interested, but not as obsessed as he actually was. Kris let the shadows hide his faint smile, for he wasn't fooled a bit.

But not once did Kris let fall the information Dirk *really* wanted to know—and finally, emboldened by the wine, he came out and asked for it.

"Look, Kris—you're the soul of chivalry, but we're blood-brothers, you can tell me safely! Were you, or weren't you?"

"Were we what?" Kris asked innocently.

"S-sleeping together, you nit!"

"Yes," Kris answered forthrightly. "What did you expect? We're neither one of us made of ice." He figured that it was far better for Dirk to hear the truth—and to hear it in such a way that he took it for the matter-of-fact thing that it was. Talia and Dirk were probably tied neck-and-neck for the position of his "best friend." And that was *all* he and Talia meant to each other. He could no more conceive of being in love with her than with the close friend he now faced. He watched Dirk covertly, weighing his reaction.

"I—I suppose it was sort of inevitable—"

"Inevitable—something more. Frankly, during that first winter it was too blamed *cold* to sleep alone." He launched into the whole tale of their blizzard-ordeal—with editing. He didn't dare reveal how Talia's Gift had gotten out of control. Firstly, it wasn't anything Dirk needed to know about. Secondly, he was fairly certain it was something that should be known by as few as possible. Elcarth and Kyril, certainly—but he was pretty well certain it just wouldn't be ethical to go around telling anyone else without Talia's express permission.

He concluded the tale with a certain puzzlement; Dirk seemed to have suddenly gone dumb, and very soon pled exhaustion and left for his own room.

Oh, Lord. Of all the damned situations to be in—his very best friend in the entire world with his hooks quite firmly in the first woman Dirk had even wanted to *look* at in years.

It wasn't fair. It wasn't any damned fair. No woman in her right mind was even going to want to look at him with Kris around. And Kris—

Kris—was *he* in love with Talia? And if he were . . .

Gods, gods, they certainly belonged together.

No, dammit! Kris could have any female he wanted, Herald or no, without even lifting a finger! By all the gods, Dirk was going to fight him for this one!

Except that he hadn't the faintest idea how to go about fighting for her. And—Kris was like a brother, more than a brother. This wasn't any kind of fair to him—

He lay sleepless for hours that night, staring into the darkness, tossing and turning restlessly, and cursing the nightjar that was apparently singing right outside his window. By dawn he was no closer to sorting out his own feelings than he had been when he threw himself down to rest.

Two

"Talia!"

Elspeth greeted Talia's appearance at breakfast with a squeal, and a hug that threatened to squeeze the last bit of breath out of her. The last year and a half had added inches to the young Heir's height; she stood a bit taller than Talia now. Time had added a woman's curves to the wraithlike child as well. Talia wondered, now that she'd seen Elspeth, if her mother truly realized how much growing she'd done in the time Talia had been gone.

The wood-paneled common room was full of youngsters in student Grays, as most of the instructors had eaten earlier. The bench-and-table-filled room buzzed with sleepy murmuring, and smelled of bacon and porridge. Except for the fact that she recognized few of the faces, and the fact that the room was completely full, it all looked the same as it had when Talia was a student; she slid into the warm, friendly atmosphere like a blade into a well-oiled sheath, and felt as if she had never left.

"Bright Lady, catling, you're going to break all my ribs!" Talia protested, returning the hug with interest. "I got your message from Keren—I take it Skif *did* tell you I got in last night, didn't he? I rather expected to find you on my doorstep."

"I had foal-watch last night." One of the duties imposed on the students was to camp in Companion's Field around the time of a foaling, each taking the watch in turn. Companions did not foal with the ease of horses, and if there were complications, seconds could be precious in preserving the life or health of mare and foal.

"Skif told me you were here, and that he'd given you my screech for help—so I knew I didn't need to worry anymore, and I certainly didn't need to disturb *your* sleep."

"I heard Cymry dropped. Who else?"

"Zaleka." Elspeth grinned at Talia's bewildered look of nonrecognition. "She Chose Arven just after you left. He's twenty if he's a day, and when Jillian was here during break between assignments—well, you know Jillian, she's as bad as Destria. Seems her Companion was like-minded. We haven't half been giving Arven a hard time over it! Zaleka hasn't dropped yet, but she's due any day."

Talia shook her head, and slipped an arm around the Heir's shoulders. "You younglings! I don't know what the world's coming to these days—"

Elspeth gave a very unladylike snort, narrowed her enormous brown eyes, and tossed her dark hair scornfully. "You don't cozen me! I've heard tales about you and *your* year-mates that gave me gray hairs! Climbing in and out of windows at the dead of night with not-so-ex-thieves! Spying on the Royal Nursemaid!"

"Catling—" Talia went cold sober. "Elspeth—I'm sorry about Hulda." She met Elspeth's scrutiny squarely.

Elspeth grimaced bitterly at the name of the nursemaid who had very nearly managed to turn her into a spoiled, unmanageable monster—and came close to eliminating any chance of her being Chosen.

"Why? You caught her red-handed in conspiracy to keep *me* from ever getting to be Heir," she replied with a mixture of amusement and resentment—the amusement at Talia's reaction, the resentment reserved for Hulda. "Sit, sit, sit! I'm hungry, and I refuse to have to crane my neck up to talk to you."

"You—you aren't angry at me?" Talia asked, taking a seat beside Elspeth on the worn wooden bench. "I wanted to tell you I was responsible for her being dismissed, but, frankly, I never had the courage."

Elspeth smiled a little. "You didn't have the courage? Thank the Lady for that! I was afraid you were perfect!"

"Hardly," Talia replied dryly.

"Well, why not tell me your end of it now? I just got it secondhand from Mother and Kyril."

"Oh, Lord—where do I begin?"

"Mm—chronologically, as you found it out." Elspeth seized a mug of fruit juice from a server and plumped it down in front of her seatmate.

"Right. It really started for me when I tried to get to know you. Hulda kept blocking me."

"How?"

"Carrying you off for lessons, saying you were asleep, or studying, or whatever other excuse she could come up with. Catling, I was only about fourteen, and a fairly unaggressive fourteen at that; *I* wasn't about to challenge her! But it just happened too consistently not to be on purpose. So I enlisted Skif."

Elspeth nodded. "Good choice. If there was anybody likely to find out anything, it would be Skif. I know for a fact he still keeps his hand in—"

"Oh? How?"

Elspeth giggled. "Whenever he's in residence he leaves me sweets hidden in the 'secret' drawer of the desk in my room. With notes."

"Oh, Lord—you haven't told anybody, have you?"

Elspeth was indignant. "And give him away? Not a chance! Oh, I've told Mother in case he ever gets caught—which isn't likely—but I swore her to secrecy first."

Talia sighed in relief. "Thanks be to the Lady. If anybody other than Heralds found out . . . "

Elspeth sobered. "I know. At worst he could be killed before a Guard knew he was a Herald and it was a prank. Believe me, I know. Mother was rather amused—and rather glad, I think. It can't hurt to have somebody with skills like *that* in the Heralds. Anyway, you recruited Skif . . ."

"Right; he began sneaking around, and discovered that Hulda, rather than being the subordinate as everyone thought, had taken over control of the nursery and your education. She was drugging old Melidy, who was *supposed* to be your primary nurse. Well, that seemed wrong to me, but it wasn't anything I could prove because Melidy *had* been ill—she'd had a brainstorm. So I had Skif keep watching. That was when he discovered that Hulda was in the pay of someone unknown—paid to ensure that you could never be Chosen, and thus, never become Heir."

"Bitch." Elspeth's eyes were bright with anger. "I take it neither you nor he ever saw who it was?"

Talia shook her head regretfully, and took a sip of fruit juice. "Never. He was always masked, cloaked, and hooded. We told Jadus, Jadus told the Queen—and Hulda vanished."

"And I only knew that I'd lost the one person at Court I was emotionally dependent on. I'm not surprised you kept quiet." Elspeth passed Talia a clean plate. "Oh, I might have gotten angry if you'd told me two or three years ago, but not now."

There was a great deal of cold, undisguised anger in the Heir's young brown eyes. "I still remember most of that time quite vividly."

Talia lost the last of her apprehension over the indignation in Elspeth's voice.

"There's more to it than just my being resentful, though," Elspeth continued, "Looking back at it, Talia, I think that woman who called herself my 'nurse' would quite cheerfully have strangled me with her own hands if she thought she could have profited and gotten away with it! Yes, and enjoyed every minute of it!"

"Oh, come now—you weren't that much of a little monster!"

"Here, you'd better start eating or Mero'll throw fits at us when we get downstairs to clean; he's fixed all your favorites." Elspeth took some of the platters being passed from hand to hand, and heaped Talia's plate with crisp oatcakes and honey, warm bacon, and stir-fried squash, totally oblivious to the incongruity of the Heir to the Throne serving one who was technically an underling. She had indeed come a long way from the Royal Brat who had been so very touchy about her rank. "Talia, I lived with Hulda most of my waking hours. I *know* for a fact she enjoyed frightening me. The bedtime stories she told me would curl the hair of an adult, and I'd bet my life that she got positive pleasure out of my shivers. And

I can't tell you why I feel this way, but I'm certain she was the most coldly self-centered creature I've ever met; that nothing mattered to her except her own well-being. She was very good at covering the fact, but—"

"I don't think I doubt you, catling. One of your Gifts is Mindspeech, after all, and little children sometimes see things we adults miss."

"You *adults?* You weren't all *that* much older than me! You saw a fair amount yourself, and you'd have seen more if you'd been able to spend more time with me. She was turning me into a little copy of herself, when she wasn't trying to scare me. Once she'd cut me off from everyone else so that there was no one to turn to as a friend, she kept schooling me in how I shouldn't trust anyone but her—and how I should fight for every scrap of royal privilege, stopping for no one and nothing on the way. There's more, something that turned up after you left. When they told me the truth, I got very curious."

"Which is why I call you 'catling'—" Talia interrupted with a grin, "—since you're fully as curious as any cat."

"Too true. Curiosity sometimes pays, though; I started going through the things she left, and doing a bit of discreet correspondence with my paternal relatives."

"Does your mother know this?" Talia was a bit surprised.

"It's with her blessing. By the way, I get the feeling that Uncle-King Faramentha likes me as much as he disliked my father. We've gotten into quite a cozy little exchange of letters and family anecdotes. I like him, too—and it's rather too bad we're so closely related; he's got a whole tribe of sons, and I think anybody with a sense of humor like his would be rather nice to get to know. . . ." Elspeth's voice trailed off wistfully, then she got back to the subject at hand with a little shake of her head. "Anyway, *now* we're not altogether certain that the Hulda who left Rethwellan is the same Hulda who arrived here."

"What?"

"Oh, it's so much *fun* to shock you. You look like somebody just hit you in the face with a board!"

"Elspeth, I may kill you myself if you don't get to the point!"

"All right, I'll be good! It's rather late in the day to be checking on these things now, but there was a span of about a month after Hulda left the Royal Nursery in Rethwellan to come here where she just seems to have vanished. She wasn't passed across the Border, and no one remembers her in the inns along the way. Then— poof!—she's here, bag and baggage. Father wasn't among the living anymore through his own stupid fault, and she had all the right papers and letters; nobody thought to doubt that she *was* the 'Hulda' he'd sent for. Until now, that is."

"Bright Lady!" Talia grew as cold as her breakfast, thinking about the multitude of possibilities this opened up. Had the unknown "my lord" she and Skif had seen her conspiring with brought her here? They had no way of knowing if that one had been among those traitors uncovered and executed after Ylsa's murder, for neither of them had ever seen his face. They thought he had been, for there were no other stirrings of trouble after that, but he *might* only have gone to ground for an interval. Had even "my lord" guessed that she was not what she seemed? And where had she vanished to after she was unmasked? No one had seen her leave; she had not passed the Border, at least by the roads (and that was an echo of what Elspeth had just detailed), yet she was most assuredly gone before anyone had a chance to detain her. And who—or what—had given her warning that she had been uncovered? A danger that Talia had long thought safely laid to rest had suddenly resurrected itself, the cockatrice new-hatched from the dunghill.

"Mero is going to have my hide," Elspeth warned, and Talia started guiltily and finished her meal. But she really couldn't have told what she was eating.

"—and that was the last incident," Kris finished. "The last couple of weeks were nothing but routine; we finished up, Griffon relieved us, and we headed home."

He met the measuring gazes of first Elcarth, then Kyril. Both of them were shocked cold sober by his revelation of the way Talia's Gift had gone rogue—and *why*. They had evidently assumed this interview was going to be a mere formality. Kris' tale had come as an unpleasant surprise.

"Why," Kyril asked, after a pause that was much too long for Kris' comfort, "didn't you look for help when this first happened?"

"Largely because by the time I knew something was really wrong, we were snowed into that Waystation, Senior."

"He's got you there, brother." Elcarth favored the silver-haired Seneschal's Herald with a wry smile.

"By the time we got out, she was well on the way to having her problems solved," Kris continued doggedly. "She had the basics, had them down firmly. And once we got in with people again, we found that those rumors had preceded us. At *that* point, I reckoned we'd do irreparable harm by leaving the circuit to look for other help. We'd only have confirmed the rumor that there was something wrong by doing so."

"Hm. A point," Kyril acknowledged.

"And at that point, I wasn't entirely certain that there *was* anyone capable of training her."

"Healers—" Elcarth began.

"Don't have Empathy *alone*, nor do they use it exactly the way she does—the way she *must*. She's actually used it offensively, as I told you. They rarely invoke the use of it outside of Healing sessions; she is going to have to use it so constantly it will be as much a part of her as her eyes and ears. At least," Kris concluded with an embarrassed smile, "that's the way I had it figured."

"I think that in this case you were right, young brother," Kyril replied after long thought, during which time Kris had plenty of leisure to think about all he'd said, and wonder if he'd managed to convince these two, the most senior Heralds in the Circle.

Kris let out a breath he didn't even realize he'd been holding.

"There was this, too," he added. "At that point, letting out word that we, and the Collegium, had failed to properly train the new Queen's Own would have been devastating to *everyone's* morale."

"Bright Goddess—you're right!" Elcarth exclaimed with consternation, his eyebrows rising to meet his gray cap of hair. "For that to become well known would be as damaging to the faith of Heralds as it would to that of nonHeralds. I think, given the circumstances, you *both* deserve high marks. You, for your good sense and discretion, and your internee for meeting and overcoming trials she should never have had to face."

"I agree," Kyril seconded. "Now, if you'll excuse us, Elcarth and I will endeavor to set such safeguards as to ensure this never happens again."

With a polite farewell, Kris thankfully fled their presence.

In the hour after breakfast, Talia covered a great deal of ground. She first left the Herald's Collegium and crossed to the separate building that housed Healer's Collegium and the House of Healing. The sun was up by now, though it hadn't been when she'd gone to breakfast, and from the cloudless blue of the sky it looked as if it were going to be another flawless spring day. Once within the beige-brick walls, she sought out Healer Devan, to let him know of her return, and to learn from him if there were any Herald-patients in the House of Healing that needed her own special touch.

She found him in the still-room, carefully mixing some sort of decoction. She entered very quietly, not wanting to break his concentration, but somehow he knew she was there anyway.

"Word spreads quickly; I knew you'd gotten back last night," he said without turning around. "And most welcome you are, too, Talia!"

She chuckled a little. "I should know better than to try and sneak up on someone with the same Gift I have!"

He set his potion down on the table before him, stoppered it with care, and turned to face her. As a smile reached and warmed his hazel eyes, he held out brown-stained hands in greeting.

"Your aura, child, is unmistakable—and right glad I am to feel it again."

She took both his hands in her own, wrinkling her nose a little at the pungent odors of the still-room. "I hope you're glad to see me for my own sake, and not because you need me desperately," she replied.

Much to her relief, he assured her that there were *no* Heralds at all among his patients at the moment.

"Just wait until the Midsummer storms South, or the pirate-raids West, though!" he told her, his dark eyes rueful. "Rynee will have her Greens by winter; she's got every intention of going back South to be stationed near her home. You're back in good time; you'll be the only trained mind-Healer besides Patris here when she leaves, and it's possible we may need you for patients other than Heralds."

Next she returned to the Herald's Wing for an interview she had not been looking forward to.

She knocked hesitantly on the door to Elcarth's office; and found that not only was Elcarth there, but that the Seneschal's Herald was with the Dean.

During the next hour she reported, as dispassionately as she could, all that had happened during her internship. She did not spare herself in the least, admitting fully that she had concealed the fact that she was losing control over her Gift; admitting that she did not confess the fact until forced to by Kris. She told them what Kris had not; that she had nearly killed both of them.

They heard her out in complete silence until she had finished, and sat with her hands clenched in her lap, waiting for their verdict on her.

"What have *you* concluded from all this?" Elcarth asked unexpectedly.

"That—that no one Herald can stand alone, not even the Queen's Own," she replied, after thought. "Perhaps *especially* the Queen's Own. What I do reflects on all Heralds, and more so than any other just because I'm so much in the minds of the people."

"And of the proper usage of your Gift?" Kyril asked.

"I—I don't really know, entirely," she admitted. "There

are times when what I need to do is quite clear. But most of the time, it's so—so nebulous. It's going to be pretty much a matter of weighing evils and necessity, I guess."

Elcarth nodded.

"If I have time, I'll ask advice from the Circle before I do anything irrevocable. But most of the time, I'm afraid I won't have that luxury. But if I make a mistake . . . well, I'll accept the consequences, and try and make it right."

"Well, Herald Talia," Elcarth said, black eyes bright with what Talia finally realized was pride, "I think you're ready to get into harness."

"Then—I passed?"

"What did I tell you?" Kyril shook his head at his colleague. "I knew she wouldn't believe it until she heard it from our lips." The iron-haired, granite-faced Herald unbent enough to smile warmly at her. "Yes, Talia, you did very well; we're quite pleased with what you and Kris have told us. You took a desperate situation that was not entirely of your own making, and turned it around, by yourselves."

"*And* we're satisfied with what you told us just now," Elcarth added. "You've managed to strike a decent balance in the ethics of having a Gift like yours, I think. So now that you've had the sweet compliments, are you ready for the bitter? There's a Council meeting shortly."

"Yes, sir," she replied. "I've been . . . warned."

"About more than just the meeting, I'll wager."

"Senior, that would be compromising my sources—"

"Lord and Lady!" Elcarth's sharp features twitched as he controlled his urge to laugh. "She sounds like Talamir already!"

Kyril just shook his head ruefully. "That she does, brother. Well enough, Talia—we'll see you there. You'd best be off; I imagine Selenay is wanting to discuss a few things with you before the Council meeting itself."

Talia knew a dismissal when she heard one, and took her leave of both of them, with a light foot to match her lightened heart.

*   *   *

"Talia—" Selenay forestalled all formality by embracing her Herald warmly. "—Bright Lady, how I have *missed* you! Come in here where we can have a little privacy."

She drew Talia into a granite-walled alcove holding a single polished wooden bench, just off the corridor leading to the Council chamber. As usual, she was dressed as any of her Heralds, with only the thin circlet of royal red-gold that rested on her own golden hair proclaiming her rank.

"Let me get a good look at you. Havens, you look wonderful! But you've gotten so *thin*—"

"Having to eat my own cooking," Talia replied, "that's all. I would have tried to see you last night—"

"You wouldn't have found me," Selenay said, blue eyes dark with affection. "I was closeted with the Lord Marshal, going over troop deployments on the Border. By the time we were finished, I wouldn't have been willing to see my resurrected father, I was that weary. All those damn maps! Besides, the first night back from internship is always spent with your closest friends, it's tradition! How else can you catch up on eighteen months of news?"

"Eighteen months of gossip, you mean." Talia grinned. "I understand Kris and I caused a little ourselves."

"From your offhand manner can I deduce that my thoughts of a deathless romance are in vain?" Her eyes danced with amusement and she pouted in feigned disappointment.

Talia shook her head in mock exasperation. "You, too? Bright Havens, is everyone in the Collegium determined to have us mated, whether we will or no?"

"The sole exceptions are Kyril, Elcarth, Skif, Keren, and—of all people—Alberich. They all swore that if you ever lost your heart, it wouldn't be to Kris' pretty face."

"They . . . could be right."

Selenay noted her Herald's faintly troubled expression, and deemed it prudent to change the subject. "Well, I'm more than happy to have you at my side again, and I could have used you for the past two months."

"Two months? Is it anything to do with what Elspeth sent Skif out to us for?"

"Did she? That minx! Probably—she hasn't been any more pleased over the Council's actions than I have. I've gotten an offer for Elspeth's hand, from a source that is going to be very difficult for me to refuse."

"Say on."

Selenay settled back on the bench, absently caressing the arm of it with one hand. "We received an envoy from King Alessandar two months ago, a formal request that I consider wedding Elspeth to his Ancar. There's a great deal to be said for the match; Ancar is about Kris' age, not too great a discrepancy as royal marriages go; he's said to be quite handsome. This would mean the eventual joining of our Kingdoms, and Alessandar has a strong and well-trained army, much larger than our own. I'd be able to spread the Heralds into his realm, and his army would make Karse think twice about ever invading us again. Three quarters of the Councillors are for it unconditionally, the rest favor the idea, but aren't trying to shove it down my throat like the others are."

"Well," Talia replied slowly, twisting the ring Kris had given her, "you wouldn't be hesitating over it if you didn't feel there was something wrong. What is it?"

"Firstly, unless I absolutely *have* to, I don't want Elspeth sacrificed in a marriage of state. Frankly, I'd rather see her live unwedded and have the throne go to a collateral line than have her making anything but a match that is *at least* based on mutual respect and liking." Selenay played with a lock of hair, twisting it around one of her long, graceful fingers, thereby betraying her anxiety. "Secondly, she's very young yet; I'm going to insist she finish her training before making a decision. Thirdly, I haven't seen Ancar since he was a babe in arms; I have no idea what kind of a man he's grown into, and I want to know that before I even begin to seriously consider the match. To tell the truth, I'm hoping for her to have a love-match, and that with someone who is at least Chosen if not a Herald. I saw for myself the kind of problems that can come when the Queen's consort is not co-ruler, yet has been trained to the idea of rule. And you know very well that Elspeth's husband will not share the Throne unless he, too, is Chosen."

"Good points, all of them—but you have more than that troubling you." Talia had fallen into reading the Queen's state of mind as easily as if she'd never been away.

"Now I know why I've missed you! You always manage to ask the question that puts everything into perspective!" Selenay smiled again, with delight. "Yes, I do, but it wasn't the kind of thing I wanted to confess to the Council, or even to Kyril, bless his heart. They'd put it down to a silly woman's maunderings and mutter about moon-days. What's bothering me is this: it's too pat, this offer; it's too perfect. Too much like the answer to everyone's prayers. I keep looking for the trap beneath the bait, and wondering why I can't see it. Perhaps I'm so in the habit of suspicion that I can't trust even what I know to be honest."

"No, I don't think that's it." Talia pursed her lips thoughtfully. "There is something out of kilter, or you wouldn't be so uneasy. You've Mindspeech and a touch of Foreseeing, right? I suspect that you're getting foggy Foresight that something isn't quite right about the idea, and your uneasiness is being caused by having to fight the Council with no real reasons to give them."

"Bless you—that's exactly what it must be! I've been feeling for the past two months as if I were trying to bail a leaky boat with my bare hands!"

"So use Elspeth's youth and the fact that she *has* to finish her training as an excuse to stall for a while. I'll back you; when Kyril and Elcarth see that I'm backing you, they'll follow my lead," Talia said with more confidence than she actually felt. "Remember, I have a full vote in the Council now. Between the two of us we have the power to veto even the vote of the full Council. All it takes is the Monarch and Queen's Own to overturn a Council vote. I'll admit it isn't politic to do so, but I'll do it if I have to."

Selenay sighed with relief. "How have I ever managed all these years without you?"

"Very well, thank you. If I hadn't been here, I expect

you'd have managed to stall them somehow—even if you had to resort to Devan physicking Elspeth into a phony fever to gain time! Now, isn't it time to make our entrance?"

"Indeed it is." Selenay smiled, with just a hint of maliciousness. "And this is a moment I have long waited for! There are going to be some cases of chagrin when certain folk realize you are Queen's Own in truth, vote and all, and that the *full* Council will be in session from now on!"

They rose together and entered the huge, brass-mounted double doors of the Council chamber.

The other members of the Council had assembled at the table; they stood as one as the Queen entered the room, with Talia in her proper position as Queen's Own, one step behind her and slightly to her right.

The Council Chamber was not a large room, and had only the horseshoe Council table and the chairs surrounding it as furnishings, all of a dark wood that age and much handling had turned nearly black. Like the rest of the Palace, it was paneled only halfway in wood; the rest of the room, from about chin-height to the ceiling, being the gray stone of the original Palace-keep. A downscaled version of Selenay's throne was placed at the exact center of the Council table, behind it was the fireplace, and over the fireplace, the arms of the Monarch of Valdemar; a winged, white horse with broken chains about its throat. On the wall over the door, the wall that her throne faced, was an enormous map of Valdemar inscribed on heavy linen and kept constantly up-to-date; it was so large that any member of the Council could read the lettering from his or her seat. The work was exquisite, every road and tiny village carefully delineated. The chair to the immediate right of the Queen's was Talia's; to the immediate left was the Seneschal's. To the left of the Seneschal sat Kyril, to Talia's right, the Lord Marshal. The rest of the Councillors took whatever seat they chose, without regard for rank.

Talia had never actually used her seat until this moment; by tradition it had to remain vacant until she completed her training and was a full Herald. She had been seated with the rest of the Councillors and had done nothing except voice an occasional opinion when asked, and give her observations to Selenay when the meetings were over. While her new position brought her considerable power, it also carried considerable responsibility.

The Councillors remained standing, some with visible surprise on their faces; evidently word of her return had not spread as quickly through the Court as it had through the Collegium. Selenay took her place before her chair, as did Talia. The Queen inclined her head slightly to either side, then sat, with Talia sitting a fraction of a second later. The Councillors took their own seats when the Queen and Queen's Own were in their places.

"I should like to open this meeting with a discussion of the marriage envoy from Alessandar," Selenay said quietly, to the open surprise of several of her Councillors. Talia nodded to herself; by taking the initiative, Selenay started the entire proceedings with herself on the high ground.

One by one each of those seated at the table voiced their own opinions; as Selenay had told Talia, they were uniformly in favor of it, most desiring that the match be made immediately.

Talia began taking stock of the Councillors, watching them with an intensity she had never felt before. She wanted to evaluate them *without* using her Gift, only her eyes and ears.

First was Lord Gartheser, who spoke for the North— Orthallen's closest ally, without a doubt. Thin, nervous, and balding, he punctuated his sentences with sharp movements of his hands. Though he never actually looked directly at Orthallen, Talia could tell by the way he oriented himself that his attention was so bound on Orthallen that no one else made any impression on him at all.

"There can be *no* doubt," Gartheser said in a rather thin and reedy voice, "that this betrothal would bring us an alliance so strong that no one would ever dare dream of attacking us again. With Alessandar's army ready to spring to our rescue, not even Karse would care to trifle with us. I venture to predict that even the Border raids would cease, and our Borders would be truly secure for the first time in generations."

Orthallen nodded, so slightly that Talia would not have noticed the motion if she had not been watching him. And she wasn't the only one who caught that faint sign of approval. Gartheser had been watching for it, too. Talia saw him nod and smile slightly in response.

Elcarth and Kyril were next; Elcarth perched on the edge of his chair and looking like nothing so much as a gray snow-wren, and Kyril as nearly motionless as an equally gray granite statue.

"I can see no strong objections," Elcarth said, his head slightly to one side, "But the Heir *must* be allowed to finish her training *and* her internship before any such alliance is consummated."

"And Prince Ancar must be of a suitable temperament," Kyril added smoothly. "This Kingdom—forgive me, Highness—this Kingdom has had the bitter experience of having a consort who was *not* suitable. I, for one, have no wish to live through another such experience."

Lady Wyrist spoke next, who stood for the East; another of Orthallen's supporters. This plump, fair-haired woman had been a great beauty in her time, and still retained charm and magnetism.

"I am totally in favor—and I do *not* think this is the time to dally! Let the betrothal be as soon as possible—the wedding, even! Training can wait until *after* alliances are irrevocable." She glared at Elcarth and Kyril. "It's my Border the Karsites come rampaging over whenever they choose. My people have little enough, and the Karsites regularly reive away what little they have! But it is also my Border that would be open to new trade with our two Kingdoms firmly united, and I can see nothing to find fault with."

White-haired, snowy-bearded Father Aldon, the Lord Patriarch, spoke up wistfully. "As my Lady has said, this alliance promises peace, a peace such as we have not enjoyed for far too long. Karse would be forced to sue for a lasting peace, faced with unity all along two of its borders. Renewing our long friendship with Hardorn can only bring a truer peace than we have ever known. Though the Heir is young, many of our ladies have wedded younger still—"

"Indeed." Bard Hyron, so fair-haired that his flowing locks were nearly white, was speaker for the Bardic Circle. He echoed Father Aldon's sentiments. "It is a small sacrifice for the young woman to make, in the interests of how much we would gain."

Talia noted dubiously that his pale gray eyes practically glowed silver when Orthallen nodded approvingly.

The thin and angular Healer Myrim, spokeswoman for her Circle, was not so enthralled. To Talia's relief she actually seemed mildly annoyed by Hyron's hero worship; and something about Orthallen seemed to be setting her ever so slightly on edge. "You all forget something—though the child *has* been Chosen, she is not yet a Herald, and the law states clearly that the Monarch *must* be a Herald. There has never been a reason strong enough to overturn that law before, and I fail to see the need to set such a dangerous precedent now!"

"Exactly," Kyril murmured.

"The child *is* just that; a child. Not ready to rule by any stretch of the imagination, with much to learn before she is. Nevertheless, I am—cautiously—in favor of the betrothal. But only if the Heir *remains* at the Collegium until after her full training is complete."

Somewhat to Talia's surprise, Lord Marshal Randon shared Myrim's mild dislike of Orthallen. Talia wondered, as she listened to that scarred and craggy warrior measuring out his words with the care and deliberation of a merchant measuring out grain, what could have happened while she'd been gone to so change him. For when she'd last sat at the Council board, Randon had been one of Orthallen's foremost supporters. Now, however, though he favored the betrothal, he stroked his dark beard with something like concealed annoyance, as if it galled him, having to agree with Orthallen's party.

Horselike Lady Kester, speaker for the West, was short and to the point. "I'm for it," she said, and sat herself down. Plump and soft-spoken Lord Gildas for the South was equally brief.

"I can see nothing to cause any problems," said Lady Cathan of the Guilds quietly. She was a quiet, gray, dovelike woman, of an outer softness that masked a stubborn inner core. "And much that would benefit every member of the Kingdom."

"That, I think, is a good summation," Lord Palinor, the Seneschal, concluded. "You know my feelings on the matter, Majesty?"

The Queen had held her peace, remaining calm and thoughtful, but totally noncommittal, until everyone had spoken except herself and her Herald.

Now she leaned forward slightly, and addressed them, a hint of command tingeing her voice.

"I have heard you all; you each favor the match, and all of your reasons are good ones. You even urge me to agree to the wedding and see it consummated within the next few months. Very well; I can agree with every one of your arguments, and I am more than willing to return Alessandar's envoy with word that we will be considering his offer with all due gravity. But one thing I cannot and *will* not do—I will never agree to anything that will interrupt Elspeth's training. That, above all other considerations, must be continued! Lady forbid it, but should I die, we cannot risk the throne of Valdemar in the keeping of an untrained Monarch! Therefore I will do no more than indicate to Alessandar that his suit is welcome— and inform him in no uncertain terms that serious negotiations cannot begin until the Heir has passed her internship."

"Majesty!" Gartheser jumped to his feet as several more Councillors started speaking at once; one or two growing angry. Talia stood then, and rapped the table, and the babble ceased. The argumentive ones stared at her as though they had forgotten her presence.

"My lords, my ladies—forgive me, but any arguments you may have are moot. My vote goes with the Queen's decision. I have so advised her."

It was fairly evident from their dumbfounded expressions that they had forgotten that Talia now carried voting rights. If the situation had not been so serious, Talia would have derived a great deal of amusement from some of the dumbfounded expressions—Orthallen's in particular.

"If that is the advice of the Queen's Own, then my vote must follow," Kyril said quickly, although Talia could almost hear him wondering if she really knew what she was doing.

"And mine," Elcarth seconded, looking and sounding much more confident of Talia's judgment than Kyril.

There was silence then, a silence so deep one could almost hear the dust motes that danced in the light from the clerestory windows falling to the floor.

"It seems," said Lord Gartheser, the apparent leader of those dissenting, "that we are outvoted."

Faint grumbling followed his words.

At the farthest end of the table, a white-haired lord rose; the faint grumbling ceased. This gentleman was the one Talia had been watching so closely, and the only one who had not spoken. Orthallen; Lord of Wyvern's Reach, and Kris' uncle. He was the most senior Councillor, for he had served Selenay's father. He had served Selenay as well, throughout her entire reign. Selenay often called him "Lord Uncle," and he had been something of a father-figure to Elspeth. He was highly regarded and respected.

But Talia had never been able to warm to him. Part of the reason was because of what he had attempted to do to Skif. While he did not have the authority to remove any Chosen from the Collegium, he had tried to have the boy sent away for two years' punishment duty with the Army. His ostensible reason was the number of infractions of the Collegium rules Skif had managed to acquire, culminating with catching him red-handed in the office of the Provost-Marshal late one night. Orthallen had claimed Skif was there to alter the Misdemeanor Book. Talia, who had asked him to go there, was the only one who knew he had broken into the office to investigate Hulda's records. He was going to try to see who, exactly, had sponsored her into the Kingdom, in an attempt to ferret out the identity of her co-conspirator.

Talia had saved her friend at the cost of a lie, saying that she had asked him to find out whether her Holderkin

relatives were claiming the Privilege Tax allowed those
who had produced a child Chosen.

Since that time she had been subtly, but constantly, at
loggerheads with Orthallen; when she first began sitting
on the Council it seemed as if he had constantly moved
to negate what little authority she had. He had openly
belittled so many of her observations (on the grounds of
her youth and inexperience) that she had very seldom
spoken up when he was present. He always seemed to
her to be just a little too careful and controlled. When he
smiled, when he frowned, the expression never seemed
to go any deeper than the skin.

At first she had chided herself for her negative reaction to him, putting it down to her irrational fear of
males; handsome males in particular, for even though
past his prime, he was a strikingly handsome man—there
was no doubt which side of Kris' family had blessed him
with his own angelic face. And there was no sin in being
a trifle cold, emotionally speaking, yet for some reason,
she was always reminded of the wyvern that formed his
crest when she saw him. Like the wyvern, he seemed to
her to be thin-blooded, calculating, and quite ruthless—
and hiding it all beneath an attractively bejeweled skin.

But there was more to her mistrust of him now—because
she had more than one reason to suspect that *he* was the
source of those rumors about her misusing her Gift, and
she was certain that he had started them because he
knew how such vile rumors would affect an Empath who
was well-known to have a low sense of self-esteem. She
was equally certain that he had deliberately planted doubts
in Kris' mind—*knowing* that she would feel those doubts
and respond.

But this time she had cause to be grateful to him; when
Orthallen spoke, the rest of the Councillors paid heed,
and he spoke now in favor of the Queen's decision.

"My lords, my ladies—the Queen is entirely correct,"
he said, surprising Talia somewhat, for he had been one
of those most in favor of marrying Elspeth off with no
further ado. "We have only one Heir, and no other
candidates in the direct line. We should not take such a
risk. The Heir must be trained; I see the wisdom of that,

now. I withdraw my earlier plea for an immediate betrothal. Alessandar is a wise monarch, and will surely be
more than willing to make preliminary agreements on the
strength of a betrothal promised for the future. In such
ways, we shall have all the benefits of both plans.''

Talia was not the only member of the Council surprised by Orthallen's apparent about-face. Hyron stared
as if he could not believe what he had heard. The members of his faction and those opposed to him seemed
equally taken aback.

The result of this speech was the somewhat reluctant—
though unanimous—vote of the Council to deal with the
envoy just as Selenay had outlined. The vote was, frankly,
little more than a gesture, since together Selenay and
Talia could overrule the entire Council. But though the
unanimous backing of her stance gave Selenay a position
of strong moral advantage, Talia wondered what private
conversations would be taking place when the Council
session concluded—and who would be involved.

The remaining items on the Council's agenda were
routine and mundane; rescinding tax for several villages
hard hit by spring floods, the deployment and provisioning of extra troops at Lake Evendim in the hope of
making life difficult enough this year that the pirates and
raiders would decide to turn to easier prey, the fining of
a merchant-clan that had been involved in the slave-
trade. The arguments about just how many troops should
be moved to Lake Evendim and who would fund the
deployment went on for hours. The Lord Marshal and
Lady Kester (who ruled the district of the fisherfolk of
the lake) were unyielding in their demands for the extra
troops; Lord Gildas and Lady Cathan, whose rich
grainlands and merchant-guilds would supply the taxes
for the primary support of the effort, were frantic in their
attempts to cut down the numbers.

Talia's sympathy lay with the fisherfolk, yet she could
find it in her heart to feel for those who were being asked
to delve into their pockets for the pay and provisioning
of extra troops who would mostly remain idle. It seemed
that there was no way to compromise, and that the

arguments would continue with no conclusion. *That* would be no solution for the fisherfolk, either!

Finally, as the Lord Marshal thundered out figures concerning the numbers needed to keep watch along the winding coastlines, a glimmering of an idea came to her.

"Forgive me," she spoke into one of the sullen silences "I know little of warfare, but I know something of the fisherfolk. Only the young, healthy, and whole go out on the boats in season; unless my memory is incorrect, the old, the very young, pregnant women, those minding the young children for the rest of the family, and the crippled remain in the temporary work-villages. Am I right?"

"Aye—and that's what makes these people so damned hard to defend!" the Lord Marshal growled. "There isn't a one left behind with the ability to take arms!"

"Well, according to your figures, a good third of your troopers would be spending all their time on coastwatch. Since you're going to have to be feeding that many people anyway, why not provision the dependents instead, and have *them* doing the watching? Once they're freed from having to see to their day-to-day food supplies, they'll have the time for it, and what does a watcher need besides a pair of good eyes and the means to set an alert?"

"You mean use *children* as coastwatchers?" Gartheser exclaimed. "That—that's plainly daft!"

"Just you wait one moment, Gartheser," Myrim interjected. "I fail to see what's daft about it. It seems rare good sense to me."

"But—how are they to defend themselves?"

"Against what? Who's going to see them? They'll be *hidden*, man, in blinds, the way coastwatchers are *always* hidden. And I see the girl's drift. Puttin' them up would let us cut down the deployment by a third, just as Gildas and Cathan want," Lady Kester exclaimed, looking up like an old gray warhorse hearing the bugles. "Ye'd still have to provision the full number, though, ye old tightfists!"

"But they'd not have to pay 'em," one of the others chuckled.

"But—children?" Hyron said doubtfully. "How can

we put children in that kind of vital position? What's to keep them from running off to play?"

"Border children are not very childlike," Talia said quietly, looking to Kester, and the Speaker for the West nodded emphatic agreement.

"Silverhair, lad, the only thing keepin' *these* children off the boats is size," Kester snorted, though not unkindly. "They're not your soft highborns; they've been *working* since their hands were big enough to knot a net."

"Aye, I must agree." Lady Wyrist entered this argument for the first time. "I suspect your fisherfolk are not unlike my Holderkin—as Herald Talia can attest, Border-bred children have little time for childish pursuits."

"All the more chance that they'll run off, then," Hyron insisted.

"Not when they've seen whole families burned out by the selfsame pirates they're supposed to be watching for," said Myrim. "I served out there. I'd trust the sense of any of those 'children' before I'd trust the sense of some highborn graybeards I could name."

"Well said, lady!" Kester applauded, and turned sharp eyes on the Lord Marshal. "Tell ye what else, ye old wardog—an ye can persuade these troopers of yours to turn to and lend a hand to a bit of honest work now and again—"

"Such as?" The Lord Marshal almost cracked a smile.

"Taking the landwork; drying the fish and the sponge, mending the nets and lines, packing and crating, readying the longhouses for winter."

"It might be possible; what were you planning to offer?"

"War-pay; with the landwork off my people's hands, and knowing their folk on land are safe, we should be able to cover the extra bonus ourselves, and *still* bring in a proper profit."

"With careful phrasing, I think I could manage it."

"Done, then. How say you, Cathan, Gildas?"

They were only too happy to agree. The Council adjourned on this most positive note. Selenay and Talia stood as one, and preceded the rest out; Kyril a pace behind them.

"You *have* been learning, haven't you?" Kyril said in Talia's ear.

"Me?"

"Yes, you; and don't play the innocent," Elcarth joined his colleague as they stood in a white-clad knot outside the Council Chamber door, waiting for Selenay to finish conferring with the Seneschal on the agenda for the afternoon's audiences. He pushed a lock of gray hair out of his eyes and smiled. "That was cleverly done, getting the Border Lords on your side."

"It was the only way to get a compromise going. Cathan and Gildas would have agreed to anything that saved them money. With the Borderers and those two, we had a majority, and everybody benefited." Talia smiled back. "It was just a matter of invoking Borderer pride, really; we're *proud* of how tough we are, even as littles."

"Lovely. Truly lovely." Selenay joined them. "All those sessions of dealing with hardheaded Borderers in the middle of feuds taught you more than a little! Now tell me this; what would you have done if you *hadn't* absorbed all that fisherfolk lore from Keren, Teren, and Sherrill? Sat dumb?"

"I don't think so, not when it was obvious that there'd never be agreement." Talia thought for a moment. "I think . . . if one of you hadn't done so first . . . I would have suggested an adjournment until we could dig up an expert on the people of the area, preferably a Herald who has done several circuits there."

"Fine—that's what I was about to do when you spoke up; we are beginning to think as a team. Now I have a working lunch with Kyril and the Seneschal. I don't need you for it, so you can go find something to gulp down at the Collegium. At one I have formal audiences, and you have to be there. Those will last about three hours; you're free then until seven and Court dinner. After dinner, unless something comes up, you're free again."

"But Alberich is expecting you at four—" Elcarth grinned at Talia's groan. "—and Devan at five. Welcome home, Talia!"

"Well," she said with a sigh, "It's better than shovel-

ing snow, I guess! But I never thought I'd begin missing
field work so soon!"

"Missing field work already?"

Talia turned to find Kris standing behind her, an inso-
lent grin on his face. "I thought you told me you'd never
miss field work!"

She grinned back. "I lied."

"No!" He feigned shock. "Well, what of the Council
meeting?"

She wanted to tell him everything—then suddenly, remembered who he was—who his uncle was. Anything
she told him would quite likely get back to Orthallen,
and Kris would be telling Orthallen in all innocence,
never dreaming he was handing the man weapons to use
against her by doing so.

"Oh—nothing much," she said reluctantly. "The betrothal's being held off until Elspeth's finished training.
Look, Kris, I'm sorry, but I'm rather short on time right
now. I'll tell you later, all right?"

And she fled before he could ask anything more.

Lunch was a few bites snatched on the run between the
Palace and her room; audiences required a slightly more
formal uniform than the one she'd worn to the Council
session. Talia managed to wash, change, and get back in
time to discuss the scheduled audiences with the Seneschal. Talia's role here was as much bodyguard as anything else, although her duties included assessing the
emotional state of those coming before the Queen and
giving her any information that seemed appropriate.

The audience chamber was long and narrow; the same
gray granite and dark wood as the rest of the old Palace.
Selenay's throne was on a raised platform at the far end.
Behind the throne the wall had been carved into the
Royal arms; there were no curtains for assassins to hide
behind. The Queen's Own spent the entire time positioned behind the throne to the Queen's right, from
which position the Queen could hear her least whisper.
Petitioners had to travel the length of the chamber, giving Talia ample time to "read" their emotional state if
she thought it necessary to do so.

The audiences were quite unexciting; petitioners ranged from a smallholder seeking permission to establish a Dyer's Guildhouse on his property to two noblemen who had called challenge on each other and were now trying desperately to find a way out of the situation without either of them losing face. Not once did she deem the situation grave enough to warrant "reading" any of them.

When the audience session concluded, Talia sprinted back to her room to change into something old and worn for her weapons drill with Alberich.

Walking into the salle was like walking into the past; nothing had changed, not the worn, backless benches against the wall, not the clutter of equipment and towels on and beneath the benches, not the light coming from the windows. Not even Alberich had changed so much as a hair; he still wore the same old leathers, or clothing like enough to have been the same. His scar-seamed face still looked as incapable of humor as the walls of the Palace; his long black hair held neither more nor less gray than it had the last time Talia had seen him.

Elspeth was already there, going full out against Jeri under Alberich's critical eye. Talia held her breath in surprise; Elspeth was, (to her judgment, at least) Jeri's equal. The young weapons instructor was not holding anything back, and more than once only saved herself from a "kill" by frantically wrenching her body out of the way of the wooden blade. Both of them were sodden with sweat when Alberich finally called a halt.

"You do well, children; both of you," Alberich nodded as he spoke. Both Elspeth and Jeri began walking slowly in little circles to keep their muscles from stiffening, while drying their faces with old towels. "Jeri, it is more work you need on your defense; working with the students has made you sloppy. Elspeth, if it was that you were not far busier than any student should be, I would make you Jeri's assistant."

Elspeth raised her head, and Talia could see she was flushed with the praise, her eyes glowing.

"However, you are very far from perfect. Your left side is too weak and you are vulnerable there. From now on you are to work left-handed, using your right only when I tell you, to keep from losing your edge. Enough for today, off to the bath with you—it is like your Companions you smell!"

He turned to Talia, who bit her lip, then said, "I have the feeling I'm in trouble."

"In trouble? It *is* possible—" Alberich scowled; then unexpectedly smiled. "No fear, little Talia; it is that I am well aware how few were the chances for you to keep in practice. Today we will start slowly, and I will determine just how much you have lost. *Tomorrow* you will be in trouble."

Talia was thanking the gods an hour later that Kris had insisted they both keep in fighting trim as much as possible. Alberich was reasonably pleased that she had lost so little edge, and kept his cutting remarks to a minimum. Nor was she the recipient of more than one or two bruising *thwacks* from his practice blade when she'd done something exceptionally stupid. On the whole, she felt as if she'd gotten off very lightly.

Another run, this time to wash and change yet again, and she was back at Healer's Collegium, going over the past eighteen months with Devan and Rynee. Both were blessedly succinct; there had not been any truly major mental traumas for Rynee to deal with among the Heraldic Circle. As a result, Talia was able to flee to Companion's Field just as the warning bell for supper sounded at the Herald's Collegium.

Rolan was waiting at the fence, and she pulled herself onto his back without bothering with going for a saddle.

"I think," she told him, as he walked off into a quiet copse, "that I may die of exhaustion. This is worse than when I was a student."

He lipped her booted foot affectionately; Talia picked up a projection of reassurance and something to do with time.

"You think I'll get used to it in a few days? Lord, I hope so! Still—" She thought hard, trying to remember just what the Queen's schedule was like. "Hm. Council sessions aren't more than three times a week. Audiences, though, they're every day. Alberich will torture me every day, too. But I *could* reschedule, say, Devan before breakfast and just after lunch—save weapons drill for just before dinner, so I'm only changing twice a day. You, my darling, whenever I can squeeze a free moment."

Rolan made a sound very like laughing.

"True, with the tight bond *we* have, I don't have to be with you physically, do I? What did you think of the audiences?"

To Talia's delight, he hung his head and did a credible imitation of a human snore.

"You, too? Lord and Lady, they're as bad as State banquets! Why did I ever think being a Herald would be exciting?"

Rolan snorted, and projected the memory of their flight across country to get help for the plague-stricken village of Waymeet, following that with the fight with the raiders that had attacked and fired Hevenbeck.

"You're right; I think I can live with boredom. What do you think of how Elspeth's coming along?"

To her surprise, Rolan was faintly worried, but could give her no clear idea why he felt that way.

"Is it important enough to trance down to where you can give me a clearer idea?"

He shook his head, mane brushing her face a little.

"Well, in that case, we'll let it go. It's probably just the usual rebelliousness—and I can't say as I blame her. Her schedule is as bad as mine. *I* don't like it, and I can't fault her if she doesn't either."

Talia dismounted beside a tiny, spring-fed pool, and sat in the grass, watching the sun set, and emptying her mind. Rolan stood beside her, both of them content with a quiet moment in which to simply be together.

"Well, I'm into it at last," she said, half to herself. "I thought I'd never make it, sometimes. . . ."

This had been the first day she had truly *been* Queen's Own—with all the duties and all the rights; from the right to overrule the Council to the right to overrule Selenay (though that was one she hadn't exercised, and still wasn't sure she had the nerve for!); from her duty to ease the fears of her fellows in the Circle to the duty to see to the Heir's well-being.

It was a frightening moment in a way, and a sobering one. On reflection, it almost seemed as if the Queen's Own best served the interests of Queen and country by *not* being too forward; by saving her votes for the truly critical issues and keeping her influence mostly to the quiet word in the Queen's ear. That suited Talia; she hadn't much enjoyed having all eyes on her this afternoon—especially not Orthallen's. But Selenay had been more at ease just because Talia was *there;* there had been no mistaking that. In the long run, that was what the job was all about—giving the Monarch one completely honest and completely trustworthy friend. . . .

The dying sun splashed scarlet and gold on the bottoms of the few clouds that hung in the west, while the sky above them deepened from blue to purple, and the Hounds, the two stars that chased the sun, shone in unwinking splendor. The tops of the clouds took on the purple of the sky as the sun dropped below the horizon, and the purple tinge soaked through them like water being taken into a sponge. The light faded, and everything began to lose color, fading into cool blues. Little frogs began to sing in the pool at Talia's feet; night-blooming jacinth flowers opened somewhere near her, and the cooling breeze picked up the perfume and carried it to her.

And just when she was feeling totally disinclined to move, a mosquito bit her.

"Ouch! Damn!" She slapped at the offending insect, then laughed. "The gods remind me of my duty. Back to work for me, love. Enjoy your evening."

Three

As if that tiny insect bite had been an omen, things began to go wrong, starting with the weather.

The perfect spring turned sour; it seemed to rain every day without a letup, and the rain was cold and steadily dismal. The sun, when Talia actually saw it, gave a chill, washed-out light. Miserable, that was what it was; miserable and depressing. The few flowers that managed to bloom seemed dispirited, and hung limply on their stems. The damp crept into everything, and fires on the hearths all day and all night did little to drive it out. The whole Kingdom was affected; there were new tales reaching the Court every day of flooding, sometimes in areas that hadn't flooded in a hundred years or more.

This was bound to have an effect on the Councillors. They worked like heroes at all hours to cope with emergencies, but the grim atmosphere made them quarrelsome and inclined to snipe at each other at the least opportunity. Every Council session meant at least one major fight and two ruffled tempers to be soothed. The names they called each other would have been ample cause for dueling anywhere else.

At least they treated Talia with that same lack of respect—she came in for her share of sniping, and that was a positive sign, that she had been accepted as one of them, and their equal.

The sniping-among-equals was something she could cope with, though it was increasingly difficult to keep her temper when everyone around her was losing theirs. Far harder to deal with in any rational way were Orthallen's subtle attempts at undercutting her authority. Clever, those attempts were; frighteningly clever. He never said anything that anyone could directly construe as criticism; no, what he did was hint—oh, so politely, and at every possible opportunity—that perhaps she was a bit young and inexperienced for her post. That she might be going overboard because of the tendency of youth to see things always in black and white. That she surely meant well, but . . . and so on. It made Talia want to scream and bite something. There was no way to counteract him except to be even more reasonable and mild-tempered than he. She felt as if she were standing on sand, and he was the flood tide washing it out from under her.

Things were not going all that well between herself and Kris either.

"Goddess, Talia," Kris groaned, slumping back into his chair. "He's *just* doing what he sees as his duty!"

Talia counted to ten, slowly, counted the Library bookshelves, then counted the rings of the knothole in the table in front of her. "He was claiming *I* was overreacting at the same time that Lady Kester was calling Hyron a pompous peabrain at the top of her lungs!"

"Well—"

"Kris, he's said the same damn things every Council session and at least three times *during* each session! Every time it looks as if the other Councillors are beginning to listen to what I'm saying, he trots out the same speech!" She shoved her chair away from the table, and began pacing restlessly, up and down the length of the vacant Library. This had been a particularly bad session, and the muscles of her neck felt as tight as bridge cables.

"I just can't see anything at all sinister in my uncle's behavior—"

"*Dammit*, Kris—"

"Talia he's old, he's set in his ways—you're frighteningly young to him, *and* likely to usurp *his* position! Have some pity on the man, he's *only* human!"

"So what am I?" She struggled not to shout, but the argument was giving her a headache. "I'm supposed to *like* what he's doing?"

"He's not *doing* anything!" Kris scowled, as if he had a headache, too. "Frankly, I think you're hearing insult and seeing peril that *isn't* there."

Talia turned abruptly, and stared at him, tight-lipped, fists clenched. "In that case," she replied, after a dozen slow, careful breaths of dust-laden air, "maybe I should take my irrational fantasies elsewhere."

"But—"

She turned again and all but ran down the staircase. He called something after her, in a distressed voice. She ignored it, and ran on.

So now they didn't talk about much of anything anymore. And Talia missed that; missed the closeness they used to have, the way they used to be able to confide their deepest secrets to each other. Truth to be told, she missed that more than the physical side of their relationship—though now that she was no longer used to being celibate she missed that, too. . . .

Then there was her relationship—or more accurately, lack of one—with Dirk.

His behavior was baffling in the extreme; one moment he would seem determined to get her alone somewhere, the next, he shied away from even being in the same room. He would be lurking in the background everywhere she went for a day or two, then just as abruptly would vanish, only to reappear in a few days. Half the time he seemed determined to throw Kris at her, the other half, equally determined to block Kris from getting anywhere near her—

Talia saw her elusive quarry leaning on the fence surrounding Companion's Field. He was staring, broodingly, off into the far distance. For a wonder, it wasn't raining, although the sky was a dead, dull gray and threatening to pour any moment.

"Dirk?"

He jumped, whipped about, and stared at her with wide, startled eyes.

"W-what are you doing here?" he asked, somewhat ungraciously, his back pressed hard against the fence as if that barrier was all that was keeping him from running away.

"The same as you, probably," Talia replied, forcing herself *not* to snap at him. "Looking for my Companion, and maybe somebody to ride with."

"In that case, shouldn't you be looking for Kris?" he asked, his expression twisted as if he'd swallowed something very unpleasant.

She couldn't think of a reply, and chose not to answer him. Instead she moved to the fence herself, and stood with one booted foot on the first railing and her arms folded along the top, mimicking the pose he had held when she saw him.

"Talia—" He took one step toward her—she heard his boot squelch in the wet grass—then stopped. "I—Kris is—a very valuable friend. More than friend. I—"

She waited for him to say what was on his mind, hoping that *this* time he'd finish it. Maybe if she didn't look at him, he'd be able to speak his piece.

"Yes?" she prompted when the silence went on so long she'd almost suspected him of sneaking away. She turned to catch his blue, blue eyes staring almost helplessly at her before he hastily averted them.

"I—I've got to go—" he gasped, and fled.

She was ready to scream with frustration. This was the fourth time he'd pulled this little trick, *starting* to say something, then running away. And with things somewhat at odds between herself and Kris, she really didn't feel as if she wanted to ask Kris to help. Besides, she hadn't seen Kris much since their last little set-to.

With an exasperated sigh she Mindcalled Rolan. They both needed exercise—and he, at least, would be a sympathetic listener.

Kris was avoiding Talia on purpose.

When he'd first returned, his uncle had taken time out to give him familial greetings; that was only to be expected. But Orthallen lately seemed to be going out of his way to speak to his nephew two or three times a week, and the conversation somehow always turned to Talia.

Not by accident, either. Kris was mortally sure of that.

Nor were they pleasant conversations, though they seemed to be on the surface. Kris was beginning to get an impression that Orthallen was *looking* for something— weaknesses in the Queen's Own, perhaps. Certainly, whenever he happened to say something complimentary about Talia, his uncle would always insinuate a "Yes, but surely . . ." in a rather odd and confiding tone.

Like the latest example.

He'd been on his way back from a consultation with Elcarth about some of his latest Farseeing pupils, when Orthallen had just "happened" to intercept him.

"Nephew!" Orthallen had hailed him, "I have word from your brother—"

"Is anything wrong?" Kris had asked anxiously. The family holdings were in the heart of some of the worst flooding in a generation. "Does he need me at home? I'll be free in a few weeks—"

"No, no; things are far from well, but it's not an emergency yet. The smallholders have lost about a tenth of their fields, in total; obviously some are worse off than others. They've lost enough livestock that the spring births are barely going to make up for the losses—oh, and your brother lost one of his Shin'a'in cross-bred stallions."

"Damn—he's not going to find another one of those in a hurry. Are we needing any outside help?"

"Not yet. There's enough grain in storage to make up for the losses. But he wanted you to know exactly how things stood, so that you wouldn't worry."

"Thank you, uncle. I appreciate your taking the time to let me know."

"And is your young protégée settling in, do you think?" he then asked smoothly. "What with all the emergencies that have come up lately, I wonder if she has more than she can cope with, sometimes."

"Havens, Uncle, I'm the *last* one to ask," Kris had said with a little impatience. "I hardly see her anymore. We both have duties, and those duties don't let us cross paths too often."

"Oh? Somehow I had gotten the impression that you

Heralds always knew what was happening in each others' lives."

Kris really hadn't been able to think of a response to that; at least not a respectful one.

"I only asked because I thought she looked a bit careworn, and I thought perhaps she might have said something to you," Orthallen continued, his cold eyes boring into Kris'. "She has a heavy burden of responsibility for one so young."

"She's equal to it, Uncle. I've told you that before. Rolan wouldn't have Chosen her otherwise."

"Well, I'm sure you're correct," Orthallen replied, sounding as if he meant the opposite. "Those rumors of her using her Gift to manipulate—"

"Were absolutely unfounded. I told you that. She has been so circumspect in even *reading* others that she practically has to be forced to it—" Kris broke off, wondering if he was saying too much.

"Ah," Orthallen said after a moment. "That *is* a comfort. The child seems to have a wisdom out of keeping with her years. However, if she should feel she's having problems, I would appreciate it if you'd tell me. After all, as the Queen's eldest Councillor, I should be aware of possible trouble. I'd be only to happy to help her in any way I can, but she still seems to be carrying over that grudge from her student days, and I doubt she'd ever give me the correct time of day, much less confide in me."

Kris had mumbled something noncommittal, and his uncle had gone away outwardly satisfied—but the whole encounter had left a very bad taste in Kris's mouth. He was regretting now the fact that he'd confided to his uncle in one of those early conversations his belief that Talia and Dirk were lifebonded; the man had seized on the tidbit as avidly as a hawk on a mouse. But at the same time, he didn't want to have to face Talia herself with these suspicions awakened; she'd get it out of him, no doubt of it. And while she wouldn't *say*, "I told you so," she had a particular look of lowered eyelids and a quirk at one corner of her mouth that spoke volumes, and he wasn't in the mood to deal with it.

Besides, it was only too possible that she'd infected *him* with her paranoia.

If only he could be sure of that—but he couldn't. So he avoided her.

Dirk straddled an old, worn chair in his room, staring into the darkness beyond the windowpane. It was nearly dusk—and as black as midnight out there. He felt as if he were being torn into little bits.

He couldn't make up his mind *what* he wanted to do; part of him wanted to battle for Talia by all means fair or foul, part of him felt that he should be unselfish and give Kris a clear field with her, part of him was afraid to find out what *she* thought of all this, and a fourth part of him argued that he really didn't want any commitments to females anyway—look what the *last* one had gotten him.

The last one. Lady Naril—oh, gods.

He stared at the sullen flickers of lightning in the heart of the clouds above the trees. It had been so long ago—and not long enough ago.

Gods, I was such a fool.

He and Kris had been posted to the Collegium, teaching their specialties—Fetching and Farsight. It had been *his* first experience of Court and Collegium as a full Herald.

I was a stupid sheep looking for a wolf.

Not that he hadn't had his share of dalliances, even if he'd always had to play second to Kris. He hadn't minded, not really. But he'd been feeling a little lost; Kris had been born to Court circles, and flowed back into them effortlessly. Dirk had been left on the outskirts.

Then Naril had introduced herself to him—

I thought she was so pure, so innocent. She seemed so alone in the great Court, so eager for a friend. And she was so young—so very beautiful.

How could he have known that in her sixteen short years she'd had more men in her thrall than a rosebush had thorns?

And how could he have guessed she intended to use *him* to snare Kris?

Gods, I was half out of my mind with love for her.

He stared at the reflection in the window, broodingly. *I saw only what I wanted to see—that's for certain. Lost most of my few wits.*

But there had been just enough sense left to him that when she'd asked him to arrange a private meeting between herself and his friend, he'd hidden where he could overhear her. The artificial grotto in the garden that she had chosen was secluded—but had ample hiding space in the bushes to either side of the entrance.

Dirk probed at the aching memory as if it were a sore tooth, taking twisted pleasure from the pain. *I could hardly believe my ears when I heard her issuing Kris an ultimatum: come to her bed until she tired of him, or she would make my life a living hell.*

He had burst in on them, demanding to know what she meant, crazy-wild with anger and pain.

Kris had slipped away. And Naril turned to him with utter hatred in her enormous violet eyes. When she'd finished what she had to say to him, he'd wanted to kill himself.

Again he stared at his reflection. *Not everything she said was wrong—* he told himself sadly. *What woman with any sense would want me? Especially with Kris in reach. . . .*

It had been a long time before he'd stopped wanting to die—and a longer time before life became something he enjoyed instead of something he endured.

Now—was it all happening again?

He was doing his level best to come to terms with himself, and being stuck at the Collegium with Talia in sight at least once a day wasn't helping. The whole situation was comical, but somehow when he tried to laugh it off, his "mirth" had a very hollow sound even to his ears. He had thrown himself into his work, only to find that he was watching for her constantly out of the corner of his eye. He couldn't help himself; it was like scratching a rash. He knew he shouldn't, but he did it anyway, and it gave him a perverse sort of satisfaction. And even though it troubled him to watch her, it troubled him more not to.

Gods, gods—what am I going to do?

The reflection gave him no answer.

After three weeks of rain, the weather had cleared for a bit. To Talia's great relief, things were emotionally on a more even keel, at least where the tempers of Court and Collegium were concerned. The evening had been warm enough to leave windows open, and the fresh air had made a gratifying change in the stuffiness of her quarters. Talia was fast asleep when the Death Bell shattered the peace of the night with its brazen tolling.

It woke her from a nightmare of flame, fear, and agony. That nightmare had held her in a grip so tenacious that she expected to open her eyes to find her own room an inferno. She clutched the blankets to her chest, as she slowly became aware that the air she breathed was cool and scented with night mist, not smoke-filled and choking. It took several moments for her to clear her mind of the dream enough to think clearly again, and when at last she did, it was to realize that the dream and the Death Bell's tolling had related causes.

Fire—her nails bit into her palms as she clenched her hands. When fire was involved, the Herald most likely to be involved with it was—Griffon! Dear gods—let it not be Griffon, not her year-mate, not her friend—

But as she stared unseeing into the darkness and forced herself into a calmer frame of mind, she *knew* without doubt that it was not Griffon, after all. The name and the face that hazed into her now-receptive mind were those of a student of the year following hers—Christa, whom she remembered as one of Dirk's pupils in the Gift of Fetching.

And in many ways, this was an even greater tragedy, for Christa had still been on her internship assignment.

When the pieces were all assembled from the various fragments the Heralds at the Collegium had "read" when the Death Bell began ringing, the result was almost as confusing as having no information at all. This much alone they knew; Christa was dead; the Herald assigned as her counselor, the cheerfully lascivious Destria, was badly hurt, and the cause had something to do both with raiders and a great fire.

The information they received from the Heralds stationed with the Healing Temple to which Destria had been carried was nearly as fragmentary. Their Gifts of Mindspeech weren't nearly as strong as Kyril's or Sherrill's. But they made it plain that Destria needed more help than they could provide—and that there was urgent need of a different kind of aid. They were sending Destria back to Healer's Collegium and the Palace, and with her would come clarification.

Within the week they came; one uninjured Herald, Destria (a pitiful thing carried on a litter swung between two Companions, one of them Destria's Sofi), and a battered and bruised farmer whose clothing still bore the smoke stains and ash of a fire. All three of them had to have traveled day and night with scarcely a pause to rest to reach the capital so quickly.

Selenay called the Council into immediate session, and the petitioner came before them. He sagged wearily into the chair they set for him, his eyes sunken deeply into their sockets, his hair so full of ash it was hard to tell what color it was. It was plain he had wasted not even a single hour, but had gotten on with the journey without taking time for his own comfort. And the tale he told, of well-armed, organized raiders, and the near-massacre of everyone in his town, was enough to chill the blood.

They had given him a seat, since he was plainly too weary to stand for very long, and he seemed like an omen of doom, sitting before the Council Table, both hands bandaged to the elbow. The taint of smoke had so permeated his clothing that it was carried even to the Councillors, and the smell of it brought his message home with terrible force.

"It was slaughter, pure and simple," he told the Council in a voice roughened by the smoke. "And we walked into it like silly sheep. Up until this spring we've had so much problem with brigands, little bands of them, pecking away at us, that we'd come to expect them, like spring floods. Then, when they all vanished this winter— gods, you'd think we'd have had the sense to realize something was up. But we didn't; we just thought they'd gone off to richer pickings. Ah, fools, fools and blind!''

He dropped his face into his hands for a moment, and when he lifted it again, there were tears on his cheeks from eyes already red. "They'd gotten together, you see; one of the wolves had finally proved the strongest, and they'd gotten together. We'd prided ourselves on having put the village in an unassailable valley; sheer rock to our back and sides, and only one narrow pass that let into it. We couldn't be starved or forced out from thirst; we had our own wells, and plenty of food stockpiled. Well, they had an answer to that. A handful of them killed the sentries, and poisoned the dogs that patrolled the heights, then rained fire arrows down on the village by night. We build with wood and thatch, mostly; the buildings went up like pitch torches. The rest waited outside the pass, and picked off those of us that got as far as the cleft. Have you ever seen rabbits running before a grass fire? That was us—and they were the hungry wolves waiting for dinner to leap into their jaws. Men I've known all my life I watched getting their legs shot out from underneath them. Children hardly old enough to be wearing knives, too—even graybeards and grannies. Anybody likely to be able to take up a weapon. They shot to cripple, not to kill; dead mouths can't tell where they've hid their little treasures, y'see. A good half of those they shot may never walk right again. A good quarter bled to death where they lay. And a full quarter of the children burned to death in the houses they set fire to.''

A muted murmur of horror crept around the table; Lady Kester hid her own face in her hands.

A beam of late afternoon sunlight spotlighted the speaker as it poured in through the high windows. It touched him with a clear gold that made his eyes seem even more like burned-out pits in his face. "Your Heralds were not far; overnighting in a Waystation, I think. How they knew our plight, I'll never know—must've been more of your magic, I guess. They came charging up on the backs of the raiders, two of 'em like a blessed army. Those white horses—the Companions—they *were* damn near an army by themselves. They broke up the

ambush at the head of the pass, got them scattered off
into the woods for a bit. Then the older one started
getting us organized, got us clearing the snipers off the
heights; the younger one took off into the burning buildings, hearing cries and looking for somebody to save, I
guess. The older one didn't even notice she was gone—
until—"

He swallowed hard, and his hands were shaking. "I
heard screaming, worse than before; the older Herald,
she jerked like she'd been shot. She shouted at us to take
the brigands before they got themselves over their fright,
then she headed into the fires herself; I followed—my
hands were too burned to hold a weapon, but I thought I
might be able to help with the fires. The younger one
had gotten trapped on the second floor of one of the
houses; I was right behind the older one and I could see
her against the fire. Calm as you please, she's tossing
younglings out to their parents. At least I *think* she was
tossing 'em—she'd have a little one in her hands one
moment, then the next, his mum or dad would be holding it. The older one ran up, started shouting at her to
jump. She just shook her head, and turned back one
more time—the floor collapsed then. That damn horse of
hers crashed through the wall and went in after her—the
other Herald was right on his heels. She'd no sooner
cleared the door when the whole roof caved in. We got
her out, but the other—"

One of Selenay's pages brought him wine, and he
drank it gratefully, his teeth chattering against the rim of
the tankard.

"That's what happened. For us, we beat 'em back, but
we didn't get more than a handful of them compared to
the numbers we know they've got. They're comin' back,
we know they are. 'Specially since they must know the
Heralds are—gone. We lost half the town—most of the
able-bodied. I was about the only one that could make
the ride here. We need help, Majesty, m'lords—we need
it bad—"

"You'll have that help," Selenay pledged, her eyes
hard and black with anger as she stood. "This isn't the
first incursion of these bastards we've heard of, but it's

by far and away the worst. It's obvious to me that there is no way we can expect you folk to handle brigands as organized as these are. Lord Marshal, and good sir, if you'll come with me we'll mobilize a company of the Guard." She looked inquiringly at the rest of the Council.

Lady Cathan spoke for all of them. "Whatever is needed, Highness. You and the Lord Marshal are the best judge of what that is. We'll stand surety for it."

Talia nodded, with all the other Councillors. What Selenay had told the man was true; for the past few months there had been tales of bandits growing organized in Gyrefalcon's Marches. Sporadic raids had occurred before this—but never had the brigands dared to put an entire town to the sword! It was obviously more than local militia could handle; the entire Council was agreed on that.

Talia slipped away then, knowing with certainty that Selenay did not need her at the moment, and that another most definitely did. The tug at her was unmistakable. She opened the door to the Council chamber just enough to slip through—and once she was out into the cool, dark hallway, broke into a run.

She ran out through the old Palace and passed the double doors of Herald's Collegium—then down the echoing main hall, heading for the side door and for Healer's. She felt the pull of a soul in agony as clearly as if she were being called by voice. She all but collided with Devan, who was on his way to look for her.

"I might have known you'd know," he said gratefully, hitching up his green robes so that he could run with her. "Talia, she's fighting us, and we can't get past her shielding to do even the simplest painblocks. She blames herself for Christa, and all she wants to do now is die. Rynee can't do anything with her."

"That's what I thought; Lord and Lady, the guilt is so thick I can almost *see* it. Well, let's see if I can get through to her."

They had accomplished a certain amount of Healing at the site of the battle, while Destria was still unconscious; enough to enable moving her safely. She still was a most unpretty sight, lying on a special pad in one of the rooms

reserved for burn patients. The room itself was bare
stone; scrubbed spotless twice a day when unoccupied,
and not so much as a speck of dust was ever allowed to
settle there. The one window was sealed tight so that
nothing could blow in. Everything that was brought in
was removed as soon as it was no longer needed, and
scalded.

It was a tribute to the onsite Healers that Destria was
still among the living. The last person Talia had seen
with burns like hers had been Vostel, who had taken the
full fury of an angry firebird on his fragile flesh. Where
her burns had been relatively light—though the skin was
red, puffed, and blistering—she was unbandaged. But
her arms and hands were wrapped in special poultices of
herbs and the thinnest and most fragile of tanned rabbit
and calfskin, and Talia knew that beneath those bandages the skin was gone, and the flesh left raw. They had
laid her on a pallet of lambskin, tanned with the wool on;
the fibers would cushion her burned skin and prevent too
much pressure from being exerted on it. Talia knelt at
the head of the pallet and rested both her hands on
Destria's forehead. Destria's face and head were the only
portions of her that were relatively untouched. As Talia
reached into the whirlwind of pain, delirium, and guilt
with her Gift, she knew that this was likely to be the
hardest such fight she'd ever faced.

Guilt, black and full of despair, surrounded Talia from
all directions. Pain, physical and mental, lanced through
the guilt like red lightning. Talia knew her first priority
was to find out *why* the guilt existed in the first place,
and where it was coming from—

That was easy enough; she simply lowered her shielding a fraction more, and let herself be drawn in where
the negative emotions were the thickest.

The fading core that was Destria spun an ever-tightening
cocoon of bleakness around herself. Talia reached for
that cocoon with a softly glowing mental "hand" and
withered it until that which was Destria stood cringing
before her.

Talia paid no heed to her attempts at escape, but drew

her into a rapport in which nothing was hidden; not from her—and not from Destria. And she let Destria read *her* as she strove to begin the Healing of the other Herald's mental hurts.

I failed— that was the most overwhelming. *They counted on me, and I failed.*

But there was something more, something that kept the guilt feeding on itself until Destria loathed her own being. And Talia found it, hiding underneath, festering. *And I failed because I wanted something for me. I failed because I was selfish; I don't deserve my Whites—I deserve to die.*

This was something Talia was only too familiar with; and was something Rynee wouldn't understand. Healers were firm believers in a little honest selfishness; it kept a person sane and healthy. Heralds, though—well, Heralds were supposed to be completely unselfish, totally devoted to duty. That was nonsense, of course; Heralds were only people. But sometimes they started to believe in that nonsense, and when something went wrong, because of their natures, the first people they tended to blame were themselves.

So now Talia had to prove to Destria that there was nothing wrong with being a Herald *and* human. No small task, since Destria's guilt was akin to doubts she shared about herself.

How often had she berated *herself* for wanting a little corner of life to call her own—some time when she didn't *have* to be a Herald—when she had been so tired of having to think first of others before taking the smallest action? How many times had she yearned for a little time to be lazy, a chance for a bit of privacy—and then felt guilty because she had?

And hadn't she had been ready to assume that she *was* guilty of unconsciously using her Empathy to manipulate others?

Hadn't she been angry enough to strangle someone more than once, and then been angry at herself for giving in to the weakness of rage?

Oh, she understood Destria's self-loathing, only too well.

*   *   *

Rynee and the rest of the Healers watched soberly, sensing the battle Talia fought, though (except for the perspiration beading Talia's brow) there were no outward signs of a struggle. They all remained in the same positions they had first taken as the shadows cast through the window lengthened almost imperceptibly and the light slowly faded; and still there was no outward indication of success or failure.

Then, after the first half-hour, Rynee whispered to Devan, "I think she's getting somewhere; Destria threw me out after the first few minutes and wouldn't let me in again."

When a full hour had passed, Talia sighed, then carefully broke her physical contact with the other Herald, and slumped with exhaustion, her hands lying limply on her thighs.

"Go ahead; I've got her convinced for now. She won't fight you at the moment."

As she spoke, the waiting Healers converged on Destria like worker-bees on an injured queen. Rynee, whose Gift of Healing was (like Talia's) for minds rather than bodies, helped Talia to her feet.

"Why couldn't *I* get through to her?" she asked plaintively.

"Simple; I'm a Herald, you're not," Talia said, edging past the Healers and out into the hall. "She reacted to you the way you would react to a nonHealer trying to tell you that a gut-stab was nothing to worry about. Gods, I'm *tired!* And I'll have it all to do again tomorrow, or she'll fight you again. And *then,* when I finally convince her permanently that it wasn't her fault, I'll have to convince her she isn't going to revolt men with—the way she'll look when you're done. And that the scarring isn't some punishment set on her for being a bit randy."

"I was afraid of that." Rynee bit her lip. "And she is going to scar; I can't tell you how badly yet, but there's no getting around it. Her face wasn't touched, but the rest of her—some of it isn't going to be at all pretty. The only burn victim I've ever heard of that was as bad was—"

Despite her weariness, Talia's eyes lighted when she saw an idea begin to form behind Rynee's frown. "Out with it, milady—you've the same Gift as I have, and if you've gotten a notion it's probably going to work." She paused in the hallway and leaned against the wood-paneled wall; Rynee rubbed the bridge of her long nose with her finger.

"Vostel—what does he do now? Could he be recalled here for a while?" she asked finally, hope in her cloud-gray eyes.

"Relay at the Fallflower Healing Temple; and yes, anyone on relay work can be replaced. What are you thinking of?"

"That he'll be the best 'medicine' for her; he went through it all himself. He knows how it hurts, and when it'll stop, and how you have to force yourself to work through the pain if you intend to get the full use of your limbs back. And he's a Herald, so she'll believe what he says. Besides all that, despite the old scars he's still a better-than-passable-looking man. And he *doesn't* believe in the fates dealing out arbitrary punishments for a little healthy hedonism."

Talia chuckled in spite of herself. "Oh, very good! If we have him at her side coaxing and encouraging, he'll do half our work for us! You're right about his beliefs, too. All I had to do was keep reassuring him that the pain *would* end, and that he wasn't being a coward and a whiner for occasionally wanting to give up. I've no doubt they'll find each other quite congenial when Destria's back to something like her old self and her old appetites. I'll see Kyril and get Vostel sent here as soon as he can be replaced; he'll be here by the time she starts to need him."

Talia moved away from the wall and stumbled as her knees wobbled a little. They had only gotten a few feet down the hall, and already her exhaustion was threatening to overwhelm her. Rynee steered her toward a soft and comfortable-looking padded bench, one of many placed at intervals along the walls, for Healers were apt to catch oddments of rest wherever and whenever they could.

"And you—you get yourself down onto that couch and take a short nap. I'll wake you, but if you don't take some recovery time you won't be of any use to any of us. You know the saying—never argue with a Healer—"

"And I never do!"

"See that you keep it that way."

About a week later Talia was on her way from the Audience Chamber to her own room to change for arms practice, and her mood was a somber one. The audiences were no longer dull, and that was unfortunate. More and more often those seeking audience with the Queen were from Gyrefalcon's Marches reporting the depredations of what was obviously a small army of bandits. It was the wild and rocky character of the countryside that had let them organize without anyone realizing it; that same wild countryside enabled them to vanish before the Guard could pin them down.

Orthallen was using the existence of these bandits as a political tool—a tactic that disgusted Talia, considering the suffering that they were causing, not to mention that they were preying on some of the lands supposedly in his jurisdiction.

She had just endured one such session.

There were six Heralds out there now—along with the Guard company Selenay had sent. The Heralds were organizing the common folk to their own defense, since the Guard could not be everywhere at once. One of those Heralds, Herald Patris, sent a messenger that had only arrived today.

" 'They seem to know exactly where the Guard is at all times,' Patris had written. 'They strike, and are away before we can do anything. They know these hills of stone and the caves that honeycomb them better than we guessed; I suspect them of traveling a great deal underground, which would certainly answer the question of how they move about without being spotted. At this point, we are beyond saving the livestock or the harvest; Majesty, I must be frank with you. It will be all we can do just to save the lives of these people. And I must tell you worse yet—having stripped them of all possessions, the bastards have taken to carrying off the only thing these folk have left. Their children.' "

"Great Goddess!" Lady Wyrist had exclaimed.

"I'm on it, Majesty," Lady Cathan had said grimly at almost the same moment. "They won't get children out past my Guildsmen—not after that slaver scandal—with your permission?"

Selenay had nodded distractedly, and Lady Cathan sprinted from the room in a swirl of colorful brocades.

"Majesty," Orthallen said then, "It is as I have been saying. We need a larger standing army—and we need more autonomy in *local* hands. If I had been given two or three companies of the Guard and the power to order them, this emergency would *never* have become the disaster it is!"

Then the debate had broken out—yet again. The Council had split on this issue of granting power at the local level and increasing the size of the Guard; split about equally. On Orthallen's side were Lord Gartheser, Lady Wyrist, Bard Hyron, Father Aldon and the Seneschal. Selenay—who did not want the size of the army increased, because to do so would mean drafted levies and possibly impressment—preferred to keep the power where it was, with the Council, and was lobbying for hiring professional mercenaries to augment the existing troops. Backing her were Talia, Kyril, Elcarth, Healer Myrim, and the Lord Marshal. Lady Kester, Lord Gildas, and Lady Cathan remained undecided. They weren't especially pleased with the notion of foreign troops, but they also weren't much in favor of hauling folk away from their lands and trades either.

Talia was pondering the state of things when her sharp ears caught the sound of a muffled sob. Without hesitation she unshielded enough to determine the source, and set out to find out was wrong.

Her sharp ears led her into a seldom-used hallway near the Royal Library, one lined with alcoves which could contain statues or suits of plate-mail or other large works of art, but which were mostly vacant and screened off by velvet curtains. This was a favored place for courting couples during great revels, but the lack of seating tended to confine assignations to those conducted standing.

She had a little problem finding the source of the sob, as it was hiding itself behind the curtains in one of those alcoves along this section of hall. Only a tiny sniffle gave her the clue as to which of three it was.

She drew the heavy velvet curtain aside quietly; curled up on a cushion purloined from a chair in the audience chamber was a child.

He was a little boy of about seven or eight; his eyes were puffy from crying, his face was smeared where he'd scrubbed tears away with dirty fingers, and from the look of him, he hadn't a friend in the world. She thought that he must have been adorable when he wasn't crying, a dark-haired, dark-eyed cherub; the uniform Selenay's pages wore, sky-blue trimmed in dark blue, suited his fair complexion. He looked up when the curtain moved, and his face was full of woe and dismay, his pupils dilated in the half-light of the hall.

"Hello," Talia said, sitting on her heels to bring herself down to his level. "You look like you could use a friend. Homesick?"

A fat tear trickled slowly down one cheek as he nodded. He looked very young to have been made one of Selenay's pages; she wondered if he weren't a fosterling.

"I was, too, when I got here. There weren't any girls my age when I first came, just boys. Where are you from?"

"G-g-gyrefalcon's Marches," he gulped, looking as if her sympathy had made him long for a comfortable shoulder to weep on, but not daring to fling himself on a strange adult.

"Can I share that pillow?" she asked, solving the problem for him. When he moved aside, she settled in with one arm comfortingly around his shoulders, projecting a gentle aura of sympathy. That released his inhibitions, and he sobbed into the velveteen of her jerkin while she soothingly stroked his hair. He didn't need her Gift, really. All he needed was a friend and a chance to cry himself out. While she gentled him, she pummeled her memory for who he could be.

"Are you Robin?" she asked finally, when the tears had slowed a bit. At his shaky affirmative she knew she'd identified him correctly. Robin's parents, who held their land of Lord Orthallen, had prevailed on Orthallen to take their only child to the safest haven they knew—Court. Understandable, even laudable, but poor Robin didn't see their reasoning. He only knew that he was alone for the first time in his young life.

"Haven't you found any friends yet?"

Robin shook his head and clutched her sleeve as he looked up to read her expression. When he saw that she was still sympathetic and encouraging he took heart enough to explain.

"They—they're all bigger an' older. They call me 'tag-along' an' they laugh at me . . . an' I don't like their games anyway. I—I can't run as fast or keep up with 'em.''

"Oh?" She narrowed her eyes a little in thought, trying to remember just what it was she'd seen the pages playing at. You took them so for granted, they were almost invisible—then she had it.

"You don't like playing war and castles?" That was understandable enough, when fighting threatened his parents.

The flicker of the oil-lamp opposite their alcove showed her his sad, lost eyes. "I—I don't know how to fight. Da said I wasn't old enough to learn yet. That's *all* they want to do—an' anyway, I'd rather r-r-read—but all my books are still at h-h-home."

And if she knew the Seneschal, he'd strictly forbidden the pages to enter the Palace Library. Not too surprising, seeing as most of them would have played catapults using the furniture, with the books as ammunition. She hugged his slight shoulders, and made a quick decision.

"Would you like to be able to read and take lessons at the Herald's Collegium instead of with the pages?" Selenay had all of her pages schooled, but for most of them it was a plague to be endured or a nuisance to be avoided.

He nodded, his eyes round with surprise.

"Well, my master Alberich is going to have to wait a little; you and I are going to go see Dean Elcarth." She rose and offered her hand, he scrambled to his feet and clutched it.

Fortunately there were plenty of other youngsters being schooled at the Collegia—though few were as young as this one. They were the unaffiliated students—the "Blues" —who belonged to no Collegium, but were attending classes along with the Bardic, Healer and Heraldic students. They, too, wore uniforms, of a pale blue, and not unlike the page's uniform. A good many of them were well-born brats, but there were others that were well-intentioned—those studying to be builders, architects, or scholars in many disciplines. They'd be well pleased to welcome Robin into their ranks, and they'd probably adopt him as a kind of mascot. Talia knew she'd have no trouble in arranging with Selenay for this little one to spend most of his time at the Collegium when he wasn't standing his duty—and at his age, his "duty" was probably less than an hour or two a day. She was pretty certain she'd be able to convince Elcarth as well.

She was right. When she took the child to Elcarth's cramped office, piled high with books, the Dean seemed to take to Robin immediately; Robin certainly did to him. She left him with Elcarth, the gray-haired Herald explaining some of the classes, Robin snuggled trustingly against his chair, both of them oblivious to the dust and clutter about them. It seemed that she'd unwittingly brought together a pair of kindred spirits.

So it proved; she met Robin from time to time thereafter—once or twice when he'd unthinkingly sought her out as a never-failing wellspring of comfort for homesickness, the rest of the time trudgingly merrily about the Collegium, his arms loaded with a pile of books almost as tall as he—and more than once, in the Library, with Elcarth. Once she found both of them bent over an ancient tome of history written in an archaic form of the language that little Robin couldn't read himself, but just *knew* Elcarth could—and said so. He was convinced that Elcarth was the original fount of all knowledge. He was bringing Elcarth all his questions, as naturally as breathing.

Until now Talia frequently found both of them immersed in something so dry that she needed a drink just thinking about it! Kindred souls, indeed.

Four

Dirk sprawled in his favorite chair in his quarters, a battered old piece of furniture long ago faded to indeterminate beige, but one that was as comfortable as an old boot. He wished that he could be as comfortable inside as he was outside.

He stared at the half-empty glass in his hand morosely. He shouldn't be drinking on such a fine night. He was drinking far too much of late, and he knew it.

But what's a man to do when he can't sleep? When all he thinks of is a certain pair of soft brown eyes? When he doesn't know whether to betray his own heart or his best friend?

The only cure for his insomnia was to be found at the bottom of a bottle; so that's where he usually was at day's end.

Of course the cure had its drawbacks; wretched hangovers, increasingly ill temper, and the distinct feeling that avoiding problems was the coward's way out. He longed for a field assignment—oh, gods, to get away from the Collegium and Her! But nothing of the kind was forthcoming—and anyway, they wouldn't assign anything to Kris or him until their current batch of students was fully trained in the use of their Gifts.

Their students—gods, there was another reason to drink.

He finished the glass without even noticing he'd done so, eyes burning with unshed tears.

Poor little Christa. He wondered if anyone else had figured out she had been using her Gift to save the little ones in that fire.

Any time I close my eyes, I can almost see her—

The self-conjured vision was horrific. He could picture her only too easily; surrounded by an inferno, steadfastly *concentrating* with all her soul—because moving anything alive by means of the Fetching Gift was hard; hard and dangerous—while the building went up in flames around her. And it was all his fault that she'd sacrificed herself that way.

He raised his glass to his lips, only to discover that it was empty already.

I'm drinking this bottle too fast—

And the way she'd died—it was all his fault.

Before Christa had finished training with him she'd asked him if it was possible to move *living* things by Fetching. Anyone else he'd have told "no"—but she was so good, and he was so infernally proud of her. So he told her the truth, and what was more, done what he'd never done before and and showed her how; how to move live creatures without smothering them, without twisting them up inside. And he'd told her (gods, how well he remembered telling her) that when it had to be done, it was far safer to move a living thing from your hands to where you wanted it to go, than from where it was to your hands.

I am definitely drinking this too fast—the bottle's half empty already.

That was why she'd gone in to send the babies out, not Fetched them out to her. If only he'd known when he'd taught her what he'd discovered since, researching in the Library—that under great stress it was often possible for someone with their Gift to transport *themselves* short distances. He'd *meant* to tell her—but somehow he never found the time.

Now she's dead, horribly, painfully dead, because I "never found the time."

He shook the bottle, surprised to find it empty already.

Oh, well, there's another where that one came from.

He didn't even have to get up; the second bottle was cooling on the windowsill. He reached out an unsteady hand and somehow managed to grab the neck of it. He'd already taken the cork out when he was sober, then stuck it back in loosely. If he hadn't, he'd never have gotten the bottle open.

Gods, I'm disgusting.

He knew this was not the way to be handling the problem; that he should be doing what his heart was telling him to do—find Talia, and let *her* help him work it all out. But he couldn't face her. Not like this.

I can't let her see me like this. I can't. She'll think I'm—I'm worse than what Naril called me.

Besides, if he did go to her, she'd read the rest of what was on his mind, and then what would he do? Gods, what a tangle he'd gotten himself into.

I—I need her, dammit. But—do I need her more than Kris does? I don't know. I just don't know.

He couldn't ask Kris for help, not when Kris was the other half of the problem. And music was no longer a solace, not when every time he played he could hear *her* singing, haunting every line.

Damn the woman! She steals my friend, she steals my music, she steals my peace of mind—

In the next instant he berated himself for even thinking such things. That wasn't fair, it wasn't her fault. She hadn't the least notion of what she'd done to him.

And so far as he'd been able to tell, she really hadn't been spending all that much time with Kris since she'd gotten back. Maybe there *was* hope for him, after all. She and Kris surely weren't behaving like lovers.

But what would he do if they *were* in love?

For that matter, what would he do if they *weren't*?

The level in the bottle continued to go down as he tried—and failed—to cope.

Robin trotted happily down the hall to the Herald's quarters. He adored the Heralds, and was always the first to volunteer when someone had a task that would involve his helping them in any way. In this case it was twice the pleasure, for the Queen's Own, Herald Talia, had come looking for a page to return some manuscripts she'd borrowed from Herald Dirk for copying. Robin loved Herald Talia better than all the others put together— excepting only Elcarth. Heralds were wonderful, and

Talia was even more than usually wonderful; she always had time to talk, she never told him he was being a baby (like Lord Orthallen did) when he was homesick. His Mama had told him how important Lord Orthallen was, but so far as Robin was concerned, Talia was worth any twelve Orthallens. He had often wished he could make her smile the way she could cheer him up. She wasn't looking very happy lately and anything he could do to make her brighten a little, he would, and gladly.

There was a swirl of somber robes ahead of him—one of the Great Lords. Maybe even his own Lord. Robin kept his eyes down as he'd always been told to do. It wasn't proper for a little boy to gawk at the Great Lords of State, especially not when that little boy was supposed to be running an errand. If it *was* Orthallen, it was important for him to see that Robin was properly doing his duty.

So it was rather a shock, what with the fact that he *was* watching where he was going and all, when he tripped and went sprawling face-first, all his scrolls flying about him.

If the one ahead of him had been a fellow page, he would immediately have suspected he'd been tripped a-purpose. But a Great Lord could hardly be suspected of a childish prank like that.

The Great Lord paused just a moment, papers fluttering around his feet, then went on. Robin kept his eyes down, blushing scarlet in humiliation, and began collecting them.

Now that was odd. That was *very* odd. He'd had fourteen scrolls when he'd been sent on this errand. He knew, because he'd counted them in Talia's presence twice. Now he had fifteen. And the fifteenth one was sealed, not just rolled up like the others.

He could have gotten muddled, of course.

But he could almost hear Dean Elcarth's voice in his ear, because he'd asked Elcarth just this very week what he should do if he was asked to do something that didn't seem quite right, or if something happened in the course of his duties that seemed odd. One of the older boys had been sent on a very dubious errand by one of the ladies of the Court, and there'd been trouble afterward. The page involved hadn't had the nerve to tell anyone until it was too late, and by then his memory was all confused. So Robin had asked the wisest person he knew what he should do if he found himself in a similar case.

"Do it, don't disobey—but remember, Robin," Elcarth had told him, "remember *everything*; what happened, who asked you, and when, and why, and who was with them. It may be that what you're being told to do is perfectly legitimate. You could have no way of knowing. But if it isn't, you could be the only person to know the real truth of something. You pages are in a very special position, you know, people look at you, but they really don't *see* you. So keep that in mind, and if anything ever happens around you that seems odd, remember it; remember the circumstances. You may help someone that way."

"Isn't that being a little like a sneak?" Robin had asked doubtfully.

Elcarth had laughed and ruffled his hair. "If you ask that question, you're in no danger of becoming one, my little owl. Besides, it's excellent training for your memory."

Very well then. Robin would remember this.

There was no answer when Robin tapped at Herald Dirk's half-open door. When he peeked inside, he could see Herald Dirk slumped in a chair at the farther end of the room by his open window. He seemed to be asleep, so Robin slipped inside, quiet as a cat, and left the scrolls on his desk.

Talia didn't need a summons that morning; anyone with the vaguest hint of her Gift of Empathy would have come running to the Queen's side. Emotional turmoil— anger, fear, worry—was so thick in the air Talia *could* taste it, bitter and metallic.

She caught the first notes of it as she was dressing, and ran for the royal chambers as soon as she was decent. The two Guards outside the door looked very uncomfortable, as if they were doing their level best to be deaf to the shouting behind the double doors they guarded. Talia tapped once, and cracked one door open.

Selenay was in her outer chamber, dressed for the day,

but without her coronet. She was sitting behind her work-table in her "public" room; there was a sealed scroll on the table before her. With her were Lord Orthallen (looking unbearably smug), a very embarrassed Kris, an equally embarrassed Guardsman, and an extremely angry Dirk.

"I don't give a fat damn how it got there—*I didn't take it!*" Dirk was shouting as Talia glanced at the sentry outside and entered. She shut the door behind her quickly. Whatever was going on here, the fewer people there were who knew about it, the better.

"Then why were you trying to hide it?" Orthallen asked smoothly.

"I wasn't trying to hide it, dammit! I was *looking* for my headache-powders when this idiot barged in without a by-your-leave!" Dirk did look slightly ill; pale, with a pain-crease between his brows, his sapphire-blue eyes thoroughly bloodshot, his straw-blond hair more than usually tangled.

"We have only your word for that."

"Since when—" Talia said clearly and coldly "—has a Herald's word been subject to cross-examination? Your pardon, Majesty, but what in the Haven's name is going on here?"

"I discovered this morning that some rather sensitive documents were missing," Selenay answered, looking outwardly calm, though Talia knew she was anything but untroubled. "Lord Orthallen instigated a search, and he found them in Herald Dirk's possession."

"I haven't been anywhere near the Palace wings for the past week! Besides, what use could I possibly make of the damned things?" Dirk's mental anguish was so intense that Talia wanted to weep.

"Look, Uncle, you *know* my quarters are just down the hall from his. I can pledge the fact that he didn't leave them all last night."

"Nephew, I know this man is your friend."

"If I have to be brutally frank, then I will be," Kris said, flushing an angry and embarrassed red. "Dirk couldn't have moved anywhere because he wasn't in any shape to move. He was dead drunk last night, just like he's been *every* night for the past couple of weeks."

Dirk went almost purple, then deathly white.

"So? Since when has inability to move physically hampered anyone with *his* Gift?"

Now it was Kris' turn to pale.

"I haven't heard an answer to a very good question—Orthallen, what on earth would Dirk *want* with those documents?" Talia asked, trying to buy a little time to think.

"They would put someone in this Court in a rather indelicate position," Orthallen replied, "And let us say that the person is entangled with a young lady with whom Herald Dirk was at one time very much involved himself. Their parting was somewhat acrimonious. His motivation could be complex—revenge, perhaps. Blackmail, perhaps. The Queen and I have been attempting to keep this situation from escalating into scandal, but if anyone excepting us saw the contents of these letters, it could throw the entire Court into an uproar."

"I can't believe I'm hearing a Councillor accuse a *Herald* of blackmail!" Talia cried out indignantly.

"You just heard my nephew—his best friend—say he's been drinking himself insensible every night for the past few weeks. Does *that* sound like normal behavior for a Herald?" Orthallen turned to the Queen. "Majesty, I am not saying that this young man would have purloined these documents were he in his proper mind, but I think there is more than enough evidence to indicate that—"

"Orthallen," the queen interrupted him, "I—"

"Wait just a moment—don't anyone say anything." Talia held one hand to her temple, feeling pain stab through her head. The hot press of the emotions of those around her was so intense she was getting a reaction-headache from trying to shield herself. "Let's just assume for one moment that Dirk is telling the absolute truth, shall we?"

"But—"

"No, hear me out. Under that assumption, in what way—*other than someone deliberately going into his room and planting them there*—could those documents have gotten where they were found? Dirk, were they there after dinner?"

"Before I started drinking, you mean?" Dirk replied bitterly. "No. My desk was perfectly clean, for a change. When I woke up this morning, there were about a dozen scrolls there, and this was one of them."

"Fine. I know if someone had gone into your room that normally didn't belong there, you'd have woken up, no matter what. I can tell you that *I* sent Robin to you last night with those poems I borrowed. There were exactly fourteen scrolls, and *that* wasn't one of them. Now unless Lord Orthallen would like to accuse *me* of purloining those documents—"

"I still had them after you left, Talia," the Queen said, a distinct edge to her voice.

"I also know that none of the Heralds would wake up for a page entering their room unless the page deliberately woke them. The little devils are too ubiquitous; practically invisible, and we all *know* they're harmless. So, it is possible that some time between when Robin left me and when he got to your room, Dirk, an extra scroll got added to his pile."

"Guard," Selenay addressed the fourth person in the room, and the Guardsman turned to the Queen with gratitude suffusing his face, "Fetch Robin, please, would you? He'll be having breakfast in the page's room about now. Just ask for him."

The Guard left, plainly happy to be out of the situation.

When he returned with Robin, Talia took the child to one side, away from the others, and closer to the Queen than to Orthallen. She spoke quietly and encouragingly, taking the initiative before Orthallen had a chance to try and bully him.

"Robin, I gave you some papers to take to Herald Dirk last night. How many were there?"

"I—" He looked troubled. "I *thought* there were fourteen, but—"

"But?"

"I fell down, and when I picked them up, there were fifteen. I know, because Dean Elcarth told me to remember things that were funny, and that was funny."

"When did you fall down?"

"Near the staircase, by the lion tapestry."

"Was anyone else nearby? Did you run into anyone?"

"I wasn't running," he said indignantly. "There was a m'lord, but—m'lady, Mama always told me not to stare at m'lords, so—I didn't see who it was."

"Bright Stars!" Orthallen suddenly looked shamefaced—almost horror-stricken—though somehow Talia had the feeling that he was putting on an act. Certainly there was nothing she could sense empathically behind his expression. "That was *me*—and I had the scroll at the time. Stars, I must have dropped it, and the child picked it up!" He turned to Dirk, a faint flush creeping over his face, and spread his hands with an apologetic grimace. "Herald Dirk, my most *profound* apologies. Majesty, I hardly know what to say."

"I think we've all said quite enough for one morning," Selenay replied tiredly. "Dirk, Kris, I am terribly sorry. I hope you'll all put this down to an excess of zeal. Talia—"

Talia just shook her head a little, and said, "We can all talk about it when we've cooled down. Right now is not the time."

Selenay gave her a smile of gratitude as Orthallen used this as a cue to excuse himself.

Talia was not sorry to see him leave.

Selenay detailed the Guard to escort Robin back, and asked Talia, "Have you had anything to eat yet? I thought not. Then go do so, and I'll see you in Council."

The three Heralds left together, the Guardsman right behind them, escorting a mystified Robin back to the page's quarters. Talia could feel Dirk seething, and braced herself for the explosion.

As soon as they were a sufficient distance from the Queen's chambers that they were likely to have no audience, it came.

"Thanks a lot, *friend!*" Dirk all but hissed. "Thanks ever so much, *brother!* How I ever managed without your help, I'll never know!"

"Look, Dirk—I'm sorry—"

"Sorry! Dammit, you didn't even believe me! My best friend, and you didn't believe a single word I said!"

"Dirk!"

"Then telling everyone I'm some kind of drunken fool—"

"I didn't say that!" Kris was beginning to get just as angry as Dirk was.

"You didn't have to! You implied it very nicely! *And* gave your precious uncle more ammunition to use on me!"

"Dirk, Kris has every right to worry about you if you've been acting oddly. And Kris, Dirk's right. Even I could tell you didn't believe him without having to read you." Talia knew she should have kept her mouth shut, but couldn't help herself. "And he's right about Orthallen."

They both turned on her as one, and spoke in nearly the same breath.

"And I don't need any more help from you, 'Queen's Own'—"

"Talia, I'm getting very tired of listening to your childish suspicions about my uncle—"

She went white-lipped with anger and hurt. "*Fine,* then—" she snarled, clenching her fists and telling herself that she *would not* deliver a pair of hearty blows to those stubborn chins. "I wash my hands of both of you! You can *both* go to Hell in a gilded carriage for all of me! With purple cushions!"

Unable to get another coherent word out, she spun on her toe and ran to the closest exit, and didn't stop running until she reached the Field and the sympathetic shoulder of Rolan.

"*Now* look what you've done!" Dirk sneered in triumph.

"What *I've* done?" Kris lost what little remained of his temper and groped visibly for words adequate to express his anger. "Gods, I hope you're satisfied—now that you've managed to get her mad at both of us!"

In point of fact, a nasty little part of him Dirk hadn't dreamed existed *was* pleased, for now, at least, they were on an equally bad footing with Talia. He could hardly admit it, though. "Me? All *I* did was defend myself—"

"I," Kris interrupted angrily, "have had just about enough of this. I'll talk to you about this mess if and when you decide to stop behaving like a damn fool and when you quit drinking yourself into a stupor every night. Until then—"

"This is just a little too public a place for you to start making threats."

Kris bit back the angry words that he knew would put any hope of reconciliation out of reach. "Far too public," he replied stiffly, "and what we have to say to each other is far too private, and can and should wait until then."

Dirk made an ironic little bow. "At your pleasure."

There didn't seem to be any way to respond to that, so Kris just nodded abruptly, and stalked off down the corridor.

Dirk found himself standing alone in the deserted corridor, temples pounding with a hangover, feeling very much abused. He wanted to feel vindicated, and all he really felt like was a fool. And very much alone.

By the time Talia arrived for her weaponry lesson, Alberich had heard the rumors that Kris and Dirk had had a falling-out. He was not too terribly surprised when Talia appeared for her practice session wearing an expression so coldly impassive it might have been a mask. Few even at the Collegium would have guessed how well he could read the Queen's Own, or how well he knew her. She had quite won his heart as a student—so very alone, and so determined to do everything perfectly. She seldom tried to make excuses for herself, and never gave up, not even when she knew she had no chance of success. She had reminded him of times long past, and a young and idealistic student-cadet of Karse—and his sympathy and soul had gone out to her. Not that he would ever have let her know. He never betrayed his feelings to his students while they were still students.

He had a shrewd idea of how matters stood with her in regard to her feelings about Dirk and Kris. So he had a fairly good idea what her reaction to the quarrel might be.

This afternoon the lesson called for Talia to work out alone against the Armsmaster. She did not hold back in the least—began attacking him, in fact, with blind fury as soon as the lesson began. Alberich let her wear herself out for a bit, scar-seamed face impassive, then caught her with a feint not even a beginner would have fallen for and disarmed her.

"Enough—quite enough," he said, as she stood white and drained and panting with exhaustion. "Have I not told you many times, it is with your intellect you fight, not with your anger? Anger you are to leave at the door. It will kill you. Look how you have let it wear you out! Had this been a real fight, your anger would have done half your enemy's work for him."

Talia's shoulders sagged. "Master Alberich—"

"Enough, I have said it," he interrupted, picking up her blade from the floor. He took three soundless steps toward her, and placed one calloused hand on her shoulder. "Since the anger cannot be left at the door, you will confide it?"

Talia capitulated, letting him push her gently toward the seats at the edge of the floor. She slumped dispiritedly down onto a bench pushed up against the wall as he seated himself beside her. After a long moment of silence, she gave him a brief outline of the morning's events. She kept her eyes for the most part on a beam of the late afternoon sunlight that fell upon the smooth, sanded, gray-brown wooden floor. No sound penetrated into the salle from the outside, and the ancient building smelled of dust and sweat. Alberich sat beside her, absolutely motionless, hands clasped around the ankle that rested on his right knee. Talia glanced at him from time to time, but his harsh, hawklike face remained unreadable.

Finally when she had finished, he stirred just a little, raising his hand to rub the side of his nose.

"I tell you what I have never admitted," he said after a long pause, tapping his lips with one finger, thoughtfully. "I have never trusted Lord Orthallen. And I have served Valdemar fully as long as he."

Talia was taken aback. "But—"

"Why? Any number of small things. He is too perfect the servant of the State, never does he take for himself any reward. And when a man does not claim a reward visibly, I look for a reward hidden. He does not openly oppose the Heraldic Circle, but when others do, he is always just behind them, pushing, gently pushing. He is everyone's friend—and no one's intimate companion. Also, my Companion does not like him."

"Rolan doesn't either."

"A good measure by which to judge the man, I think. I believe that your suspicions are correct; that he has been striving to undermine your influence with Selenay. I think that since he has failed at that, he turns to eliminating your friends, to weaken your emotional base. I think he well knows how it hurts you to see young Dirk injured."

Talia blushed.

"You are the best judge of the truth of what I say." He shifted on the hard, worn bench and recrossed his legs, ankle over knee. "My guess—he knows Kris is your partisan; he could not get Kris to repudiate you so he decided to set the two great friends at odds with each other in hopes you would be caught in the middle."

"Me? But—"

"If he *is* of the mind to undermine your authority, this is one way of it," Alberich added quietly, hands clasped thoughtfully over one knee. "To chip away at those supporting you until they are so entangled in their own misfortune that they can spare no time for helping you."

"I see what you're getting at, now. He's removing my support in such a way that *I'm* set off-balance. Then, when I'm in a particularly delicate position, give me a little shove—" Talia flicked out a finger, "—and with no one to advise me or give me backing, I vacillate, or start making mistakes. And all the things he's been whispering about my not being quite up to the job look like something more than an old man's mistrust of the young. I thought you didn't deal with Court politics . . ." She smiled wanly at her instructor.

"I said I do not play the game; I never said I did not know how the game was played." His mouth turned up a little at one corner. "Be advised, however, that I have never told anyone of my suspicions because I seemed to be alone in them—and I did not intend to give Lord Orthallen a reason to gaze in my direction. It is difficult enough being from Karse—without earning high-placed enemies."

Talia nodded with sympathy. It had been hard enough on her during *her* first years at the Collegium. She could hardly imagine what it had been like for someone hailing from the land that was Valdemar's traditional enemy.

"Now I do think he has miscalculated, perhaps to his eventual grief. It is that he has badly underestimated the unity of the Circle, I think, or it is that he cannot understand it. Among the courtiers, such a falling out as is between Kris and Dirk would be permanent—and woe betide she caught between them!"

Talia sighed. "I know they'll make up eventually—Lord of Lights, though, I'm not sure I can deal with the emotional lightnings and thunders till they do! Why couldn't Ahrodie and Tantris get their hooves into this and straighten it out?"

"Why do you not?" Alberich retorted. "They are our Companions and friends, *delinda*, not our overseers. They leave our personal lives to ourselves, nor would any of us thank them for interfering. Yes, they will most probably be whispering sensible things into their Chosen's minds, but you know well they will not force either of the two into anything."

She sighed wistfully. "If I were a little less ethical, I'd fix both of them."

"If you were a little less ethical, you would not have been Chosen," Alberich pointed out. "Now, since the anger is gone, shall we return to the exercise of the body in place of the tongue?"

"Do I have a choice?" Talia asked, as she rose from her place on the bench.

"No, *delinda*, you do not—so guard yourself!"

Elspeth had encountered Orthallen during one of her rare moments of leisure; she was dawdling a bit on her way back to her suite in the Palace to dress for dinner with the Court. She took dinner with the Court once a week—"to remind everyone" (in her own wry words) "that they still have a Heir."

She was standing before an open second-story window; some of the gardens were directly below her. She was wearing a rather wistful expression and hadn't realized there was anyone else in the corridor with her until Orthallen touched her elbow.

She jumped and started back (one hand brushing a hidden dagger) when she realized who it was and relaxed.

"Havens, Lord-Un—Lord Orthallen, you startled me out of a year's life!"

"I most sincerely hope not," he replied, "But I do wish you would continue to call me 'Lord-Uncle' as you started to. Surely now that you're nearly through with your studies you aren't going to become formal with me!"

"All right, Lord-Uncle, since you ask it. Just remember to defend me for my impudence when Mother takes me to task for it!" Elspeth grinned, and leaned back on the window-frame a little.

"Now what is it that you were watching with such a long face?" he asked lightly, coming close enough to look out of the window himself.

Below the window were some of the Palace gardens; in the gardens a half-dozen couples—children of courtiers or courtiers themselves—ranging from Elspeth's age upward to twenty or so. They were involved in the usual sorts of activities that might be expected from a group of adolescents in a sunny garden in the spring. One couple was engaged in a mock-game of "tag," one girl was embroidering while her gallant read to her, two maids were giggling and gasping at the antics of two lads balancing on the basin of a fountain, one young gentleman was peacefully asleep with his head in the lap of his chosen lady, two couples were simply strolling hand in hand.

Elspeth sighed.

"And why aren't you down there, my lady?" Orthallen asked quietly.

"Havens, Lord-Uncle, where would I get the time?" Elspeth's reply was impatient and a touch self-pitying. "Between my classes and everything else—besides, I don't know any boys, at least not well. Well, there's Skif, but he's busy chasing Nerissa. Besides, he's even older than Talia."

"You don't know any young men—when half the swains of the Court are near dying just to speak to you?"

Orthallen's expression of incredulity held as much of bitter as playful mockery, though Elspeth was so used to his manners that she hardly noted it.

"Well if they're near-dying, nobody told *me* about it, and nobody's bothered to introduce us."

"If that's all that's lacking, I will be happy to make the introductions. Seriously, Elspeth, you are spending far too much of your time among the Heralds and Heraldic Students. Heralds make up only a very small part of Valdemar, my dear. You need to get to know your courtiers better, particularly those of your own age. Who knows? You may one day wish to choose a consort from among them. You can hardly do that if you don't know any of them."

"You have a point, Lord-Uncle," Elspeth mused, taking another wistful glance out the window, "But when am I going to find the time?"

"Surely you have an hour or two in the evenings?"

"Well, yes, usually."

"There's your answer."

Elspeth smiled. "Lord-Uncle, you're almost as good at solving problems as Talia!"

Her face fell a trifle then, and Orthallen's right eyebrow rose as he took note of her expression.

"Is there some problem with Talia?"

"Only—only that there's only one of her. Mother needs her more than I do, I know that—but—I wish I could talk to her the way I used to when she was still a student. She doesn't have the time anymore."

"You could talk to me," Orthallen pointed out. "Besides, Talia's first loyalty is to your mother; she might feel obliged to tell her what you confided in her."

Elspeth did not reply to this, but his words made her very thoughtful.

"At any rate, we were speaking of those young gentlemen who are perishing to make your acquaintance. Would you care to meet some of them tonight, after dinner? In the garden by the fountain, for instance?"

Elspeth blushed and her eyes sparkled. "I'd *love* to!"

"Then," Orthallen made her a sweeping bow, "it shall be as my lady commands."

* * *

Elspeth thought a great deal about that conversation as she sat through dinner. On the one hand, she trusted Talia; on the other, if there *were* a conflict of loyalties there was no doubt who her first allegiance was due. She hadn't thought about it before—but the idea of her mother knowing *everything* about her wasn't a comfortable one.

Especially since Selenay didn't appear to be taking Elspeth's maturity very seriously.

But Elspeth had gained inches since Talia had gone—and with the inches, a woman's curves. She was taking more care with her appearance; she'd seen the glances given some of her older friends by the young males of the Collegium and recently those glances had seemed very desirable things to collect. She found that lately she was looking to the young men of Collegium and Court with an eye less bemused and more calculating. And to the eyes of a stranger—

She'd looked at herself in her mirror before dinner, trying to appraise what she saw there. Lithe, taller than Talia by half a head, wavy sable hair and velvety brown eyes—the body of a young goddess, if certain people were to be believed, and the look of one more than ready to know more of life—yes. There was no doubt that to a stranger, she looked more than ready to be thinking about wedding or bedding, certainly old enough by the standards of the Court.

Or so Elspeth thought, setting her chin stubbornly. Well, if her mother wouldn't see on her own that Elspeth was quite fully grown now, perhaps there were ways to to bring that knowledge home to her.

And, she thought, catching sight of Lord Orthallen among a group of quite fascinating-looking young men, *it just might be rather exciting as well . . .*

Five

The weather, which had briefly taken a turn for the better, soured again. Talia's mood was none too sweet either.

The rains returned, and with them, spoiled tempers among the Councillors. Again Talia found herself spending as much time intervening in personal quarrels as helping to make decisions. Orthallen, strangely enough, seemed content now to let her alone. He brooded down at his end of the Council table like some huge white owl, face blank and inscrutable, pondering mysterious thoughts of his own. This alarmed her more than it reassured her. She took to examining every word she intended to say, and weighing it against all the possible ways Orthallen might be able to use what she said against her at some later date.

Dirk split his free time either lurking in her vicinity or hiding out in the wet. The one was as frustrating as the other. Either she didn't see him at all, or she saw him but couldn't get near him. For whenever she tried to approach him, he turned pale, looked around—wearing a frantic expression—for the nearest exit, and escaped with whatever haste was seemly. He seemed to have a sixth sense for when she was trying to catch him; she couldn't even trap him in his rooms. Either that, or he somehow knew when she was at the door, and pretended he wasn't there.

Kris all but hibernated in *his* room. And Talia was determined *not* to see him until he apologized for what he'd said to her. While their quarrel of itself was of no great moment, she was tired to death of having to justify her feelings about his uncle. After her little talk with Alberich, she was certain—with a surety that came all too seldom—that in the case of Orthallen she was entirely in the right, and he was entirely in the wrong. And *this* time she was going to hold out until he acknowledged the fact!

Meanwhile she made up for the absence of both of them by trying to be everywhere at once.

She was shorting herself of sleep to do so, and still felt there was much she wasn't doing. But there was just so much *work*; Selenay had asked her to take on the interviews of petitioners from the flooded areas, Devan needed her with three profoundly depressed patients, and there were all those quarrels among the Councillors.

It was with heartfelt gratitude that she found the sessions with Destria going well; Vostel's arrival put the cap on their success. It was plain to Talia that his reaction to Destria's appearance comforted her immensely. It helped that he regarded her scars as badges of honor and told her so in as many words. And as Rynee had thought, he was of tremendous aid when they began Destria's rehabilitative therapy—for he had gone through all this himself. He coaxed her when she faltered, bolstered her courage when it ran out, goaded her when she turned sulky, and held her when she wept with pain. He was doing so much for her that she needed Talia's Gift less with every day.

Which was just as well, for Selenay needed it the more. As soon as one crisis was solved, another sprang up like a noxious weed, and Selenay's resources were wearing thin. And when some of the choices she made turned out to be the wrong ones—as, soon or late, happened—Talia found herself exercising her good sense and Gift to the utmost.

A drenched and mud-splattered messenger from Herald Patris stood before the Council; when the door-Guard had learned his news, he'd interrupted the session to bring him there himself.

"Majesty," the man said, with a blank expression that Talia found very disconcerting, and which made her very uneasy, "Herald Patris sends this to tell you that the outlaws are no more."

He held out a sealed message pouch as those at the Council board erupted in cheers and congratulations. Only the Queen, Kyril, and Selenay did not join in the rejoicing. There was something about the messenger's expression that told them there was much he had not said.

Selenay opened the message and scanned it, the blood draining from her face as she did so.

"Goddess—" the parchment sheet fell from her nerveless fingers, and Talia caught it. The Queen covered her face with trembling hands, as the tumult around the Council table died into absolute silence.

Her Councillors stared at their monarch, and at an equally pale Queen's Own, as Talia read Patris' grim words in a voice that shook.

" 'We ran the brigands to earth, but by the time they were brought to bay, the temper of the Guard was fully aroused. We cornered them at their own camp, a valley overlooked by Darkfell Peak. It was then that they made the mistake of killing the envoy sent to parley. At that point the Guard declared "no quarter." They went mad— that is the only way I can describe it. They were no longer rational men; they were blood-mad berserkers. Perhaps it was being out here too long, chasing phantoms—perhaps the foul weather—I do not know. It was hideous. Nothing I or anyone else could say or do was able to curb them. They fell on the encampment—and the outlaws were slaughtered to the last man.' "

Talia took a deep breath, and continued. " 'It was not just the outlaws themselves; the Guard slew every living thing in their bolt-hole, be it man, woman, or beast. But that was not the worst of the horrors, though that was horror enough. Among the dead—' "

Talia's voice failed, then, and Kyril took the message from her, and continued in a hoarse half-whisper.

" 'Among the dead were the very children we had hoped to save. All—all of them, dead. Slain by their captors when it became obvious that they would get no mercy from the Guard.' "

The Councillors stared in dumb shock, as Selenay wept without shame.

Selenay blamed herself for not replacing the Guard companies with fresher troops or for not sending someone who could have controlled the weary Guardsmen no matter what strain the troops were under.

Nor was the murder of the children the only tragedy, although it was the greatest. Vital intelligence had been lost in that slaughter—who their leader had been, and whether or not he had been acting under orders from outside the Kingdom.

It took days before Selenay was anything like her normal self.

The one blessing, so far as Talia was concerned, was that Orthallen exercised a little good sense and chose to back down on his militant stance for more local autonomy; just as well, for Lady Kester's people began having the expected troubles with pirates and coastal raiders, and the promised troops had to be shifted to the West. But before they could reach their deployments, Herald Nathen was seriously hurt leading the fisherfolk in beating off a slaving raid.

And that opened up another wonder-chest of troubles.

Nathen himself came before them, although the Healers protested that he was not yet well enough to do so. He was a sharp-featured man, not old, but no longer young; brown-haired, brown-eyed—quite unremarkable except for the intensity in those eyes, and an anger that kept him going when nothing else was left to him. He sat, rather than stood, facing the entire Council. He was heavily bandaged, with his arm bound against his side, and still physically so weak he could scarcely speak above a whisper.

"My ladies, my lords—" he coughed, "—I did not dare trust this to anyone but myself. Messengers can be waylaid, documents purloined —"

"My lord Herald," Gartheser said smoothly, "I think you may be overreacting. Your injuries . . ."

"Did *not* cause me to hallucinate what I heard," Nathan snapped, his anger giving him a burst of strength. "We captured a prisoner, Councillors; I interrogated him myself under Truth Spell *before* I was hurt. The brigands are serving those slavers we thought banished!"

"What?" Lady Cathan choked out, as she half-stood, then collapsed back into her seat.

"There is worse. The slave-traders are not working unaided. I have it by my prisoner's confession *and* by written proofs that they have been aided and abetted by Lord Geoffery of Helmscarp, Lord Nestor of Laverin, Lord Tavis of Brengard, and TradeGuildsmen Osten Deveral, Jerard Stonesmith, Petar Ringwright, and Igan Horstfel."

He sank back into his own chair, eyes still burning with controlled rage, as the Council erupted into accusation and counter-accusation.

"How could this have occurred without your knowl-edge, Cathan?" Gartheser demanded. "By the gods, I begin to wonder just how assiduous you were in rooting out the *last* lot—"

"You were right up there in the front ranks to accuse me the last time, Gartheser," Cathan sneered "but I seem to remember you were also the one who insisted I do all the dirty work. I am only one woman; I can't be everywhere at once."

"But Cathan, I *cannot* see how this could have escaped your knowledge," Hyron protested. "Those four named are of first-rank."

"And the other three are Kester's liegemen," added Wyrist, suspiciously. "I'd like to know how *they* managed to operate a slaving ring under Kester's nose."

"And so would I," Lady Kester snapped. "More than you, I reckon."

And so it went, as Selenay mediated the strife among her Councillors. Talia had her hands full seeing that she remained sane during all of it.

All this, of course, meant that she had no time to pay heed to her own problems—most particularly that of the rift between Dirk and Kris, Kris and herself, and Dirk and herself.

It was bad enough that the quarrel existed—but to add yet another pine-bough to the conflagrations, Rolan was causing her considerable discomfort.

He was the premier stallion of the Companion herd and while Talia had been on internship, had only had another stallion—Kris' Tantris—for company. Now he was making up for his enforced celibacy with a vengeance—and the partner he dallied with most often was Dirk's Ahrodie.

And Talia shared it—couldn't block it if she tried. Not that she blamed Rolan; Ahrodie was sweet, attractive, and a most cooperative partner. She ought to know; she was on the empathic receiving end of all of it. But to have this going on, two and three times a week, while she positively ached for Ahrodie's Chosen—well, it was unpleasantly like torture. Rolan evidently had no notion of what he was doing to his Chosen, and Talia refused to spoil his pleasure by letting him know.

So she lost further sleep at night; either in suffering through what Rolan was unknowingly inflicting on her or in dreams in which she worked desperately to knit up some undefined but important object that kept unraveling.

She didn't see Elspeth except at training sessions with Alberich, occasional meals, or now and again with Gwena out in the Field. She seemed a little distracted, and maybe a touch shy, but that was normal for a girl just into puberty, and besides, Talia had her hands full to overflowing. So Talia never once worried about her—until one day she realized with a chill of foreboding that she hadn't seen the girl in several days, not even at arms practice.

Well, that could have been simple circumstance, but it was a situation that needed rectifying. So Talia went looking for her.

She found the Heir in the garden, which was not a place where Elspeth usually spent any time. But she was reading, so she could have decided simply that she needed some fresh air.

"Hello, catling," Talia called cheerfully, seeing Elspeth's

head snap up at the sound of her voice. "Are you waiting for someone?"

"No—no, just got tired of the Library—" Had she hesitated a fraction of a second before denying that? "Say, you've been so busy, I'll bet you haven't heard the latest scrape Tuli's gotten himself into, and I'll *bet* you could use a good laugh—"

With that, Elspeth kept the conversation on Collegium gossip, and then pled tasks elsewhere before Talia could gain control of the situation.

The incident left Talia very disconcerted, and when she began seeking the girl out on a regular basis, she only got repetitions of the same. Then Talia began to take note of the specific changes in the girl's behavior. She was secretive—which was unlike her. There was just the vaguest hint of guilt in the way she evaded Talia's questions.

Talia took an indirect approach then, and began checking on her through her year-mates and teachers. What she found made her truly alarmed.

"Havens," Tuli said, scratching his curly head in puzzlement. *"I* don't know where she is. She just sort of vanishes about this time of day."

"Uh-huh," Gerond agreed, nodding so hard Talia thought his head was going to come off. "Just lately. She's swapped me chores a couple times so she had the hour free—an' she *hates* floorwashing! Somethin' wrong?"

"No, I've just been having trouble finding her today," Talia replied, taking care to seem nonchalant.

But she was unnerved. These two were Elspeth's closest friends among her year-mates, and they only confirmed what Talia had begun to fear. There were gaps of an hour or so in Elspeth's day during which she was vanishing, and no one seemed to have any idea of where she was.

It was time she checked her other sources—the Palace servants.

Talia perched herself on a settle, next to the cold fireplace in the Servant's Hall. She had come to her

friends—for many of the servants *were* her friends, and
had been since she was a student—rather than raise
anyone's attention by having them come to her. Seated
about her were a half-dozen servitors she had found to
be the most observant and most trustworthy. Two of
them, a chambermaid called Elise and a groom named
Ralf, had pinpointed the guilty parties when a group of
the "Blues" (or unaffiliated students) had tried to murder her as a student by attacking her and throwing her
into the ice-covered river. Elise had seen several of Talia's
attackers coming in mucky, and thought it more than
odd; Ralf had spotted the entire group hanging about the
stable earlier. Both had reported their observations to
Elcarth when word spread of the attempt on Talia's life.

"All right," Talia began, "I have a problem. Elspeth is
going off somewhere about midafternoon every day, and
I can't find out where or why. I was hoping one of you
would know."

From the looks exchanged within the group, she knew
she'd found her answer.

"She's—this goes no farther, young Talia—" this from
Jan, one of the oldest there. He was a gardener, and to
him, she would *always* be "young" Talia. Talia nodded
and he continued. "She's hangin' about with young m'lord
Joserlin Corby's crew. Them as is no better'n rowdies."

"Rowdies!" Elise snorted. "If 'tweren't for their highborn da's, they'd been sent home long ago for the way
they paw over every girl they can catch unawares." "Girl"
here meant "female servant"; if Elise had intended to say
that the young men had been mishandling other females,
she'd have said "m'ladies." Not that this difference was
very comforting; it meant that they were only confining
unwanted attentions to the women who dared not protest
overmuch.

"It's said," added another chambermaid, "that at home
they gets t' more'n pawings."

"Such as?" Talia replied. "You know I won't take it
elsewhere."

"Well—mind, m'lady, this is just tales, but it's tales I
hear from *their* people—this lot is plain vicious."

Besides forcing their attentions on the servants of their

estates, it seemed that "Corby's Crew" was given to so-called pranks that were very unfunny. A cut saddle-girth before a rough hunt was no joking matter, not when it nearly caused a death. And some of these same adolescents were the younger brothers and sisters of those who had tried to murder Talia.

But thus far—that anyone knew—Elspeth had not been a participant in any of their activities. It seemed that at the moment she was simply being paid elaborate court to—something new to her that she evidently found very enjoyable. But it could well be only a matter of time before they lured her into some indiscretion—then used that indiscretion to blackmail her into deeper participation.

Elspeth's good sense had probably protected her so far, but Talia was worried that it might not be enough protection for very much longer.

This required active measures.

She tried to set a watch on the girl, but Elspeth was very clever and kept eluding her. She tried once or twice to read her with a surface probe, but Elspeth's shields were better than Talia's ability to penetrate without forcing her.

Something was going to have to be done, or among the three of them, Elspeth, Dirk, and Kris were going to drive *her* mad in white linen.

So she decided to try to do something about Dirk first, as being the easiest to get at—and since he wasn't talking to Kris, the way to him was through her blood-brother Skif.

"I'm as baffled as you are, little sister," Skif confessed, running a nervous hand through his dark curls, "I haven't got the vaguest notion why Dirk's making such an ass of himself."

"Lord and Lady," Talia moaned, rubbing her temple and collapsing onto an old chair in Skif's room, "I'd hoped he'd have said *something* to you—you were my last hope! If this doesn't clear up soon, I think I'm going to go rather noisily mad!"

When she had finally given up on trying to manage the problem of Dirk by herself, and had sought out Skif's aid, he'd invited her up to his quarters. He'd been to hers a time or two, but this was the first time she'd seen his. Skif's room was much like Skif himself; neat, decked with odd weapons and thick with books. Lately Talia hadn't had much time to devote to picking her own rooms up, and she found his quarters a haven from chaos. He had only one window, but it looked out over Companion's Field—always a tranquilizing view.

"First things first—this bond you've got. Kris was right. It's a lifebond—and he's got it, too. I have no doubt whatsoever of that. I can tell by the way he looks at you."

"He looks at me? When? I never *see* him anymore! Since the fight he spends all of his time out in the mud."

"Except at meals—any meal you take at the Collegium—he spends so much time watching you that he hardly eats. And I think he knows your schedule by heart. Any time you might be passing under a window, he's got an excuse to be near that window." Skif paced the length of the room restlessly as he spoke, his arms folded. "He's wearing himself to a thread. That's why I wanted to talk to you alone here."

"I don't know how I'm supposed to be able to help when the man won't let me near him."

"Oh, great!"

"He acts like I was a plague-carrier. I've *tried* to get him alone; he won't let me. And that was before all this mess with the argument with Kris. Now it's twice as bad."

"Havens, what a mess." Skif shook his head ruefully. "He hasn't said anything to me. I can't imagine why he's acting this way. I've had it though, and I know you're at your wits' end. It's about time we brought this out into the sunlight. Since he won't talk to you, I'm going to make damned sure he talks to me. I'm going to have it out with him as soon as I can corner him, and I'll do it if I have to trap him in the bathing-room and steal his clothes! I'm going to get things settled between him and Kris and him and you if I have to tie you all together in a bundle to do it!"

Neither of them had reckoned on the whims of Fate.

* * *

Dirk had been fighting what he thought was a slight cold—one of the many varieties that were currently decimating Court and Collegium alike—for about a week. Perversely he refused to care for it; continuing to escape Talia and Kris by retreating into the dismal weather out-of-doors. In a bizarre way, he didn't really *mind* feeling miserable; concentrating on his symptoms kept him from thinking about Her and Him. Physical misery provided a relief from emotional misery.

So he ducked in and out of the cold and rain, day after day, getting soaked to the skin more often than not, but not doing much about it except to change his clothing. Added to that, the emotional strain was taking a greater toll on him than anyone—including himself—realized.

It was midweek, and Talia was taking dinner with the Collegium instead of the Court. She was watching Dirk out of the corner of her eye the entire time, and hoping that Skif was going to be able to fulfill his promise. She was worried—very worried. Dirk was white to the ears; he kept rubbing his head as if it ached. She could see him shiver, although the common-room was warm. He seemed to be unable to keep his mind on what anyone was saying, and he couldn't speak more than two words in a row without going into a fit of coughing.

She could also see that Kris was watching him, and looking just as concerned.

He pushed his food around without eating much. Kris finally seemed to come to some conclusion, visibly steeled himself, and walked over to sit down next to him.

Kris said something to him, which he answered with a shake of his head. Then he stood up—and Kris had to catch him as he started to crumple.

Kris had decided he'd had enough. He couldn't stand watching his dearest friend fret himself to pieces—and he'd come to some unhappy conclusions over the past couple of weeks. He'd gone over to sit next to Dirk before the Herald was aware that he was even in the common room, and spoke his piece before Dirk had a chance to escape.

"I was wrong; I was wrong to put so much trust in my uncle, wrong to have doubted you, and wrong to have said anything about your private life. I apologize. Are you going to forgive me, or will I have to throw myself from the battlements in despair?"

Dirk had started a little when Kris first began speaking in his ear, but hadn't moved away. He'd listened with a mixture of relief and bemusement, then shook his head with a weak smile at Kris' last sally. Then he stood up—

And the room faded from before his eyes, as he felt his legs give under him.

Half a dozen instructors and field Heralds made a rush for him as Kris caught him. They lowered him back down into his seat, as he protested weakly that he was all right.

"I—" he coughed, rackingly. "I just was dizzy a minute—" he bent over in a fit of coughs, unable to continue, hardly able to catch his breath.

"Like Hell!" replied Teren, one hand on his forehead, "You're on fire, man. You're for the Healers, and I don't want to hear any nonsense out of you about it."

Before he could regain enough breath to object, Teren draped one of his arms over his own shoulders, while a very worried Kris did the same on Dirk's other side. The rest surrounded the three of them, allowing no opportunity to escape, and escorted them out the door.

By the time they'd reached their goal, his breath was rattling in his chest and there was little doubt of what ailed him. The Healers isolated him and ran everyone else off, and there was very little that anyone could do about it.

Talia had turned ashen when he'd collapsed, and had left her dinner uneaten, waiting for Kris' return.

Kris finally reappeared, to be engulfed by everyone who'd been present, demanding to know what the Healers had said.

"They tell me he has pneumonia, and it's going to get a lot worse before it gets better," he replied, his voice carrying easily across from the doorway to the bench where Talia sat. "And they won't let anyone see him for at least a day or two."

Talia made a little noise like a strangled sob, stood quickly, and pushed blindly away from the table. The knot of people surrounding Kris had blocked the door nearest her; she stumbled against benches twice as she fled to the door opposite and to her room. She ran all the way down the corridors of the Collegium and through the double doors leading to the Herald's Wing. She hurled herself up the darkened spiral staircase of the tower that held her room, pushed the door open and flung herself down on the couch in the outer room of her suite, sobbing with a lost despair she hadn't felt since that awful moment in the Waystation. . . .

She hadn't closed the door behind her in her flight, and wasn't in much shape to pay attention to sounds around her. She only realized that she was not alone when she heard someone settle beside her, and somehow knew it was Keren and Sherrill.

She tried to get herself back under control, but Keren's first words, spoken in a tone of such deep and unmistakable love that Talia hardly believed her ears, completely undid her.

"Little centaur, dearheart, what cause tha' greeting?"

Keren had slipped into the dialect of her home, something she only did on the rarest of occasions, and then mostly with her twin or her lifemate—moments of profound intimacy.

That broke down the last of her reserve, and she turned with gratitude into Keren's arms and wept bitterly on her ready shoulder.

"Everything's gone wrong!" she sobbed, "Elspeth isn't talking to me anymore, and I *know* there's something going on—something she doesn't want either Selenay or me to know about—but I can't find out *what*! And Dirk—and Kris—we fought, and now they won't talk to me either and—and—now Dirk's sick, and I can't *bear* it! Oh, gods, I'm a total failure!"

Keren, wisely, said nothing, and let the hysterical words and tears wear themselves out. Sherrill meanwhile went

quietly about the room, closing the door and lighting
candles against the growing darkness. That done, she
seated herself at Keren's feet to wait.

"For tha' problem of Elspeth I can think of no solution," Keren said thoughtfully when Talia was in a better
state to listen. "But if there was anything truly wrong,
her Gwena would surely seek out Rolan—and thee would
know."

"I hadn't even thought of that." Talia looked up into
Keren's eyes from where she rested on her shoulder,
crestfallen at her own stupidity.

"Why should thee? She's never given thee anxiety
before." Keren almost-smiled.

"I'm not thinking very clearly. No, that's not true. I'm
not thinking *at all*. It's wrong of me, but—Keren, I don't
know how much longer I can bear this trouble with Dirk
without flying to pieces. Keren, I want to be with him so
much sometimes I think it would be easier to die!"

Keren sighed. "Lifebond, then, is it? And with Dirk—
gods, what a tangle! Well, that explains *his* madness, for
certain. Lady only knows what cracked notion the lad
has in his head, and 'tis sure the thing's got him all
turned round about."

"We know how it can be—an agony." Sherrill rose
from her place, sat next to Talia, and slipped her arm
around Talia's waist, joining Keren in supporting her.
"It's hellish, being pulled inside out by something that
can't be denied and won't be turned to anything else. Is
anyone trying to help you get this straightened out?"

At Talia's nod, Keren pursed her lips thoughtfully. "I
can't think of anything at all to help thee, little centaur.
First it's a matter of getting Dirk and Kris speaking, then
getting Dirk's mind made up about thee. Hopefully the
first is done already. But the second—my best guess is
that he's gotten confused somewhere, and has been chasing his own tail. Time, dearling. That's all it will take.
Time."

"If I can just hold out a little longer—" Talia relaxed
herself with an effort while Keren and Sherrill held her in
a circle of love and comfort for long moments.

"You know we understand, dearling," Sherrill said at

last for both of them. "Who better? Now, let's change the subject. We're determined to make you smile again."

With that she and Keren took turns telling her the most hilarious stories that they could think of—mostly of some of the goings-on at the Collegium during her absence. No few of them were libelous; all of them were at least undignified. Talia wished profoundly that she had been present to witness the grave and aloof Kyril picking himself out of the fish pond with a strand of waterweed behind his ear. Between the two of them, they soon had her laughing again, and had drained at least some of the tension from her.

Finally, Keren nodded to her lifemate and gave Talia a comforting hug. "I think you're cheered enough to survive the night, dear one," the older woman said. "Yes?"

"I think so," Talia replied.

"Then let tomorrow take care of tomorrow, and have a good long sleep," Keren advised, and she and Sherrill departed as quietly as they had come.

Talia wandered back into her bedroom to shed her uniform. She dressed for bed, then changed her mind and wrapped a robe about herself and settled down on her couch with a book. She must have dozed off without meaning to, because the next thing she knew, Kris was standing beside her and touching her arm lightly to wake her, and the candles were burned down to stubs in their holders.

He was hardly what she expected to see. "Kris!" she exclaimed joyfully, then fear took the place of joy. "Is Dirk—worse?" she asked, feeling the color drain from her face.

"No, little bird, he's no worse. I've just come from there. He's asleep, and the Healers say he'll be all right in a week or two. And we're friends again. I thought you'd want to know—and I wanted to make up with you, too."

"Oh, Kris—I—I've never been so miserable in my life," she confessed. "I was so *angry* with you, that I swore I wasn't going to speak to you until you came to me and apologized, but my pride isn't worth wrecking our friendship over."

His expression softened a little, and she realized he'd been tensed against her answer. "I've never been so miserable either, little bird. And I've never felt like quite so much of an idiot."

"You aren't an idiot. Your uncle is—"

"My uncle is—not what I thought," he interrupted. "I have to apologize to you, like I apologized to Dirk. I was wrong about my uncle. I'm not certain what his problem is, but he *is* trying to undermine you. And he's trying to wean me away from you. I've extracted information from the unwary often enough that I ought to have recognized it when he was doing it to me—but I didn't until just recently. He became a little too eager, and failed to cover his trail." Kris' expression was troubled. "I *hope* that what he did to Dirk was unintentional, but I'm afraid I can't be certain anymore. I wish I *knew* what his game is. At the moment if I were to hazard a guess, it would be this: he wants the postion he had as Selenay's closest advisor, and he wants me slightly disaffected from the Heralds so that my family loyalty is just a trifle stronger than my loyalty to the Circle. You were right; I was wrong."

"I—I'm almost sorry to hear you say that." A little breeze from the open window behind her made the candles flicker and stirred locks of his hair as she assessed his rueful expression. "What happened to change your mind?"

"Mostly that he tried too hard after the squabble; as I said, he tried to pump me for information about you, and made one too many slighting remarks about Dirk. You were right, that he has a grudge against you, though why, I have no idea. And I think he used that incident with the scrolls as a chance to get at you through Dirk . . . and as a chance to come between *me* and Dirk. I can only hope he didn't manufacture it, too."

She almost said angrily that the dropped scroll was no accident, that Orthallen *had* manufactured the incident, but decided to hold her tongue. He was in a receptive mood, but the quickest way to close his mind would be to make further accusations. "I have to admit I'm of two minds about this. I'm glad you're coming around to my way of thinking, but I'm sorry to have changed your faith in your uncle."

"Don't be, it isn't you that has problems, it's him."

"Well, this is the first time anything has gone right in weeks. Kris, I'm glad we're friends again."

He dropped easily to the floor beside her couch. "So am I. I've missed talking to you. But as for things not going right . . . I don't know about that." He grinned ironically. "That advice you gave me on how to deal with Nessa certainly worked."

"I meant to ask you about that," she said, grateful for the way they dropped back into easy conversation, and glad of his company. "I noticed she seems to be pursuing Skif these days."

He sighed, and drooped like a mime displaying dejection. "Once she had her way with me, she was off to other conquests. Oh, the perfidy of women! When will I ever learn? My heart is forever broken!"

"That's the first time I ever heard that 'forever' equaled the time it takes to boil an egg," she replied wryly.

"Oh, less, I assure you. I had a chance to drop Skif a word on the subject of the fair Nessa. Now *he* happens to be very appreciative of Nerissa's quite real charms. So now that he knows the means of keeping her attention—which is to play hard-to-get—she may very well find herself in the position of hunter-turned-hunted."

"Like the old man said about that handfasted couple in Fivetree . . . do you remember?"

Kris screwed his face up into a fair imitation of the old man's age-twisted countenance. "Lor' help you, Herald!" he croaked. "Chased 'er? 'Deed he did, in very deed. Chased 'er till *she* caught *him!*"

Talia smiled wistfully. "We had some good times out there, didn't we?"

"There'll be more. Don't worry, little bird. I'll get this tangle straightened as soon as the Healers will let me near to talk to Dirk. You know, this illness may be a blessing in disguise; he won't be able to avoid me *or* find something that urgently needs his attention, and hopefully he'll believe the things I tell him."

He stood to leave, and Talia gently touched his hand in thanks.

"Take heart, little bird. Things will get better. I can always slip Dirk love-potions with his medicines!" He winked, and ran lightly down the staircase.

She laughed, feeling much eased, and rose; laying her book down on the table beside the couch. She went slowly about the room and extinguished her lights, and then went to bed with a happier heart and mind.

By the next morning Talia felt far more optimistic—and far readier to tackle her problems face on. And since Dirk was out of reach, the logical problem to tackle was Elspeth.

Now she was determined to corner Elspeth and confront her about her behavior. Council and Court kept her occupied most of the day, she missed the girl at arms practice by scant moments. Finally she tried tracking her down after dinner—but Elspeth managed to elude Talia again. She had no doubt this time that it was no accident, but a purposeful avoidance.

Talia was badly worried. All her instincts told her that things were about to come to a head. She opened her shields and was unsuccessfully trying to locate the girl when she felt an urgent and unmistakable summons from Rolan. With a sinking heart she left the Collegium and ran for the Field. When she reached the fence that surrounded it she saw her worst fears realized. Waiting with Rolan was Elspeth's Gwena, both of them like marble statues in the moonlight.

The images she received from both of them—especially Gwena—were blurred and chaotic, though there was no mistaking Gwena's anxiety. Talia touched both their necks and concentrated in an effort to make some sense of the images. Finally she got a series that came clear . . . and Orthallen was at the center of them. Orthallen, and a young courtier who was his creature, one of "Corby's Crew"—and they were planning Elspeth's disgrace!

She threw herself onto Rolan's back without a moment's hesitation. He galloped at full speed to the fence that separated the Field from the barn and stables of the ordinary horses, with Gwena barely keeping up beside him. They vaulted the fence like a pair of great white birds, and headed straight for the haybarn. Talia flung herself off Rolan's back before they had fully stopped.

As she sprinted for the barn, she heard a young male voice murmuring something in the darkness, and she flung open the great door with a strength she never even knew she had.

Moonlight poured in on the pair disclosed, and Talia saw with relief that matters had not yet had a chance to proceed very far between Elspeth and her would-be lover. *He* was rattled considerably by Talia's sudden appearance. If Elspeth was, she wasn't showing it.

"What do *you* want?" Elspeth asked flatly, refusing pridefully to snatch her jerkin closed where it was unlaced.

"To prevent you from making the same mistake your mother did," Talia replied just as coldly. "The mistake of thinking that fine words mean a lofty mind, and a pretty face goes with a noble heart. This young peacock has little more in *his* mind except to put you in a position where you have no choice but to take him as your consort or disgrace yourself, your mother, and your Kingdom."

"You're wrong!" Elspeth defended him passionately. "He *loves* me! He told me so!"

"And you believed him, even when your own Companion would have nothing to do with him?" Talia was white-hot with anger now. Elspeth was not willing to listen to reason. Very well then, she should have evidence that she *would* accept—in plenty.

Talia ruthlessly forced rapport on the young courtier. His petty evil was no match for some of the minds Talia had been forced to touch, though his slimy slyness made her skin crawl. Before Elspeth had a chance to shield herself, Talia pulled her in as well—and forced her to see for herself the true thoughts of one who had *claimed* that he cared for her.

With a cry of revulsion, Elspeth tore herself away from him and fled to the opposite side of the barn, while Talia released her mind from the enforced union. She was less gentle with the young popinjay. She had him in a crushing mental grip, and fed his fear without compunction as he gazed at her in dumb terror.

"You will say nothing of this to anyone," she told him, burning each word into his mind. "Because if you dare, you'll never sleep again—for every time you shut your misbegotten eyes, *this* is what you'll see—"

She tore the memory of his worst nightmare out of the bowels of recollection and flung it in his face, brutally invoking terror and forcing that on him as well. He whimpered and groveled at her feet until she threw him violently out of rapport.

"Get out of here," she growled. "Get out, go back to your father's holding, and don't come back."

He fled without a single backward glance.

She turned to face Elspeth, trying to control her anger by slowing her breathing. "I thought better of you than that," she said, each word built of ice. "I thought you would have had better taste than to let a creature like that touch you."

Elspeth was crying, but as much out of anger as unhappiness. "Fine words from the Herald Vestal," she spat. "First Skif, then Kris—and now who? Why *shouldn't* I have my lovers as well as you?"

Talia closed her hands into fists so tightly that her nails cut her palms. "I think I hear the Brat speaking," she replied. "The little bitch who wants all the glory of being the Heir, but none of the responsibilities. Oh, Hulda taught you very well, didn't she? Grab and take—snatch all you can, think only of yourself, and never mind what repercussions your actions may have on others. Others don't matter. Oh, no, not now that you're Heir. After all, your word is law, right? Or it should be. And if somebody tries to make you see reason, well, dredge up the worst you can about them and throw it in their faces— then they'll be afraid to try and stop you from doing what you want. Well, that doesn't work with me, young woman. For all the importance it has, I could be sleeping with men, women, or chirras, because *I'm* not the Heir. You seem to have conveniently forgotten that you will sit on the Throne when your mother dies. You may have to make a marriage of state to save us from a powerful enemy. That was what this business with Alessandar and Ancar was all about, or have you forgotten that, too? No one will want you *or* respect you outKingdom after dallying with a petty schemer like *he* is. And I, at least, have never been intimate with anyone that I didn't know, and who wasn't willing to let me inside his thoughts. He wouldn't let you do that, would he? Didn't that make you the least bit suspicious? Lady's Breasts, girl—where was your *mind?* Your own Companion wouldn't have anything to do with him! Didn't that *tell* you anything? If you're so hot to have a man between your legs, why the *hell* didn't you choose a fellow student or someone from the Circle? *They* will at least never betray you and they know when to keep their mouths shut!"

Elspeth burst into frantic tears. "Go away!" she wailed. "Leave me alone! It wasn't like that at all! I thought—I thought—he loved me! I hate you—I never want to see you ever again!"

"That pleases me very well," Talia snapped. "I'm ashamed that I wasted so much of my time trying to help a damned fool."

She stalked out of the barn, vaulted onto Rolan's back, and returned to the Palace without a backward glance.

But before she was halfway there, she was already rueing half of what she had said.

She reported to Selenay in an agony of self-accusation.

The Queen was in her private quarters, which were as spartan as her public rooms were opulent. She had wrapped herself in a robe of old and shabby brown velveteen, nearly the same age and color as the couch she curled up on. Talia stood before her, unable to look her in the eyes, as she related the entire bitter tale.

"Goddess, Selenay, I couldn't have made a bigger mess of the situation if I'd planned it out in advance," she finished, rubbing one temple and very near to weeping with vexation. "I'm as big an idiot as I accused Elspeth of being. I let all my training go flying merrily out the window, let my own problems get the better of me, and completely lost my temper. Maybe you'd better send me back through the Collegium with the babies again."

"Just wait a moment. I'm not sure that your reaction was the wrong one, and I'm not sure that you didn't do the right thing," the Queen replied thoughtfully, candle-light reflecting in her wide eyes. "Sit down, little friend, and hear me out. Firstly, we've been very gentle with Elspeth up until now insofar as exposing her to the kind of emotional blackmail and double-dealing perfidy that we *both* know is fairly commonplace at Court. Well, now she's learned that deceit can arrive packaged very attrac-tively, and that isn't a bad thing. She was hurt and frightened—but that will send the lesson home the more deeply. I believe you were correct in thinking that this experience will prevent her from making the same kind of mistake I made. That's not to say that you didn't overreact and say some things you shouldn't have, but on the whole, I think the good will outweigh the mistakes."

"How can you say that after the way I've alienated her? I'm supposed to be her friend and counselor!"

"And when, in all the time you've known her, have *you* ever lost your temper with her? Not *once*. So she learns something else—that it's possible to go too far with you, and that you're as human and fallible as the rest of us. I doubt she'll ever provoke you that far again."

"There isn't likely to be another chance," Talia said bitterly. "Not the way I've fouled things up."

"I disagree." Selenay shook her head emphatically. "Since you've been gone I've gotten to know my daugh-ter very well. She meant what she said . . . for now. She has a temper, but once it cools she doesn't hold a grudge. And when she realizes that you were right—and acting in her defense—she'll come around. If you were to disap-pear for a while, I think she'll eventually realize that while you *did* overreact, so did she."

The Queen pondered for a moment. "I think I have the perfect solution. Remember Alessandar's marriage proposal? I intended to make a state visit there in the next few weeks, and I wanted to send an envoy on ahead to look the prince over. As my own personal advisor you would be perfect for that, the more especially as I intend to send Kris as well. I heard about the quarrel between Kris and Dirk, and I had figured on giving *them* a bit of time for things to cool as well. I *was* going to send Dirk and Kyril, until Dirk fell ill last night, so I'll separate the pair by sending Kris off."

"*That's* mended," Talia sighed.

"I still want to send Kris; he has the manner and the blood to be acceptable, and I would as soon keep Kyril here. You and Kris worked outstandingly well as a team, and I trust your judgment completely. I think that rather than canceling the visit, I'll move the date up and send the two of you on ahead to spy things out for me. I'll take Elspeth with me. And I'll have a word with Orthallen about those protégés of his." Selenay's eyes grew cold. "It's about time he stopped being their defender and stopped letting them use his good name to get away with whatever they please."

Talia realized then that she had *not* told Selenay her belief that Orthallen had put the boy up to the attempted seduction. But—what proof did she have? Nothing, except the vague image of Orthallen in the boy's mind—and that could have been because he was hoping to escape punishment by sheltering behind his protector. *Best not to mention it,* she thought wearily. *I'm not up to going through the same arguments I faced with Kris.*

"By the time we all meet again," Selenay was saying, "Elspeth will have had time to think. Do you think you could be ready in the morning? The sooner you drop out of Elspeth's sight, the better."

"I could be ready in an hour," Talia replied. "Although I'm not sure you should be so quick to trust me after tonight."

"Talia, I trust you even more," Selenay replied, as Talia seemed to read understanding in her eyes. "You've come to me hot from the quarrel to claim it was all your fault—how many people, how many Heralds, even, would have done the same? But you haven't told me what has set you so on edge. Is it something to do with Kris? Did you get caught in the middle of his feud with Dirk? If you have problems with Kris, I'll send a different Herald with you."

"Kris?" Talia's honest surprise seemed to relieve the Queen. "No, thank the Lady, we've more than made up our differences, just as he and Dirk made up. Bright Havens, if anything he'll help straighten out this awful tangle! It's nothing that can't be worked out with time, just like this row with Elspeth; it's just that the time it's taking to set everything straight is driving me out of patience and out of temper."

"Good. Then the plan stands. You and Kris will leave in the morning."

"Selenay, if you don't think it's a bad idea . . ." Talia began hesitantly.

"I doubt that it would be. What is it you'd like to do?"

"I'd like to write a note of apology to Elspeth and leave it with you. There's no doubt in my mind that I was partially in the wrong, that I overreacted, and that I said a great many hurtful things because I was unhappy and I wanted to hurt someone else. I certainly was far too hard on her. You can use your own judgment whether or not to give it to her, and when."

"It sounds reasonable to me," Selenay replied, "although a bit unnecessary. We'll be following a week or two behind you, and apologies are always more effective in person."

"That's quite true—but you never know what's likely to happen, and you may to want to give it to her before you start off. I don't like the idea of leaving unfinished business behind me, especially something as wretched as this. Who knows? I might never get another chance."

"Bright Havens, dear! I should hire you out as my official doomsayer!" Selenay laughed, but it was a little uneasy.

Talia shook her head with a vague smile. "Gods, I'm seeing everything miserable just because I'm miserable. I will leave that note with you, but because the catling may well decide to be a human being again once I've left. Now—are they expecting any two Heralds, or Dirk and Kyril? Will there be any problem with me showing up?"

"The underlings are probably just expecting two Heralds," Selenay said. "I hadn't specified. I'll send the appropriate papers with you, of course. The guards on

Alessandar's side of the Border will send the specifics on ahead of you. I've heard he has some special way of relaying messages, faster than birds or couriers. I would appreciate it if you could find out more details on that, if it's possible. It might not be. . . ."

"It depends on whether it's supposed to be kept secret from allies or not—or whether it's a secret at all. We'll do our best," Talia managed half a smile. "You know, having the two of us on this assignment will work rather well at ferreting secrets out. Anybody involved with state secrets will be nervous; I can pick that up, and Kris can follow my anchor to Farsee what's going on. My Queen, you are very sly."

"Me?" Selenay contrived to look innocent, then caught her eyes squarely. "Are you *sure* you're ready for this? I won't send you if you don't feel capable of political intrigue and all the rest that this will entail. It is likely to be simple and straightforward, but it *could* involve ferreting out secrets, and at the very least you'll be dealing with the same amount of scheming you have here."

"I'm ready," Talia sighed. "It can't be worse than the mess I've already been dealing with."

Six

"I feel like I'm **running** away."

Talia's voice was quiet, but in the hush of pre-dawn Kris had no trouble hearing her.

"Don't," Kris replied, tightening Tantris' girth with a little grunt.

Their Companions stood patiently side by side in the tackshed, as they had so many times during Talia's internship, waiting for their Chosen to finish harnessing them. The rain that had blown up just past midnight had died away to nothing, but the skies were still overcast; both Heralds wore their cloaks against the chill damp. Tantris and Rolan were being decked out in full "formal" array; the silver brightwork gleamed in the light from the lantern just above Tantris' shoulder and the bridle bells tinkled softly as the Companions shifted. The homey scent of leather and hay made Talia's throat ache with tears she refused to shed.

"Look, there isn't anything either of us can do here at the moment, right?" Kris threw his saddlebags over Tantris' hindquarters and fastened them to the saddle's skirting. "Elspeth won't talk to you, and Dirk can't. So you might as well be doing something useful—something different. There won't be anybody who's going to *need* you during the few weeks we'll be gone, will there?"

"No, not really." Talia had been very busy this past evening; her lack of sleep was apparent from the dark circles under her eyes. "Destria is doing fine; anything she needs now Vostel is more than competent to give her. I talked to Alberich; he took me to see Kyril. They promised me that they'd keep an eye on your uncle—I'm sorry, Kris. . . ."

"Don't apologize; I'm just a little surprised you managed to convince Kyril he needed watching. Tantris, *stand*, dammit!"

"I didn't, really, Alberich did."

"Huh. Alberich? Nobody convinces *him* of anything; he must have had reasons of his own to agree with you." He digested this in silence for a moment. Tantris shifted over another step.

"Alberich is going to have a word or two with Elspeth, too," she continued after the silence had become a little uncomfortable. She ran her hands down Rolan's legs to confirm that the bindings on his pasterns and fetlocks were firm. "And Keren promised to beard Dirk in his lair as soon as she can bully her way past the Healers. So did Skif."

"Skif said as much to me. Poor Dirk, I could almost feel sorry for him. He's not likely to get much sympathy from either of those two." Tantris' bridle bells tinkled as he shifted again.

"Sympathy isn't what he needs," she replied a little waspishly, straightening up. "He's been wallowing in self-pity long enough . . ." her voice trailed off, and she concluded shamefacedly: "for that matter, so have I."

"Work is the best cure I know for self-pity, little bird," Kris said, self-consciously. "And—hey!"

With that last step Tantris had managed to shift over far enough that Kris and Talia were trapped between the two Companions, breast-to-breast.

:*Kiss and make up, brother-mine. And be nice. She's having a hard time.*:

Kris sighed with exasperation, then looking down at Talia's wistful eyes, softened.

"It'll be all right, little bird—and you have every reason to feel sorry for yourself." He kissed her softly on the forehead and the lips.

She relaxed just a little, and leaned her head for a short moment on his shoulder. "I don't know what I've done to deserve a friend like you," she sighed, then took hold of herself. "But we have a long road ahead of us—"

Tantris had moved away so that they were no longer trapped, and Kris could hear him laughing in his mind. "—and we've got a limited time to cover it," Kris finished for her. "And since my Companion has decided to cooperate again, we ought to get moving." He gave Tantris' harness a final tug and swung into the saddle. "Ready to go?"

"As ready as I'll ever be."

They took with them only what Tantris and Rolan could carry. They needed to carry no supplies; they would be housed and fed at inns along the way until they reached the Border, and thereafter would be using the hostels of King Alessandar. They also needed to bring a minimum in the way of personal belongings. The Queen and her entourage would be following at a pace geared to her baggage train, and they would bring whatever might be required for the term of official visits. Selenay and Alessandar were long-time allies; he and her father had been that rarest of things among rulers—personal friends. Although it was a slim chance, the possibility of Elspeth being willing to make a marriage with Alessandar's own heir was not to be dismissed offhand. Alessandar had not been discouraged by Selenay's initial reply to his offer— rather he had urged this visit on her, so that she and Elspeth could see Ancar for themselves. He had argued convincingly that such marriages took years to arrange; even were they to agree now, Elspeth would be past her internship when it became a reality.

Since Selenay had not seen the young man since he was an infant, on the occasion of his naming and her last state visit, she agreed. This would be the ideal time for such a visit. Since the Collegium was about to go into summer recess, she *could* bring Elspeth with her. She was still determined that Elspeth would not be forced into any marriage unless the safety of the entire realm rested on it. She was equally determined that any young man that Elspeth chose, be he royal or common, would at least be of the frame of mind to agree with the principles that governed her Kingdom. If possible, he should be of Heraldic material himself. Ideally, Elspeth's consort would be someone who was either Chosen already or who would be Chosen once he was brought to the attention of the Companions. If this came to pass, it would fulfill Selenay's highest hopes, for the Heir's consort would be co-ruler if also a Herald.

Besides preceding their Monarch and making certain all was in readiness for her, Kris' and Talia's primary duty was to examine the proposed bridegroom—and to determine how his own people felt about him—for themselves; and then give Selenay their opinions of his character. It was no small trust.

This was all in the back of Talia's mind as they rode away in the darkness before dawn. Troubling her thoughts was her feeling that, in spite of the importance of this mission, she was running away from unfinished business by accepting it.

She had labored for hours over the simple note to Elspeth, tearing up dozens of false starts. It still wasn't right; she wished she'd been able to find better words to explain why she had overreacted, and nothing she could say would unspeak some of the hurtful things she'd said. The incident was evidence that she and Elspeth had drawn apart during Talia's interning, and the rift that had come between them needed to be healed, and quickly. She couldn't help but berate herself for not seeing it when she'd first returned.

Then there was Dirk . . .

She couldn't help but think she was being cowardly. Anyone with any courage at all would have remained, despite everything. And yet—what could she truly do back there besides fret? Kris was right; Elspeth would refuse to speak with her, and Dirk was out of bounds in the Healers' hands.

It seemed appropriate that they rode away through darkness, and that the sky was so gloomy and overcast there was no bright dawn at all, merely a gradual lightening of the dark to gray, leaden daylight.

Kris was not very happy with himself at the moment. :*I haven't been doing too well by my friends lately, have I?*: he sent to Tantris' backward-pointing ears.

:*No, little brother, you haven't,*: his Companion agreed.

He sighed, and settled himself a little more comfortably in the saddle. Now that he looked back on it, there were things he *should* have done. He should have told Dirk right off about the way Talia felt—about Dirk, and about himself. When Dirk started acting oddly, he should have had it out with him. He should never have let things get to the point where Dirk was leaning on the bottle to cope.

Lord and Lady, I'd be willing to bet gold he thinks it's me Talia's in love with. Gods, gods, I've been tearing his heart and soul into ragged bits and I never even noticed. No wonder he picked a fight with me, no wonder he was drinking. Ah, Dirk, my poor brother—I did it to you again. How am I going to make it up to you?

Then there was Talia. He should have believed that Talia wasn't indulging in a grudge. He should have known, what with all the time he'd spent with her, that she wasn't inclined to hold grudges, even though she wasn't inclined to forgive a hurt too easily. He should have believed that her feeling about his uncle was rooted in fact, not dislike. Alberich obviously believed her—and the Armsmaster was hardly noted for making hasty judgments.

:Might-have-beens don't mend the broken pot,: Tantris said in his mind. *:Little brother,* why *didn't you do these things?:*

Good question. Kris thought about that one while the road passed under Tantris' hooves. There weren't many folk out this early, so they had the road to themselves, and there was nothing to distract him.

One thing at a time. Why hadn't he done anything about Dirk?

He came to the sobering conclusion that he hadn't done anything because he hadn't seen the problem until Dirk was drinking himself to sleep every night. And he hadn't seen it because he was so pleased with himself for the completion of a successful assignment on his own—so wrapped up in a glow of self-congratulation—that he hadn't noticed anything else. He'd been like a child on holiday; selfishly intent only on his own pleasures now that the onerous burden of school was done with for the

nonce. Teaching the classes in Farseeing was so very easy
for him that it was like having no duty at all, and he'd
been spending the rest of his time up to his eyebrows in
his own pleasures.

:Very good,: Tantris said dryly. *:Now don't go overboard
in beating your breast about it. I wasn't too remiss in
enjoying myself, either. It had been a long time to be
out—and Ahrodie and I missed each other.:*

:Hedonist,: Kris sent, a little relieved that his Companion was being so reasonable.

*:Not really. We're as close as you and Dirk—in a slightly
different fashion. More like you and Talia, really.:*

Yes, Talia—it was easy to figure out why he'd been so
slow to see her plight. Orthallen was, in all honesty, a
politician, a schemer, and power-hungry. Kris had been
forced to defend his uncle's actions to other Heralds
more than once, although never against an accusation of
deliberate and malicious wrongdoing. *Kris* knew Orthallen
never did anything for just one reason; yes, he might well
manage to gain a little more power, influence, or put
someone in his debt by the things he did, but there was
always a profit for the Kingdom as well. Heralds though—
the use of authority for personal benefit bothered them,
probably because such usage was forbidden *them*, both
by training and by inclination. Most Heralds *weren't* highborn, and didn't grow up with the intrigue and politics that
were a part of the rhythm of Court life. Things Kris
accepted matter-of-factly disgusted them. But the fact
was that Heralds were very sheltered creatures—except
the ones who lived and worked in the Court, or were
highborn. Court politics were a reality most Heralds could
remain blissfully unaware of, for they dealt only with the
highest level of Court life—the Queen, her immediate
entourage, and the Seniors—where for all intents and
purposes, the politicking didn't exist. It was at Orthallen's
level, the mid-to-upper level nobility, that the competi-
tion was fiercest. And it was very possible he had seen
only the political implications of the ascension of the new
Queen's Own. More than possible. Most likely . . .

Which meant he'd seen Talia as a political rival to be
trimmed down; seen her *only* as a political rival. Her

duties and responsibilities as a *Herald*—Orthallen probably didn't understand them, and certainly discounted them
as irrelevant. Old Talamir had been no threat to Orthallen,
but this quick, intelligent, *young* woman was.

All of which boiled down to the fact that Talia was
likely dead-accurate in reading Orthallen's motives
toward her.

Yes, Kris had dealt with fellow Heralds' censure of his
uncle before. But Talia's accusations had been different—
and he had been as shocked by the idea that a member of
his family could be suspected of *real* wrongdoing as Talia
had been that a Herald was accused of it. He'd taken it
almost as an attack on himself, and had reacted just as
unthinkingly.

:*I wish you'd spoken your mind to me before this,*: Kris
told Tantris, just a hint of accusation flavoring the
thought.

:*It doesn't work that way, little brother,*: Tantris replied, :*and you know that perfectly well. We only give
advice when we're asked for it. It isn't our job to interfere
in your personal lives. How do you think poor Ahrodie
was feeling, with her Chosen making a muck of things and
not even talking to her, hm? And Rolan can't even properly
talk with his Chosen. But now that you are finally asking—:*

:*Impart to me your deathless wisdom.*:

:*Now, now, there's no need to be sarcastic. As it happens, I don't like Orthallen either, but he's never given
anyone any real evidence of ill-will before this. All I've
ever had to go on were my instincts.*:

:*Which are far better than any human's,*: Kris reminded him.

:*Well, don't blame yourself for not seeing anything,*:
Tantris continued. :*But when someone like Talia insists
on a thing, it's probably a good idea to lay aside your
feelings about it and consider it as dispassionately as possible. Now that she's got that Gift of hers in full control,
her instincts in these matters are as good as mine.*:

:*Yes, graybeard,*: Kris thought, his good humor somewhat restored by the fact that Tantris wasn't trying to
make him feel guilty about the mess.

:*Graybeard, am I?*: Tantris snorted and shook his mane.

:We'll see about that.: And he performed a little caracole, a half-buck that shook Kris' bones, and a kick or two before settling back down to his original steady pace.

While Rolan could not Mindspeak Talia as Tantris could Kris, he was making his feelings abundantly clear. It was quite plain to Talia that her Companion thought she was indulging in a good deal more self-pity than the occasion warranted. Perversely, his disapproval made her feel all the sorrier for herself.

Eventually he gave up on her, and let her wallow in her misery to her heart's content.

The weather, unseasonable for the edge of summer, was certainly cooperating; it was a perfect day for being depressed. The chill, leaden skies threatened rain, but it never quite made up its mind to fall. The few people they met on the roadway were taciturn and scant in their greetings. The threat of rainfall made folk in the villages they passed inclined to stay indoors.

Because they were traveling light, they would make the best possible time to the Border, even though they would be stopping to rest at night. According to Kyril, it was probable that they would proceed still on their own as far as the capital, since the Companions would be able to make far better time than any steeds the King could send with an escort. Which meant, given the probable speed of Selenay and her entourage, they would have several days at least to assess the prince and the situation before one of them rode back to meet the Queen on the Border.

That likeliest would be Kris; Talia, as Queen's Own, was the better choice for envoy. Although her reason acknowledged the wisdom of this, her emotions rebelled, wanting it to be *her* who made that first contact with Selenay—and with Elspeth—and possibly, with Dirk, if he were well enough by then.

Nothing was going as she would have chosen; and on top of it all, she had been experiencing an odd foreboding about this trip from the moment Selenay mentioned it. There was no reason for it, yet she couldn't shake it.

It was as if she were riding from bad into worse, and there was no way to stop what was coming.

Talia remained turned inward, determined to control her own internal turmoil by herself. Weeping on Kris' shoulder would accomplish nothing. Rolan was a solace— but this was a matter of dealing with her own emotions and her own control. A Herald, she told herself for the thousandth time, was supposed to be self-sufficient, able to cope no matter how difficult the situation. She would, by the Havens, control herself—there was no excuse for her own emotional weakness. She had learned to control her Gift—she would learn to school her emotions to the same degree.

The hard pace they were setting left little opportunity for conversation, but Kris was very aware of her unhappiness. Talia had told him in detail about the confrontation with the Heir as they were saddling up. He was sadly aware that there was little he could do to help her; it was extremely frustrating to see her in such emotional pain and be unable to do anything constructive about it. Not long ago, he would have fled the prospect of emotional demands. Now in the light of this morning's introspection his sole regret was that he could not find some way to help.

When she'd lost control over her Gift, there had been something he could do. He was a teacher; he knew the fundamentals of training any Gift, and he had Tantris and Rolan to help him with the specifics of hers. Now . . .

Well, maybe there was one small way in which he could help her. If he talked to his uncle, perhaps he could make him understand that Talia was *not* a political threat. With that pressure off, the problem of dealing with Elspeth and Dirk might assume more manageable proportions.

They stopped for a brief lunch at an inn, but mindful of the time constraints they were under, they ate it standing in the stable-yard.

"How are you doing so far?" he asked around a mouthful of meat pie.

"I'm all right," she replied. She'd already bolted down

her portion so fast she couldn't have tasted it. Now she
was giving Rolan a brisk rubdown, and was putting far
more energy into Rolan's currying than was strictly
necessary.

"Well I know you haven't ridden much at forced pace;
if you have any problems, let me know."

"I will," was her only reply.

He tried again. "I hope the weather breaks; it's bad
for riding, but I would think it's worse for crops."

"Uh-huh."

"We'll have to ride right up until dark to make Trevale,
but the inn there should make up for the ride. I've been
there before." He waited. No response. "Think you can
make it that far?"

"Yes."

"Their wine is good. Their beer is better."

"Oh."

"Their hearthcats have two tails."

"Uh-huh."

He gave up.

They stopped long after dark when Kris was beginning
to go numb in his legs, and staggered into an inn neither
of them really saw. The innkeeper saw that both of them
were exhausted, and wisely kept his other customers
away from them, giving them a table right on the hearth
and a good dinner.

The inn was a big one, and catered to traders, carters,
and other mercantile travel. The common room was nearly
full, and noisy enough that Kris did not attempt conversation. Talia was just as glad; she knew she wasn't decent
company at the moment, and she rather hoped he'd
ignore her until she was. After a meal which she did not
even taste and choked down only because she needed to
fuel her body, they went straight to their beds. She was
able to force herself to sleep, but she could do nothing
about her dreams. They were tortured and nightmarish,
and not at all restful.

They again left before dawn, rising before any of the
other guests of the inn, breaking their fast with hot bread

and milk before swinging up into their saddles and resuming the journey.

Talia, having found no answers within, began resolutely turning her attention without. The skies had begun clearing, and by late morning they were able to roll up their cloaks and fasten them behind their saddles. When birds began voicing their songs, her spirits finally began to lighten. By noon she had managed to regain enough of her good humor to speak normally with Kris, and the whole mess she'd left behind her began to assume better proportions. She was still conscious of a faint foreboding, but in the bright sunlight it seemed hardly more than the remnants of her nightmares.

Toward midday Talia suddenly perked up and became more like her old self, for which Kris was very grateful. Riding next to a person who strongly resembled the undead of the tales was not his idea of the way to make a journey.

Diplomatic missions were not entirely new to Kris, though he'd not been senior Herald before. This *was* Talia's first stint as an envoy, and they really needed to talk about it while it was possible to do so unobserved.

Kris was relieved by her apparent return to normal, and ventured a tentative prompting. She responded immediately with a flood of questions, and *that* was more like the Talia he knew, but he could not help but note (with a feeling of profound sympathy) her dark-circled eyes. While he was no Empath, he knew her sleep must have been scant.

By the time they reached the Border itself at the end of a week of hard riding, things were back on their old footing between them. They had discussed every contingency that they could think of between them (ranging from the possibility that Ancar should seem to be perfect in every way, to the possibility that he was a worse marital prospect than Selenay's late consort) and talked over graceful ways to get them all out if the latter should be the case. Kris was fairly sure she was ready to face whatever the fates should throw at her.

* * *

As they rounded a curve, late in the afternoon of the fourth day of the journey, Talia got her first sight of the Border. The Border itself, here where two civilized and allied countries touched, was manned by small outposts from each Kingdom.

On the Valdemar side stood a small building, a few feet from the road, and a few feet from the simple bar that marked the Border itself. It served as dwelling and office for the two pairs of Guardsfolk stationed there. The pair on duty were checking the papers of an incoming trader; they looked up at the sound of hoofbeats, and grinned to see the two Heralds. The taller of the two left the trader's wagon and took down the bar for them, waving them through with an elaborate mock bow.

A few lengths farther on was a proper gate, marking Alessandar's side of the Border. It was manned by another pair of guards, this time in the black-and-gold uniforms of Alessandar's army. With them was a young man in a slightly more elaborate uniform; a Captain of Alessandar's army.

The Captain was young, friendly, and quite handsome; he passed them in without more than a cursory glance at their credentials.

"I've been waiting for you," he told them, "but I truly didn't expect you here this soon. You must have made very good time."

"Fairly good," Kris replied, "and we started out a bit sooner than planned. We've been out in the field for the last year or so. Field Heralds are used to being ready to go at a moment's notice."

"As opposed to folks with soft bunks at Court, hm?" the Captain grinned. "Same with us. That lot stationed at Court couldn't have a half-day of maneuvers without a full baggage train and enough supplies to feed a town. Well, I do have some basic orders about what to do with you . . ."

"You do?" Talia said, raising her eyebrows in surprise.

"Oh, it isn't much—just wait until you arrive, then inform the capital."

Talia recalled then what Selenay had said, that Alessandar was rumored to have some new system of passing messages swiftly. She also remembered that Selenay had asked her to find out what she could about it.

Evidently Kris had gotten similar instructions.

"Now *how* are you going to get further instructions about us in any reasonable amount of time?" Kris asked. "I know the nearest authority is several days away on horseback, and you don't have Heralds to carry messages quickly."

The young Captain smiled proudly. "It's no secret," he replied, his brown eyes frank. "In fact, I would be honored to show you, if you aren't too tired."

"Not likely—not when you're offering to show us what sounds like magic!"

The Captain laughed. "From what *I* understand, you're fine ones to talk about wonders and magic! Well, one man's magic is another man's commonplace, so they say. Come along then, and I'll show you."

Out of courtesy to him, since he was afoot, Talia and Kris dismounted and walked with him up the packed-gravel roadway to his outpost; a building much bigger than the one on the Valdemar side, and shaded on three sides by trees.

"Will it interest you to know that I may very well get my orders within a matter of hours, if someone is found of high enough rank to issue them before the sun sets?"

"That's amazing! We can't even do that," Talia replied. "But what does the sun setting have to do with it?"

"You see the tower attached to the outpost?" He shook dark hair out of his eyes as he pointed to a slim, skeletal edifice of gray wood. This tower rose several feet above the treetops, and was anchored on one side to the main barracks of the Border station. It had had both of them puzzled since it seemed to have no real use except perhaps as a lookout point.

"I must admit we were wondering about that," Kris told him. "Are forest fires that much of a danger around here? I wouldn't have thought so, what with all the land under cultivation."

"Oh, it's not a firetower, though that's where the design is from." The young Captain laughed. "Come up to the top with me, and I'll show you something to set you on your ears."

They followed him up the series of ladders that led to the broad platform on the top. Once there, though, Talia didn't see anything out of the ordinary—just two men in the black uniform tunics of Alessandar's army, and an enormous concave mirror, as wide as Talia was tall. Although it was not quite perfect, its surface a bit wavering, it was an impressive piece of workmanship. Talia marveled at the skill that had gone into first producing and then silvering such an enormous piece of glass.

The mirror stood on a pivoting pedestal, and as they watched, one of the two men turned it until it reflected a beam of the westering sunlight at the southwestern corner of the platform. When he'd done that, the second man picked up a smaller mirror about three handspans across and took his position in the beam of reflected light.

That was when Talia realized just how they were going to pull off the trick. It was a very clever variant on the old scheme of signaling across distance by means of the sun flashing off a reflective object. It was clever because in this case there was no need to hope that the sun was in the correct position when you needed to send a message.

The Captain smiled broadly as he saw understanding in their faces. "It was the idea of some savant in Ancar's entourage. We started building these towers last year at all the outposts; when we realized how useful they are we sped up the building and put towers up as fast as we could get the mirrors for them. We have relay towers all across the Kingdom now," he continued, with cheerful pride. "We can transmit a message from one end of the Kingdom to the other in a matter of hours. That's rather better than you Heralds can do, from what I understand."

"That's quite true, but anyone who knows your code has no trouble in learning the content of any messages you send," Kris pointed out. "That makes it a bit difficult to keep anything secret, doesn't it?"

The Captain laughed. "In that case, the couriers need never fret that there will be no job for them, true? Solan," he addressed the man holding the smaller mirror, "tell them down the line that Queen Selenay of

Valdemar's two envoys are here, and waiting for instructions on how to proceed."

"Sir!" The signalman saluted smartly, and carried out his orders. In the far distance the Heralds could just barely make out what might be the top of another tower above the treetops. Shortly after their man had completed his message, a series of flashes winked back at them from this point.

"He's repeating our entire message back to us," the Captain explained. "We started this check after a few too many misreadings had caused some serious tangles. Now if he's mistaken any of it, we can correct him before he sends it on."

"Sir. Message correct, sir," the signalman replied.

"Send the confirmation," the Captain ordered, then continued his commentary. "Now the closer you get to any of the major cities, especially the capital, the more men we have on each tower. That makes sure that several incoming messages can be handled at once. If the originator doesn't get confirmation, he assumes that there was a momentary jam-up, and keeps sending until he does."

"It's really brilliant," Talia said, and she and the Captain exchanged a grin at her pun, "but what do you do on cloudy days or at night?"

He laughed. "We go back to the old, reliable courier system in bad weather. We back it up by making our posting stations part of the tower system, so as soon as the clouds break or the sun rises, the message can be relayed. Even when conditions have been at their worst the towers usually still manage to beat the courier. At night, of course, we can signal with lanterns, but that won't be of any help in this case, since no one is going to want to trouble envoys with orders after they've presumably retired. That's assuming anyone highborn enough to issue those orders is willing to take the time to do so after the sun sets!"

They followed him back down the ladders. Once back on the ground, since neither of them showed any signs of fatigue, he gave them a tour of the post that lasted until darkness fell. Talia was intrigued, and not just by the signal towers. This was more than simply a Border-guard station; there was a company of Alessandar's army on permanent duty here. When not patrolling the road for bandits or standing watch on the relay tower, the men (there were no women in Alessandar's army) performed policing functions for local villages.

It was an interesting contrast to the Valdemar system, where Selenay's soldiery was kept in central locations, and shifted about at need. But then, Alessandar had a much larger standing army.

In addition to the army company, there were four Healers—all women—permanently assigned here. There were three buildings, not including the tower; the barracks, the Border station where the Healers lived and where Customs checks were made and taxes collected from those passing across the Border, and a kind of all-purpose building that included the kitchen and storage facilities.

"Well," the Captain said with resignation, when the tour was over and no one had appeared from the tower with a message. "It looks like the folks at the other end couldn't find anyone with enough authority to issue orders about you before it became too late. That means you'll have to spend the night here—unless you'd rather recross the Border?"

"Here will be fine, providing it's no imposition," Kris answered.

The Captain looked doubtfully from Kris to Talia and back again, and coughed politely.

"I haven't got private quarters for you," he said a bit awkwardly. "I could easily find you space in the barracks, of course, and the young lady could take a bed with the Healers, since they're all women. But if you'd rather not be separated. . . ."

"Captain, Herald Talia and I are colleagues, nothing more." Kris looked sober enough, but Talia could read his amusement at the Captain's embarrassment.

"Your arrangements are perfectly fine," Talia said smoothly. "We're both used to barracks-style quarters; I promise you that they're quite a luxury compared with some of the Waystations I've spent my nights in."

Talia had been careful to use "I" instead of "we" in speaking of the Waystations. She saw out of the corner of her eye Kris winking at her to congratulate her on her tact.

"If that's the case, I'll escort you to the officer's mess for some dinner," the Captain replied, apparently relieved that they'd made no awkwardness over the situation.

His attitude made Talia wonder if other guests at this outpost had been less than cooperative, or if it was simply that he'd heard some of the more exaggerated tales about Heralds.

While somewhat restrained by the presence of outsiders, the officers were a very congenial lot. They were terribly curious about Heralds, of course, and some of the questions were as naive as any child's. If all of Alessandar's people were as open-handed and content with their lot as these men were, Talia was inclined to think he was every bit as good a ruler as Selenay.

Although Kris got a real bed, Talia had to make do with a cot in the Healer's quarters. She didn't mind in the least. The nightmares that had plagued her nightly all the way here had left her so weary she thought that she could quite probably sleep on a slab of stone.

This night, however, the nightmares seemed to have been partially thwarted. That might have been due to the soothing presence of the Healers bedded all around her. After all, she *was* an Empath; Kris was not. There had been enough bad fortune this spring that it was possible she might well have been picking up the general air of disaster *everyone* was sharing lately. She'd thought she'd made her shields strong enough to block just about anything, but she *had* been stressed, and that put a strain on her shielding.

Or the fact that the nightmares went away might have been just because she had worn herself out past the point of being disturbed by them. For whatever reason, she slept soundly for the first time since leaving, and had only the vaguest memories of disturbing dreams in the morning.

Seven

If Kris had been deaf, he *might* have been able to sleep through the noise of the night guards coming in and the day guards getting up. Since he wasn't, he made a virtue of the inevitable and got up with them. He found Talia, still sleepy-eyed, waiting for him in the mess hall; she'd had the foresight to claim two breakfasts from the cook. Their host put in an appearance just as they were finishing.

"Well, I've got your instructions. I'm to give you maps, and you're not to wait for an escort but to go on to the capital. You're to check in with relay stations at sunset before you stop for the night."

"Sounds simple enough," Kris replied. "I really wanted to get on—not that your hospitality isn't appreciated, but I'd rather not strain your resources. Just as well we're not going to have to wait for an escort."

"I'll admit I was glad to hear I didn't need to supply you with one," their host said frankly. "I'm shorthanded enough, and if half of what I've heard is true, none of our beasts could ever hope to keep pace with yours, anyway."

"It's true enough," Kris replied with pardonable pride. "There isn't a horse born that can match the speed and endurance of a Companion."

"All right, what you'll do is follow the main road to the capital—it's easy enough—and stay overnight at Alessandar's hostels. They'll always be on the main square of town; there'll be a Guardpost nearby, and they'll look like inns. The only difference between a hostel and an inn is that the sign outside will have a wheat sheaf in a crown. Oh—you do speak our language, don't you?"

"Perfectly," Kris replied in Hardornen.

"Oh, good—I thought they wouldn't have sent anybody that didn't, but you never know—and once you get a few miles off the Border nobody speaks Valdemaren."

"I can't say that surprises me too much," Talia put in, in slow, clear Hardornen. "Once you get a few miles off *our* Border no one except Heralds speaks *yours!*"

"Right then, you can be on your way as soon as you're ready. Here's your map," he handed Kris a folded packet "and best of luck to you."

"Thanks," Kris said, both of them rising and heading for the door.

"And don't forget," he called after them as they headed for the stables, "Check in with the relay towers every night. The capital wants to be able to keep track of you."

The first day passed without incident. Alessandar's people seemed as content as Selenay's; they were friendly, and looked quite prosperous, at least from a distance.

"Isn't there supposed to be a village along here soon?" Talia asked around noon.

Kris pulled the map they'd been given out of his beltpouch and consulted it. "Assuming I haven't been misreading this—let's see if we can find a native."

One more turning of the road brought them to a grove of trees in the road-side corner of a fenced field. Beneath those trees was a group that could have been exchanged for farmers of Valdemar without anyone noticing the difference. They were stolidly munching their way through a dinner of thick, coarse bread and cheese, but when one of them noticed that the two Heralds were approaching them with purpose, he stood, brushed crumbs off his linen smock, and met them halfway.

"Eh, sir, and can I be of any help to ye?" he asked, as friendly as the Captain had been.

"I'm not quite used to this map," Kris replied, "And I wonder if you could tell me how far it is to Southford?"

"That be just a league or so a-down the road; there's that hill yonder in the way, or ye could see it from here."

The man grinned. "A'course, if the hill bain't there, ye wouldn't have to ask, eh?"

Kris laughed along with him. "That's only true," he said, "And thank you."

"Nice man," Talia commented when Kris returned to her side. "He could have been one of ours." She squinted across the fields of swiftly-growing green grain, and Kris followed her gaze. "They seem to be thriving, too. So far Alessandar gets high marks from me."

"Ah," Kris replied, "But it isn't Alessandar that's the prospective bridegroom."

"That's true." The face she turned toward him was a sober one. "And I wish I didn't know so many tales of black-sheep sons. . . ."

They were to stay only at the hostels, or so their orders went, so as sunset neared they checked the map for the first town ahead of them likely to have one.

The hostels were an innovation of Alessandar's, and were meant to serve as a courtesy to those moving about his Kingdom on official business. They were rather like well-run inns, save that there was no fee. Court officials, envoys of other Kingdoms, and clergy were permitted unlimited use of these facilities.

They first reported their progress to one of the relay stations in a village along the way, as had been requested. The station was easy enough to find, as it towered over every other structure in the village.

"Will ye be stayin' here, or movin' on past dark?" asked the grizzled veteran who greeted them.

"Moving on," Talia replied, "We plan on making— Keeper's Crossing, was it?" She looked to Kris for confirmation.

He checked the map and nodded.

"That's a ways—but you know best. Guess the tales 'bout them horses o' yours must be true." He looked over Rolan and Tantris with an appraising and approving eye. "Useta be cavalry, meself. Can't say I've ever seen neater beasts. Ye came all the way from the Border since this mornin'?"

Rolan and Tantris preened under his admiring gaze

and curvetted a little, showing off. "That we did, sir," Kris answered with a smile.

"Don't look winded—don't even look tired—just exercised a mite. Lord Sun, I'd not have believed it if I hadn't a' seen it. Well if ye can make that kinda time, ye'll be at the Crossings 'bout a candlemark after sunset. Hostel's in the town square, right-hand side as you come in."

"Many thanks," Talia called as they turned the Companions' heads back to the road.

"Fair wind at yer back!" he called after them, his admiring gaze following them until they were out of sight.

The hostel was indeed like an inn, complete with innkeeper. They had been told that the accommodations were as plain as the food, but adequate.

They showed their credentials to the businesslike Hostelmaster when they dismounted at the door. He examined them quite carefully, paying close attention to the seals of Valdemar and Hardorn. When he was satisfied that they were genuine, he summoned a stableboy with a single word. The lad came at a run to take the Companions, and the Hostelmaster waved them inside.

The common room was hot, smoky, and crowded, and it took them a little time to find themselves places at smooth, worn wooden trestle-tables. Finally Talia squeezed in beside a pair of travelers in priestly garb—apparently from the rival sects of Kindas Sun-Kindler and Tembor Earth-Shaker. They were having a spirited discussion of the deficiencies of their various congregations and simply nodded to her as she took her place on the very end of the bench. Kris sat opposite her, with his neighbor a thin, clerkly-looking sort with ink-stained fingers, whose sole interest was the contents of the stoneware platter in front of him.

A harried serving girl placed similar platters before the two Heralds; meat, bread, and stewed vegetables. A boy followed her with a tray of wooden mugs of thin ale, and the keys to their rooms.

They ate quickly; the food wasn't anything to linger over, and Talia's bench, at least, was so crowded she had barely enough room to perch. And there were more people coming in, waiting with expressions of impatience for seats. With their hunger appeased, they took their keys and their mugs to the other side of the lantern-lit room, where there was a fire and a number of benches and settles scattered about.

Talia felt curious eyes on them—not hostile, just curious. She decided that they were the only foreigners among the guests, for she couldn't detect any accents among those speaking. She picked a seat, and took it quickly, feeling very conspicous in her white uniform that stood out so sharply in the otherwise dark room.

"Heralds out of Valdemar, be you?" asked a portly fellow in brown velvet as Kris took a corner of a bench.

"You have us rightly, good sir," Talia answered him.

"Don't see Heralds often." His inquisitive glance left no doubt but that he was curious about what brought them.

"You should be seeing more before summer's over," Talia replied with what she hoped was just enough friendliness. "Queen Selenay will be making a visit to your King. We're here to help get things ready for her."

"Ah?" he replied, his interest piqued. "That so? Well— maybe things be taking a turn for the better, after all."

"Have things been bad lately?" she asked as casually as possible. "Valdemar's had its share of troubles, what with floods and all."

"Oh, aye—floods and all," he replied, a bit too hastily, and turned to the men on the other side of him, joining the conversation in progress.

"'Scuse me, milady, but could you tell me what the grain prices look to be on your side of the Border?" A tall, thin merchant interposed himself between Talia and the man she had first spoken to, and it would have been plain rudeness to ignore him. He kept her engaged with so many questions that she had no chance to ask any of her own. Finally she'd had enough of being monopolized, and signaled Kris that she was ready to leave.

When Kris yawned, pled fatigue, and rose to head for his room and bed, Talia followed. The guest rooms were monklike cells arranged along the walls; they had no fireplaces or windows, but slits in the walls near the ceiling gave adequate ventilation. Kris raised one eyebrow interrogatively at her as he unlocked his door; she gave him the little nod that meant she'd learned something interesting, and the hand motion that meant they'd talk about it later.

Even without a window, Talia knew when it was sunrise. She wasn't much surprised to discover that Kris had beaten her to breakfast by a few minutes. No one else was even stirring. She didn't pay much attention to what she was eating; some kind of grain porridge with nuts and mushrooms, she thought. It was as bland as the dinner had been.

"The boy is harnessing for us," Kris said around a mouthful. "We can be on the road as soon as you're ready."

She washed down the last bite of the gluey stuff with a quick gulp of unsweetened tea. "I'm ready."

"Then let's get going."

They cantered out the village until they reached the outskirts before settling back to a slower pace.

"Well?" Kris asked, when they were well out earshot of the village.

"There's something not quite right around here," Talia replied, "but I can't put my finger on anything. All I've got is a feeling—and that no one wants to talk about 'bad times' around here. It may just be an isolated case of discontent—"

She shook her head, suddenly feeling dizzy.

"What's the matter?"

"I don't—know. I feel a little funny all of a sudden."

"You want to stop a minute?" Kris asked, sounding concerned.

She was about to say "no" when another wave of disorientation hit. "I think I'd better—"

Their Companions moved over to the grassy verge of the road on their own. Rolan braced all four legs and stood rock-still, while waves of dizziness washed over her. She didn't dismount—she didn't dare; she was afraid she wouldn't be able to get back up again. She just clung to the saddle, and hoped she wouldn't fall off.

"Want to go back?" Kris asked anxiously. "Think you need a Healer?"

"N-no. I don't think so. I don't know—" The disorientation didn't seem quite so bad, after a bit. "I think it's going away by itself."

Then, as the dizziness faded, so did the empathic awareness of those around her; an awareness she always had, no matter how tightly shielded.

"Goddess!" Her eyes snapped open and she looked frantically around her, as Kris grabbed her elbow, anxiously. "It's—" She unshielded. It was the same. She could sense nothing, not even Kris, beside her. "It's gone! My Gift—"

Then it was back—redoubled. And she, unshielded and wide open, bent over in physical pain at the mental clamor of what seemed to be thousands of people. Hastily she shielded back down—

Only to have the clamor vanish again.

She remained bent over, head in hands. "Kris—Kris, what's happening to me? What's wrong?"

He was steadying her as best he could from his saddle. "I don't know," he said tightly, "I—wait—wasn't there some kind of mushroom in that glop they fed us?"

"I—" she tried to think. "Yes. Maybe."

"Goatsfoot," he said grimly. "It has to be. That's why you're getting hit and I'm not."

"Goatsfoot? That—" She sat up slowly, blinking tears away. "That's the stuff that scrambles Gifts, isn't it? I thought it was rare—"

"Only Thoughtsensing and Empathy and yes, it is rare in most places. It's not *common* around here, but it's not rare either, and it's been a wet spring, just what goatsfoot likes. The damned fools must have gotten hold of a lot and just chucked it in the food without checking beyond seeing that it was edible."

She was able to think a little clearer now. "This is going to make anything I read pretty well worthless for the next couple of days, isn't it?"

He grimaced. "Don't even try; it'll make you sick.

Those damned fools were just lucky they didn't have a Healer overnighting there! If you can ride, I think we'd better go back—"

"I can ride, if we take it easy. Why?"

He had already turned Tantris' head back the way they had come. "What if they have more of that stuff—and a Healer as a guest tonight?"

"Great good gods!" She let Rolan follow in Kris' wake.

It wasn't more than a league back; they hadn't traveled far before the effect of the fungus hit her. She fought off successive waves of dizziness and disorientation, and was vaguely aware that they'd stopped and Kris was giving someone a sharp-tongued dressing-down. She caught frantic apology; it seemed genuine enough—what her Gift was feeding at her was anything but a reliable gauge. Waves of paralyzing fear, apprehension, guilt—followed immediately by waves of delirious joy, intense sexual arousal, and overwhelming hunger.

Finally, another "blank" moment, and she drew a shuddering breath of relief.

"Little bird?"

She opened her eyes to look down on Kris standing at her right stirrup.

"Do you want to stay here? I can go back to the signal tower and get them to send a message that you've been taken ill—and whose fault it is."

"No—no. I'll be better—better away from people. You can shield; they can't. I won't fall off; Rolan won't let me."

"If that's the way you want it . . . "

"Please—" She closed her eyes. "Let's get out of here—"

She heard him mount; felt Rolan start off after him. She didn't open her eyes; the disorientation didn't seem so bad when she could keep them closed. And she was right; as distance increased between herself and the village, the worst of the effects decreased. She felt a second shield snap up around her—Kris'—then a third—Rolan's—

She opened her eyes cautiously. It was like looking

up through water, but bearable. She felt Kris touch her arm, and saw that he was riding beside her.

"This couldn't have been on purpose," she asked, slowly, "Could it?"

He gave the idea serious thought; she could tell by the blank expression on his face. "I don't think so," he said at last. "They couldn't have known what hostel we'd overnight in, and they couldn't have counted on goatsfoot being available. They swore they only had that one batch, that it was in a lot of edible fungus some boy sold them this morning. I made them dump the rest of the porridge in the pig trough. No, I think it's just a damned bad accident. Can you go on?"

She closed her eyes, and took a kind of internal tally. "Yes."

"All right, then let's get on with it. I'd like to get you to bed as early as we can."

But Talia wondered—because with the relay towers, someone *could* have known what hostel they intended to stay in—and as a former farmchild, she knew that *some* mushrooms could be preserved indefinitely when dried. . . .

Kris pushed both of them to the limit, hoping to get Talia into the haven of a bed long before sundown. He managed; better still, that night they were the only travelers making use of the hostel. The quiet did her some good; so did the rest. Unfortunately, he knew from old lessons that there was no remedy for goatsfoot poisoning except time.

The accident was more than annoying; he really needed her abilities on this trip. Without them, they'd have to go on wit alone.

With a good night's sleep she was back to normal—except that her Gift was completely unreliable. She was either completely blocked, or so wide open she couldn't sort out what emotion was coming from whom.

Neither one of them wanted her to try projecting under *these* conditions. They couldn't predict what would happen and didn't really want to find out.

So he pushed to make the best time they could to the

next hostel—and hoped they could make training, wit, and skills serve.

When Kris stopped to try to inquire about hostels at noon, people seemed overly quiet, and not inclined to talk much beyond the simple courtesy of answering their questions. And the townspeople in the hamlet they finally reached were the same; hurrying to be about their business and showing only furtive curiosity about the strangers who had ridden in.

That night the Guard at the relay station they reported to was cold and somewhat brusque, and advised them against changing their plans for stopping at Ilderhaven.

"Them at the capital need to know where ye be; they'll be takin' it amiss if they can't find ye should they need ye," he said, making it sound as if "they" would be taking it more than "amiss" if the Heralds changed their stated plans.

Kris exchanged a flickering, sober glance with his partner, but made no retort.

At the hostel, which held a scant handful of travelers, they split up, each taking a likely prospect, and began trying to eke a little more information out of them.

Talia had chosen a shy priestess of one of the Moon-oriented orders, and hoped she could get something useful out of her without her Gift. She began her conversation with ordinary enough exchanges; the difficulties women faced when making long journeys, commiseration over the fact that men in authority seemed to take them lightly—Hostelmasters serving the men in the room first, no matter what the order of their arrival was, and much more in the same vein. Carefully, over the entire evening, she began steering the talk to the topics that seemed to be the most sensitive.

"Your King—I must say, he certainly seems to be a good ruler," Talia said casually, when the topic of Alessandar came up. "From what I can see, everyone seems to be prospering. That ought to be making for good days with your temple."

"Oh, yes . . . Alessandar is a fine ruler to us; things

have never been better . . ." The priestess trailed off into hesitant uncertainty.

"And he has a fine, strong son to follow him? Or so I'm told."

"Yes, yes, Ancar is strong enough . . . has there been much flooding in Valdemar? We've never seen the like of it this spring."

Had there been uneasiness when the woman spoke Ancar's name?

"Flooding, for fair. Crops and herds wiped out, rivers changing course even. Young Elspeth has been at the Queen to let her be about the countryside doing what she can—but of course that's out of the question while she's still in schooling. Once she's older though, I've no doubt she'll be the Queen's own right hand. Surely Ancar has been seeing to things for his father?"

"No . . . no, not really. The . . . the factors take care of all that, you know. And . . . we really don't want to be seeing Ancar . . . it isn't fitting for someone in his station to be going among the common folk. He has his own Court—has since he came of age, you know. He has—other interests."

"Ah," Talia replied, and allowed the conversation to turn to another topic.

"Not very conclusive," Kris mused. "But it's looking odd."

Talia nodded; they'd waited again until they were on the road before talking.

"I've gotten a similar sort of impression," he began.

"As if things were reasonably well *now,* but that folk are not entirely sure of what the morrow might bring."

"*Damn* that goatsfoot! If we could just have some idea how deeply this goes—if it's more than just the usual worries about 'better the straw king than the lion king' —*gods,* we need your Gift!"

"It's still not reliable," she told him regretfully.

"Well, we just have to muddle along on our own." He sighed. "This is exactly the kind of reason we've been sent on ahead, and we *have* to have clearer information than we've got. Selenay can't act on anything this vague."

"I know," she said, biting her lip. "I know."

That night Talia tackled an elderly clerk. When she brought up the topic of the King, he was voluble in his praise of Alessandar.

"Look at these hostels—wonderful idea, wonderful! I remember when I was just a lad, my first post as tax-collector—Lord Sun, the inns I had to stay in, verminous, filthy, and costing so high you wondered why they didn't just put a knife to your throat and have done with it! And he's cleaned out most of the brigands and robbers, him and his Army; Karse daren't even think about invading anymore. Oh, aye, he's a great King—but he's old . . ."

"Surely Ancar—"

"Well, that's as may be. The Prince is a one for protocol and position; he doesn't seem to be as open-handed as his sire. And there's the rumors. . . ."

"Oh?"

"Oh, you know, young m'lady—there's always rumors."

Indeed there were rumors; and now Kris actually suspected listeners, so he signaled Talia to wait to talk until they were on an open stretch of road the next day, with no one else near.

She told him what she'd gotten, and what she'd guessed.

"So Ancar has his own little Court, hm?" Kris mused. "And his own circle of followers and hangers-on. I can't say as I like the sound of that. Even if the Prince is innocent and fair-minded, there's likely to be those that would use him in a situation like that."

"He doesn't sound innocent or fair-minded from the little I've pried out of anyone," Talia replied. "Granted in fairness—he may just be a naturally cold and hard man. Goddess knows he's seen enough warfare at his age to have turned him hard."

"Oh? This is news to me—say on."

"At fourteen he participated in a series of campaigns that wiped out every trace of the Northern barbarians along their North Border. That set of campaigns lasted almost two years. At seventeen he led the Army against the last raid Karse ever dared make on them—and again, the raiders were utterly wiped out. At twenty he personally mounted a campaign against highwaymen, with the result that nearly every tree from here to the capital was bearing gallows' fruit that summer."

"Sounds like he should be regarded as a hero."

"Instead of with fear? It was apparently the *way* he conducted himself that has people afraid. He makes no effort to hide the fact that he enjoys killing—and he's utterly, utterly ruthless. He hanged more than a few of those 'highwaymen' on merest suspicion of wrongdoing, and lingered with a winecup in his hand to watch while they died."

"Lovely lad. Sounds like just the mate for our Elspeth."

"Don't even say that as a joke!" Talia all but hissed. "Or haven't you been granted any of the tales of his conduct with women? *I* was told it isn't a good idea to attract his attention, and to stay out of his sight as much as possible."

"Probably more than you; if you believe what you hear, young Ancar's taste runs to rape, and the younger, the better, so long as they're nubile and attractive. But that's the tale only if you read between the lines. Nobody's told me anything about that straight out."

:*They haven't said anything straight out about the wizards he keeps either,*: Tantris put in unexpectedly.

"What?" Kris replied in surprise.

:*I've been keeping my ears open in the stable. The hostelkeepers have been frightening the stablehands into line with threats about turning them over to Ancar's wizards if they don't move briskly and keep to their work.*:

"So? That's an old wives' trick."

:*Not when it's being used on "stableboys" old enough to have families of their own. And not when the threat genuinely terrified them.*:

"Lord of Light, this is beginning to look grim—" Kris relayed Tantris' words to Talia.

"We've *got* to find someone willing to speak out," she replied. "We daren't turn back with nothing in our hands but rumors. Selenay needs *facts*—and if we turned back now, we might well precipitate a diplomatic incident."

"I agree," Kris replied, even more firmly. "And if we're being watched, well—we just might not reach the Border again."

"You think it's possible? You think he'd dare?"

"I think he would, if what the rumors hint at is true, and enough was at stake. And the only way we're going to get any idea of what Ancar is like and what his plans are, is to get in close to him. And I'm afraid we *need* that information; I'm afraid more than Elspeth's betrothal hinges on us now."

"That," she replied, "is what I feared you'd say."

A day from the capital they finally found someone who would discuss the "rumors." It was pure luck, plainly and simply.

As they rode into town, Talia spotted a trader's caravan that she thought she recognized. Traders' wagons were all built to the same pattern, but their gaudy painting was highly individual. The designs rarely included lettering, since most of a trader's customers were far from literate, but they were meant to be memorable for the selfsame reason. And Talia thought she remembered the design of cheerful blue cats chasing each other around the lower border.

A few moments later, she saw the shaggy black head of the bearded owner, and couldn't believe her good fortune. This trader, one Evan by name, was a man who owed Talia his life. He had been accused of murder; she had defended him from an angry mob and found out the real culprit. Having cast Truth Spell on him and touched his mind, she knew she could trust not only his words, but that he would not betray them to anyone.

His wagon was parked in a row of others, in the stableyard of the "Crown and Candle," an inn that catered to trade.

When they reached the hostel, and settled down to dinner, Talia tapped Kris' toe with her own. They didn't like to use this method of communicating; it was awkward and very easy to detect unless their feet were hidden. But the hostel was nearly empty, and they'd been given a table to themselves in the back; she reckoned it was safe enough this time.

Follow my lead, she signaled.

He nodded, eyes half closed, as if in response to a thought of his own.

"I saw an old friend today," she said—and tapped *Trader—Truth Spell*—knowing that he would readily remember the only circumstance that combined those two subjects.

"Really? Wonder if we could get him to stand us a drink?"

And—*Information source?*—he tapped back.

"Oh, I think so," she replied cheerfully. *Yes.*

"Good! I could stand a drop of good wine. This stuff is not my idea of a drink." *Reliable?*

"Then I'll see if we can't talk him into a round or two." *Yes—Debt of honor.*

"Hm." He pushed his stew around with a bit of bread. *Gods—your Gift?*

Back.

Do it.

She summoned one of the little boys that hung around the hostel hoping for just such an opportunity to earn a coin, and sent a carefully worded message to Evan. He replied by the same messenger, asking her to meet him, not at his inn, but at his wagon.

He did not seem surprised to see Kris with her. He opened the back of the wagon and invited both of them inside the tiny living area. The three of them squeezed into seats around a tiny scrap of a table, and Evan poured three cups of wine, then waited expectantly.

Talia let down her shields with caution, and searched about the wagon for any human presence near enough to hear anything. There was nothing, and no one.

"Evan—" she said quietly, then, "traders hear a lot. To come straight to the point, I need to know what *you've* heard about Prince Ancar. You know you can trust me—and I promise we aren't being spied on. I'd know if we were."

Evan hesitated, but only a moment. "I . . . expected something of this sort. If I did not owe you so very much, Lady Herald—but there it is. And you have the right of it, a trader hears much. Aye, there's rumors, black rumors, about young Ancar. Five, six years agone, when he first came of age and warranted his own court, he began collecting some unchancy sorts about him. Scholars, he calls 'em. And, aye, some good has come of it—like the signal towers, some aqueducts and the like. But in the last year his scholars have gotten more of a reputation for wizardry and witchcraft than they have for knowledge."

"Well, now, isn't that what they say of Heralds here, too?" Kris smiled uneasily.

"But I never heard anyone say your witchcraft was anything but of the Light, young man," Evan replied, "And I've never heard anything but darksome tales of late where Ancar's friends are concerned. I've heard tales that they raise power with the spilling of blood—"

"How likely?" Kris asked.

Evan shrugged. "Can't say. To be fair, I've been places where the same is said of the followers of the One, and you of Valdemar know how wrong *that* is. This I *can* tell for true—he has in the past year turned to wenching. Wenching of the nastier sort. He has his way with any poor young maid that catches his eye, highborn or low, and none dare gainsay him—and his tastes run to leaving them with scars. Well, and that isn't all. He has men of his own about the countryside these days—'intelligencers' they call themselves. They claim to be like you twain, being the King's eyes and ears, to see that all's well—but I misdoubt that they're speaking their information in any ears but Ancar's, and I doubt the King knows they exist."

"I don't like that," Talia whispered.

"I don't either. I've been questioned by 'em fair often since I crossed the Border, and I mislike some of the questions they're asking. Who bought like they'd gotten prosperous, who'd told me aught, who bends knee to what god—aye, you can believe old Evan the Shrewd became Evan the Stupid 'round 'em."

His expression changed to one of thick-headed opacity. "Aye, milord, no, milord, talk t' *me* milord?" He wiped the look from his face. "Even let 'em cheat me right royally t' convince 'em. That's not the end of it. I've heard from those I trust that Ancar has raised his own private Army; at least three thousand men, and all of them the scum of the prisons, given their lives on condition they serve him. Well, I'll likely be gone before I find what this was all about, but I pity anybody who's here when Ancar takes the throne. Oh, yes," he shook his head, "I pity them."

They rode away from their hostel the next morning with grim faces, and paused in a little copse of trees just outside of town, where they could see anyone approaching, but no one could see them.

"I don't like it," Talia said flatly. "My vote is to turn around and head back for the Border—but there's the fact that a move like that could be construed as an insult."

She wanted badly to run; she was more afraid now than she'd ever been except when she'd lost control over her Gift. She was feeling very like she was walking into something she couldn't handle now, too—but this was exactly why Selenay had sent them in the first place—to uncover anything that might threaten Valdemar. And there was just the faintest of premonitions that some of this might lead back to Orthallen.

"All the more reason to stick it out," Kris replied soberly. "We've heard the rumors; we need to learn *exactly* how much danger there is, or we can't properly advise the Queen of the situation. We don't learn the depth of the problem by turning tail and running. And like I said before—if we turn now, they might decide we've learned something, and stop us before we made it back across the Border. If we stick, we should be able to bluff our way out."

"Kris, it's dangerous; we're playing with fire, here."

"I know it's dangerous, but no more dangerous than any number of other missions Dirk and I pulled off. And we have to find what his long-term plans are, if there's any chance at all to do so."

"I know, I know," Talia shivered. "But Kris, I don't like it. I feel like I'm walking into a darkened room, knowing that as soon as I light a candle I'll discover I've walked into a den of serpents and the door's been locked behind me."

"You're the ranking Herald, little bird. Do we go on and find out exactly what the situation is and whether or not there's immediate threat to the Kingdom, or do we head back to Selenay with what we know now—running like our tails are on fire and hope they can't stop us?"

"How could we get back if they come after us?"

Kris sighed. "I wouldn't give very good odds. What we'd have to do is cut across country, avoiding roads—unfamiliar country, I might add, and we'd have to go night and day. *Or* we send Rolan and Tantris back alone, with messages, get rid of our rather conspicuous uniforms, steal disguises, try to get back afoot. With accents that damn us and every 'intelligencer' in the country knowing our exact descriptions. Frankly, the odds are with playing stupid and bluffing our way out."

"Could I pretend to be sick again?"

"Then they'd expect us to go straight to the capital and the King's Healers, not head back to our Border."

Talia shut her eyes and weighed all the possible consequences; then bit her lip, and steeled herself for the decision she knew she had to make.

"We go on," she said, unhappily. "We haven't got a choice."

But when they met their escort just outside the capital at the end of a six-day journey from the Valdemar Border, Talia almost heard the click of the lock behind her.

They announced their arrival at the gates of the city, and were asked, courteously enough, to wait. After about an hour, spent watching the usual sort of foot-and-beast traffic pass in and out of the city, there was a blast of trumpets and the common folk vanished from the vicinity as if whisked away by a spell.

Talia had expected an official escort; she had *not* expected that they would be met by what amounted to a royal procession. For that was exactly what emerged from the city gates.

Prancing out of the gateway came a procession of dozens of brightly-bedecked nobles and their liveried attendants, all mounted on high-bred palfries.

Prince Ancar and his entourage rode at the head of it.

Talia had *definitely* not expected *him*—and from the very brief flash of surprise on his face, neither had Kris.

Ancar rode toward them through a double row formed by his mounted courtiers and his guards; it was all very staged, and meant to impress. It impressed Talia, but hardly in the way she assumed he intended. On seeing him for the first time, Talia felt like a cat that has suddenly been confronted by a viper. She wanted to arch her back, hiss, and strike out at him.

"Greetings, from myself, and my honored Father," he said coolly, bowing slightly but not dismounting. "We have come to escort the envoys of Queen Selenay to the palace."

Talia was mortally certain that the "we" he used was the royal plurality, and noted that his horse was at least two hands higher than either Companion, allowing his head to be that much higher than theirs.

Gods—I don't think he's left anything to chance—

There was no superficial reason for the violent feeling of animosity that struck her; as they exchanged courtesies the Prince seemed perfectly amiable. He was darkly handsome with smooth, even features and a neat black beard and mustache. He spoke to them fairly enough and accorded them every honor. As he rode beside them, back into the city and toward the palace, he discoursed on neutral topics—the harvest to come, the recent spring floods that had occurred in both countries, his wish for continuing good relations between the two Kingdoms. All perfectly natural topics, and all spoken in tones of good-will.

None of this made the slightest bit of difference to Talia. There was something indefinably evil about the man, something cold and calculating, like a snake judging when it would be best to strike.

He was paying very little attention to Talia, who was riding with Kris between them; as if, because of her sex, she was not quite of an exalted enough station for him to bother with. That was all to the good; since he was busy directing his attention to Kris, she decided that this was no time for ethical quibbling; she would try to probe him. This was neither diplomatic nor particularly moral, but she didn't much care. There was something lurking beneath the smooth, careful surface of this cultivated Prince, and she was determined to discover what it was.

She was stopped by a powerful shield—one unlike anything she had ever touched before. There were no cracks in it that she could discover, not by the most careful probing. Startled, she cast a surreptitious glance at Ancar; he continued his conversation without seeming the least disturbed. So *he* was not the one doing the shielding. Who was?

Then her sharp glance was intercepted by a nondescript man in gray riding to the left of the Prince. He looked at her with eyes like dead brown pebbles, then permitted himself a faint smile and a nod. She shivered, and looked hastily away.

They couldn't reach the Palace grounds any too soon for Talia, who only wanted out of the Prince's presence. When they reached the courtyard of the Palace the entire entourage dismounted and dozens of liveried grooms appeared to lead the horses away—and with them, their Companions. Shaken by the encounter with the Prince's mage, Talia scanned the grooms quickly for any evidence of harmful intent.

Thank the gods—

To her relief there was nothing there but admiration for the beautiful creatures and the honest wish to make them comfortable. She tried to link with Rolan, and caught an impression of concern, but in the confusion it was hard to make out what the concern was for.

Kris began to say something—the Prince interrupted him before he'd even gotten a single syllable out.

"The Palace is quite remarkable," said Ancar, a kind of glint in his eye that Talia didn't understand and didn't at all like. "You really *must* see it *all*."

What could they do but consent?

And the Prince seemed determined that they see every inch of his father's Palace, conducting them all over it himself. He kept himself at Kris' side, and one of his ubiquitous toadies at Talia's, effectively separating them. They couldn't even signal to one another—and Talia was

nearly stiff with apprehension before the enforced tour
was over. Her anxiety, carefully concealed, redoubled
every moment they spent in his presence, and she longed
for one single moment alone with Kris. It almost seemed
as if the Prince were deliberately attempting to prevent
any contact between the two Heralds that did not take
place under his gaze, for he kept them at his side until it
was nearly time for the state banquet that was to welcome them.

At last they were left alone in their sumptuous suite.

Talia scanned about her for listeners, but could detect
none. But then—could she if they were shielded?

Make discretion the better part, then.

"Lord of Light," she sighed, "I didn't think I could
ever be so tired . . ."

Hand-sign; *Trap—listeners?* She sat down on a couch,
and patted the fabric next to her in invitation.

He took a seat next to her, and her hand. Squeezed.
Gift?

She squeezed back. *Shields?*

His eyebrows arched in surprise. *How?*

"Did you see that odd little man on the Prince's right?"
she asked. *Him.* "I wonder what on earth he could be."
Shielded Ancar. Maybe more.

"Who knows? Some sort of tutor, maybe." *Trouble.*

"Hm. I could use a little air." *For true.*

They moved to the open window, arms around one
another, loverlike.

"Little bird," Kris whispered in her ear, "There's another problem—there aren't enough guards visible here."

Talia giggled and nuzzled his neck. "I'm not sure I
understand you," she murmured back.

He laughed, and kissed her with expertly feigned passion. "Look, Selenay is well-loved, so she keeps a minimum of guards about her for safety—but they're still
there, still visible. Alessandar is just as highly regarded,
so I would expect to see about the same number of
guards. I didn't see them. If they're not *in* sight, they
must be *out* of sight. Why should he hide his guards?
Unless he doesn't know that they're hidden—and if you

can hide one, you can hide a dozen just as easily. I don't like it."

"Kris, please—" Talia whispered urgently. "I've changed my mind about staying. I think we should get out of here. Now. Tonight."

"I agree; I think we've walked into a bit more than we can handle by ourselves." He led her back to the couch, where they continued the mock-loveplay. "I've got no doubt now after seeing that magician and watching the way people react to Ancar that every one of the rumors is true. So we'd better leave tonight—but not quite yet. I want to find out what's going on with Alessandar first." He stayed quiet for a moment, deep in thought, hands resting in the small of her back, and face buried in her hair. "I think we should send substitutes into the banquet and do some spying before we leave."

"All right, but I'll do the spying. If I unshield I'll be able to detect people coming long before you would."

"Could you tell if there's a shielded spy watching us by the shield on him?"

"Alone—no."

"I see what you're getting at. Link—"

By linking their two Gifts, her Empathy and his Farsight, they were able to scan their entire vicinity for "null" areas. And discovered, to their mutual chagrin, that there *were* no spies, shielded or otherwise.

"Well—" he pulled away from her, embarrassed. "I certainly feel like a fool."

"Don't." She ran her hands nervously through her hair, and smiled wanly at him. "Better we take the precaution needlessly. If we send in substitutes, won't they be recognized?"

"No one from the Prince's party will be at the banquet, remember? There won't be anyone there who's ever seen us. And if we use a couple of the servants there should be no problems. After all, no one ever looks at servants. The two they assigned to us should do. They're enough like us in size and appearance that our uniforms will fit reasonably well. I'll get their attention, and you deep-trance, and take them over."

Talia shivered. She didn't like doing this, but Kris

couldn't. His Gift of Farsight would do him no good in implanting a false personality. It was only by virtue of the fact that her Gift of Empathy was a particularly strong one that Talia could do it at all—this was normally a trick only Mindspeakers could manage.

Kris rang for the two who had been assigned to them. As he had pointed out, they were similar enough in height and build to the two of them that the uniforms should fit well enough to cause no comment.

The servants arrived, and with them, their baggage; Kris instructed them in the unpacking of the formal uniforms. While he engaged their attention, Talia put herself into deep-trance.

Forgive me—she thought, then reached out and touched their minds—*lightly*—*there*—first the man, then the woman—

Kris caught them as they fell, easing them down onto the bed.

Talia insinuated herself carefully into their minds, sending their real selves into a kind of waking sleep.

Now—for the next part she would need help—

:Rolan?:

In a moment he was with her, still anxious, but in agreement with the plan, or at least as much of it as she was able to show him without being able to Mindspeak him in words instead of images.

Together they emplanted false personalities and memories in their two substitutes; he could do some things she couldn't, she could make them *believe* that they were the foreigners. For the next several hours the servants would be a sketchy sort of Kris and Talia, and remain that way until they returned to these rooms after the banquet. Their behavior would be rather stilted and wooden, but the formal etiquette such occasions demanded would cover most of that.

Talia let Rolan go, and eased herself up out of trance, feeling very stiff, quite exhausted, and just a bit guilty.

"Is it—"

"They're ready," she replied, moving her head around to ease the stiffness in her neck, and getting slowly to her feet. "Let's get some clothes on them."

They clothed the pair in the waiting formal Whites as if they were dealing with two dolls, it being easier to handle them in the entranced state. Talia cut their hair in imitation of Kris' and her own, and applied her skill with makeup to both of them. When she'd done, they bore at least enough of a superficial resemblance to the two of them to get them safely through the doors.

"All right." Kris looked at her as they got the two substitutes on their feet. "I'm for the stables. It's going to take a little time to find the Companions and their tack without being detected. If I can, I'll get everything and get them all saddled up. If you have the chance, you meet me at the stable doors."

"Fine," Talia replied nervously. "I'm going to sneak up to the second floor and the minstrel's gallery. I ought to learn something there; with luck I may be able to pick up something from one of Ancar's toadies, and I'll definitely be able to probe Alessandar and find out if he knows what his son is up to. I won't take long, if I can help it."

"If the worst happens, and you have to run for it, tell Rolan, and I'll pick you up on the run in the courtyard." Kris gave her a tight grin, and she returned it.

Talia took her substitute by the elbow; Kris did the same with his. Together they led them as far as the doors to the suite; then Talia released their minds and gave hers a little push. The young woman blinked once, then her implanted personality took over. She took the young man's arm; he opened the door, and led her toward the banquet hall. Kris and Talia followed behind them long enough to be certain that the ruse would work, then separated.

Thanks to the Prince's enforced tour they were both familiar with the layout of the entire Palace. Kris made for one of the servants' stairs that led to the stables; once she saw him safely on his way, Talia headed for the gallery that overlooked the banquet hall.

She dropped all her shielding and slipped from shadow to shadow along the corridor, taking another of the servants' stairs to the second floor. The activity in the banquet hall aided her; the servants hadn't yet had time to light more than a few of the candles meant to illuminate the maze of corridors. She detected no one as she moved to the wall that backed the gallery.

She sensed the presence of many men as she paused there, hiding herself in the folds of drapery along the wall. This was very wrong. There were to be no minstrels playing in the gallery until much later this evening; at the moment they were playing from behind a screen on the floor of the hall. There should be no one at all in the gallery at this time.

She closed her eyes and carefully extended her other sense past the wall, hoping that one of them might be nervous enough to let her read what he was seeing, carried on the wind of his emotions.

It was easy—too easy. The images came charging into her mind—she knew who and what they were, and what their intent was, and her heart leapt into her throat with terror.

Ranged at about three-foot intervals around the gallery, which ran the entire circumference of the hall, were crossbowmen. Their weapons were loaded and ready, and each had a full quiver of bolts beside him. These were not members of Alessandar's guard, nor soldiers from his army; these were ruthless killers recruited personally by Ancar.

The Prince was impatient, and no longer prepared to wait for his father's natural death to bring him to the seat of power. He was also ambitious, and not content with the prospect of ruling only one kingdom. Here in one room sat his father and everyone who might be opposed to Ancar's rule, as well as the two Heralds who might have warned their Queen of his intent. The opportunity was far too tempting for him to pass by. Once the banquet was well underway, the doors would be locked—and all who might oppose Ancar's desires would die.

With the exception of the Heralds; Ancar's orders concerning *them* were to disable, not kill. And if anything, that frightened Talia even more.

Ancar must have had this whole scheme planned for months, and had only waited for the perfect moment to put it in motion. The six days' warning he'd had when they crossed the Border was sufficient for him to mobilize what was already prepared.

When the slaughter was over he would ride with his own army to the Border, overwhelm the Queen and her escort as soon as they'd crossed it, kill her, seize Elspeth, and present himself as Valdemar's ruler by fait accompli.

Talia longed for Kyril's ability to Farspeak; even at this distance she would have been able to get some kind of warning back to the Heralds near the Border. And she would have been able to Mindcall Kris, and warn him as well. All she could do was to Mindcall to Rolan, carrying her message on a burst of purest fear, and hope he could convey the whole to Kris through Tantris.

She slipped back to the staircase as silently and carefully as she had come, and made her way down to the lower floor.

The hall here was lighted well, and Talia feared to set foot in it; feared it doubly when she sensed the presence of more of Ancar's men standing at intervals along it, presumably to take care of any stragglers. She clung, half paralyzed with terror, to the inside of the door, and tried to think. Was there any other way out?

Then she recalled the smaller rooms of state, meant for receptions and the like, that faced the forecourt on the second floor. Many of them had balconies, and windows or doors that opened out onto the balconies. For the second time she climbed the staircase, heart pounding, her Empathic-sense extended to the utmost.

She moved along the wall, between it and the musty draperies lining it, until she came to the door of one of those rooms. Mercifully it was unoccupied and unlocked; not even a single candle was lit within. She crept out from behind the drape, ignoring the itch of dust in her eyes and nose, and slipped inside.

There was only the gleam of torchlight and moonlight through the windows, but that was enough to show her a room with a polished-wood floor empty of all furniture. She edged around the walls, grudging the time, but not wanting to silhouette herself against those windows for anyone passing by the hall door.

The door to the balcony was locked, but from the

inside. Talia realized this after an instant of panic-stricken struggle with it. The catch was stiff, but finally gave. She eased the door open and stepped out onto the balcony, crouched low so as to be below the balustrade. A moment's surveillance of the courtyard showed no eyes to be watching it; she slipped over the balustrade and was about to drop to the court, when the killing began.

With her Empathic senses extended as they were, that nearly killed *her* along with the rest. She felt the deaths of dozens of people in her own flesh; she lost her grip on the railing and dropped to the cobblestones below. Shock, pain, and fear drove any other thoughts out of her, she could not even move to save herself. She was falling—and couldn't think, couldn't move, couldn't do anything but *react*—react to the agony, the terror—and the anguished guilt of Alessandar's guards seeing him pinned to his throne by dozens of crossbow bolts before they themselves were cut down—

But Alberich had foreseen the day when something like this might happen; he had drilled her until some reactions had become instinctive. Though her mind might be helpless beneath that onslaught, her body wasn't—

She twisted in midair, rolled into a limp ball—hit the pavement feet-first, and turned the impact into a tumble that left her sprawled and bruised, but otherwise unharmed.

Her face twisted with agony as she struggled to her feet and staggered toward the entrance to the stable area, trying to shut her shields down and the pain out. It seemed like an eternity between each stumbling step, yet she had hardly taken half a dozen when she heard the pounding of hooves on stone and saw a white form surging toward her.

It was Rolan—unsaddled. He did not pause as he passed her, knowing that she would not be able to mount unless he came to a dead stop. Hard on his heels came Tantris carrying Kris—who was leaning over as far as he dared, one hand wrapped in Tantris' mane, the other extended toward her, his legs clenched so tightly she could almost feel the muscles ache. As Companion and rider passed her, Talia caught him, hands catching forearms, as she leaped and Kris pulled her up in front of him. Tantris had had to slow a trifle, and Rolan was ahead of him, but they'd not had to stop.

But there was one last obstacle to pass—the narrow passage between the inner and outer walls that led to the portcullis and the outer gate. And Talia had succeeded in shielding herself once again—so they had no warning that the walls were manned.

They galloped straight into a hail of arrows.

It was over in seconds. Fire lanced through Talia's shoulder—just as Tantris screamed in agony, shuddered, and crashed to the ground. She was thrown forward and hit the ground stunned, with the impact breaking off the shaft of the arrow and driving the head deeper. But more agonizing than her own pain was what Kris was enduring.

Rolan paused in his headlong flight—the marksmen had let the unburdened beast go by. There was one thought only in Talia's mind besides the agony of pain—that *one* of them must escape.

"Rolan—*run!*" she screamed with voice, heart, and mind.

He hesitated no longer, but shot through the gate just as the portcullis came crashing down, so close that she felt the sharp pain and his surge of fear as it actually carried away a few hairs from his tail.

Kris lay crumpled beside the motionless body of Tantris, so racked with agony that he could not even cry out. She tried to rise, and half-stumbled, half-dragged herself to his side. She took his pain-tortured body into her arms, desperately trying to think of *anything* that would help him. He was transfixed by arrows so that he looked like a straw target—but a target that bled; it had been his body and Tantris' that had shielded her. Even in the flickering torchlight she could see that his Whites were dyed in creeping scarlet blotches that spread while she held him. She groped mindlessly for the Healing energy Kerithwyn had used; not sure what she could do with it, but driven beyond sanity with the overwhelming need to take the burden of his torment from him. She felt a kind of pressure building within her, as it had in those past times when desperation had driven her to pass the bounds of what she knew. It built past the point where she was conscious of anything outside of herself, conscious even of the agony lancing her own shoulder—

Then it found sudden release.

She opened her eyes to find Kris' own eyes holding hers; free from pain and feverishly clear. Although she could feel his pain still, *he* could not. She had somehow come to stand between it and him.

But he was dying, and they both knew it.

She looked around, expecting to see soldiers surrounding them.

"No."

Kris' hoarse whisper brought her attention back to him. "They—it is a maze. While I live, they will not come."

She understood. His Gift had shown him that there was a maze of stairs and corridors to traverse before the soldiers reached an entrance to this area. But it had also shown him how little time he had left.

"Kris—" She couldn't get anything more past the tears that rose and choked off her words.

"No, little love, little bird. Weep for yourself, not for me."

She nearly fell to pieces with grief at his words.

"I don't fear Death; gladly, willingly would I seek the Havens, if I but knew my Companion waits for me there— but to leave you—how can I leave you with all my burden and yours as well?" He coughed, and blood showed at the corner of his mouth. Somehow he managed to raise one hand to touch her cheek; she seized it with her own and wept into it.

"It isn't fair—to leave you alone—but warn them, heartsister. Somehow warn them. I cannot carry the task to the end, so it ends with you."

She nodded, so choked with tears she could not speak.

"Oh, little bird, I love you—" He seemed to be trying to say more when another spate of coughing shook him. He looked up again, but plainly did not see her; his eyes brightened and gladdened as if he were seeing something wonderful and unexpected. "So—bright! T—"

For one fleeting moment Talia sensed—joy; joy and the touch of awe and a strange glory that was like nothing she'd ever sensed before. Then his body shuddered once in her arms, and the light and life left his eyes. He went limp within her embrace—and then there was nothing but the empty husk she held.

The soldiers came then, tore them apart, and took her away; she was too numb with shock and grief to resist.

Eight

Her guards were anything but gentle.

They bound her hands behind her and kicked and shoved her down countless rock-faced corridors and a flight of rough stone stairs; when she stumbled they kicked her until she rose, when she faltered they sent her onward with blows. They gave her a final push that sent her sprawling into the center of a bare room. There they put her in the custody of three hulking brutes, creatures who looked more beast than man.

These three stripped her to the skin, indifferent to the agony of her shoulder, and brutally searched her. Then one by one, they raped her with the same brutality and indifference. By that time, she was nearly senseless with shock and pain, and it hardly seemed to matter. It was just one more torture. She couldn't even concentrate enough to use her Gift to defend herself, and when she'd tried feebly to fight back, the one using her had knocked her head against the stone floor so hard she was barely conscious.

When they had finished with her they hauled her to her feet by one arm, and threw her into a dirt-floored, stone-walled cell, then tossed what was left of her blood-stained clothing in behind her. It was the cold that finally roused her, cold that chilled her and made her shake uncontrollably, and awoke her lacerated shoulder to new pain. She roused enough then to crawl to where they'd tossed her things and pull them on over her abused flesh.

Not surprisingly, nothing had been done about the

wound in her shoulder, which continued to bleed sluggishly.

I've—got to do something—she thought, through the pain and cold clouding her mind, —*got to—get it out.*

She got a firmer grip on reality; thought she remembered that the arrows she'd seen the guards carrying had had leafpoints. *Right*— She steeled herself against the inevitable, got a good grip on what was left of the slippery, blood-soaked shaft, and pulled.

It came free—she passed out briefly as it did. When her vision cleared, she bound the wound with one hand using a scrap from her shredded shirt as a bandage, and hoped that this would at least stem the blood loss.

Selenay. Elspeth. She had to warn the Queen—

That goad was driving her past the point where she should have collapsed, and continued to drive her. She had to warn the others. For that she *must* stay aware— and alive, much as she longed to die. She curled in on herself, forcing herself into trance, driving herself regardless of the pain of her brutalized body. With this much pain behind it, even *she* should be able to reach the Border.

But she met with the same wall that had protected the Prince from her probe. She battered herself against it like a wild bird against the bars of a cage, and with as much effect. There were no cracks, no weak points in it. Try as she might, she could not reach her Mindcall past it. Weeping with bitter pain and tortured frustration, she gave up, and lay in a hopeless huddle on the floor in the darkness.

There was no way of telling how long she lay there before an anomalous sound roused her from a nightmare of shock, pain, and confused grief. She listened again. It was the sound of someone whispering.

"Herald! Lady Herald!" The voice sounded vaguely familiar.

"Herald!" It was coming from a small opening in the ceiling.

She crawled on hands and knees across the dirt floor to lie beneath it, for her legs trembled so much she doubted they'd hold her, and coughed several times before she could speak.

"I'm—here."

"Lady Herald, it's me, Evan—Evan, the trader from Westmark in Valdemar. The one you talked to a day ago."

As she reached out tentatively with her Gift she wondered briefly if this, too, was a trap.

Gods—if it is—but what do I have to lose? Please, Lady—

She nearly fainted with relief when her Gift confirmed that it was the same man.

"Oh, gods—Evan, Evan, Lady bless you—" she gulped and got control over her babbling. "Where are you?"

"Outside the walls in the dry moat. Some of my acquaintances have worked in the Palace and Guard and told me of these ventilation holes. I arrived after you, late this evening—I was drinking with some of the Guard when—there were screams. They told me some of what was happening, and warned me to hold my tongue if I wanted to live. They aren't bad men, but they are afraid, Herald, very much afraid. The Prince is making no secret now that he has evil magicians, and an entire army that answers only to him."

—if only I'd overruled Kris—he'd be alive now—

"Later they told me they'd captured you—I—couldn't leave you without trying to help. I bribed a guard to learn which cell they had taken for you. Lady—" he seemed to be groping for words. "Lady, your friend is dead."

"Yes—I—I know." She bowed her head as the tears fell anew and she did not try to hold them back.

He was silent for a long moment. "Lady, you saved my life; I am still in your life-debt. *Is* there some way I can help you? The Prince means to keep you living; I am told he has plans for you."

Hope rose to faltering life. "Can you help me escape this place?"

And died. "No, Lady," he said sadly. "That would require an army. I would gladly try alone—but it would not serve you. You would still be here, and I would be quite dead."

Half a dozen ideas flitted through her mind; one stayed.

"Are these holes straight? Could you lower something to me, or bring something up?"

"If it were something small, yes, Lady; easily done. My guide told me that they were quite straight, and unobstructed."

"Can you find me two arrows—if you can, see that the barbs of the fletching are heavy—and—" She faltered, and forced herself to continue. "—and at least ten drams of argonel."

"Have they hurt you, Lady? There are safer ways to ease pain than argonel. And Lady, that much—"

"Trader, do not argue. I have my reasons, and argonel it must be. Can you do it?"

"Within the hour, Lady."

There was a thin whisper of sound as he left. She propped herself against the wall and tried to use the pain-deadening tricks she'd been taught to ease her shoulder and her throbbing loins. She would not let herself hope that the trader would keep his promise, but strove to remain passive, unfeeling, in a kind of numbness. It was still dark when she heard a scratch and the trader's voice.

"Lady, I have all you asked for. It's coming now."

She pulled herself up the wall and reached for the bundle that dangled from the ceiling with her good hand, feeling more of the injured shoulder muscles tear as she reached up.

"The bottle holds fourteen drams, and it is full."

"May the Lord of Lights and the Fair Lady shine on you, friend, and all your kin and trade—" she replied fervently, loosening the stopper enough to catch the distinctive sweet-sour odor of argonel. The bottle *was* completely full. "Leave the string. You will be taking something up in a moment and doing me another service— one last office that will free you of life-debt entirely."

"I am yours to command," he replied with simple sincerity.

She snapped the head from the first arrow by holding

it under one foot. She let the tears flow freely as she patterned it with Kris' fletching pattern, grateful that she'd been made to learn to do the task in the dark, and finding it hard to continue with the memory fresh of him teaching her his own pattern. The headless arrow—code for a Herald dead. Now for the most important half of the message—code for herself; and code for the mission in such ruins that no attempt at rescue should be made. She broke the second arrow in half and patterned the fletching as her own. She tore the remains of one sleeve from her shirt, secured the arrows into a compact bundle with it, and fastened the whole to the string dangling down from the hole in the ceiling.

"Trader, pull it up."

It gleamed for a moment against the stone, then was gone.

"Now listen carefully. I want you to leave now, before dawn, before the Prince tries to seal the city. You must get outside the city gates."

"There is a guard at the night-gate I know I can bribe."

"Good. Just out of sight of the guardpost on the main highway that runs from the Triumph Gate there is a shrine to the god of wayfarers."

"I know the place."

"My horse will find you there." The one thing that damned magician *couldn't* block was her bond with Rolan! "Tie the bundle around his neck, just as it is, then take whatever plan seems good to you. If I were you, I would make a run for the Border; you'll be safe enough on the Valdemar side. Know that you have all my thanks and all my blessings."

"Lady—a horse?"

She remembered then that he was Hardornen, and couldn't know how unlike horses the Companions were.

"He is more than horse; think of him as a familiar spirit. He will return to my people with my message. Will you do this for me?"

He was close to weeping himself. "Is there nothing more I can do?"

"If you do that, you will have done more than I dared

hope. You take with you all my gratitude, and my blessings. Now go, please, and quickly."

He did not speak again, and she heard the scrape that signaled his departure.

She felt for her contact with Rolan. Her bond with him was at too deep a level for the magician even to sense, let alone block. Although alternating waves of pain and faintness threatened to overwhelm her, she managed to remain aware until she knew with total certainty that Rolan had gotten her message-bundle from the trader.

Rolan did not need any instructions to know what to do. Her contact with him weakened and faded as she weakened with effort and blood loss and he headed for the Border at his fastest pace, until it vanished altogether as he reached the edge of her fast-shrinking range. By then it was almost dawn.

Now, there were just two more tasks, and she would be able to give way to her anguish, her hurts, her grief.

First, the bottle. The trader had been right to be nervous about argonel. It was chancy stuff. Sometimes even the normal dose of four drams killed—but the Healers used it now and again to end the suffering of one they could not save. It had the advantage that no matter how great the overdose, there were no painful side effects such as there were with other such drugs—nothing but a peaceful drifting into sleep. If four drams could kill, fourteen should make death very sure.

Using the broken-off arrowhead, she scraped a hole in the floor beneath the pile of molding straw that was supposed to be her bed, a hole just deep enough to bury the bottle. Alessandar had not been the kind of monarch that often used his dungeons; by the grace of the gods the floors were packed earth rather than stone, with a pit dug in one corner for a privy.

She would not use the drug yet—not until she was *certain* that the Queen had received the warning. *Soon, Bright Lady—make it soon—*

Then she scraped a second hole, and a third, and hid the arrowhead from the broken arrow and the one she'd pulled from her own shoulder. If by some mischance they should find the bottle, she could still cut her wrists with one of them.

Her shoulder was aflame with pain and bleeding again, and a little gray light was creeping down the ventilation hole when she'd finished.

She lay on the straw and let herself mourn at last.

Tears of sorrow and of pain were still pouring from her eyes when blood loss and exhaustion finally drove her into unconsciousness.

When she came to herself again, there was a single spot of sunlight on the floor, making the rest of the room seem black by comparison. She blinked in hurt and confusion, as the door clanked once and opened.

She saw one of her jailors strolling toward her, wearing a sadistic grin and unfastening his breeches as he walked. For the space of a second she was ready to cry out and shrink away from him—but then a cold and deadly anger came over her, and abruptly she could bear no more. She took all her agony and Kris' (still rawly part of her), all her loss, all her hatred, and hurled them into his unprotected mind in a blinding instant of forced rapport.

Hatred couldn't sustain her long—she couldn't maintain it for more than a single moment—but that moment was enough.

He screamed soundlessly, and flung himself wildly at the door, nearly knocking himself senseless when he reached it. He slammed it after himself, and threw the bolt home. She could hear him babbling in panic to his comrades on the other side. As she slumped back, she knew that they would not dare to molest her again, not unless the magician was with them. That was very unlikely. *That* one was too busy protecting his Prince and keeping her from Mindspeaking to have time to spare to protect menials so that they might amuse themselves.

They shoved in a pail of water and a plate of some sort of slop later in the day. She ignored the food, but drank the stale, fusty-tasting water avidly. Her terrible thirst woke her to the fact that she was beginning to feel both overheated and chilled.

Gingerly she touched the skin next to the arrow-wound. It was hot and dry to the touch, and badly swollen.

She was taking wound-fever.

While she was still able, she relieved herself down the privy hole in the corner, telling herself that she should be grateful that there was nothing in her stomach and bowels to make a flux of. It was cold comfort, that. She pulled the bucket within reach of the straw and propped herself against the wall in case someone should try to take her unaware. When the hallucinations and fever-dreams began, she was more or less ready for them.

There was no pattern to the fever. When she was able to think, she would tend to herself as best she could. When the fever took her, she endured.

There were horrible visions of the slaughter in the banquet hall, and the victims paraded their death-wounds before her and mutely asked why she hadn't warned them. In vain she told them that she hadn't known—they pressed in on her, shoving mutilated limbs and dripping wounds in her face, smothering her—

Her bestial guards multiplied into a horde, and used her, and used her, and used her—

Then Kris came.

At first she thought it was going to be another dream like the first, but it wasn't. Instead, he was whole, well; even happy—until he saw her. Then, to her distress, he began weeping—and blamed himself for what had happened to her.

She tried to put on a brave face for him, but when she moved, she hurt so much that her fragile pretense shattered. He shook off his own distress at that, and hurried to kneel at her side.

He somehow drove away some of the pain, spoke words of comfort, bathed her feverish brow with cool water. When she whimpered involuntarily as movement sent lances of hurt through her shoulder, he wept again with vexation at his own impotence, and berated himself for leaving her alone. When the other, horrible dreams came, he stood them off.

The next time she came to herself, she found that there was a scrap torn from her sleeve near the bucket, still damp. After trying to puzzle it out, she decided that she'd done it herself, and the dream had been a rationalization of it.

As delirium began to take her again, she tried to tell herself that it was unlikely that her hallucinations would include Kris a second time.

But they did, and Kris continued to guard her from the hideous visions, all the while trying to give her courage.

Finally she gave up even trying to pretend to hope, and told Kris about the argonel.

"No, little bird," he said, shaking his head at her. "It isn't your time yet."

"But—"

"Trust me. Trust me, dearheart. Everything is going to come out fine. Just try to hold on—" He faded into the stone, then, as she woke once more.

That puzzled her. Why should a fever-dream of her own making be trying to urge her to live, when she only wanted release?

But for the most part, she simply suffered, and endured the waiting, watching for some sign that her message had safely reached Selenay. The Queen and her entourage should have reached the Border about two days after she and Kris had ridden through the palace gates. They would have been expecting Kris about three or four days after they arrived—a week after she'd been thrown in here. With luck and the Lady with him, Rolan should reach them about that time. She added the days in her head—that meant he would reach the Queen in six to ten days at his hardest gallop—six if he could take the open roads, ten if he had to backtrack and hide.

When Hulda first appeared, at the end of the third day, Talia thought initially that she was another hallucination.

If it hadn't been that Hulda's sharp features and strange gray-violet eyes were unmistakable, Talia wouldn't have recognized her. She was swathed in a voluptuous gown of burgundy-wine velvet, cut low and daringly across the bosom, and there were jewels on her neck and hands and the net that bound her hair. But most amazing of all, she appeared to be hardly older than Talia herself.

She stood peering into the darkness, eyes darting this way and that; a cruel smile touched her lips when she finally spotted Talia huddled against the wall. She moved from the center of the room with an odd, gliding step to stand above Talia, eyes narrowed in pleasure, and nudged her sharply with one dainty shoe.

The pain she caused made Talia gasp and pull in on herself—and her heart leapt into her throat when she realized that the woman was still standing there—real, and no hallucination.

When Talia's eyes widened with shock and recognition, Hulda smiled. "You remember me? How very touching! I had no hope you'd have any recollection of little Elspeth's adored nurse."

She moved a few steps farther away and stood artfully posing in the light that came through the ventilation hole. "And how low the mighty Herald has fallen! You'd have been pleased to see me brought so low, wouldn't you? But I am not caught so easily, little Herald. Not half so easily."

"What—what are you?" The words were forced out almost against Talia's will.

"I? Besides a nurse, you mean?" She laughed. "Well, a magician, I suppose you'd call me. Did you think the Heralds held all the magic there was in the world? Oh, no, little Herald, that is far, far from being the case."

She laughed again, and swept out of the cell, the door clanging shut behind her.

Talia struggled to think; but—Lord and Lady, this meant there was more, much more at stake here than she'd dreamed.

Hulda—so young-looking, and claiming to be a magician. And she hadn't any trace of a Gift, Talia knew *that* for certain. Put that together with the mage who guarded Ancar and kept her from Mindspeaking to other Heralds— gods protect Valdemar! That meant that old magic, *real* magic, and not just Heraldic Mind-magic, was loose in the world again. And in the hands of Valdemar's enemies—

And Hulda had been—*must* have been—playing a deeper game than anyone ever guessed, and for far longer.

But to what purpose?

Hulda came again, this time after dark, bringing some kind of witchlight with her. It was an odd, misty ball that gave off a red glare that flickered and pulsated; it floated in behind her and hovered just above her shoulder, bathing the entire cell in an eerie, reddish glow.

This time Talia was more or less ready for her. She was free from delirium for the moment, and feeling light-yet clear-headed. She had managed to put her own emotions and the helplessness of her position in the back of her mind, hoping for some stroke of luck that might bring her a chance to strike back at her tormentors.

She had figured that Hulda was warded, even as the Prince was; she probed anyway, and discovered her guess was correct. So rather than making any other moves, she simply shifted her weight where she sat so that she might be able to get to her feet at a moment's notice.

Hulda smiled mockingly; Talia glared right back.

"You might rise to greet me," she mocked. "No? Well, I shan't ask it of you. You'll be dancing to my little Prince's tunes soon enough. Or should I say, 'King'? I suppose I should. Aren't you at all curious as to why and I how I came here?"

"I have the feeling you'd tell me whether I cared or not," Talia said bitterly.

"Spirited! You're right, I would. Oh, I spent years looking for a child like Ancar—one of high estate, yet one who could readily incline himself to what I would teach him. Then once I found him, I knew within a year that one land would never be enough for him. So once I taught him enough that he could do without me for a time, I turned my attention toward finding him a suitable mate. Dear Elspeth seemed so perfect—" she sighed theatrically.

"Oh?"

"You are so talented, little Herald! What volumes of meaning you convey with a single syllable! Yes, dear Elspeth seemed perfect—coming from a long line of those

Gifted magically, *and* with such a father! Plotting against his own wife! Delicious!"

"If you're trying to convince me that treachery is inherited, you're wasting your breath."

She laughed. "Very well then, I'll be brief. I intended Elspeth to be properly trained and eventually consolidate an alliance with Ancar. As you probably guessed, I substituted myself for the original Hulda. Things were progressing quite well—until you intervened."

This time the glance she shot at Talia was venomous. "Fortunately I was forewarned. I returned to my dear Prince, and when he was of an age to begin taking part in the making of plans, we put together a quite tidy plot."

She began pacing the room, restlessly, the folds of her vermilion gown collecting loose dirt from the floor, dirt which she ignored.

"What *is* it," Talia asked the ceiling above her head, "what is it about would-be tyrants that makes them speak and posture like third-rate gleemen in a badly-written play?"

Hulda pivoted sharply about and glared, her hands twitching a little as if she'd like to settle them about Talia's neck. Talia braced herself, hoping she'd try. Granted, she was as weak as water, but there were some tricks Alberich had taught her. . . .

"Haven't you got anything better to do than boast about your petty triumphs to a captive audience?" she taunted.

Hulda's face darkened with anger; then to Talia's disappointment she regained control of herself, and slowly straightened and smoothed the folds of her gown while she calmed her temper.

"You're to be a part of this, you know," she said abruptly. "Ancar wanted both of you alive, but you alone will do. We'll all ride together to the Border and wait for your Queen there. She'll see you with us, and be reassured. Then—"

"You don't seriously think you'll get me to cooperate, do you?"

"You won't have a choice. Just as my Prince's servant can keep you from sending your little messages, so I can take control of your own body from you—particularly since you're in rather poor condition at the moment."

"You can try."

"Oh, no, little Herald. I can bring in more help than you could ever hope to hold against. I will succeed."

She laughed, and swept out the door, then, the witchlight following.

As Talia had hoped, on the tenth day of her captivity, the door to her cell opened, and Prince Ancar and his magician stood before her. And with him was Hulda.

She was in another of the periods of clear-headedness between bouts of delirium. She debated facing them standing, but decided that she didn't have the strength. She simply stared at them with undisguised contempt.

"My messengers have sent signals telling me that the Queen of Valdemar has turned back at the Border," Ancar said, gazing at her with basilisk-eyes. "And now they say she gathers an army to her side. Somehow you warned her, Herald. How?"

She returned him stare for stare. "If you two are so all-powerful," she asked contemptuously, "why don't you read my thoughts?"

His face reddened with anger. "*Damn* you Heralds and your barriers—" he spat, before Hulda managed to hush him.

Talia stared at him in astonishment. *Brightest Lady—he can't read me—they can't read me, can't read Heralds—no wonder we almost caught Hulda before—* For one moment, she felt a stirring of excitement, but it faded. The information was priceless—and useless. It only meant they would not be able to pluck truth from her thoughts, and so would never know when and if she lied.

So start now. Tell them a truth they would never believe. According to Elspeth, Hulda had never believed that the Companions were more than very well trained beasts. She had been convinced it was the Heralds who picked the Chosen, not the Companions.

So. "My horse," she said after a long pause, "My horse escaped to warn them."

Ancar smiled, and ice rimed her blood. "An imagination, I trow. You should have been a Bard. This will only delay things, you must realize. I have been working toward my goals for years, and I can easily compass a little more delay." He turned toward Hulda, and brushed his lips along her hair. "Can't I, my dear nurse?"

"Easily, my Prince. You have been a most apt pupil."

"And the pupil has exceeded the teacher, no?"

"In some things, my love. Not in all."

"Perhaps you will be interested to hear that I know of your quarrel with the young Heir, little Herald. It would seem that she is quite crestfallen, and determined to make it up with you, since my informant tells me she is most eager to be meeting with you again. A pity that won't happen. It would have been amusing to watch the meeting—and you under my dear nurse's control."

Talia tried not to show any reaction, but her concentration slipped enough that she bit her lip.

"Do tell her who our informant is, my love," Hulda murmured in Ancar's ear.

"None other than the trusted Lord Orthallen. What, you are not surprised? How vexing. Hulda discovered him, you know—found that he had been working at undermining the Heralds and the Monarchs so long and so cleverly that no one even guessed how often he'd played his cards."

"Some of us guessed."

"Really?" Hulda pouted. "I *am* disappointed. But have you guessed why? Ancar has promised him the throne. Orthallen has wanted that for so very long, you see. He thought he had it when he arranged for an assassin to take Selenay's father in battle. But then there was Selenay—and all those Heralds who persisted in protecting her. He decided to do away with them first—it's a pity how little luck he's had. He has been so surprised at the way you keep eluding his traps. He'll be even more amazed when Ancar gives him the dagger instead of the crown. But I *am* disappointed that you had guessed at his perfidy already."

"My poor dear—two disappointments in one day." Ancar turned his cold gaze back on Talia. "Well, since you have denied me one pleasure, you can hardly blame anyone but yourself when I use you for another, can you? Perhaps it will make up for the entertainments your actions denied my dear nurse."

"Ah, but be wary of this wench, my lord King," Hulda cautioned. "She is not without weapons, even now. Your servant must not let the barrier break for even a moment."

He smiled again. "Small chance of that, my love. He *knows* the penalty should he fail to keep her trapped within her own mind. Should he weaken, my heart—he becomes *yours*."

She trilled with delight as he signaled to the hulking guards that stood behind him.

They seized Talia and dragged her to her feet, pinioning her arms behind her back. Anguish threaded her body as the wound broke open anew, but she bit her lip and suffered silently.

"Stubborn as well! How entertaining you will be, Herald. How very entertaining."

He turned and led the way from the cell with the magician and Hulda in close attendance and the guards following with Talia. There was a long corridor that smelled of mold and damp, and an iron door at the end of it. Beyond it was the smell of fear, and blood.

They shackled her arms to the cold stone above her head, putting an almost intolerable strain on her wounded shoulder.

"I consider myself an artist," Ancar told her, "There is a certain artistry in producing the most pain without inflicting permanent damage, or causing death." He removed a long, slender iron rod from the fire and regarded the white-hot tip thoughtfully. "There are such fascinating things to be done with this, for instance."

As from a century distant she recalled Alberich discussing some of the more unpleasant realities of becoming a Herald with a small knot of final-year students in which she was included.

"The possibility of torture," Alberich had said on that long ago afternoon, "is something we cannot afford to ignore. No matter what it is that the stories say, anyone can be broken by pain. There are mental exercises that will enable one to escape, but they are not proof against the worst that man can devise. All I can advise you if you find yourself in the hopeless situation is that you must lie; lie so often and with such creativity that your captors will not know the truth when they hear it. For the time will come when you will tell them the truth—you will be unable to help yourself. But by then, I hope, you will have muddied the waters past any hope of clarity. . . ."

But Ancar did not want information; he was getting that in plenty from Orthallen. All he wanted was to make her hurt. She was damned if she'd give him satisfaction before she had to.

So the "fascinating things" failed to drive a sound from her, and the Prince was displeased.

He proceeded to more sophisticated tortures, involving complicated apparatus. He handled all of this himself, his long hands caressing the bloodstained straps and cruel metal as he described in loving detail what each was to do to her helpless body.

Talia did her best to keep herself shielded, and to retreat behind those mental barriers to pain and the outside world she had long ago learned to erect, but as he continued his entertainment, her barriers and shielding gradually eroded. She became nauseatingly aware of every emotion he, Hulda, and the nameless magician were experiencing. The intensely sexual pleasure he derived from her pain was worse than rape; and she was in too much agony to block it out. Hulda's pleasure was as perverted, and as hard to bear. In fact, both of them were erotically aroused to a fever-pitch by what they were doing to her, and were a scant step from tearing the clothing from each other's backs and consummating their passion there and then.

Twice she tried to turn her agony back on him, but the magician always shielded him. The magician was deriving nearly as much enjoyment from this as Ancar and his "dear nurse" were, and Talia wished passionately (while she was still thinking coherently enough to wish) to be able to strike out at all of them.

After a time, she was no longer capable of anything but screaming.

When they crushed her feet, she was not even capable of that.

They dragged her back to her cell when her voice was gone, for the Prince did not derive half the pleasure from her torture when she could not respond to his experiments. He stood over her, gloating, as she lay unable to move on the straw where they'd left her.

"So, child, you must rest, and recover, so that we can play my games again," he crooned. "Perhaps I will tire of the game soon; perhaps not. No matter. Think on tomorrow—and think on this. When I tire of you, I shall still find a use for you. First my men will again take their pleasure of you, for they shall not mind that you are no longer as attractive as you once were; some of them would find your appearance as stimulating as *I* do, my dear. Then you shall be *my* messenger. How will your beloved Queen react to receiving her favorite Herald, but a small piece at a time?"

He laughed, and swept out with Hulda at his side, already fondling one of her breasts as the door thudded shut behind him.

It took every last bit of her will, but she remained where she was until it was dark, dark enough that she knew that no one would be able to see what she was doing. She rolled to one side then, pushed aside the straw, and uncovered the place where she'd buried her precious bottle of argonel. It had been the knowledge that she had it that was all that had sustained her this day, and she prayed that they had not searched the cell and found it.

They hadn't.

She kept her mind fastened on each tiny movement, knowing that otherwise she would never be able to continue.

Her fingers were so swollen as to be all but useless, but she had anticipated that. She managed to scrape back the loosely-packed dirt with the sides of her hands, clearing away enough so that she could get her teeth around the neck and pull the bottle out of the hole that way.

The effort nearly caused her to black out and left her

gasping and weeping with pain, unable to stir for long moments. When she could move again, she braced the bottle between wrists rubbed raw and pulled the stopper out with her teeth.

She lay for a long, long moment again, while her mind threatened to retreat into blackness. That would only be a temporary escape, and she needed a permanent one.

She spat the stopper out and rolled onto her side while her body howled in anguish, and poured the entire bottle into her mouth. It burned all the way down her raw throat, and burned in her stomach where it lay like molten lead. It felt as if it were eating a hole through to the outside.

She wept with pain, conscious of nothing but pain, for what seemed to be an eternity. But then numbness began to spread from the fire, pushing the pain before it. It spread faster as it moved outward, and soon she could no longer feel anything, anything at all. Her mind seemed to be floating in warm, dark water.

A few thoughts remained with her for a while. Elspeth; she hoped the child really had forgiven her—she hoped the next Queen's Own would love her as much as Talia did. And Dirk. Perhaps it was the best thing that he should *not* know how much she loved him; he would be spared much anguish that way. Wouldn't he? She was glad of one thing; that he and Kris had made up before they'd left. It was going to hurt him badly enough when he learned of Kris' death as it was.

If only she'd been able to tell them—if only she'd known for certain about Orthallen. *He* still was there, the unsuspected enemy, waiting to try yet again. And Ancar—master of magicians and possessed of an army of killers. If only she could tell them somehow. . . .

While she still had the strength and the will, she tried again to Mindcall, but was foiled by the mage-barrier.

Then her will went numb, and all she could do was drift.

It was odd . . . Bards always claimed that all the answers came when one died, but there were no answers for her. Only questions, unanswered questions, and unfinished business. Why were there no answers? One would think that at least one would know *why* one had to die.

Maybe it didn't matter.

Kris had said it was bright. The tales all said the Havens were bright. But it wasn't bright. It was dark—darkness all around, and never a hint of brightness.

And so lonely! She would have welcomed anything, even a fever-dream.

But perhaps that was just as well, too. In the darkness that damned magician couldn't find her to bring her back. If she fled away far enough, he might get lost in trying to find her. It was worth the effort—and the warm, numbing darkness was very soothing, if the loneliness could be ignored.

Perhaps elsewhere, where the mage couldn't follow, she would find the Havens . . . and there would be light.

She let the darkness pull her farther along, closing behind her, and thoughts began to numb and fall away as well.

As she retreated away down into the darkness, her very last thought was to wonder why there still was no light at all, even at the end of it.

Nine

When the Queen and her entourage set out at last, Dirk was part of her honorguard despite the vehement protests of Healers and fellow Heralds that he was not well enough for such an expedition.

He had responded that he was needed. This was true; the Collegium had suspended classes and all Heralds normally teaching were serving as bodyguards, with the sole exceptions being those too sick or old to travel. He also argued that he was far healthier than he looked (which was not true), and that he would rest just as well at the easy pace of the baggage train as he would fretting in the infirmary (which was marginally true). The Healers threw up their hands in disgust when Selenay agreed to his presence, and pronounced her to be insane and him to be the worst patient they had ever had since Keren.

He knew very well that Teren and Skif had quietly detailed themselves to keep an eye on him, not trusting his protestations of health in the slightest. He didn't care. *Anything* was worth not being left behind—even being hovered over.

But he was right about the leisurely quality of the journey—this was to be an easy trip; the most exciting thing likely to occur would be when they met Talia or Kris at the Border. The bodyguard of Heralds was more because of tradition than suspected danger. After all, Alessandar was a trusted ally and a firm friend of Valdemar, and it was as likely for harm to come to Selenay and Elspeth in her own capital as it was for them to come to harm in Hardorn. Dirk figured he should be as safe with them as in his own bed.

There were other reasons why Dirk wanted to accompany the others, although none that he was willing to disclose to anyone else. His enforced idleness had given him ample time for thought, and he was beginning to wonder if he hadn't made a bad mistake in his assumptions about the relationship between Talia and Kris. While he hadn't precisely left the field clear, Kris hadn't spent much (if any!) time alone with her since they'd returned. Instead, he'd had a brief fling with Nessa, then returned to his old semi-monastic habits. Nor had Talia sought him out. He knew these things to be facts, since he'd been keeping track of their whereabouts rather obsessively. Now that he thought back on it, Kris' frequent paeans of praise for the Queen's Own seemed less like those of a lover lauding his beloved, and more like a horsetrader trying to convince a reluctant buyer! And the one whose company Talia *had* been seeking was the one person who had been trying to avoid her—himself.

Then there was that odd incident with Keren, right after he'd damn near collapsed. She'd bullied her way past the Healers the morning Kris and Talia had left, while he was still fairly light-headed with fever, and had delivered a vehement lecture to him that he couldn't quite remember. It was maddening, because he had the shrewd notion that it was important, and he couldn't quite bring himself to confront Keren again and ask her what her diatribe had been all about. But if what vague memories he *did* have were not totally misleading—and they very well could be—she'd spoken of lifebonds, and more than once. And she'd gone on at some length about what an idiot he was being, and how miserable he was making Talia feel.

Besides all that, he had had some very frightening dreams that he didn't think could all be laid to the fever, and had been entertaining very uneasy feelings about the whole expedition from the moment he had learned that Talia and Kris were gone. If something were to go wrong, he wanted to know about it firsthand. And he wanted to be in a position where he could do something, not just wonder what was happening; although in the kind of shape he was in, he was not too sanguine that he'd be able to do much.

Technically, he was still an invalid, so he was sent to the rear of the company before the baggage animals, to share Skif's bodyguard duty on Elspeth. Skif's Cymry had foaled in early spring, and the youngster was just barely old enough to make this kind of easy trip.

Elspeth was anxious, and Dirk had a notion that he and Skif were the best possible company for the young Heir; the antics of Cymry's offspring and Skif's easy patter kept her spirits up, and Dirk was more than willing to talk about the one subject that overwhelmed her with guilt and dominated her thoughts—Talia.

Selenay had given Talia's note to Elspeth when the Heir had searched for the Queen's Own without success and had finally demanded to know what her mother had done with her. She had recalled her promise of many years' standing with heartfelt remorse almost as soon as Talia had turned her back on her and ridden away. "I'll never get mad at you," she had pledged. "No matter what you say, unless I go away and think about it, and decide what you told me just wasn't true."

And a great deal of what Talia had said that night, though harsh, *was* true. She hadn't thought past her own pleasure and her own wishes. She hadn't once considered her "affair" in the light of the larger view.

Her would-be lover's betrayal had hurt—but not nearly so much as the thought that she'd driven away a friend who truly loved her with that broken promise. Talia's words had been ugly, but not unearned—and Elspeth had returned her own share of harsh and ugly words.

If truth were to be told, though Elspeth was even more ashamed when she thought about it, the name-calling had begun with her. She wanted desperately, now that she'd read the note, to make her own apologies and explanations, and to regain the closeness they'd had before Talia's stint in the field. Her remorse was very real, and she had the urge to talk about it incessantly.

She found a sympathetic ear in Dirk, who never seemed to find her own repetitive litany boring.

She gradually managed to purge some of her guilt just by pouring her unhappiness into his ears, and slowly it became less obsessive.

But it was still very much with her.

"Daydreaming, young milady?"

The smooth, cultivated voice startled Elspeth out of deep thought.

"Not daydreaming," she corrected Lord Orthallen, just a shade stiffly. "Thinking."

He raised an inquisitive eyebrow, but she wasn't about to enlighten him.

He nudged his chestnut palfrey a little closer; Gwena responded to her unspoken twinge of revulsion and moved away.

"I must admit to being caught up in a great deal of thought, myself," he said, as if unwilling to let her escape from him. "Thought—and worry—"

Damn him! she thought. *He is so smooth—he makes me want to trust him so much! If Alberich hadn't said what he did to me—*

:I'd trust Alberich with my life,: Gwena said unexpectedly in her mind. *:I wouldn't trust that snake with my hoof-parings!:*

:Hush, loveling,: she replied the same way, amusement at her Companion's vehemence restoring her good humor. *:He won't catch me again.:*

"Worry about what, my Lord?" she asked ingenuously.

"My nephew," he replied surprising the boots off her with his expression and the tinge of *real* concern in his voice. "I wish that Selenay had consulted me before sending him on this mission. He's so young."

"He's quite experienced."

"But not in diplomacy. And not alone."

:Bright Havens, loveling, I could almost believe he really is anxious!:

:He is.: Gwena sounded just as surprised. *:And somehow—somehow that frightens me. What does he know that we don't?:*

"It's a simple mission to an ally," she said aloud. "What could possibly go wrong?"

"Nothing, of course. It's just an old man's foolish fancies." He laughed, but it sounded forced. "No, never mind. I actually came back here to see if you were pining over one of those young men you've left back at Court."

"Them?" She produced a trill of very artificial gaiety. "Lady bless, my lord, I can't for the life of me wonder what I ever saw in them. I never met a pack of puppies with emptier heads in my life! I'm afraid they bored me so I was only too pleased to escape them—and I think I'd better head to the rear and take my turn making sure poor Dirk doesn't fall out of his saddle. Farewell, my lord!"

:*Oh*, that's *putting a kink in his tail, little sister!*: Gwena applauded as she spun and cantered to the rear. :*Well done indeed!*:

"Dirk?" Elspeth cantered up next to him.

"What imp?" He'd been almost half-asleep; the sun was gentle and warm, Ahrodie's pace was smooth, and the gentle chime of bridle bells and the ringing of hooves on the road had been very soporific.

"Do you think it'll be Talia that meets us on the Border?" Elspeth's tone was wistful, her face full of undisguised hope. Dirk hated to disappoint her, but he didn't have much choice.

He sighed. "Not likely, I'm afraid. Fact is, as Queen's Own she's really your mother's first representative, so chances are she'll still be with Alessandar."

"Oh." She looked rather crestfallen, but apparently was feeling like continuing the conversation. "Are you feeling all right? You've been coughing a lot."

She looked sideways at him with a certain amount of concern in her glance.

"Don't tell me *you're* going to nursemaid me," Dirk replied with some exasperation. "It's bad enough with those two playing mother-hen." He nodded back in the direction where Skif and Teren were riding, just out of earshot.

The bright noontide sun, so welcome after all those

weeks of cold rain, made their white uniforms difficult to look at without squinting, Teren positively glistened.

And how in blazes, Dirk found himself wondering, _does he manage to look so immaculate with all the dust we're kicking up?_

Elspeth giggled. "Sorry. It does get to be a bit muchish, doesn't it? Now you know how I feel! It was all right back at the Collegium, but I can't even slip off into the woods to—you know—without two Heralds pounding up to bodyguard me!"

"Don't blame anybody but your mother, imp. You're the only offspring. She should have whelped a litter, then you wouldn't have these problems."

Elspeth giggled even harder. "I wish some of the court-iers could hear you, talking about her like she was a prize bitch!"

"They'd probably call me out for insulting her. She, on the other hand, might very well agree with me. What are you doing for classes since you're not warming a desk?"

Much to his own surprise, Dirk realized he was inter-ested in hearing Elspeth's answer. Some of the lethargy of his illness was ebbing, replaced by a little of his old energy, and he was beginning to realize that a good deal of his mental distress had vanished as well. Whether this was as a result of mending his quarrel with Kris or something else he had no idea, but it was a welcome change.

"Alberich told Skif to teach me knife-throwing. I'm getting pretty good at it, if I can be forgiven a boast. Watch—"

Her hand flicked out sideways and forward, and a small knife appeared almost magically, quivering in the bole of a tree ahead of them. Dirk hadn't even seen it leave her hand.

"Not bad—not bad at all."

Elspeth cantered up to retrieve it, cleaning the blade of sap on her sleeve, then rejoined Dirk. "He gave me a wrist sheath with a trick release—see?" She pushed up her sleeve to display it proudly. "Just like Talia's."

"So that's where she got them! Figures it'd be him. If there's a way to hide anything, that boy knows it." Dirk grinned, and realized with surprise that it had been a long while since he'd smiled. "Not that I've got any objections, mind you. I'm just as glad you've got a hidden sting, imp."

"Whyfor? Mother wasn't all that happy about my learning 'assassin's tricks,' as she so tactfully put it. It was only my saying that Alberich ordered it that made it right with her."

"Call me a little more pragmatic, but if you know the assassin's tricks, you're one up on the assassin—and there's only one of you, imp. We can't afford to lose you."

"Funny, that's just what Skif said. I guess I'm out of the habit of thinking of myself as important." She grinned, and Dirk thought fleetingly that a charming young woman had been born out of the haughty Brat Talia had taken in charge. No small miracle had been wrought there.

"I hope you're also learning that in a dangerous situation you react with reflexes, not with your head."

She made a face. "Am I not! It hasn't been so long ago that Alberich, Skif and Jeri were ambushing me every time I wasn't looking, solo or in groups! Anyway, other than that, I'm just supposed to be talking with Heralds. I guess they figure I'll pick things up by contamination, or something."

"That's a fine way to talk about your elders! Although I hate to admit it—but with Skif, 'contamination' is pretty accurate."

"Do I hear my name being taken in vain?"

Skif nudged Cymry up to ride beside them.

"Most assuredly, my fine, feathered felon. I was just warning our innocent young Heir about associating with you."

"Me?" Skif went round-eyed with innocence. "I am as pure—"

"As what they shovel out of the stables."

"Hey, I don't have to sit here and be insulted!"

"That's right," Elspeth giggled. "You could ride off and let us insult you behind your back like we were doing already."

As if to echo her, a bold scarlet jay called down filthy names on him just as he rode beneath it. It hopped along the branch that overhung the road and continued catcalling after he'd passed.

"I do believe I am outnumbered—you're even getting the wildlife on your side! It's time, as Master Alberich would say, for a strategic retreat."

He reined Cymry in and dropped back to resume his place beside Teren, making a face at Elspeth when he saw she was sticking her tongue out at him. Dirk was hard put to keep a straight face.

But a moment later Elspeth's mood abruptly shifted. "Dirk? Can I ask you something?"

"That's what I'm here for, imp. Part of it, anyway."

"What's evil?"

Dirk nearly lost his teeth. Philosophy was *not* what he was expecting out of Elspeth. "Ouch! Don't believe in asking the easy ones, do you?"

He sat silent for a long moment, aware after a sidelong glance at her that he had won Elspeth's heart forever by taking her question seriously. "Have you ever asked Gwena that one?" he said at last. "She's probably a better authority than I am."

"I did—and all she did was look at me like I'd grown horns and say, 'It just *is!*' "

He laughed, for the answer sounded very like the kind of response Ahrodie used to give him. "They do seem to have some peculiar blind spots, don't they? All right, I'll give it a try. This isn't the best answer by a long road, but I think it might be somewhere in the right direction. It seems to me that evil is a kind of ultimate greed, a greed that is so all-encompassing that it can't ever see anything lovely, rare, or precious without wanting to possess it. A greed so total that if it can't possess these things, it will destroy them rather than chance that someone else might have them. And a greed so intense that even having these things never causes it to lessen one iota—the lovely, the rare and the precious never affect it except to make it want them."

"So—'good' would be a kind of opposite? Unselfishness?"

He frowned a little, groping for the proper words. "Oh, partially. Evil can't create, it can only copy, mar, or destroy, because it's so taken up with itself. So 'good' would also be a kind of self*less*ness. And you know what a lot of sects preach—that ultimate good—Godhead—can only be reached by totally forgetting the self. What brought this on?"

"When Skif mentioned Master Alberich—he—I—" she hesitated, looking shamefaced, but Dirk did his best to look kind and understanding, and his expression evidently encouraged her to continue. "You know about what happened—with Talia and me. I was still angry with her the next day, even though I was almost as angry with myself; well, that showed up in practice. Master Alberich made me stop, and took me out to the Field for a walk to cool off. You know, I never thought he was—I don't know, understanding, I guess. Nice. He seems so hard, most of the time."

"Perhaps that's to mask the softness underneath," Dirk replied quietly. He knew Alberich better than almost any other Herald, except for Elcarth and Jeri; and despite all the time he spent in the field, he had come as close as anyone was ever likely to get to the Armsmaster. "Being easy with any of us might be a quick way to get us killed in the field. So he's hard, hopefully harder than anything we'll have to face. That doesn't make him less a human, or less a Herald. Think about it a minute. He's the *one* teacher in the Collegium whose lessoning will make a difference whether we live or die. If he eliminates one little thing—no matter for what reason—it might be the cause of one of his pupils finding an early grave. You can't say that about any other instructor in the Collegium. You might notice the next time the Death Bell rings that you won't see him anywhere around. I don't know where he goes, but I saw him leaving, once. He looked like he was in mortal agony. I think he feels more than most of us would credit him with."

"I guess I know that now. Anyway, he started talking, and you know how it is with him, when he talks, you automatically listen. Somehow I ended up telling him about everything—about how, since Talia seemed so busy, I started talking to Lord-Un—I mean, Lord Orthallen. And how that was why I—started being with—some people. The wild crowd, I guess. That boy. Lord Orthallen introduced us; he told me he thought I ought to be spending more time with the other people of the Court. It all made sense when *he* was saying it, and the boys he introduced me to seemed so . . . attentive. Flattering. I . . . like the attention; I told Alberich that. That's when he said something really odd, Alberich, I mean. He said, "I tell you this in strictest confidence, Herald to Herald, for I think I would have to guard my back at all times should he come to learn of it. Lord Orthallen is one of the only three truly evil persons I have ever encountered. He does nothing without a purpose, my lady, and you would be wise never to forget this.'"

She glanced at Dirk; he had the feeling she wanted to see the effect of her words.

He made no effort to hide that he was quite sobered by them. The first time she had spoken Lord Orthallen's name, it had felt as if a cloud had passed between himself and the gentle warmth of the sun. And her account of Alberich's words had come as something of a revelation.

"I'm not sure what to say," he replied finally. "Alberich is hardly inclined to make hasty judgments though; I'm sure you realize that. But at the same time, I am hardly one of Orthallen's supporters. I'll just say this; Kris and I quarreled largely because Orthallen insisted he be there when I was accused, and because Orthallen did his best to force him to make a choice between himself and me. I can't think why he would want to do that—except for what I already have said about evil; that it can't see a precious thing without wanting to own or destroy it. And our friendship, Kris' and mine, is one of the most precious things in my life."

Elspeth rode silently by his side for a good many miles after that, her face very quiet and thoughtful

This was only the first of many such conversations they were to have. They discovered that they were very much alike, sharing a bent toward the mystical that might have surprised those who didn't know them well.

* * *

"Well?" Elspeth asked aggressively, "Why *don't* they interfere? If I'm making an ass of myself, why won't Gwena *say* anything?"

Dirk sighed. "Imp, I don't know. Have you ever asked her?"

Elspeth snorted, sounding rather like her own Companion when impatient. "Of course—after I'd made a total fool of myself I asked her right off why she didn't just forbid me to have anything to do with that puppy."

"And what did she tell you?"

"That I knew very well Companions didn't do things that way."

"And they don't . . . until we, their Chosen, come to them." Dirk harbored no small amount of chagrin for not having asked Ahrodie's advice when he'd quarreled with Kris.

"But *why?* It isn't *fair!*" At Elspeth's age, Dirk knew from his *own* experience, "fair" achieved monumental importance.

"Isn't it? Would it be fair to us, in the long run, if they stepped in like nursemaids and prevented us from falling on our noses every time we tried to learn to walk?"

:Good answer, Chosen,: Ahrodie told him, *:Even if a bit simplistic.:*

:Unless you've got a better one—:

:Oh, no!: she said hastily. *:You go right on as you were!:*

"You mean, we have to learn from experience by ourselves?" Elspeth asked, as Dirk fought down a grin at Ahrodie's hurried reply.

Elspeth brooded over that while Gwena and Ahrodie amused themselves by matching paces with such absolute precision that they sounded like one Companion rather than two.

"Don't they *ever* interfere?" she asked, finally.

"Not in living memory. In some of the old chronicles, though . . ."

"Well?" she prompted, when his silence had gone on too long.

"*Some* Companions, very rarely, have intervened. But only when the situation was hopeless, and only when there was no other way out of it except by their aid. They were always Grove-born, though, and the only one of those we have now is Rolan. And they have *never* done so except by freely volunteering, which is why Heralds never ask them to."

"Why only then? Why shouldn't we ask?"

"Imp—" He was doing his best to try and express what until now he had only sensed. "What's the one governing law of this Kingdom?"

She looked at him askance. "Are you changing the subject?"

"No. No, I'm not, trust me."

"There *is* no 'one true way.' "

"Take it a step further. Why are the clergy *forbidden* by law to pray for Valdemar's victory in war?"

"I . . . don't know."

"Think about it. Go away, if you like, and come back when you're ready."

She chose not to leave his side, and simply rode next to him with her expression blank and her attention turned so inward that she never noticed Skif coming up from behind them.

Skif pulled up on Dirk's other side, and gave the young Heir a long and curious look.

"Isn't this a bit deep for her?" he asked, finally. "I mean, I've been trying to follow this, and I'm lost."

"I don't think so," Dirk replied slowly. "I really don't. If she weren't ready, she wouldn't be asking."

"Lord and Lady," Skif exclaimed, shaking his head in honest bewilderment, "I give up. You *are* two of a kind."

At length the party reached the Border; Selenay ordered that they make camp there on the Valdemar side since the outpost was far too small to accommodate all of them. The last of the baggage train actually reached it very near dark, and so the Queen was hardly surprised that neither of the two envoys was waiting for them when they arrived. But when the next day passed, she felt a building uneasiness. When two more went by without any sign whatsoever, the uneasiness became alarm.

"Kyril—" Selenay did not remove her gaze from the road as she spoke to the Seneschal's Herald. "—I have the feeling something has gone terribly, terribly wrong. Am I being alarmist?"

"No, Majesty." Kyril's usually controlled voice held an unmistakable tenor of strain.

Selenay looked at him sharply. Kyril's brow was lined with worry. "I've tried Farspeech; I can't reach them— and Kris, at least, has enough of that Gift to be able to receive what I send. He's done so in the past. I don't know what's gone awry, but Majesty, I—I am afraid for them."

She did not hesitate. "Order the camp moved back from the Border, and now. There's a good place about half a mile back down the road; it's a flattish hill, barren except for grass. Should there be need, it won't be hard to defend."

Kyril nodded. He did not seem surprised by her paranoia.

"When you've gotten the rest on the move," she continued, "order the local reserves of the Guard to meet us there. I'm going to have the Border Guards stand alert and keep a watch down the Hardorn side of the trade road."

Her Companion, Caryo, came trotting up at her mental summons, and she pulled herself up on the Companion's bare back, without bothering to call for saddle or bridle. As she rode away, Kyril was going in search of the Herald in charge of the camp to begin seeing to the first of her orders.

The new camp was uncomfortable, but as Selenay had planned, was far more easily defensible than the old. When the Guardsmen arrived, Selenay ordered them to bivouac between their camp and the Border. She had sentries posted as well—and ominously, she noticed that the Companions began taking up stations about the perimeter, providing their own kind of sentry-duty.

Elspeth attached herself to Dirk and seldom left his side. Neither of them voiced their fears until late in the fifth day, a day spent in an atmosphere of tension and anxiety.

"Dirk," Elspeth finally said, after Dirk watched her try to read the same page in her book ten times, and apparently never once see a word of it, "do you suppose something's happened to them?"

Dirk hadn't even been making a pretense of doing anything but watching the road. "Something must have," he answered flatly, "If it had been simple delay, they would have gotten word to us. It's not like Kris—"

He broke off at the sight of her frightened eyes.

"Look imp, I'm sure they'll be all right. Kris and I have gotten out of a lot of tight situations before this, and Talia's no faint-hearted Court flower. I'm sure they're making their way back to us right now."

"I hope you're right . . ." Elspeth said faintly, but she didn't sound to Dirk as if she really believed his words.

For that matter, he wasn't sure he believed them either.

The sixth day dawned, with Selenay—in fact, all of them—waiting for the axe to fall.

Late in the afternoon, when one of the lookouts—a Herald with Farsight as well as Mindspeech—reported that a Companion was approaching at speed, the entire encampment was roused within moments, and lined the roadside. Selenay was one of the first; eyes straining to catch the first glimpse.

She, Kyril, and several others of her immediate entourage stood in a tense knot at the edge of the encampment. She noticed vaguely that Dirk, Teren, Skif, Elspeth, and Jeri had formed their own little huddle just within earshot. None of them moved or spoke. The sun beat down on them all without pity, but no one made a move to look for shade.

As Dirk waited with mouth going dry with unspoken fear, a second lookout sprinted up and whispered in the Queen's ear. Selenay grew pale as ice; Elspeth clutched Dirk's arm and the rest stirred uneasily.

Then a dust-cloud and hoofbeats signaled the arrival of

the Companion, and hard on the sound itself Rolan pounded into their midst.

Rolan—alone. Without saddle or bridle; gaunt, covered with dust and sweat, and completely exhausted, a state few had ever seen a Companion in before.

He staggered the last few feet up the hill to the Queen, tearing a bundle from his neck with his teeth and dropping it at her feet. Then he sagged with exhaustion, standing motionless except for his heaving flanks and his quivering muscles, head nearly touching the ground, eyes closed, suffering written in every line of him.

Keren was the first to break from her shock. She ran to him, throwing her cloak over him for lack of any other blanket and began to lead him to a place where he could be tended properly, step by trembling step.

Selenay picked up the filthy, stained package with hands that shook so hard she nearly dropped it, and undid the knots holding it together.

Into the grass at her feet fell two arrows; one headless, one broken.

A ripple of shocked dismay passed over the crowd. The Queen felt as frozen as a snow-statue.

As Kyril bent to pick them up, Elspeth whimpered once beside her, and swayed with shock. Jeri caught and supported her just as Dirk's agonized cry of negation broke the silence.

Selenay started, and turned to see Dirk struggling to break away from Skif and Teren.

"Damn you, let me *go!*" he cried in agony, as Skif held him away from Ahrodie. "I've got to go to her—I've got to help her!"

"Dirk, man, you don't even know if—" Teren choked out the words "—if she's still alive."

"She's *got* to be. I'd know if she weren't. She's *got* to be!" He fought them still, as Kyril's low tones carried to where they stood.

"The headless arrow is Herald Kris," he said, his expressionless face belying the anguish in his voice. "The broken is Herald Talia."

"You see? I was right! Let me *go!*"

Skif caught his chin in one hand and forced his head around so that Dirk was forced to look him in the eyes, with a strength that matched Dirk's own, even augmented by the latter's frenzy. There were tears flowing freely down his cheeks as he half sobbed his words. "*Think*, man! That's the broken arrow she sent. She was as good as dead when she sent it, and dammit, she knew it. There's no hope of saving her, but she gave us the warning to save ourselves. Do you want to kill yourself, too, and make us mourn three of you?"

His words penetrated Dirk's madness, and the wild look left his eyes, replaced by anguish and torture.

"Oh, *gods!*" The fight left him, and he sagged to his knees, buried his face in his hands, and began weeping hoarsely.

At this moment Selenay wished with all her aching heart that she could do the same. But this message could have only one meaning; a friend to her and her people had suddenly turned his coat, and her land was in danger. Her Kingdom and the lives of her folk were at stake and she had her duty just as surely as any other Herald. There was no leisure time to spend on personal feelings. Later, when all was safe, she would mourn. Now she *must* act.

She emptied herself of emotion, knowing she'd pay for this self-denial later. There was the Guard to be alerted, the Lord Marshal to be brought; her mind filled with plans, making it easier to ignore (for the moment) the sorrow she longed to give vent to.

She gave orders crisply, sending one Herald after another flying for his Companion, carrying messages to warn, to summon, to prepare. She turned on her heel with Kyril at her side and strode hastily to her tent. Those with experience in armed conflict followed; as did those who might still be needed to bear messages. Those who were not of either group headed for the baggage train to break out the weaponry, or down the hill to organize the tiny force of the Guard to protect the Queen.

*   *   *

Left in their wake were Skif, Teren, and Dirk.

Skif reached out his hand to his friend, then pulled it back. Dirk was curled in on himself, still kneeling in the dust of the road. Only the shaking of his shoulders showed that he still wept.

Skif and Teren stood awkwardly at his side for long moments, both unsure of what, if anything, they could do for him. Finally Teren said in an undertone, "He won't try anything stupid now. Why don't we give him a little privacy? Ahrodie's the only one likely to be able to comfort him at all."

Skif nodded, biting his lip to keep from sobbing himself; and they withdrew after the others, as Ahrodie moved up beside Dirk and stood with her head bowed next to his, almost, but not quite, touching his shoulder.

Lost in his own travail, Dirk heard nothing of another approaching, until a hand lightly touched his shoulder.

He raised his head slowly, peering through blurred, burning eyes, to see that the one touching him was Elspeth. Grief matching his stared out of her eyes, and her features were as tear-streaked as his own. It was growing dark; the last rays of sunset streaked the sky like bloodstains and stars were showing overhead. He realized dimly that he must have been crouching there for hours. And as he stared at her, he began to have the beginnings of an idea.

"Elspeth," he croaked. "Do you know some place no one is likely to be right now? Some place quiet?"

"My tent, and the area around it," she said. He thought he had surprised her out of her own tears by the question. "I'm at the back of the camp, not close to mother's tent. Everybody is with her right now."

"Can I use it?"

"Of course—why? Have you—can you—oh, Dirk, have you thought of something? You have—you have!"

"I think . . . maybe . . . I might be able to 'Fetch' her. But I need a place where my concentration won't be broken."

Elspeth looked hopeful—and dubious. "It's an awfully long way."

"I know. That doesn't matter. It isn't the distance that

worries me, it's the weight. I've never Fetched anything that big before; gods, nothing alive even close to that size." His face and heart twisted with pain. "But I've got to try—something, anything!"

"But Kris—" her voice broke. "Kris isn't here to See for you—no, wait—" she said, kneeling next to him as his hope crumpled. "I can See. I'm not trained, but I've got the Gift. It came on me early—it's been getting a lot stronger since I was Chosen and I know I've got more range than anybody else I've talked to. Will I do?"

"Yes! Oh, gods, yes!" He hugged her shoulders and they rose together and stumbled through the dusk to her tent.

Elspeth slipped inside the tent and tossed two cushions out for them to sit on. Dirk set his hands lightly on her wrists and calmed his own thoughts as best he could. He tried to pretend to himself that this was just another student he was training in her Gift, and began coaxing her into a light trance. The last of the light faded, and the stars grew brighter overhead, while they sat oblivious to their surroundings. She was silent for a very long time, and Dirk began to fear that her untrained Gift would be useless against all that distance, despite the power of the emotions fueling it.

Then, abruptly, Elspeth whimpered in fear and pain and her own hands closed convulsively on his wrists. "I've found her—oh, gods! Dirk, they've done such horrible things to her! I—think I'm going to be sick—"

"Hold on, imp. Don't break on me yet! I need you—*she* needs you!"

Elspeth gulped audibly, and held. He followed her mind to where it had reached, found his target, took hold, and pulled with all his strength.

He could not tell how long he strove against the weight of it—but suddenly pain rose in a wave to engulf him, and he blacked out.

He found himself slumped over, with Elspeth shaking him as hard as she could.

"All of a sudden—you stopped breathing," she said fearfully. "I thought you were dead! Oh, gods, Dirk—it—it's no good, is it?"

He shook his head numbly. "I tried, Goddess save me, I *tried*. I found her all right, but I can't pull her here. I just don't have the strength."

He felt hot tears splash on his hand from Elspeth's eyes, and decided they would make a second attempt. He knew with conviction that he'd rather die in trying to bring Talia back than live with the knowledge that he wasn't brave enough to make the second trial.

But before he could say anything, the matter was taken out of his hands.

:*Man*,: said a voice in his mind. :*Dirk—Herald*.:

The voice was not Ahrodie's; it was masculine. He looked up to find three Companions standing beside them; Ahrodie, Elspeth's Gwena, and leading them, Rolan. They had moved up on them without so much as a twig stirring. Behind them, at the edge of the enclosure that held Elspeth's tent, were gathered more Companions— every Companion in the encampment, down to Cymry's foal.

Rolan looked ghostlike, gaunt, and seemed to glow, and the back of Dirk's neck prickled at the sight of him. He looked like something out of legend, not a creature of the solid, everyday world.

:*You have the Gift and the will to use it. She has the Sight. We have the strength you need.*:

"I—but—are you saying—"

:*That we may yet save her, if our love and courage are enough. But—be prepared—if we succeed, it will not be without high cost to you. There will be great pain. You may die of it.*:

Wordlessly, Dirk looked at Elspeth, and knew by her nod that Rolan had spoken to her as well.

Dirk looked into Rolan's glowing eyes—and they *were* glowing, a sapphirine light brighter than the starshine. "Whatever the cost is, we'll pay it," he said, knowing he spoke for both of them.

They stood up and made room for the three Companions between them. They stood in a circle; Rolan, Elspeth, Gwena, Ahrodie, and Dirk. Elspeth and Dirk clasped hands and rested their arms over the backs of the Companions, obtaining the needed physical contact among the five of them in that way.

It was much easier for Elspeth to find her target the second time.

"I have her," she said softly when she'd touched Talia again, then sobbed, "Dirk—I think she's dying!"

Once more Dirk sent his own mind along the path Elspeth had laid for him, took hold, and pulled.

Then a second strength was added to his, and it built, and grew. Then another joined the second, and another. For one awful, pain-wracked moment—or was it an eternity?—Dirk felt like the object of a tug-of-war game, being pulled apart between two forces far greater than his own. Only his own stubbornness kept him to the task, as he felt his mind being torn in two. He held; then felt himself being stretched thinner and thinner, tighter, and tighter, quivering like a harpstring about to snap. All his strength seemed to flow out of him; he felt consciousness fading again, fought back, and held on with nothing left to him but his own stubborn will. Then, one of the two forces broke—and not theirs. And together they pulled their target toward them, cushioning and protecting it against further damage.

Their combined strength was enough. Barely, but enough.

The conference of war was proceeding in Selenay's tent, with Council members, Officers of the Army and Guard, and Heralds perched wherever there was room. Kyril was pointing out weak spots in their own defenses— places that appeared to be candidates to be attacked—on the map laid over her table. Then a cry of horror from someone standing just outside the tent flap made everyone look up with startlement.

Someone shoved tent flap and those standing inside it abruptly out of the way, and Elspeth stumbled inside, face paper-white and drained, pushing others from her path. Following her was Dirk, who looked even worse. When those inside saw what he bore in his arms, the cry of horror was echoed inside the tent as well—for it was a mangled, bloody wreck of a human body and it had Talia's face.

No one moved—no one but Dirk and the Heir. Elspeth emptied Selenay's bed of the five Heralds perched on the edge of it, pushing them out of the way without a word. Dirk went straight to the bed and set Talia down gently on it. Without even looking around he reached out a blood-smeared hand and seized the most senior Healer present by the arm, pulling her to Talia's side. Then he straightened up with exaggerated care, moved two or three steps out of the way, and passed out, dropping to the ground like a felled tree.

When the furor was over and Selenay had a chance to look around, she discovered that Elspeth had done the same—but less dramatically and more quietly, in the corner.

Elspeth's recovery was rapid—which, as she remarked somewhat astringently, was fortunate for the sanity of those who could not imagine how the impossible rescue had been accomplished.

She was the center of attention for all those who were not involved with the attempt to save Talia. Kyril was her particular demon, insisting on being told every detail so many times she thought she could recite the tale in her sleep, and coming up with countless questions. Eventually Elspeth's patience reached a breaking point, and she told him, in a quiet, but deadly voice, that if he wanted to know any more he should ask his own Companion about it—*she* was going to see what she could do about helping the Healers with Talia and Dirk.

Healer Thesa was worried; Dirk's recovery was not as rapid. He was still unconscious the next day, and it was some time before she and the other Healers diagnosed the problem as a relapse of his pneumonia coupled with incredible psychic strain. She had charge of his case; her old friend Devan had charge of Talia's, though they shared every germ of expertise they had on both cases. Dirk had inadvertently brought the bottle Talia had drunk the argonel out of with her; and the traces of it within the bottle told Devan what it was they had to fight besides her terrible injuries. Within a day or two he and Thesa decided between them that they had done all they possibly could for both of the patients under the primitive conditions of the encampment. They decided that while it was dangerous to move them, it was far more dangerous to leave them there. There might be warfare waged there at any moment, and they both badly needed the expert touch of the teachers at the Healer's Collegium.

Yet there was no time to spare—and assuredly no Heralds to spare—to move them back to the capital. Instead, after a hasty conference, Thesa and her colleague decided to take the patients a few miles up the road, and install them in the stone-walled home of the Lord Holder, who gladly gave up his dwelling to the Queen—and was equally glad to move himself and his family well out of the way of possible combat.

The Queen had called for all the Healers of the Collegium that could be spared. The Lord Holder's residence was more than half fortress; it was readily defensible at need. The Healers were installed there as soon as they arrived with Thesa organizing them as soon as Dirk began showing signs of improvement. Thesa knew with grim certainty that although they had only Talia and Dirk to treat now, if there should be war, they would have other patients, and soon.

Elspeth spent most of her time there; her mother had asked her—*asked* her, and not ordered her, a sign that Selenay trusted her good sense and was tacitly acknowledging that she was becoming adult—to stay with the Healers and some other of the officials of the Court who began arriving as she called them.

"But—" Elspeth began to protest, until the haunted expression in her mother's eyes stopped her. "Never mind. What do you want me to do?"

"I'm giving you powers of regency," Selenay replied. "The rest of the Kingdom isn't going to cease to exist while we wait here. You've sat through enough Council meetings, catling; you have a good idea what to do. You handle the day-to-day needs of the Kingdom unless you *have* to have a decision from me. And one other thing—if the worst happens, you and the Council and whatever Heralds are left escape together into the west and north; Sorrows should hold you safe."

"But what about you?" she asked, around a lump in her throat.

"Elspeth—if it goes that badly—you'll be their new Queen."

That was an eventuality Elspeth preferred not to contemplate. She had enough worries as it was. Talia looked far more dead than alive, and the Healers were obviously baffled and frightened by something about her condition, though they would not reveal to Elspeth what it was.

It was stalemate at the Border, and stalemate in the sickroom, and in neither case could Elspeth do anything about the matter. It was not a position she enjoyed—and she began to realize just how often it was a position the Queen was in. All she could do was pray.

So she did, with a fervor that matched that of her ancestor, King Valdemar—and she hoped that fervor would make her prayers heard.

Ten

Dirk came to himself shortly after being put in the Healers' hands, but he was confused and disoriented, as well as fevered. And the reaction-backlash he was suffering had him near-blind with a headache no amount of herb tea could remedy. They had to darken his room almost completely until the pain ebbed. In living memory—or so Healer Thesa told him multitudinous times—no Healer had ever seen anyone suffering from a case of backlash as profound as his—not and still be alive to tell about it.

Once again he found himself alone in a small room—but this time it was not in the House of Healing. For several days it was all he could do to feed himself and respond to the orders the Healers gave him. This time he was far too weak to even protest at the regime the Healers directed for him—unlike his previous encounter with them. For a while he remained pliant and well-behaved—but as he recovered, he began to grow suspicious and worried when his questions about Talia remained unanswered or were evaded.

The more they evaded the subject, the more frustrated and angry he became. He even queried Gwena, as soon as his reaction-headache wore off. Gwena couldn't help; she tried to tell him what was wrong with Talia, but her answers were frightening and confusing. She couldn't seem to convey more than that there *was* something seriously ailing the Queen's Own. Finally he decided to take matters into his own hands.

* * *

Little Robin had been brought by Lord Orthallen—although he had the feeling that his lord did not realize it. The boy was a part of his household, though Orthallen seemed to have long since forgotten the fact; and when the order came to pack up the household and move to the Border, Robin found himself in the tail of the baggage train, with no small bewilderment. He'd been at a loss in the encampment, wandering about until someone had seen him and realized that a small child had no place in a camp preparing for warfare. So he was sent packing; first off with Elspeth, then pressed into service by the Healers. They'd set him to fetching and carrying for Dirk, thinking that the child was far too young to be able to pick anything up from the casual talk around him, and that Dirk wouldn't think to interrogate a child as young as he.

They were wrong on both counts.

Robin was very much aware of what was going on—not surprising, since it concerned his adored Talia. He was worried sick, and longing for an adult to talk to. And Dirk was kind and gentle with him—and had he but known it, desperate enough for news to have questioned the rats in the walls if he thought it would get him anywhere.

Dirk knew all about Robin and his adoration of Talia. If anyone knew where she was being kept and what her condition was, that boy would.

Dirk bided his time. Eventually the Healers stopped overseeing his every waking moment. Finally there came a point when they began leaving him alone for hours at a time. He waited then, until Robin was sent in alone with his lunch—alone, unsupervised, and more than willing to talk—and put the question to him.

"Robin," Dirk had no intention of frightening the boy, and his tone was gentle, "I need your help. The Healers won't answer my questions, and I need to know about Talia."

Robin had turned back with his hand still on the doorknob; at the mention of Talia's name, his expression was one of distress.

"I'll tell you what I know, sir," he replied, his voice quavering a little. "But she's hurt real bad and they won't let anybody but Healers see her."

"Where is she? Do you have any idea who's taking care of her?"

The boy not only knew *where* she was, but the names and seniority of every Healer caring for her—and the list nearly froze Dirk's heart. They'd even pulled old Farnherdt out of retirement—and he'd sworn that no case would ever be desperate enough for them to call on him.

"Robin, I've got to get out of here—and I need you to help me, all right?" he said urgently.

Robin nodded, his eyes widening.

"Check the hall for me—see if there's anybody out there."

Robin opened the door and stuck his head out. "Nobody," he reported.

"Good. I'm going to get dressed and sneak out. You stand just outside, and if anybody comes this way, knock on the door."

Robin slipped out to play guard, while Dirk pulled on his clothing. He waited just a few moments more, then left his room, giving Robin a conspiratorial wink on the way out, determined to discover the truth.

The Healer in charge was Devan. Though not the most senior, he was the one with the most expertise and the strongest Gift for dealing with wounds and trauma. He was also one of Talia's first and best friends among the Healers, and had worked with her on many other cases where Heralds were involved. There were times when loving care was more important than seniority—and Devan would have been one of Dirk's first choices to care for her, had he been consulted.

Dirk had a fairly good idea of where to find him at this hour—and most castle-keeps were of the same design; Devan would be in the still-room, just off the herb garden near the kitchen—snatching lunch with one hand while he worked with the other. Dirk used all his expertise at shadow-stalking to avoid being caught while making his way to the little first-floor workroom, redolent with the odors—pleasant, and not so pleasant—of countless medicines.

He heard someone moving about behind the closed door, and slipped inside quickly and quietly, shutting it behind him and putting his back up against it. Devan, his back to the door, didn't seem to notice his presence.

"Devan, I want some answers."

"I've been expecting you," the Healer said calmly, without taking his attention from the task in front of him. "I thought you might not be satisfied with what you were being told about Talia. I said so, but I wasn't in charge of your case, and Thesa felt you shouldn't be worried."

"Then—how is she?" Dirk demanded and at the sight of the Healer's gloomy face, asked fearfully, "Is she—?"

"No, Herald," Devan replied with a sigh, stoppering the bottle he'd been decanting liquid into and turning to face him. "She's not dying; not yet, anyway. But she isn't alive, either."

"What's that supposed to mean?" Dirk asked, becoming angry. "What do you mean, 'she's not alive'?"

"Come with me, and you'll see for yourself."

The Healer led the way to a small room in the infirmary, one of several that were interconnected, such as were used for patients that needed to be isolated. There was little there besides a bedside table with a candle and the bed in which Talia lay without moving.

Dirk felt his throat constrict; she looked as if she'd been laid out for a funeral.

Her face was pale and waxen. By watching very closely, Dirk could see that she was breathing—but just barely.

"What's wrong with her?" His voice cracked with strain.

Devan shrugged helplessly—feeling a lot less helpless than he looked, now that Dirk had finally approached him. "I wish we knew. We think we counteracted the argonel in time—well, the pain she was in neutralized a great deal of it, and if we hadn't taken care of the rest she *would* be dead; argonel doesn't allow for mistakes. We've restored some of the blood loss, we're doing painblockages on most of the major injuries—we've done everything we can to restore her, but she simply doesn't wake. No, it's more than that—it's as if 'she' wasn't there anymore, as if we were dealing with an unensouled body. The body works, the reflexes are all there, it breathes, the heart beats—but there's no one 'home.' And we don't have the slightest notion why. One of the older Healers speculates that her soul has 'gone somewhere,' perhaps trying to escape some kind of mental coercion. I suppose that's possible; tradition claims many mages have had Gifts like ours, and used them for evil purposes. It may be she encountered one of them, along with her other trials. It's possible that now she fears returning to herself, not knowing she is in the hands of friends again. We were willing to try almost anything—"

"So?"

"So we asked Herald Kyril to help. He was here for a solid day, holding her hand and Mindcalling her. He pushed himself to his limits, pushed himself until he had a reaction that sent him into a state of collapse. It did no good at all. Frankly, I don't know what else we could try—" he glanced sideways at Dirk. Devan had something in mind, but from what he understood about this young man, Dirk would have to be lured into it very carefully. "—unless—"

"Unless what?" Dirk snatched at the offered scrap.

"As you know, her Gift was Empathic. She did not Mindhear or Mindcall very well. It may be that Kyril simply wasn't able to reach her. I suppose if someone who had a strong emotional bond with her were to try calling her, using that bond, she might hear. We tried communicating with her Companion, but he apparently had no better luck than Kyril, and possibly for the same reasons. Herald Kris had a strong emotional tie with her, but . . ."

"Yes."

"And no one can think of anyone else."

Dirk gulped and closed his eyes, then whispered, "Could . . . I try?"

Devan almost smiled despite the grimness of the situation. *Come on, little fishy,* he thought, trying to imbue his will with all the coercive force of a Farspeaking Her-

ald. *Take the nice bait. I know all about your lifebond.
Keren told me about the night you fell ill—and about your
performance over the death arrows and how you rescued
her. But if you don't admit that lifebond exists you might
as well be calling into the hurricane for all she'll hear you.*

He pretended to be dubious. "I just don't know, Herald. It would have to be a very strong emotional bond."

The answer he was praying for came as a nearly inaudible whisper. "I love her. Is that enough?"

Devan almost cheered. Now that Dirk had admitted
the existence of the lifebond, the idea stood a chance of
working. "Then by all means, do your best. I'll be just
outside if you need me."

Dirk sat heavily in the chair next to the bed, and took
one bandaged, unresisting, flaccid hand in his own. He
felt so helpless, so alone . . . how in the names of all the
gods could you call through emotions? And . . . it would
mean letting down barriers to his heart he'd erected
years ago and meant to be permanent.

But they couldn't have been permanent, not if she'd
already made him admit that he loved her. It was too late
now for anything but complete commitment—and besides, he'd been willing to die to save her, hadn't he?
Was the lowering of those barriers any greater a sacrifice? Was life really worth anything if she wasn't sharing
it?

But—where was he going to find her?

Suddenly he sat ramrod straight; he had no way of
knowing how or where to call her from, but Rolan must!

He blanked his mind, and reached for Ahrodie.

She settled gently into his thoughts almost as soon as
he called her. *:Chosen?:*

:I need your help—and Rolan's,: he told her.

*:Then you've seen—you know? You think we can help
to call Her back? Rolan has been trying, but cannot reach
Her, not alone. Chosen, my brother, I had been hoping
you would understand and try!:*

Then the other came into his mind. *:Dirk-Herald—she
has gone Elsewhere. Can you See?:*

And amazingly, as Rolan projected strongly into his

mind, he could See—a kind of darkness, with something that flickered feebly at the end of it.

:Do you call her. We shall give you strength and an anchoring. You can go where we cannot.:

He took a deep breath, closed his eyes, and sent himself into the deepest trance he'd ever managed, trying to send out his love, calling with his heart, trying to use his need of her as a shining beacon to draw her back through the darkness. And somewhere "behind" him Rolan and Ahrodie remained, a double anchor to the real world.

How long he called, he had no way of knowing; there was no time in the currents through which he dove. Certainly the candle on the table had burned down considerably when the faint movement of the hand he held broke his trance and caused his eyes to fly open in startlement.

He could *see* color coming back into her face. She moved a little, winced, and moaned softly in protest. Her free hand reached for her temple; her eyes opened, focused, and saw him.

"You . . . called me."

It was the faintest of whispers.

He nodded, unable to speak through a throat choked with conflicting joy and doubt.

"Where—I'm home? But how—" Then intelligence and urgency flooded into her eyes. And fear; terrible fear. "Orthallen—oh, my God—Orthallen!"

She began struggling to rise, whimpering involuntarily in pain, but driven beyond caring for herself by some knowledge only she possessed.

"Devan!" Dirk could see she had something obsessively important to impart. He knew better than to try and thwart her if the need was *that* urgent—and her evident fear coupled with *that* name could mean worse trouble than anyone but she knew. So instead of trying to prevent her, he gave her the support of his arms, and called for help. *"Devan!"*

Devan nearly broke in the door in his haste to respond to Dirk's call. As he stared at Talia, dumbfounded, she demanded to know who was in authority. Devan saw she would heed nothing he told her until he gave her what she wanted, and recited the all-too-brief list.

"I want—Elspeth," she said breathlessly, "And Kyril—the Seneschal—and Alberich. Now, Devan." And would not be gainsaid.

When Devan sent messengers for the four she had demanded, she finally gave in to his insistent urgings to lie quietly.

Dirk remained in the room, wishing passionately that he could take some of the burden of pain from her, for her face was lined and white with it.

The four she had sent for arrived at a run, and within a few moments of one another. From the despair on their faces, it was evident they had expected to find Talia at least at Death's door, if not already gone. But their joy at seeing her once again awake and aware was quickly turned to shock and dismay by what she had to tell them.

"So from the very beginning it has been Orthallen?" Alberich's question appeared to be mostly rhetorical. He didn't look terribly surprised. "I would give much to know how he has managed to mindblock himself for so long, but that can wait for a later day."

Both Kyril and the Seneschal, however, were staggered by the revelation.

"Lord *Orthallen*?" the Seneschal kept muttering. "Anyone else, perhaps; treason is always a possibility with any highborn—but not Orthallen! Why, he predates me in the Council! Elspeth, can you believe this?"

"I . . . I'm not sure," Elspeth murmured, looking at Alberich, and then at Dirk.

"There . . . is a very simple way . . . to prove my words." Talia was lying quite still to harbor her strength; her eyes were closed and her voice labored, but there was no doubt that she was very much alive to everything about her. "Orthallen . . . surely knows . . . where I was. Call him here . . . but do not let him know . . . that I have . . . recovered enough to speak. Devan . . . you will painblock . . . everything. Then . . . get me propped up . . . somehow. I . . . must seem to be . . . completely

well. His reaction . . . when he sees me with Elspeth . . .
should tell us . . . all we need to know."

"There is no way I will countenance anything of the
sort!" Devan said angrily. "You are in no shape to move
a single inch, much less—"

"You will. You must," Talia's voice was flat, implaca-
ble, with no tinge of anger, only of command. But Devan
folded before it, and the look in the eyes she opened to
meet his.

"Old friend, it *must* be," she added softly. "More than
my well-being is at stake."

"This could kill you, you know," he said with obvious
bitterness, beginning to touch her forehead so that he
could establish the painblocks she demanded. "You're
forcing me to violate every Healing Oath I ever swore."

"No—" Dirk couldn't quite fathom the sad, tender
little smile she wore. "I have it . . . on excellent authority . . . that it isn't my time."

She got other protests from the rest when she decreed
that only she and Elspeth should receive Orthallen.

With total painblocks established she was able to speak
normally, if weakly. "It has to be this way," she insisted.
"If he sees you, I think he might be able to mask his
reaction. At the least he'll be warned by your presence.
With us alone, I think it will be genuine; I don't think
he'll bother trying to hide it initially from two he doesn't
consider to be physically or mentally threatening."

She relented enough to allow them to conceal themselves in the room next door, watching all that went on
through the door that linked the two, provided they keep
that door open only a bare crack. Once everyone was in
place, they sent for Orthallen.

It seemed an age before they heard his slow, deliberate
footsteps following the pattering ones of the page.

The door opened; Orthallen stepped inside, his head
turned back over his shoulder, dismissing the page before
he closed the door behind himself. Only then did he turn
to face the two that awaited him.

Talia had set her stage most carefully. She was propped
up like an oversized doll, but to all appearances was

sitting up in bed normally. She was a deathly white, but the relatively dim light of their single candle concealed that. Elspeth stood at her right hand. The room was entirely dark except for the candle that illuminated both their faces—concealing the fact that the door behind the two of them was propped open a tiny amount.

"Elspeth," Orthallen began as he turned, "This is an odd place for a meet—"

Then he truly saw who was in the room besides the Heir.

The blood drained swiftly from his face, and the condescending smile he had worn faded.

As he noted their expressions, he grew even more agitated. His hands began trembling, and his complexion took on a grayish tinge. His eyes scanned the room, looking for anyone else who might be standing in the shadows behind them.

"I have met Ancar, my lord, and seen Hulda—" Talia began.

Then the staid, poised Lord Orthallen, who always preferred words over any other weapon, did the one thing none of them would ever have expected him to do.

He went berserk.

He snatched his ornamental dagger from its sheath at his side, and sprang for them, madness in his eyes, his mouth twisted into a wild rictus of fear.

For the men hidden behind the door, time suddenly slowed to an agonizing crawl. They burst through it, knowing as they did so that by the time they reached the two women, anything they did would be far too late to save them.

But before anyone else even had time to react, before Orthallen had even moved more than a single step, Elspeth's right hand flickered out sideways, then snapped forward.

Halfway to them, Orthallen suddenly collapsed over Talia's bed with an odd gurgle, then slid to the floor.

Time resumed its normal pace.

Elspeth, white-faced and shaking, reached out and rolled him over with her foot as the four men reached her side. There was a little throwing dagger winking in the candle-light that fell on Orthallen's chest. Blood from the wound it had made stained his blue velvet robe black. It was, Dirk noted with an odd, detached corner of his mind, perfectly placed for a heart-shot.

"By my authority as Heir," Elspeth said in a voice that quavered on the edge of hysterics, "I have judged this man guilty of high treason, and carried out his sentence with my own hand."

She held to the edge of the bed to keep her shaking legs from collapsing under her, as Talia touched her arm with one bandaged hand—in an attempt, perhaps, to comfort and support her. Her eyes looked like they were going to pop out of her head, and dilated with shock. When Devan threw open the door to the hall, she looked at him pleadingly.

"And now," she said in a strained voice, "I think I'd like to be sick. Please?"

Devan had the presence of mind to get her a basin before she lost the contents of her stomach; she retched until she was totally empty, then burst into hysterical tears. Devan took charge of her quickly, leading her off to clean herself up and find a quiet place where she could vent her feelings in peace.

Kyril and Alberich removed the body, quickly and efficiently. The Seneschal wandered after them, dazed and shaken. That left Dirk alone with Talia.

Devan reappeared for a moment before he could say or do anything. The Healer removed the cushions that had been propping her up, and got her lying down again to his own satisfaction. He pressed his hand briefly to her forehead, then turned to Dirk.

"Stay with her, would you? I took some of the painblocks off before they do her an injury, but all this would have been a heavy strain if she had been healthy. In the shape she's in—I can't predict the effect. She may very well be perfectly all right; she seems in no worse state than she was before. If she starts to go into shock, or looks like she's relapsing—or really, if you think *anything* is going wrong, call me. I'll be within hearing distance, getting Elspeth calmed."

What else could he do, except nod?

When Devan left, he turned hungry eyes back toward Talia. There was so much he wanted to say—and had no idea of how to say it.

Now that the impetus of the emergency was gone, she seemed confused, disoriented, dazed with pain. He could see her groping after coherent thought.

Finally she seemed to see him. "Oh, gods, Dirk—Kris is *dead*. They murdered him—he didn't have a chance. I couldn't help him, I couldn't save him. And it's all my fault that it happened—if I'd told him we had to turn back when we first knew something was wrong, he'd still be alive."

She began to weep, soundlessly, tears trickling slowly down her cheeks; she was plainly too exhausted even to sob.

Then it hit him—

"Goddess—" he said. "Kris—oh, *Kris*—"

He knelt beside her, not touching her, while his shoulders shook with the sobs she was too weary to share—and they mourned together.

He had no idea how long they wept together; long enough for his eyes and throat to go raw. But flesh has its limits; finally he got himself back under control, carefully wiped her tears away for her, and took a seat beside her.

"I knew what happened to him," he said at last. "Rolan made it through with your message."

"How did—how did I get here?"

"I Fetched you—" he groped for the right words. "I mean, I had to, I couldn't leave you there! I didn't know if it would work but I had to try! Elspeth, the Companions, we all Fetched you together."

"You did that? It—I've never heard of anything like that— It's like—like some tale. But I was lost in the dark." She seemed almost in a state of shock now, or a half-trance. "I could see the Havens, you know, I could see them. But they wouldn't let me go to them—they held me back."

"Who? Who held you back?"

"Love and duty—" she whispered as if to herself.

"What?" She wasn't making any sense.

"But Kris said—" Her voice was almost inaudible.

He had feared before. Now he was certain. It *had* been Kris whom she loved—and he'd prevented her from reaching him. He hung his head, not wanting her to see the despair on his face.

"Dirk—" Her voice was stronger, not quite so confused. "It was *you* who called me. You saved me from Ancar, then brought me out of the dark. Why?"

She'd hate him for it, but she deserved the truth. Maybe one day she'd forgive him.

"I had to. I love you," he said helplessly, hopelessly. He stood up to leave, his eyes burning with more tears— tears he dared not shed—and cast one longing glance back at her.

Talia heard the words she'd been past hoping for— then saw her hope getting ready to walk out the door. Suddenly everything fell into place. Dirk had thought that *Kris* was the one she'd been in love with!

That was why he'd been acting so crazy—wanting her himself, yet fearing to try to compete with Kris. Havens, half the time he must have loathed himself for a very natural anger at his best friend who had turned rival. No *wonder* he'd been in such a state!

And now Kris was gone, and he thought that she'd want no part of him, the constant reminder, the second-best.

Damn the man! Stubborn as he was, there would be no reasoning with him. He would never believe anything she told him; it could take months, years to straighten it all out.

Her mind felt preternaturally clear, and she sought frantically for a way out of her predicament—and found one in memory.

". . . *just like with a Farspeaker.*" Ylsa's words were clear in her memory. "*They almost always begin by hearing first, not speaking. You're feeling right now—but I suspect that one day you'll learn how to project your own feelings in such a way that others can read them, can share them.*

*That could be a very useful trick—especially if you ever
need to convince someone of your sincerity!"*

Yes, she'd done that without really thinking about it
already. There was the forced rapport, and the kind of
rapport she'd shared with Kris and Rolan. And the sim-
pler tasks of projecting confidence, reassurance—this was
just one step farther along—

She reached for the strength and the will to *show* him,
only to discover that she was too drained, too exhausted.
There was nothing left.

She nearly sobbed with vexation. Then Rolan made his
presence felt, filling her with his love—and more—

Rolan—*his* strength was there, as always, and offered to
her with open-hearted generosity.

And she had the knowledge of what to do and how to do
it.

"Wait!" she coughed, and as Dirk half-turned, she
projected everything she felt into his open mind and
heart. All her love, her need for him—forcing him to see
the truth that words alone would never make him believe.

Devan heard a strange, strangled cry that sounded as if
it were something torn from a masculine throat. He
whirled and started for Talia's room, fearing the worst.

He paused for a moment at the door, steeled himself
against what he was likely to see, and opened it slowly,
words of comfort on his tongue.

To his total amazement, not only was Talia still living—
but she was actually clear-eyed and smiling, and trembling
on the knife-edge between laughter and tears. And Dirk
was sitting on the side of her bed, trying his best to find
some way of holding her without hurting her, covering
every uninjured inch of her that he could reach with
kisses and tears.

Half stunned, Devan slipped out before either of them
noticed him, and signaled a page passing in the hall. He
absently noted that it was one whose face he had seen
often in this corridor, though he couldn't imagine why
the child should have spent so much time here. When the
boy saw who it was that had summoned him and what
door he had come out of, he paled.

Incredible, Devan thought wryly. *Is there anyone who isn't worried to death about her?*

"I need a messenger sent to the Queen, preferably a Herald-courier, since a Herald is the only one likely to be able to find her without looking for hours, and this is fairly urgent," he said.

The page's mouth trembled. "The Lady-Herald, sir," he said in an unsteady treble. "Is she—dead?"

"Lord of Lights, no!" Devan suddenly realized that he felt like laughing for the first time in days, and shocked the child with an enormous grin. "In fact, while you're getting me that messenger, spread the news! She's very much with us—and she's going to be very, very well indeed!"

Eleven

Dirk's pure joy could not last for long: all too soon he recalled that there were far more important issues at stake than just his happiness. Talia alone knew what had transpired in Ancar's capital; might know what they could expect. Surely, surely there was danger to Valdemar, and only she might be able to guess how much.

He sobered; she caught his mood immediately. "Orthallen isn't the only enemy," he said slowly.

She couldn't have gotten any paler, but her eyes widened and pupils dilated. "No—how long—was I—"

"Since we Fetched you? Let me think—" he reckoned it up. He'd been unconscious for two days; then spent six more recovering from backlash. "Just about eight days." He guessed at what she'd ask next. "We're in Lord Falthern's keep, right on the edge of the Border."

"Selenay?"

"Devan's sent for her. You're in pain—"

"No choice, you know that." She managed a wan smile. "I—"

She forgot what she was about to say completely as Selenay fairly flew in the open door, face alight with a fierce joy.

"You see, Majesty." Alberich was close on her heels. "It is only the truth I told you." Dirk was astonished to see that the Armsmaster's face wore a nearly identical expression.

"Talia, Talia—" Selenay could manage no more before she was overcome with tears of happiness. She took the hand that Dirk had not claimed gently in her own, holding it with every care, lest she cause more pain. Alberich stood beside her, beaming as if it had all been his doing. Never in his entire life had Dirk seen the Armsmaster smile so broadly.

"Selenay—?"

The anxiety in Talia's voice penetrated even their joy, and brought them abruptly back to earth.

"There's still danger?"

Talia nodded wearily. Dirk arranged the bedding so that she was spared as much pain as he could manage, and she cast him a look that made him flush with pleasure. "Ancar—has his own army."

"And he may attack with it?"

"*Will* attack. Has to, now. He meant to kill you. Then take Elspeth."

"God of Light—"

"Last I knew—planned to take Border. He—has to have—missed me. Can't guess his reaction—but he has to assume—I lived long enough to talk."

"So we're in as much danger as before, maybe more," Selenay stood, jaw clenched in anger. "He'll have a fight on his hands!"

"Magicians. He has magicians. *Old* magic. Kept me from Mindcalling—kept Heralds from knowing Kris was dead; don't know what else they can do. Just know they can block us. And Orthallen—kept him well informed."

"Orthallen?" Selenay lost some of her anger; now she looked bewildered. "Orthallen—Lady help me, I still can't believe it of him—Goddess—he was Kris' *uncle!*"

"He was unpleased that you had sent the lad, Selenay," Alberich reminded her. "I think that we know the reason, now. And his grief at hearing—that was unfeigned."

"But over—perhaps a bit too soon," the Queen replied, biting her lip. "Though he had never been one for making much of a show of feelings."

"He killed your father," Talia whispered, her eyes closed again, exhausted with the effort of speaking for so long. "During the battle—sent an assassin in the confusion."

"He—" Selenay went white. "I never guessed—I *trusted* him!"

Silence then; the silence before the tempest.

"Dirk?" Talia opened her eyes very briefly, only to close them quickly, as if she found her vision wavering when she did so.

He needed no other clue than the dazed way she looked at him; he touched her cheek gently and went looking for Devan himself.

When he came back, he brought with him not only Devan but three other Healers as well. By then the little room was rather crowded; Kyril was back, and Elspeth with him. The Seneschal had returned and had brought the Lord Marshal. Candles had been brought, lighted and stuck on every available surface; the room was bright and a little warm and stuffy.

"I hate to ask this of you and of her, Devan," Selenay said, looking guilty, "But we haven't got the choice. Can you Healers hold her together long enough for her to tell us what we need to know?"

Dirk wanted to protest—then his rebellion subsided. He knew what he'd be doing in Talia's place; using his last breath to gasp out every bit of information he could. Why should she be any different?

"Majesty," Devan bowed his head in resignation. "I will say that I do not approve, and we will not let her kill herself with exhaustion."

"But you'll do it?"

"Like Talia, we have no choice." The Healers surrounded her, touched her lightly, and went into their Healing trances. She sighed; her pain-twisted expression eased and she opened her eyes, which were alert and clear again.

"Ask—quickly."

"Ancar—what can we expect from him?" the Lord Marshal spoke first. "How large is this private army? What kind of men does he have in it?"

"Prison scum; about three thousand. No mercenaries I heard of. But they're trained, well trained."

"What about the standing army? Will he use them?"

"I don't think yet. He murdered Alessandar; don't think he controls officers in the regular army yet. Have to put down rebels in the corps before he can use them. Needs to replace all officers with his own puppets."

"Do you think—can we expect defections?"

"I think so. Whole Border Guard may come over when they learn what happened. Welcome them, but Truth Spell them."

"Where was his own army last?"

"Just outside the capital."

"Does he know you know about his three thousand?"

"No." Her eyes were almost unnaturally bright. "He didn't ask any questions of me, ever."

"The more fool, he. A bit overconfident, wouldn't you say, Alberich? So," the Lord Marshal mused, stroking his beard, his black brows knitted in thought. "Twelve to fourteen days of forced marching would get them here. Much cavalry?"

"I don't think so; these were prison scum before he recruited them. But they're trained to work together, been training for at least three years. He also has magicians. Old magic, real magic, like in tales. If he thinks he'll come up against Heralds, he'll use them."

"How good are they?" asked Kyril.

"Don't know. One of them kept me from Mindspeaking, from probing Ancar, from defending myself, and kept Kris' passing from reaching you here—but he couldn't block empathic link with Rolan. Gods—this is important—they can *block* us, but they *can't read* us. Ancar let that slip—said something about 'damn Heralds and your barriers.' "

"Which means they can't possibly use their magic to learn our plans, especially not if *we* keep shields up?" Kyril asked, with hope in his eyes.

"Think so. Didn't even bother to try to read me, and Hulda is a mage, too—taught Ancar; I don't know how good they are. This isn't mind-magic; can't guess how it works."

"Orthallen," said the Seneschal. "How long has he been working against the Queen?"

"Decades; he had an assassin take the King during battle."

"Who was he working with?"

"Nobody then. Wanted the Throne for himself; just took advantage of Tedrel Wars."

"When did he change?"

"When Hulda contacted him. He thought he was using her."

"That was years ago—!"

"Right. She came to groom Elspeth as Ancar's consort. She found Orthallen, worked with him. He warned her in time to escape. Later Ancar offered him the Throne in exchange for information and internal help."

"The magicians—?" said Kyril, anxiously.

"Not much I can tell. Told you about the mindblock. Same mage kept Ancar shielded. Hulda shielded herself, I think. She looked physically about twenty-five years old. Could have been illusion, but don't think so. She's old enough to have been actually Ancar's nurse—makes her at least forty. Saw her make a witchlight—" Talia pulled her bandaged hand away from Dirk's for a moment, and pulled her loose gown away from her shoulder. Selenay and Elspeth gasped, and the Seneschal bit back an exclamation at what was revealed there—a handprint, burned into the flesh of her chest as if with a branding iron. "She did that, while they were—playing with me. Just laid her hand there, casually. Like it was easy as breathing. Rumors were they can do worse; lots worse."

The four Healers were beginning to look drawn; even with their aid, Talia was visibly fading.

"Tired—" she said, begging with her eyes for a rest.

"We've got enough to go on for now," Selenay looked to each of the others and they nodded in confirmation. "We can get our defenses organized, at least. Rest, my brave one."

She led the others out; one by one the Healers disengaged themselves. As they did, Talia seemed to wilt, and more than a little. Devan caught Dirk's shoulder before he had a chance to panic.

"She'll live; she just needs rest and a chance to heal," he said wearily. "And she's going to get at least some of both right now—if I have to post guards to keep people out!"

Dirk nodded, and returned to her side. She opened her eyes with an effort.

"Love—you—" she whispered.

"My own—" His throat closed for a moment, and he fought down a renewal of tears. "I'm going to leave you for a while; Devan says you need rest. But I'll be back as soon as he lets me!"

"Make it—soon—"

He left, walking backward; she keeping her eyes on him until the door closed.

As Alberich had suspected would be the case, when dawn came, the bivouac on the Border as well as the smaller collection of Councillors and officials at the Keep were in an uproar. Units of the Guard—heartbreakingly small—arrived every hour. Tales, more or less garbled, of what had occurred the previous night were spreading like oil from a shattered urn, and were just as potentially flammable. Talia slept in an induced Healing-trance, blissfully unaware of the confusion.

The Guard was easiest to deal with; the Lord Marshal simply called all the officers together, and with Alberich present to verify exactly what had been said and done, related to them the entire true story. The officers of the Guard, for the most part, had never associated closely with Orthallen; thus, while they were shocked by his betrayal, they took the tale at its face value. They were far more worried about the army Ancar would bring against them, for they numbered something around a thousand to Ancar's three thousand. The magicians they dismissed out of hand.

"My lord," one veteran officer said, his face as scar-seamed as Alberich's "Begging your pardon, but there's nothing we can *do* about mages. We'll leave that in the hands of those that deal with magic—"

His gaze flickered to Alberich; the Armsmaster gave him a barely perceptible nod.

"—we've more than enough on our plate with what's coming at us."

And Ancar's army *was* on its way; Alberich and the Lord Marshal knew that for a fact. There were two

Heralds in Selenay's entourage gifted with Farsight who had also been in Hardorn on more than one mission. They had bent their talents beyond the Border during the night, at Alberich's urging. They had seen Ancar's army, plainly camped for a few hours' rest. More disturbingly, they had "looked" again for that army with the coming of dawn—and found nothing, nothing but empty country-side.

"So there's at least one mage with them," Kyril deduced, as the warleaders conferred over breakfast. "And he's concealing their movements from our Farsight somehow." Knowing what they now knew about mages being in Ancar's entourage—however little that was—Kyril and Alberich had been made co-equal with the Lord Marshal. Their task was to lead the assembled Heralds in combat—either by steel or by Gift. One of the Heralds' most important tasks was communications; each officer would have a Mindspeaking Herald with him at all times, and Kyril would be with Selenay to coordinate all of them. That was the trick that had won the Tedrel Wars for them, the one thing no other army could match.

"Doesn't matter," the Lord Marshal replied, "at least not at the moment. We know where they *were*; we know by that how fast they've come, and how soon they're likely to get here. We also know those mages haven't been moving 'em somehow—else they wouldn't have needed all the horses your Heralds 'saw.' "

"My lord?" One of his officers had appeared beyond the open tent flap, saluting smartly. He was scarcely old enough to have grown a beard; morning sun gilded his fair hair, and he was having a difficult time repressing a grin. "We're getting the recruits you warned us of."

"Recruits?" Kyril said, puzzled, as Alberich nodded.

The Lord Marshal gave a brief snort that might have been a laugh. "You'll see, Herald. Bring them on up here, lad; we've got two here that can test them."

"All of them, sir?"

"How many are there?" The Lord Marshal was surprised now.

"Over a hundred, sir."

"Lady Bright—aye, bring them all up. We'll get them sorted out, somehow."

As the three Warleaders left the tent to stand in the brilliant sunlight, there was a small dust-cloud in the vicinity of the trade road. As those who made the cloud neared, Kyril and Alberich saw that those at the front of the crowd that approached afoot were wearing the black-and-gold uniforms of Alessandar's regular army.

It appeared that the entire force guarding the Border, from officers to Healers and all their dependents, had defected when they had learned of Alessandar's murder.

Elspeth had the joyous task of breaking the news to the rest of the Council. There was no such accord among the political leaders of Valdemar as there was among her military leaders.

Lord Gartheser was speechless with outrage and shock; Bard Hyron was dazed. Lady Kester and Lady Cathan, still seething over Orthallen's accusations of complicity with the slavers, were surprised, but not altogether unhappy. Father Aldon had closeted himself in the tiny chapel of the Keep; Lord Gildas was with him. Healer Myrim made no attempt to conceal the fact that Orthallen's treachery had not surprised her. Nor did she conceal that his demise gave her a certain grim satisfaction. But then, she might well be forgiven such uncharitable thoughts; she was one of the four Healers who were tending Talia's wounds.

Once the bare bones had been told to the Councillors as a group, Elspeth went to each of these Councillors in turn, privately. She gave a simple explanation of what had occurred, but would answer no questions. Questions, she told them, must wait until Talia had recovered enough to tell them all more.

Long before then, Ancar's army arrived.

Alberich was beginning to feel hopeful. The ranks of Valdemar's forces had been swelled to nearly double the original size by deserters—partisans of Alessandar—from across the Border. The Lord Marshal was fairly dancing with glee; with the exception of the dependents, every one of the men and women who sought sanctuary with them was a well-trained fighter or Healer—and every one burned with hatred and anger for the murder of their beloved King.

For the true tale had been spread to the countryside, from the capital westward, by a most unexpected source— the members of Trader Evan's clan.

Evan, it seemed had taken to heart Talia's warning to flee—and done more than that. He had spread the word among the traders of his own clan as he fled; they in turn had carried the tale farther. Close to the capital, the people were cowed and afraid, too frightened to dare even escape; but close to the Border where Ancar's hand had not yet fallen so heavily, and where Alessandar had been served out of love, feelings ran high. High enough, that when two or three Border officers decided to defect to Valdemar's side of the Border, nearly the entire contingent of the regular army stationed in the area chose to come with them.

Ancar surely had not anticipated this, nor would Ancar have any way of knowing they had gone. A small group of volunteers had remained behind at the signal towers and continued to send messages and information—all of it false.

"They'll fade into the villages when Ancar has gone by," the Captain who had hosted Kris and Talia told Alberich. "They've got civilian clothing at hand now. If they can, they'll come across to us, but all the men who volunteered have families, and they won't leave 'em."

"Understandable," Alberich replied. "If it is that we win this battle, we shall post watchers to guide them here at every likely crossing. If not . . ."

"Then it won't matter a damn, because Ancar will have us all," the Captain answered grimly.

The Lord Marshal, with his forces doubled, was in no doubt as to the outcome.

"Randon," Selenay said anxiously, as they waited for some sign that Ancar was within striking distance, "I know it's your job to be confident, but he still has us outnumbered three to two—"

They were standing, as they had every day since the Border had been alerted, at the top of the highest hill in the vicinity. Ancar's mages probably could mask the movements of his troops from Farsight, but they'd be hard put to eliminate the dust-cloud of their passing, or the disturbance of birds, or any one of a number of other signs of the movement of many men. From this hill there was a clear line-of-sight for miles into Hardorn. Trained watchers were posted here, but Selenay and the Lord Marshal also spent most of their time not otherwise occupied squinting into the bright sunshine alongside them.

"My lady, we have more on our side than he can guess at. We have a thousand trained fighters besides our own that he knows *nothing* about. We have the choice of battleground. And we have the Heralds to ensure that there are *no* botched orders or misheard messages, or commands that come too late to be effective. The only thing I fear are his mages." Now doubt did shadow the Lord Marshal's eyes, and creep into his voice. "We have no way of knowing what they can do, how many he has, or if we can counteract them. And *they* may turn the day for him."

"And Heraldic Gifts for the most part are not much use offensively," Selenay added, sobered by the thought of the mages. "If only we had one of the Herald-mages alive today."

"Lady-Queen, will I do?"

Selenay whirled, startled. As she and Randon had been absorbed in watching the Border and in their conversation, two Heralds had climbed the hill behind them. One was Dirk, pale, but looking better than he had in days.

The other, so begrimed with dust that his Whites were gray, his face lined with exhaustion, but sporting a self-conscious grin despite his weariness, was Griffon.

"I brought him right here as soon as we'd pried him off his saddle, Majesty," Dirk said. "This lout just may be our answer to the mages—remember his Gift? He's a *Firestarter*, Majesty."

"Just point out what you want to go up in flames—or

who," Griffon added. "I guarantee it'll go. Kyril hasn't found anything that'll block me yet."

"That's no boast, Majesty; I trained him, I know what he can do. He's limited to line-of-sight, but that should be good enough."

"But—you were riding circuit up North," Selenay said, dazed with the sudden turn in their fortunes that brought Griffon there when he was most needed. "How did you even find out we were under threat, much less get here in time?"

"Pure, dumb, Herald's luck," Griffon replied. "I ran into a Herald Courier whose Gift just *happens* to be Foresight; her message was delivered and we were—ah—passing an evening together. That night she got a really strong vision; all but dragged me out of bed and threw me into the saddle stark naked. She took over my circuit, I rode for the Border as fast as Harevis could carry me. And here I am. I just hope I can do you some good."

The setting sun was turning the clouds bloody when one of the lookouts reported the first long-awaited sign of Ancar's army. Selenay prayed that the blood-red of the sunset was not an ill omen for her forces, even while she and the Lord Marshal issued the first of the orders for the battle to come.

The Lord Marshal had chosen as the battlefield a low, bare hill just on the Valdemar side of the Border. It had woods to the rear and the left of it, and open fields to the right. What Ancar couldn't know—and what even now the scouts and skirmishers heading into the woods intended to keep him from learning—was that the woods to the rear of the hill had flooded with the bursting of an earthen dam earlier this spring. Water lay two and three feet deep all through them, and the hitherto-spongy ground was a morass of mud.

Others besides those skirmishers were moving into the woods to the left of the chosen field—the thousand or so fighters who had defected to Valdemar. In groups of a hundred or thereabouts, each with a mindspeaking Herald, they were taking positions to lie in wait past any point where Ancar's scouts would be allowed to penetrate.

* * *

Teren slapped at another mosquito, and curbed his irritation. The ground was high enough here that they weren't up to their rears in mud, but the stinging insects were having a rare old party—not only acres of new-made marsh to lay eggs in, but this unexpected bonus of humans as refreshments! It was dark, the air was damp, and it was chilly. Wythra didn't like it any better than he did; he could hear his Companion blowing impatiently in the darkness to his right.

:Twin?: he mind-sent. *:We're in position, how about you?:*

:The same,: was Keren's reply, with an overtone of exasperation, *:and up to our armpits in goddamn midges!:*

:Mosquitos here.:

:Count your blessings,: came her retort. *:The midges are crawling into people's armor and you beat yourself black and blue trying to get them.:*

:They're everywhere—: That had the unmistakable overtones of Keren's stallion Dantris, and he was irritated. Unlike most other Heralds, the twins could Mindspeak as well with each other's Companions as with their own. *:Even fellis-oil isn't helping,:* Dantris concluded in annoyance.

:Sounds like you may have more casualties from the wildlife than in battle.: Teren grinned to himself despite his discomfort.

:Let's all hope you're right,: his twin answered soberly.

"Be my eyes and ears, love," Talia had begged Dirk. "They're going to need me—"

"But—" he'd protested.

"Take Rolan; you *know* you can link to him. And when they need me—"

"Not *if?*" He'd sighed. "No, never mind. I link to Rolan and he links to you? Gods, can't you rest for a *moment?*"

"Dare I?"

He'd had no answer to give her. So here he waited, in the lines behind Selenay, waiting for dawn. Praying she didn't kill herself—because if he lost her, now that he'd just found her. . . .

* * *

When dawn came, Selenay's forces were formed up along the top of the hill, with their backs to the woods. There was a heavy knot of Heralds in Whites at the end of the left flank, hard against the woods to the side. With them was Jeri, wearing some of Elspeth's student Grays; they were hoping Ancar would mistake her for Elspeth and drive for that part of the line. Elspeth herself was back at the Keep, ready to flee at a moment's notice if the tide turned against them. She had agreed to this reluctantly, but saw the sense in it, and she wanted to be certain if everything went wrong that Talia was not left behind. During one of her brief moments of wakefulness, the Queen's Own had soberly asked the Heir to personally be certain that she didn't fall back into Ancar's hands, and Elspeth had promised just as soberly. Although Elspeth had a shrewd notion that Talia meant she should see to it that the Queen's Own received coup de grace, the Heir was determined to bring her along even if it meant carrying the injured Herald herself!

In the pale light of dawn, Selenay's original thousand looked pitiful against Ancar's three thousand.

They were a shade more heavily armored than the Guard; from the way they obeyed their officers' orders, they were as well trained. About five hundred of the three thousand were still mounted; cavalry then, but light cavalry, not heavy. The good news was that their bows were all crossbows—in an open field battle, virtually useless in combat once fired, and lacking the range of a longbow.

Selenay's forces waited, patiently. Ancar would have to come to them.

"He's a good commander, I'll give him that," the Lord Marshal growled, when after an hour of waiting nothing had happened. "He's assessing his chances—and I hope to blazes we look like fools! Wait a minute, something's happening—"

A rider came forward from the ranks with a white parley flag. He rode to the exact middle of the battle-field, and paused.

The Lord Marshal rode forward three paces, his battle-harness jingling, and thundered, "Speak, man! Or are you just here to look pretty?"

The rider, a slightly foppish fellow wearing highly ornamented plate with a helmet that bore an outlandish crest, colored angrily and spoke up. "Queen Selenay, your envoys murdered King Alessandar, clearly on your orders. King Ancar has declared a state of war upon Valdemar for your heinous act. Your forces are out-numbered—will you surrender yourself now to Ancar's justice?"

An angry muttering went up along the line, as Selenay grimaced. "I wondered what sort of tale he'd concoct," she murmured to Kyril, then called to the rider: "And just what can I expect frcm Ancar's justice?"

"You must abdicate and give over your daughter Elspeth in marriage to Ancar. The Heralds of Valdemar must be disbanded and outlawed. Ancar will rule Valdemar jointly with Elspeth; you will be imprisoned in a place of Ancar's choosing for as long as you live."

"Which will be about ten minutes once Ancar has me in his hands," Selenay said loud enough for the envoy to hear. Then she stood up in her stirrups, removed her helm so that the sun shone fully on her golden hair, and called aloud, "What do you say, my people? Shall I surrender?"

The resounding "No!" that met her question rang across the hilltop and caused the envoy's horse to start and shy.

"Now hear *me*—" she said, in a voice so clear and carrying that there was no doubt that every one of Ancar's men could hear it. "Ancar murdered his own father, and my envoy as well. He consorts with evil magicians, and dabbles in blood-sacrifice, and I'd sooner set a blade across Elspeth's throat than have her spend so much as five minutes in his company! Let him beware the vengeance of the gods for his false accusations—and the only way he'll rule Valdemar is when every one of her citizens is dead in her defense!"

The envoy turned his horse back to his own lines, the cheering that followed Selenay's words seeming to push him along before it like a leaf before the wind.

"Well, now we're for it," Selenay said to her commanders, settling her sword a little more comfortably at her side. She replaced her helm, and patted her Companion's neck. "Now we see if our plans work, even at three-to-two."

"And," Kyril replied, "if a Firestarter's the equal of Ancar's mages."

"Why are they just sitting there?" Griffon asked, his expression perplexed. "Why aren't they charging?"

He was far back behind the first and second lines, with the bowmen. His Gift was far too precious to risk him anywhere near the front, but he chafed at his enforced idleness.

They found out in the next few moments as fog seemed to begin rising from the earth at a point between their lines and Ancar's. The fog was a sickly yellow, and the breeze blowing across the battle field did not disturb it at all. Then it seemed to writhe and curdle; there was an eerie green glow all about it. The breeze brought a whiff of a sulfurous stench, the whole battlefield seemed to shift sideways for an instant, and Griffon's stomach lurched—and in place of the fog was a clutch of demonic monsters.

They were easily seven feet tall, with dark pits in their skulls in place of eyes, in the depths of which a dim red fire seemed to flicker. Their mouths were fanged: their leathery yellow hides, the color of rancid butter, seemed armor enough. They each carried a double-bladed axe in one hand, a knife nearly the length of a sword in the other. There were nearly a hundred of them. A fearful murmuring arose from the ranks of Selenay's forces—a few arrows flew in the direction of the things, but those that connected merely bounced off. As they opened their fanged mouths to roar and began advancing on the center of Selenay's lines, her own troops fell back a step or two involuntarily.

Then, without warning, one of the demon-warriors stopped dead in its tracks, and let out a howl that caused men to clap their hands to their ears; then it burst into flame.

It howled again, and began staggering in circles, a walking pyre. Selenay's troops cheered again; then the cheering died, for the rest of the demons were still coming, oblivious to the fate of the burning one, which had fallen to the ground, still afire.

A second and a third ignited—and still they kept coming. They moved fairly slowly, but it was evident that they would reach Selenay's lines in a few moments.

And so they did—and the slaughter they caused was hideous. The demons waded into the line of fighters as a man might wade into a pack of yipping curs. They swung their heavy axes with deceptive slowness—and sheared through armor and the flesh beneath as if the armor were paper and the flesh as soft as melted cheese. There was no deflecting the blows of those vicious axes; a man in the way of one of them went down with his shield split, and his skull split as well. Incredibly, fighters pressed to replace those that had fallen, but their bravery was useless. The axes continued to swing, and the replacements joined their fellows, either in death or in mangled agony. The Guard swarmed to make a protective wall around Selenay and her commanders, but the demons were inexorably cutting through them. There was blood everywhere—some of it yellow, but precious little compared to the amount of red, human blood flowing. Men cried out in fear or in pain, the monsters roared, and under all was the screech of blade-edge meeting armor and the stink of demon-flesh burning.

Griffon, standing far behind the lines, brow furrowed with concentration, was focusing on yet another of the demons. As it, too, went up in flames, he looked for a new target in despair. It seemed that he alone could kill these monsters—but there were so many of them!

"Herald—" He tried to ignore the insistent voice in his ear, but the man would not go away. He turned impatiently, to see that his persistant companion was the Councillor, Bard Hyron. Hyron was enough of a trained bowman to have warranted a place back here, alongside Griffon.

"Herald—the tales say these things are dependent on their sorcerer. If you kill him, they'll vanish!"

"What if the tales are wrong?"

"You won't have lost anything," the Bard pointed out. "Look—the mage must be in that knot of people back by the standard; just to the left of the center and the rear of Ancar's lines."

"Get me a Farseer!" Before Griffon had finished speaking, the man was off, running faster than Griffon would have guessed he could.

The Bard was back in an instant—too long for Griffon, who watched, sickened, as the demons carved down another swath of the Guard.

"I'm looking, Grif—" It was Griffon's red-haired yearmate, Davan, who came stumbling up in the Bard's wake—stumbling because he had one hand pressed to his forehead, trying to "See" as he ran. "I've—bloody *hell!* I *know* he's there, but they're blocking me! *Damn* you, you bastards—"

Davan went to his knees, face twisted and unrecognizable with the effort of fighting the blockage the mages were putting on him.

"Come *on*, Davan—" Griffon glanced up; and swallowed bile and fear. The demons were continuing to advance. He concentrated, and sent the nearest up in flames, but another took its place.

Hyron froze for a moment, then ran off again. Griffon hardly noticed; he was doing what he could—and it wasn't enough.

Pounding hooves and a flash of white that Griffon saw out of the corner of his eye signaled the arrival of another Herald. Distracted, Griffon turned to see who it was.

Dirk—and not Ahrodie, but *Rolan!*

Dirk slid off the stallion's bare back, and took Davan by the shoulder, shaking him. "Break it off, little brother—that isn't going to get you anywhere," he shouted over the noise of battle. "You two—don't argue. Link with us—"

Griffon did not even bother to think, much less argue. He linked in with Dirk, as he had so often done as a student—

To find himself, not in a four-way linkage, but a *five*.

Dirk was linked to Rolan—who in his turn was linked to—Talia?

Yes, it *was* Talia.

Dirk's ability at Mindspeech was limited, but urgency made it clear and strong. *:Davan, follow Her. Mage used death to raise power—pain, despair—She can track it to him. Grif, follow Davan—I hold here.:*

Davan caught that; they all remembered how Talia had used Ylsa's dying to lead Kris' Farsight to where her body lay. The thread of Talia's sending was faint, but unmistakable. Davan caught and followed it, and Griffon, linked in as closely as he dared, was hot on his "heels."

:Yes—yes, I've got him! I See him! He's dressed in a bright sky-blue velvet robe—Grif, strike now, through me!:

Clear in Davan's mind, Griffon saw a wizened man in a robe of vivid blue just a little to one side of the knot of people around Ancar's standard. And that was all he needed.

With hatred and anger he hadn't known he could feel, born of the horror he felt watching his fellows being slaughtered, he *reached*—

And found himself blocked, as he'd never been before.

He strove against the wall blocking him, fighting his way through it with every ounce of energy he possessed, fueled by his rage—

He felt it yield just the tiniest amount, and dragged up new reserves of energy—from where, he neither knew nor cared.

There was an explosion in Ancar's lines. And a tower of flame rose next to Ancar's standard—

And the demons vanished.

Griffon's eyes rolled up into his head, he fainted dead away, and Davan went with him; Hyron and Dirk caught them as they fell.

When the demon-warriors vanished, Selenay's forces let out a cheer of relief. Selenay cheered with them, but wondered if they were being a bit premature.

When no other arcane attacks manifested, *then* she

truly felt like cheering. There must have been only the one mage, and somehow the Heralds had been able to defeat him.

"Griffon and Davan found the mage and burned him," Kyril said at Selenay's glance of inquiry. "They both collapsed, after. Griffon's still passed out, but it doesn't look as if he'll be needed again in a hurry."

No, it didn't; for now Ancar's regular troops were charging Selenay's line. The bowmen showered them with arrows—no few of which found their marks. Ancar's own crossbowmen had long since expended their own bolts—uselessly, it might be added—and had switched to charging with the rest, swords in hand. Selenay's Guardsfolk braced themselves for the shock, for now the first step of their battle plan was about to take place.

When Ancar's line hit Selenay's with a clangor of metal on metal and cries of battle-rage and pain, most of their force was concentrated on the middle, where Selenay's standard was. She waited, ignoring the sight and sound of her people killing and being killed, for several long moments—for *she,* not the Lord Marshal, was the field commander. Her Gift of Foresight was not a strong one, but it was an invaluable one, for it operated best on the battlefield. It would not tell her what was to happen, but given that there were plans already made, it *would* tell her when the exact instant occurred that those plans should be set into motion.

She waited, listening for that insistent inner prompting. Then—"Tell the left to pull in," she said to Kyril.

He Mindsent, with a frown of concentration, and almost instantly the troops on the lefthand side of the standard began making their way toward the center.

As she'd hoped, Ancar sent his cavalry to the left, with foot following—supposing that he could encircle their line at that point, or even capture the supposed Heir.

"Wheel—" she told Kyril. And relayed by the Heralds with each group, the entire force pivoted on the center, with the leftmost end being on the very edge of the swamp, where some of Ancar's cavalry were even now discovering the two and three feet of water and mud.

She waited another long moment, until all of Ancar's forces were between her line and the woods on the left.

Then—"Now, Kyril! Call them in!"

And pouring from the woods came the troops that had hidden there all night—fresh, angry, and out for blood; the defectors from Alessandar's army, and the Heralds that were their link to the command post. The defectors looked a little odd, for each of them had spent a few moments of his hours in waiting cutting away the sleeves of his uniform tunic so that the sleeves of the white, padded gambeson showed. There could now be no mistaking them on the battlefield for Ancar's troopers.

Caught between two forces, with a morass in front of them, even Ancar's seasoned veterans began to panic.

After that, it was a rout.

Griffon was the first to reach the Keep, half-blind with reaction-headache. He had stayed only long enough to assure himself that the victory was indeed Selenay's, then pulled himself onto his Companion's back and sought the Healers.

"We did it; we pulled it off," he told Elspeth, downing a swallow of headache-potion with a grimace. "Those extra troops from Hardorn turned the tide. By now what's left of Ancar's army is probably being chased across the border with its tail between its legs."

"What about Ancar himself?"

"Never got into the thick of battle; probably he's gotten away. And before you ask, I don't know if Hulda was with him, but I'd guess not. From what I've been able to pick up from you and Talia, I'd say she isn't one to put herself at any kind of risk. She's probably safely back at the capital, consolidating things for her 'little dear.' "

"What about—"

"Elspeth, my head is about ready to break open. I think I know why Lavan called the Firestorm down on himself—it probably felt better than his reaction-headache! I'm going to go pass out for a while. Thank Talia for me. We couldn't have done it without her. And you stay ready; they'll be bringing battle casualties back any minute now. The Healers will need every hand they can get, and there'll be plenty of fellows eager for the privilege of having the Heir listening to their boasts while they're being patched up."

So it proved . . . and Elspeth learned firsthand of the aftermath of battle. She grew a great deal older in the next few hours. And never again would she think of war as "glorious."

Selenay remained on the Border, as fresh troops came to help with mopping-up, but Elspeth, the Councillors, the wounded, and most of the Heralds (including Talia and Dirk) returned to the capital.

Just before the Councillors left, Selenay called them all together.

"I *must* remain here," she said, feeling gray with exhaustion. "Elspeth has full powers of regency; in my absence she heads the Council—with full vote."

Lord Gartheser looked as if he was about to protest, then subsided, sullenly. The Councillors who had been Orthallen's advocates—with the exception of Hyron—were angry and unhappy and would be Elspeth's first problem.

"You have no choice in this, my Councillors," Selenay told them, fixing her eyes on Gartheser in particular. "In war the Monarch has right of decree, as you well know. And should there be any trouble . . ."

She paused significantly.

"Be certain that I shall hear of it—and act."

Elspeth called a Council meeting as soon as they were all settled, but sent messages that it would be held in Talia's quarters.

With the more aged or slothful of the Councillors grumbling and panting their way up the stairs to the top story, the meeting convened.

Talia was by no means well; she was healed enough to manage an hour or two undrugged, but no more than that. She was propped up on her little couch, positioned just under her window. She wore bandages everywhere except her head and neck; her ruined feet were encased in odd bootlike contraptions. She was nearly as white as the uniform she wore. Elspeth sat next to her, with one eye on her at all times.

Lord Gartheser (predictably) was the first to speak. "What has been going on here?" he snapped angrily. "What's all this nonsense about Orthallen being a traitor? I—"

"It is not nonsense, my lord," Talia interrupted him quietly. "I heard it from his co-conspirators, and his own actions when confronted merely with their names proves his guilt."

Simply, and without elaboration, she told the whole story of what she and Kris had learned about Ancar, of the massacre at the banquet, of Kris' death, and her confrontations with Hulda and Ancar.

When she paused, obviously tired, Elspeth took up the tale, relating what Talia had told them after Dirk had brought her back, and the scene with Orthallen.

Lord Gartheser sat silently through it all, mouth agape, growing paler by the moment.

"So you can see, Councillors," Elspeth finished, "why my very first act as regent *must* be to ascertain your loyalty under Truth Spell. Kyril, would you be willing to administer to your fellow Councillors? I have only one question to put to all of us—where and with whom do your first loyalties lie?"

"Certainly, Elspeth," Kyril replied, nodding his gray head toward her obediently. "And Elcarth can administer the test to me."

"But—I—" Gartheser was sweating profusely.

"You have some objection, Gartheser?" Lady Cathan asked with honeyed sweetness.

"I—uh—"

"If you prefer not to take the test, you could resign your position—"

Lord Gartheser looked from face to face, hoping for a reprieve, and found none. "I—Lady Elspeth, I fear the— the stress of my position is too much for me. With your leave, I should prefer to resign it."

"Very well, Gartheser," Elspeth said calmly. "Does anyone else object? No? Then, my lord, you may leave us. I would suggest you retire to your estates for the quiet, peaceful life you have so richly earned. I do not think, given the stress you have been through, that it would be wise to entertain many visitors."

She watched Gartheser rise and stumble out the door with an impassive expression not even Selenay could have matched.

"Kyril," she said when he was gone, "you may begin with me."

"And after Elspeth, I should like to be tested," Hyron said, shamefacedly, "being as I was one of Orthallen's stronger supporters."

"If you wish. Kyril?"

The testing took a very short time; not surprisingly, all passed.

"Next, we have two Council seats to fill, speaker for the North, and speaker for the Central districts. Any suggestions?"

"For the Central, I would suggest Lord Jelthan," said Lady Kester. "He's young, he's got some good ideas, but he's been lord of his holdings for nearly fourteen years—his father died young."

"Anyone else? No? And the North?"

No one spoke, until Talia's whisper broke the silence. "If no one has any other notions, I suggest Mayor Loschal of Trevendale. He's quite able, he knows the problems of the North intimately, he has no private axe to grind that I am aware of, and he has enough years to balance Lord Jelthan's youth."

"Any other suggestions? So be it—Kyril, see to it, will you? Now, the other matter facing us is Hardorn and Ancar. We are going to have to increase the size of the Guard; that means a tax increase—"

"Why? We beat them, right soundly!"

"There's no need—"

"You're starting at shadows—"

"I know for a fact your mother gave you no such orders—"

"Quiet!" Kyril thundered out over the bedlam. When they stared at him dumbfounded, he continued, "Herald Talia wishes to speak, and she can't be heard over your babbling."

"Elspeth is right," Talia whispered wearily. "I know Ancar better than any of you. He'll be back at us, again and again, until one of our lands lacks its leader. And I tell you, this kingdom is in more danger now than we were before the battle we just won! *Now* he knows some of what we can do, and what kind of strength we can raise at short notice. The next time he comes for us, it will be with a force *he* deems overwhelming; we must be ready to meet that force."

"And that means a larger Guard; taxes to support it—"

"And your help, Councillors. Bard Hyron, the help of your Circle especially," Talia continued.

"My Circle? Why?"

"Because, as you ably demonstrated with Griffon, the Bardic Circle is the only source of information we have on old magic."

"Surely you overestimate these mages—" Lady Wyrist began.

"Look here and tell me I overestimate!" Again Talia pulled gown and bandage from her shoulder to display the handprint-brand, still livid and raw-looking. "I will bear this mark until the day I die, and this was just a *parlor-trick* for Hulda!" Lady Wyrist paled and turned her head away. "Ask the widows and children and widowers of those slain by demons if I overestimate the danger! I tell you now that what Ancar brought with him is likely to be one of his lesser mages—he would not risk the greater in battle. And Hyron, your Circle alone preserves the tradition of what we can expect and how we can defend against it. If, indeed, we can."

"We can," Hyron said thoughtfully. "It's in some of the chronicles from Vanyel's time—when the Gifts were superseding the mage-crafts. It may be that you Heralds and your Companions are all that *will* be able to guard us from Ancar's magicians."

"Sounds like a rare good reason to have them by us, if you ask me," said Lady Kester wryly.

"And we'll need you and your Circle for your traditional reason as well," Elspeth said, smiling at Hyron.

"Especially if we're not to end up conscripting for the Guard."

"Rousing patriotic fervor and spreading tales of what's happened and what we can expect? Aye, Lady Elspeth, as always, the Circle is yours to command."

"And keeping the spirits of our people high."

"Ever in your service—"

Elspeth took a quick glance at Talia, as she lay back on her pillows, face pinched and drained. "If there's no more business at hand?"

"None that can't wait," said Lord Gildas.

"Then I think we'd best dismiss, and let the Healers see to Talia."

As the Councillors filed out, Skif slipped in, Healer Devan and Healer Rynee with him.

"Little sister, Dirk's waiting downstairs—" Skif began.

Talia's face crumpled, and she began to cry. "Please— not now—I'm so tired. . . ."

"Listen to me—listen—" He caught one of her hands in his own and knelt beside her couch. "I know what's happening to you, I understand! I've seen you trying not to wince away when he touches you. I've talked him into going home to tell his parents about you; I'm going with him. By the time we get back, you'll be fine again, I know you will. Now gather your courage and give him a wonderful good-bye to keep him going, eh?"

She shuddered; he wiped her tears, and she relaxed. "Is that why you brought Rynee?"

He chuckled. "You've got it. She'll give you a little mental painblock, as it were. Let her work while I fetch Dirk."

She was able to do all Skif had asked and more, but when the two of them left, she crumbled again.

"Rynee, am I ever going to be able to—be *whole* again? I love him, I need him—but whenever he touches me, I see Ancar and Ancar's guards—"

"Hush, now, hush," Rynee soothed her as if Talia were twelve years her junior instead of four her senior.

"It was fine at first, but after the battle it started to build every time a man touched me, and it was worse

than that when the man was *him!* Rynee, I can't bear it, I
can't bear it!"

"Talia, dear friend, be easy. Yes, you'll be fine, just
like Skif said. It's just a matter of Healing, inside instead
of out. Now sleep."

"Will she Heal?" Devan looked at Rynee somberly, as
Talia dropped into Healing-trance.

"She will," Rynee replied serenely. "And it'll be mostly
her own doing. You'll see."

"I pray you're right."

"I *know* I am."

Twelve

Skif took the tower stairs at a run, though for all the sound he made, no one would ever have known there was anyone on the stairs at all. He'd been back from the North for several hours now, and he was more than impatient. "You can't see Talia yet," they'd told him. "She's with the Healers every morning, and they've left orders that they're never to be disturbed." Well, all right, but that didn't make a fellow any less twitchy, not when he was worried about her. He'd determined to get up to her room as soon as he'd finished lunch; he'd all but bolted his food and nearly choked as a consequence.

He'd evidently misjudged the timing by a bit, for as he approached the half-open door at the top of the stairs, he'd heard voices inside. He shrank back into a shadow on the landing, and peeked around the corner. From where he was hidden he could see inside the room quite easily. There were two Healers there, both easily identifiable by their Greens, one on either side of a lounge that held someone in Herald's Whites—Talia, without a doubt.

He winced inside, for her face was distorted by pain and her eyes streamed tears, although she did not utter so much as a single moan.

"Enough," said the Healer on her right; and Skif recognized Devan. "That's absolutely all for today, Talia."

Her face relaxed somewhat, and the woman on her left gave her a look of caring sympathy and a handkerchief to dry her tears with.

"You really don't need to be enduring all this, you know," Devan said, a bit crossly. "If you'd let us Heal you at the normal rate it could all be done quite painlessly."

"Dear Devan, I don't have time, and you know that perfectly well," Talia replied softly.

"Then you ought to at least let us work under painblock! And I still don't understand *why* you don't think you have time!"

"But if you worked under painblocks, I wouldn't be able to help—and if I can't help, neither can Rolan. In that case, it would take six of you to do what one does now." Her voice actually held a touch of amusement.

"She's got you there, Devan," the woman Healer—Myrim, the Healer's representative on the Council—pointed out wryly.

He snorted with disgust. "Heralds! I don't know why we put up with you! If you're not out killing yourselves, you're trying to get us to speed-Heal you so that you can go back out and get yourselves ruined that much sooner!"

"Well, old friend, if you'll recall—the first time you ever saw me, I was your patient. There'd already been an attempt to rid the world of me, and I was only a student. You could hardly expect this tabbycat to change color after such an auspicious beginning, could you?"

The Healer reached out and touched her cheek in a spontaneous gesture of affection. "It's just that it hurts me to have to put you through such agony, dearling."

She caught the hand and held it, smiling at him. The smile transformed her from a simply pretty woman (swollen and red-rimmed eyes notwithstanding) to a lovely one. "Take heart, old friend. There are not many more days of this to come; then whatever Healing is left will all be bone-Healing—and you can't speed that." She laughed. "As for why I don't have time, well, I can't tell you, because I don't know myself. I only know it's true, just as true as the fact that Rolan's eyes are blue. Besides, I know you. I'm a cooperative patient; unlike Keren and Dirk, I do exactly what I'm told. Since you can't complain of that, you have to find *something* to be annoyed about!"

Myrim chuckled, as did Healer Devan. "Oh, you know

him far too well, milady," she said, standing and stretching. "And we will see you on the morrow."

They left the room and passed Skif without ever noticing that he was there.

But Talia seemed to sense that someone was there. "Whoever's outside, please come in," she called out. "It can't be comfortable on that cold, dark landing."

Skif chuckled, and pushed the door open all the way, to see Talia regarding him with her head tilted to one side and an expectant look on her face. "I never could fool you, could I?"

"Skif!" she exclaimed with delight, and held out both arms to him. "I hadn't expected you back this soon!"

"Oh, you know me—a box of soap and a spare uniform, and I'm ready to go." He embraced her very carefully, and kissed her forehead, before sitting on the floor next to her couch. "And where Skif is—seeing as we went to the same destination—can Dirk be far behind?"

"*You* tell *me*." He was pleased to see her eyes light with carefully contained joy.

"Well, he's not. Far behind, that is. He planned to stay one day longer, but if I'm any judge, he'll have made that up on the road. I wouldn't be surprised to see him here this afternoon. Dear heart, I'm glad to see you want him again."

Her eyes glowed, and she smiled. "I didn't fool you either, did I?"

"Not a bit. That's why I came up with the notion of sending him home to tell his family in person. I could see all that old fear of men—and worse—building up in you every time he touched you, and you trying not to show it so that you wouldn't hurt him."

"Oh, Skif—what ever did I do to deserve you? You were right; it was horrible, I felt like I was at war with myself."

"Dearling, I served a Border Sector, remember? *And* my old home neighborhood was a pretty rough place. You weren't the first woman I've seen that was suffering the aftereffects of rape and abuse. I know what the reaction is. I take it you're—"

"Fine. Better than ever; and half-mad with wanting to see him again."

"That's the best news I've had for a long time. Well, don't you want to know how it all went?"

"I'm consumed with curiosity because if I know Dirk, he probably sent his family a two-line note—"I'm getting married. I'll be there in a week,"—and no further explanation whatsoever."

Skif laughed, and admitted that that was just about what Dirk *had* written, word for word. "And a fine turmoil it sent them into, I can tell you! Especially coming on top of the rest of it—well, let me take it from the beginning."

He settled himself a bit more comfortably. "We got to the farm just about a week after we left here, and it was hard riding all the way. Dirk didn't want to spend any more time traveling than he had to; well, I can't say as I much blame him. When we got there, the entire clan was out waiting for us, since they'd had the children playing lookout ever since his message. Holy Stars, what a mob! You're going to like them, heartsister, they're all as mad as he is. They got us separated almost at once; the younglings plying me with food and drink while Dirk's mother and father dragged him off for a family conference. I could tell that he'd had them fair worried, especially after the last time—that bitch Naril and the way she played with him—"

"I know all about that. I don't blame them for being worried."

"It didn't help much that he was still a bit thin and worn-looking, I'm sure. They weren't easy to convince that everything was all right, because they had him incommunicado for several hours, at least an hour past supper, and we got there just at lunch. The poor youngsters were at their wit's end, trying to find something to distract me with!" Skif's lips pursed in a mischievous smile. "And I'm afraid I didn't help much. I wasn't cooperating at all. Well, they all finally emerged; Father looked satisfied, but Mother still had doubts in her eyes. They fed us all, then it was *my* turn to come under fire. Let me tell you, Dirk's mother is a lovely lady, and she ought to be put in charge of questioning witnesses; the Truth Spell would become entirely superfluous! By the time she was done with me, she knew everything I've ever known about you, including a lot of things I'd forgotten. We were up practically all night, talking; one of the best conversations I've ever had. I didn't mind in the least, she's such a dear. It was worth every yawn to see the worry going out of her eyes, the more I told her."

Talia sighed, and Skif could feel her relief and gratitude as she wordlessly squeezed his hand. "I can't tell you how glad I was that you insisted on going with him. You're a good friend to both of us."

"Hm—you'll be even gladder, I think—none of them are going to be able to be here for the wedding. That's what I meant by 'coming on top of all the rest of it.' "

"What's happened?" she asked anxiously.

"His third sister is having a real problem with this child she's bearing. She can't travel, obviously, her older sisters don't want to leave her. Needless to say, her mother, as Healer as well as parent, feels obligated to stay. And Dirk's father's joint problem is so bad he can't even take long wagon journeys anymore, never mind riding. I did my best to assure them that you wouldn't feel slighted or insulted if they didn't come, given the circumstances."

"I'd never forgive myself if they *had* come, and something had gone wrong at home while they were here."

"Well, that's what I told them. By the next day, we were all good friends, and I was part of the family. Then I had the hardest task I've ever faced. They asked me about Kris."

He looked at his hands, his voice fogged a little with tears. "I—they loved him, little sister. He was like another son to them. I've never had to tell anyone how their son died before."

He felt her hand lightly on his shoulder, and looked up. The sadness that never quite left her face was plain in her eyes. A single tear slid slowly down her cheek, and she did not trouble to wipe it away. He reached up, and brushed it away with gentle fingers.

"I miss him," she said simply. "I miss him every day. If it weren't for what I felt when he—left—it would be unbearable. At least—I know he must be happy. I have that. They don't even have that much comfort."

"I'm glad I got Dirk to go home for that reason, too," Skif replied quietly. "Kris was something special to him—more than a friend, more than anyone else could ever be, I think. When he finally let himself grieve, he needed his family around him . . . ."

He took both of her hands in his own and they sat in silence for long moments, mourning their loss.

"Well," he coughed a little, "I wish you had the leisure to wait on this until you were entirely well again."

"I know. So do I," Talia sighed. "But as soon as I can use my feet again, I *have* to return to duty; in fact, Selenay wrote me herself yesterday that if it weren't so damnably painful for me to move, she'd have me on duty now."

"I know, too. Well, it can't be helped. Listen—I have *got* to tell you what that tribe is like—" Skif launched into a series of affectionate descriptions of the various members of Dirk's family, and had the pleasure of seeing some of the sorrow leave her eyes.

"So that's the last of them," he concluded. Then he noticed a basket of sewing beside her—and none of the garments were her own! "What's all this?" he asked, holding up an enormous shirt with both sleeves pulling out.

Talia blushed a charming crimson. "I can't go anywhere except this couch or my bed. I'm tired of reading, I can't handle my harp very long without hurting myself, and I can't stand having nothing to do. I suppose it goes back to my farmgirl days, when I wasn't even allowed to read without having a task in my hands. So since my embroidery is bad enough to make a cat laugh, I made Elspeth hunt out all of Dirk's clothing, and I've been mending it. I can't keep him from looking rumpled, but at least I can keep him from looking like a rag-bag!"

Before Skif could tease her further, the sound of a familiar footstep—taking the tower stairs three at a time—caused her to direct all her attention to the open door, her visitor momentarily forgotten.

There was no mistaking it—it could only be Dirk. Skif

bounced to his feet and took himself out of the way before Dirk reached the door, not wanting to intrude on their greeting. Every time Dirk had spoken of Talia when he'd been with his family, he'd practically glowed. It had been that, at least in part, that had convinced them that all was well. Well, if Skif had thought he'd glowed when he only spoke of Talia, he was incandescent when he saw her waiting for him, with both her hands stretched yearningly out toward him. A quick glance at her proved that she was equally radiant.

Dirk was across the room in a few steps and went to one knee beside her, taking both her hands in his and kissing them gently. What would have been a hopelessly melodramatic scene for anyone else seemed natural for them. Talia drew his hands toward her and laid her cheek against them, and the expression on her face made Skif hold his breath and freeze absolutely still lest he break the mood.

"Has it been very bad, my love?" Dirk asked, so softly Skif could barely make out the words.

"I don't know—while you were gone, all I could think of was how I wished you were here; and now you're here, I'm too busy being glad you're with me," she replied teasingly.

"Why then I must needs find a way to shrink thee, and carry thee in my pocket always," he said tenderly, falling into the speech-mode of his childhood.

Talia freed one hand from his and laid it softly along his cheek. "Would not having me in thy pocket soon make thee tired of my company?"

"Not so long as it spares thee any pain at all. Oh, have a care to thyself, little bird!" he murmured. "Thou hast my soul in thy keeping, and without thee, I would be nothing but an empty, dead shell!"

His tone was jesting, but the light in his eyes said that he spoke nothing less than the truth.

"Oh, beloved, then we are surely lost beyond redemption," she whispered "for in truth I find myself in the like case. Thou hast mine in trade for thine."

Their joy in each other seemed to brighten the very air around them.

Skif soon realized, however, that it is only possible to go without breathing for a limited amount of time. On the other hand, he couldn't bear the notion that his interference would break the mood of the two before him.

"Dearest," Talia said with laughter in her voice. "my brotherling Skif is trying to decide between disturbing us and fainting from lack of air—"

Dirk chuckled, and turned his head slightly so that he could see Skif out of the corner of his eye. "Thought I hadn't noticed you were there, did you? Come out of your corner, and stop pretending you're here to pick pockets!"

To Skif's intense relief, the mood had *not* broken. Perhaps the glow had been dimmed a little, but if so, it had been a deliberate action on their part, to make it easier for him. As he took a chair and pulled it nearer to the couch, Dirk removed the pillows behind Talia and took their place. Now she was leaning on his chest and shoulder instead, one of his arms protectively circling her. The vague shadow of anxiety was gone from his face, and the pain that had faintly echoed in her eyes was gone as well. There was a "rightness" about them that defied analysis.

No sooner were they all settled again when more footsteps could be heard running up the stairs. Elspeth came bursting into the room, her arms full of glorious scarlet silk.

"Talia, the dresses are done! Has—" She stopped short at the sight of Dirk, and gave a whoop of joy. She threw the dress at Skif (who caught it gingerly), and danced around to grab both of Dirk's ears and plant an enthusiastic kiss squarely on his mouth.

"Well!" he said, when he could finally speak. "If that's how I'm going to get greeted on my return, I'm going to go away more often!"

"Oh, horse manure," Elspeth giggled, then rescued Skif from the folds of the dress, and planted an equally enthusiastic kiss on his mouth. "I'm just glad to see you for Talia's sake. She's been drooping like a wilted lily since you left!"

"Elspeth!" Talia protested.

"I'm *just* as glad to see Skif. More—he can help me. Or hadn't you heard, oh, cloud-scraper? You get to help me with putting this wedding together. Talia can't, and Dirk hasn't been here."

"And besides that, Dirk has no idea of what is supposed to go on at weddings," Dirk said ruefully. "If you told me I was supposed to suspend myself by my knees from a treelimb, I'd probably believe you."

"Oooh—what a wonderful opportunity!" Elspeth sparkled with mischief. "Maybe I'll do that. No, I'd better not. Talia might tell you to beat me."

"I'd do worse than have Dirk beat you," Talia twinkled back. "I'd tell Alberich that I thought you were shirking your practices."

"You *are* a beast, aren't you? Are you safe to hug, dearling?"

"As of this morning, quite safe."

With that assurance, Elspeth bent over the Heralds and hugged Talia with warmth and enthusiasm, then tweaked Dirk's nose with an impudent grin.

"I have been wanting to do that for *eons*," she said, snatching a pillow from the pile that Dirk had displaced and seating herself on the floor at Talia's feet.

"The hug, or the nose?" Dirk asked.

"Both—but the hug more," she turned to Skif. "You wouldn't know, since you were gone, too—but you hardly knew where you could touch her, at first. Poor Dirk, practically all he could touch were her fingertips before he left!"

"Oh, I found a *few* other places," Dirk chuckled, and Talia blushed furiously. "So tell me, what new and wonderful plans for this fiasco have you managed to crush since I've been gone?"

"You'll adore this one—and it's new today. The Lord Marshal thought it would be a grand idea to load Talia up on a flower-bedecked platform and carry her to the priest on the shoulders of half the Heralds in the Kingdom. You know, like the image of the Goddess in a Midsummer pageant."

"Oh, *no!*" Talia plainly was torn between laughter and embarrassment.

"Oh, *yes!* And once I'd managed to convince him that poor Talia would probably die of mortification if anyone even suggested it, the Lord Patriarch came storming in, demanding to know why the thing wasn't being held in the High Temple!"

"Lord of Lights!"

"After I'd told him that since the Companions had a big part in the rescue, they were being invited, too, he agreed that the High Temple probably wasn't the best site."

"I can just see Dantris helping himself to the Goddess' lilies out of sheer mischief," Dirk muttered.

"Dantris? Bright Havens, love, Rolan and Ahrodie would probably decide to watch from the choir loft and leave hoofmarks all over the hardwood floor!" Talia replied. "And to think that all I ever wanted was a private pledging with a few friends."

"Then you shouldn't have been Chosen Queen's Own," Elspeth told her sweetly. "You're a figure of national importance, so you can't begrudge people their fun any more than I can."

"And I suppose it's too late to back out now."

"Out of the wedding, or being Queen's Own?" Dirk chuckled.

"Guess."

"I'd rather not. I might not like the answer."

"Look," Elspeth interjected, "since Skif is right here now, why don't I drag him off and tell him what I've gotten set up so far? That way we won't be interrupted."

"Good idea," Dirk approved.

Elspeth gathered up her dress and drew Skif with her into the bedroom, shutting the door after them.

"I really don't need any help in getting these things organized, but let's pretend I do, all right? And let's take lots of time about it," Elspeth said in a low voice. "Being Heir has *some* advantages. As long as it's me that's up here, nobody is going to come bursting in on them the way they do when the Healers aren't with her. You'd think people would give them a *little* time alone! But even though he's just gotten back, they won't."

"But—why?"

"Why are people always up here? A lot of reasons. The Lord Marshal always manages to think up something more about Ancar he'd like to know. Kyril and Hyron are always asking about Hulda. Only the gods know what her powers could mean. Even her friends, Lady bless 'em, are always coming in to 'make sure that she's all right.' Havens, I'm as bad as they are! Here, as long as you're here, you can help me—I want to show this off." She hid behind the wardrobe door for a moment, emerging in the scarlet dress. "Lace me up, would you? Then there's the emergencies, though gods be thanked we haven't had any really bad ones, like the backlash of a Herald getting killed." Her face clouded, "Except for poor Nessa. Well, Talia fixed that quickly enough, once she was well enough to handle it."

"Gods, does everyone in the world pop in and out of here?"

"Sometimes it seems that way. You know, I don't think anyone ever really realized how *many* lives she's touched until we thought we'd lost her. That dress, for instance—have you ever seen anything like that fabric in your life?"

"Never." Skif admired the gown, with an eye trained by thieving to evaluate it; it was of scarlet silk, and patterned through the scarlet of the main fabric were threads of pure gold and deep vermilion. It was incredible stuff.

"Neither have I—and I have seen a *lot* of Court gowns. It came by special messenger, after Dirk had them keep watch for the trader who smuggled in the argonel and the arrows to her, then got the message out to Rolan. Dirk was hoping he could find him and thank him, and let him know she was all right. Well, he managed to get back across the Border before Ancar closed his side, and he got Dirk's message and sent this in reply. The note that went with it said that among his people the bride always wore scarlet, and while he knew that this would not be the case among us, he hoped his 'little gift' could be put to good use. 'Little gift!' Mother said that the last time she saw anything like this it was priced at a rate that would purchase a small town!" Elspeth finished tying up the laces in back. "Talia thought it would be lovely to use it for attendants' dresses. *I* am not going to argue with her! Mother would never get me anything like this unless they discovered diamonds growing on the trees in Sorrows!" She wiggled sensuously. "Then there was the other truly strange gift. Did she ever tell you about the woman she helped up in Berrybay? The one they called 'Weatherwitch'?"

"A bit."

"Out of the blue came this really *elderly* Herald—I mean, he was *supposed* have retired, that's how old. He came with a message from this Weatherwitch person— the *exactly* perfect day to have the wedding, and you know fall weather. Since we're having it outside, we'd been a good bit worried about that. Talia says Maeven's never wrong, so that's why we're having it then."

She pressed her ear briefly against the door and giggled. "I think it's safe enough to go out now, but I'll bet it wasn't a few minutes ago. Let's go show off."

As far as Skif could tell, neither Talia nor Dirk had moved an inch since they'd left them—although Talia's hair was a trifle mussed, and both of them wore preoccupied and dreaming expressions.

"Well, what do you think?" Elspeth asked, posing dramatically.

"I think it looks wonderful. No one in their right mind is going to be watching me with you and Jeri around," Talia said admiringly.

"Well, Elspeth and I are agreed; we'll take care of the wedding arrangements," Skif said with a proprietary air. "That will free you up a bit more, Dirk—that is, if you don't mind."

"I don't mind at all, and I think it's very good of you," Dirk replied, surprised. "Especially since you know very well that I don't have to be freed up to do anything except spend more time up here."

"That *was* the general idea," Elspeth said mockingly.

"Enough, enough! It's settled then," he laughed, "and much thanks to you both."

"Remember that the next time I do something wrong!" Elspeth giggled back.

She teased Dirk for a few moments longer—then her face clouded with anxiety when she realized that Talia had fallen asleep. She'd been doing that a great deal lately, sometimes right in the middle of a conversation. Elspeth was afraid that this was a sign that she would never be quite well again.

But Dirk and Skif just exchanged amused glances while Dirk settled the sleeping Herald a little more comfortably on his shoulder. Elspeth heaved an audible sigh of relief at this; surely if anyone would know if something were wrong, Dirk would.

Dirk hadn't missed the anxious look or the sigh of relief.

"It's nothing important," he told her; quietly, to avoid waking Talia.

"He's right—honestly!" Skif assured her. "Dirk's mother told us she'll be dropping off like this. It's just a side-effect of speed-Healing. It has something to do with all the energy you're using, and all the strain you're putting on yourself. She says it's the same kind of effect you'd get if you ran twenty or thirty miles, swam a river, and climbed a mountain or two, then stayed up three days straight."

"According to mother," Dirk continued, "It has to do with—fatigue poisons?—I think that's what she called them. When you speed-Heal, they build up faster than the body can get rid of them, and the person you're Healing tends to fall asleep a lot. When they stop the speed-Healing, she'll stop falling asleep all the time."

"Show-off," Skif taunted.

Dirk grinned and shrugged. "See all the useless information you pick up when you're a Healer's offspring?"

Elspeth protested; "Useless, my eye! I thought for sure there was something wrong that nobody wanted to tell me about—like there was when she wouldn't wake up. Nobody ever thinks to tell me *anything* anymore!"

"Well, imp," Dirk retorted, "That's the price you pay for poking your nose into things all the time. People think you already know everything!"

The Border was officially closed, but refugees kept slipping across every night, each of them with a worse tale to tell than the last. Selenay had had a premonition that Ancar wasn't quite through with Valdemar, and had stayed on the Border with a force built mainly of the defectors from Hardorn's army, now fanatically devoted to her. She had been absolutely right.

This time the attack came at night, preceded by a storm Selenay suspected of being mage-caused. There was a feint in the direction of the Border Guardpost, a strong enough feint that it would have convinced most leaders that the attack there was genuine.

But Selenay had Davan—a Farseer—and Alberich—a Foreseer—with her, and knew better. Ancar meant to regain some of his lost soldiers—and plant some traitors in Selenay's new Border Guards. And to do both, he was going to use some of the *other* talents of what was left of his army of thieves and murderers.

But the force of black-clad infiltrators who attempted to penetrate the stockade-enclosed village that housed the defectors and their dependents met with a grave surprise.

They got all the way to the foot of the stockade, when suddenly—

Light! Blinding light burst above their heads, light nearly as bright as day. As they cringed, and looked up through watering eyes, four white-clad figures appeared above them, and out of the darkness at the top of the stockade fence rose hundreds of angry men and women armed with bows, who in no way wished to return to the man who called himself their King. Suspended from the trees by thin wires were burning balls of some unknown substance that flamed with a white ferocity.

"You could have knocked," Griffon called down to them, "We'd have been glad to let you in."

"But perhaps it is that this is no friendly visit—" Alberich dodged as one of those below threw a knife at him in desperation.

"B'God, Alberich, I believe you might be right," Davan dodged a second missile. "Majesty?"

"Take them," Selenay ordered shortly.

A few were taken alive; what they had to tell was interesting. More interesting by far was the assortment of drugs and potions they had intended to use on the village well. Drugs that, according to those Selenay questioned under Truth Spell, would open the minds of those that took them to the influence of Ancar's mages—and Ancar himself.

That told them much about what Ancar was currently able to accomplish. What happened next on Ancar's side of the Border told them more.

He fortified it, created a zone a mile deep in which he allowed neither farm nor dwelling place—then left it. And neither Foreseer nor Farseer could see him doing anything offensive for some time.

So for the moment, Ancar's knife was no longer at Valdemar's throat—and Selenay felt free to come home to resume her Throne, and in time for Talia's wedding.

Companion's Field was the only suitable place within easy reach of the Collegium that could hold all the people expected to attend. The wedding site had to be within easy reach, because Talia's feet were still not healed. The Healers were satisified that the bones had all set well (after so many sessions of arranging the tiny fragments that nonHealers had begun to wonder if her feet would ever be usable) but they had only begun to knit, and she had been absolutely forbidden to put one ounce of weight on them. That meant that wherever she needed to go, she had to be carried.

The Healers had chosen not to put the kind of plaster casts on her that they had used to hold Keren's broken hip in place. This was mostly because they needed to be able to monitor the Healing they were doing on a much finer level than they had with Keren, but also partially because such casts would have been a considerable burden on a body already heavily taxed and exhausted. Instead they constructed stiff half-boots of glue, wood strips, and hardened leather, all lined with lambswool felt. These had been made in two halves that laced together and could be removed at will. Talia had been much relieved by this solution, needless to say.

"Can you imagine trying to bathe with those plaster things on your feet?" she'd said with a comical expression. "Or trying to find some way of covering them during the wedding? Or finding someone strong enough to carry me and all that damned plaster as well?"

"Not to mention Dirk's displeasure at trying to deal with them afterward—" Elspeth had teased, while Talia blushed.

Elspeth was waiting in Talia's room, watching Keren and Jeri put the final touches on her hair and face. The Heir privately thought that Talia was lovely enough to make anyone's heart break. She was still thin, and very pale from her ordeal, but that only served to make her more attractive, in an odd way. It was rather as if she'd been distilled into the true essence of herself—or tempered and honed like an heirloom blade. They'd taken great pains with her dress of white silk and silver, designing something that draped well when the wearer was being carried and extended past her feet to cover the ugly leather boots. By the same token, nothing would fall far enough to the floor that the person carrying her would be likely to trip over it. Jeri had given her a very simple hairstyle to complement the simplicity of the dress, and her only ornaments were fresh flowers.

" 'Nobody in their right mind is going to look at me with you and Jeri around,' " Elspeth quoted to Keren under her breath, her eyes sparkling with laughter. "Bright Havens, next to her I look like a half-fledged red heron!"

"I hope after all this time you women are finally ready," Dirk announced as he came through the door, for once in his life totally immaculate, and resplendent in white velvet.

"*Dirk!*" Jeri laughed, interposing herself between him

and Talia. "Tradition says you're not supposed to see the bride until you meet before the priest!"

"Tradition be damned. The only reason I'm letting Skif carry her at all is because if I try and manage her *and* her ring, I'll drop one of the two!"

"Oh, all right. I can see you're too stubborn to argue with." She stepped aside, and at the sight of one another, they seemed to glow from deep within.

"Two hours I spend on her—" Jeri muttered under her breath, obviously amused, "—and in two eyeblinks *he* makes everything I did look insignificant."

Dirk gathered her up carefully, holding her in his arms as if she weighed next to nothing. "Ready, loveling?" he asked softly.

"I've been ready forever," she replied, never once taking her eyes from his.

The Field was alive with color; Healer Green, Bard Scarlet, Guard Blue—the muted grays, pale greens and red-brown of the students moving among them, the gilded and bejeweled courtiers catching the sun. Most prevalent, of course, was Heraldic White, and not just because even more Heralds had managed to appear for this occasion than had arrived for Elspeth's fealty ceremony. Half of the white figures in the crowd were Companions, be-flowered and be-ribboned by the loving hands of their Chosen, and looking for all the world as if it were *they* who were being wedded. Even Cymry's foal had a garland—though he kept trying to eat it.

The ceremony was a simple one, though it was not one that was often performed—for the wedding of a lifebonded couple was less of a promising than an affirmation. Despite well-meaning efforts to the contrary, Skif and Elspeth had managed to keep the pomp and ritual to an absolute minimum.

Dirk carried his love as far as the priest, handing her very carefully to Skif, who felt proud and happy enough when he did so to burst. Elspeth gave him Talia's ring, and he slipped it onto her finger. Skif and Elspeth both bit their lips to keep from shedding a tear or two at that moment; partially because she'd moved Kris' friendship

ring to the finger next to it, and partially because the
wedding ring was still so large for her.

Dirk repeated his vows in a voice that seemed soft, but
carried to the edge of the crowd. Then Talia took his ring
from Keren, slipped it onto his ring-finger and made her
own vows in her clear, sweet voice.

Dirk took her back from Skif—and as he did so, the
massed Heralds cheered spontaneously.

Somehow, it seemed totally appropriate.

The wedded couple was enthroned on a pile of cushions brought by every hand in the Collegium, with Talia
arranged so that she could see everything without having
to strain herself. Elcarth waited until most of the well-
wishers had cleared away, and Talia and Dirk were pretty
much alone before strolling over to them.

He shook his head at the sight. "I hope you two realize
this display of yours is fevering the imaginations of an
entire generation of Bards," he said with mock-severity.
"I hesitate to think of all the the truly awful creations
we'll have to suffer through for the next year from the
students alone—and every full Bard is going to be determined that *he* will be the writer of the next 'Sun and
Shadow.' "

"Oh, gods," Dirk groaned, "I never thought of that.
D'you suppose I could give her back?"

Talia eyed him speculatively. "We *could* always have a
horrible fight here and now." She hefted a wine bottle,
appraising its weight. "This would make a lovely dent in
his skull—not to mention the truly spectacular effect it
will have when the bottle breaks and the red wine splashes
all over that spotless white velvet." She considered it and
him for a long moment, then sighed. "No, it just won't
do. I might get some of the wine on me. And if I knock
him cold, how will I get back to my room?"

"And if I give her away, who will I sleep with tonight?"
Dirk added, as Talia giggled. "Sorry, Elcarth. You're
just going to have to suffer. What can we do for you?"

"Actually, there is something. I wanted to let you both
know what the Circle has decided about Dirk's assignments."

*   *   *

Talia stiffened a little, but otherwise gave no sign that she was dreading what Elcarth's next words might contain.

"First of all—I am retiring as Dean. I intend to stay on as Historian, but to handle both positions is a little more than I can manage these days. I'm a lot older than I look, I'm afraid, and I'm beginning to feel the years. Teren is replacing me. Dirk, *you* are replacing Teren as Orientation instructor, as well as working with training students in their Gifts."

Talia was stunned; she'd expected to learn that he was being given a new partner, or that he would be assigned Sector duty at the least. She had partially resigned herself to the idea, telling herself that having him part of the time was a distinct improvement over not having him at all.

"Elcarth—you can't be serious—" Dirk protested. "I'm no kind of a scholar, you know that! If the Circle is trying to do us a favor by giving us preferential treatment . . ."

"Then we'd rather you didn't," Talia finished for him.

"My dear children! It is *not* preferential treatment that you are getting. Dirk, you will still be expected to take on the kinds of special jobs you used to, make no mistake about it. The only thing we're really pulling you off is riding the problem Sectors. We've picked you to replace Teren for the same reason we picked him to replace Werda as Orientation instructor; your ability to handle children. Both of you are able to take confused, frightened children and give them warmth, reassurance, and the certain knowledge that they are in a place where they belong and have friends. Dirk, you have demonstrated that over and over in training Gifts—the way you brought Griffon along, giving him confidence without once making him feel that his Gift was a frightening or dangerous one, was nothing short of masterful—and look at the result! He trusted you so completely that he linked with you without asking the why or wherefore; he trusted you enough to follow your directions exactly, and now Griffon is the unsung hero of the Battle of Demons. That kind of ability in a teacher is much rarer than scholasticism, and it's one we need. So let's hear no more about 'preferential treatment,' shall we?"

Dirk sighed with relief, and his arm tightened around Talia. She thanked Elcarth with her shining eyes; no words were necessary.

"That isn't *quite* all. You'll also be working with Kyril—Dirk on a regular basis, Talia as time permits. This is the first we've ever heard of the Companions augmenting anyone's abilities purposefully except in chronicles so old we can't winnow fable from truth; we'd like to know if it's something that any Herald can take advantage of, or if it's something peculiar to you two and Elspeth, or even if it's peculiar to your Companions. Before Kyril's through with you, you may wish yourself back in the field again!"

They laughed a little ruefully; Kyril drove himself mercilessly in the cause of investigating Heraldic Gifts, and would expect no less from them.

"Last of all, I bring your wedding gift from the Circle; the next two weeks are yours to do with as you like. We can all get along without either of you for that long. Talia still has to have her sessions with the Healers, of course, but barring that—well, if you should choose to vanish on a few overnight trips, no one will come looking for you. After all, Talia, you may not be able to walk, but you can certainly ride! Just make sure you schedule everything with your Healers. The last thing I need or want is to have Devan after my head! That man can be positively vicious!"

Talia laughed, and promised; she could tell by the speculative glint in Dirk's eyes that he already had a destination or two in mind. They traded a few more pleasantries with Elcarth, then the Historian—Dean no longer, and that would take some getting used to—took himself off.

Dirk shook his head. "I never, ever pictured myself as a teacher," he said quietly. "That was always Kr—"

He choked off the end of the name.

"That was what Kris wanted," Talia finished, watching him. "You've been avoiding speaking about him, love. Why?"

"Fear," he replied frankly. "Fear that I'd hurt you—

fear I'd be hurt myself. I—I still don't really know how you felt about each other—"

"All you ever had to do was ask," she said softly, and drew him into rapport with gentle mental fingers.

After a moment he raised his eyes to hers and smiled. "And you said emotions don't speak clearly. So that's how it was?"

She nodded. "No more, no less. He tried to tell you, but you weren't hearing."

"I wasn't, was I?" He sighed. "Gods—I miss him. I miss him so damn much. . . ."

"We lost more than a friend when we lost him," she said, hesitating over the words. "I think—I think we lost a part of ourselves."

He was silent for a long moment. "Talia, what happened after he died? You said some very strange things when you answered my call and came back to us."

She shook her head slightly, her brow wrinkled in thought. "Love, I'm not sure. It's not very clear, and it's all mixed up with pain and fever and drug-dreams. All I can tell you for certain is that I *wanted* to die, and I *should* have died—but something kept me from dying."

"Or someone."

"Or someone," she agreed. "Maybe it *was* Kris. That's who my memories say it was."

"I have a lot to thank him for, and not just that," he said thoughtfully.

"Hm?"

"You learned from him about loving before those beasts hurt you."

"It helped," she said, after a long moment of thought.

"Loveling, are you ready to go through with this?" he asked after a pause. "Are you sure?"

For answer she kissed him with rapport still strung between them. When they came up for air he chuckled, much more relaxed.

"Hedonist," he said.

"At least," she agreed, wrinkling her nose at him, then sobered again. "Yes, there are scars—but you have them, too. The wounds are healed—I'm not the only Healer of minds, you know—just the only one that's a Herald as well. Rynee—she's very good, as good as I am. Besides, I refuse to let what happened ruin what's between us— and really, all they did was hurt my body, they didn't touch *me*. What happened to you was worse—Naril raped your soul."

"That's healed, too," he said quietly.

"Then leave it in the dead past. No one goes through life without picking up a scar or two." She nestled closer to him as someone else came to offer their congratulations.

Then suddenly sat up. "Gods!"

"What?" Dirk asked, anxious until he saw that there was no sign of pain on her face. "What is it?"

"Back on my internship—that business with Maeven Weatherwitch—she ForeSaw something for me, and I couldn't even guess what she meant, then. *Now* I know! She said that I would see the Havens but that love and duty would bar me from them—and—"

She faltered.

"And?" he prompted, gently.

"That—my greatest joy would be preceded by my greatest grief. Oh, gods—if only I'd known—if only I'd *guessed*—"

"You could never have anticipated what happened," Dirk replied with such force that she shook off her anguish to stare at him. "*No one* could. Don't ever blame yourself. Don't you think that with all the ForeSeers among the Heralds if there had been any way of preventing what happened it would have been done?"

She sighed, and relaxed again. "You're right . . ." she said, slowly. "You're right."

The celebrating continued on well past dusk, until at last, by ones and twos, the wedding guests began to drift away. Some were heading for other gatherings—like the one Talia and Dirk knew their fellow Heralds *must* be having somewhere. Some had more private affairs in mind. Finally Talia and Dirk were left alone, a state with which they were not at all displeased.

She rested contentedly on his shoulder, both of his arms lightly around her, and watched the stars blossoming overhead.

"It's getting chilly," she said at last.

"Are you cold?"

"A little."

"Well," he chuckled, "They've certainly made it easy for us to depart unnoticed."

"I'm fairly certain that was on purpose. All that cheering was embarrassing enough, without chivaree, too."

"It could have been worse. Think of the flower-bedecked platform! Think of Companions in the High Temple! Think of the life-sized sugar replicas of both of us!"

"I'd rather not!" She laughed.

"Ready to go?"

"Yes," she said, putting her arms around his neck so that he could lift her.

He took her up the stairs to her rooms—now *their* rooms—this time taking them one at a time, and slowly, so as not to jar her.

To their mutual surprise, they found Elspeth seated on the top step.

"What on earth are you doing here?" he asked.

"Guarding your threshold, oh, magnificent one. It was the students' idea. We took it turn and turn about since you left this morning. Except for during the ceremony itself that is—we left the staircase booby-trapped then. Not that we're suspicious of anyone, mind, but we did want to make certain no one could get in to play any little tricks while you were gone. Some people have very rotten ideas about what's funny. Anyway, that's *our* wedding present." With that, she skipped down the stairs without waiting for thanks.

" 'The caring heart,' " Talia said softly. "She'll be a good Queen, one day."

Dirk nudged the door open with his foot, placed Talia carefully on her couch inside, then turned to close it and throw the latch.

"Not that *I'm* suspicious of anyone," he said with a gleam in his eye, "but a certain earlier performance of yours makes me wish to be certain that we're undisturbed."

"Not *quite* yet," she said with a smile. "First I've got a bride-gift for you."

"A what?"

"One *good* custom of my people. The bride always has a gift for her husband. It's over there—on the hearth."

"But—" for a moment he was speechless. "Talia, that's My Lady. She's *your* harp, I couldn't take her!"

"Look again."

He did—and realized that there was a second harp hidden in the shadows. He pulled both of them out into the light and scrutinized them closely.

"I can't tell them apart," he admitted at last.

"Well, I can, but I've had My Lady for years, I know every line of her grain. No one else can, though. They're twins, made by the same hand, from the same wood; they're even the same age. No—" she held up a warning hand. "Don't ask me where or how I found it. That's *my* secret. But in return for this one, you'll have to promise to teach me to play My Lady as well as she deserves to be played."

"Willingly—gladly. We can play duets—like—"

"Like you and Kris used to play," she finished for him when he could not. "Love—I think it's time for one last gift—" and she touched his mind, sharing with him the incredulous joy that had marked Kris' passing.

"Gods—oh, gods, that helps . . . you must know how much that helps," he managed after a moment. "Now if only—I wish I could know for certain that he knows about us—about now."

He lifted her from the couch to move to the bedroom.

"If I were to have one wish granted, that would be mine, too," she replied, her cheek resting against the velvet of his tunic. "He told me once that it was his own dearest wish to see the two people he loved most find happiness with each other—"

She would have said more, but a familiar perfume wreathed around her, and she gasped.

"What's wrong? Did you hurt something?" Dirk asked anxiously.

"There—on the bed—"

Lying on the coverlet, in the middle and heart-high, was a spray of the little flowers known as Maiden's Hope. Dirk set her down on the bed and she picked it up with trembling hands.

"Did you put this here?" she asked in a voice that shook.

"No."

"And no one else has been here since we left—" In hushed tones she continued: "When Kris gave me this ring, it was around a Midsummer bouquet of those flowers. I'd never smelled anything like them before—and he promised he'd find some for my wedding garland if he had to grow them himself—but I've never seen them anywhere around here—"

"There's more to it than that, little bird," Dirk said, taking the flowers from her and regarding them with wondering eyes. "This flower *only* blooms for the week before and after Midsummer. We're well into fall. They can't be grown in hothouses. People have tried. To find even one bloom, much less as many as this, would take a miracle. No human could do it."

They looked from the flowers to each other—and slowly began to smile; smiles that, for the first time in weeks, had no underlying hint of sadness.

Dirk took her into his arms, with the flowers held between them. "We've had our wish—shall we give him his?"

She carefully reached behind her, and inserted the blossoms into the vase on her nightstand.

"Yes," she breathed, turning back to him, and beginning to touch him with her rapport even as she touched her lips to his, "I think we should."

APPENDIX
Songs of Valdemar

HER FATHER'S EYES

Lyrics: Mercedes Lackey   Music: Kristoph Klover

(Selenay: *Arrows of the Queen*)

How tenuous the boundary between love and hate—
How easy to mistake the first, and learn the truth too
  late—
How hard to bear what brings to mind mistakes that we
  despise—
And when I look into her face, I see her father's eyes.

He tried to steal away my throne—he tried to rule my
  life—
And I am not made to forgive, a cowed and coward wife!
My love became my enemy who sought his Queen's
  demise—
And when I look into her face, I see her father's eyes.

Poor child, we battled over her as two dogs with a
  bone—
I should not see his treachery in temper-tantrums
  thrown—
I should not see betrayal where there's naught but
  childish lies—
But when I look into her face, I see her father's eyes.

Now how am I to deal with this rebellion in my soul?

I cannot treat her fairly when my own heart is not whole.
I truly wish to love her—but I'm not so strong, nor wise—
For when I look into her face, I see her father's eyes—
Only—her father's eyes.

FIRST LOVE

Lyrics: Mercedes Lackey   Music: Frank Hayes

(Jadus: *Arrows of the Queen*)

Was it so long ago now that we met, you and I?
Both held fast in a passion that we could not deny?
If my hands gave you life, then your voice woke my
    heart—
From such simple beginnings, how such wonder may start!

Chorus:
Through my long, empty nights, through my cold, lonely
    days,
How you comfort and cheer me, delight and amaze—
And your soft silver voice could charm life into stone—
My sweet mistress of music, My Lady, my own.

With your sweet song to guide me you have taught me
    to care
How to open my soul to both love and despair
Though you're wood and bright silver, and not warm flesh
    and bone
I think no one here doubts you've a soul of your own.

And I know my own journey will too soon reach its end—
I must leave you with one I am proud to call friend.
How she opened my life when she opened my door!
Give her comfort, my dear one, when I am no more.

HOLDERKIN SHEEP-SONG

Lyrics: Mercedes Lackey   Music: Ernie Mansfield

(Talia: *Arrows of the Queen*)

Silly sheep
Go to sleep.
We will watch around you keep
Though the night be dark and deep
Nothing past us dares to creep
Go to sleep.

Wooly heads
Have no dreads
Though we'd rather seek out beds
And our eyes are dull as leads
And we long for hearths and Steads
Have no dreads.

Do not fear
We are here
Though this watch is lone and drear
Lacking in all warmth and cheer
Till the morn again draws near
We are here.

In the night
Stars shine bright
And the moon is at her height
Lending us her little light
Nothing comes to give you fright
Stars shine bright.

With the day
We'll away
Leaving you to greet the day
Other shepherds watch you play
Keep you safe from all that prey
We'll away.

Silly sheep
Go to sleep.
We will watch around you keep
Go to sleep.
Go to sleep.

IT WAS A DARK AND STORMY NIGHT

Lyrics: Mercedes Lackey   Music: Leslie Fish

(Talia: *Arrows of the Queen*)

It was a dark and stormy night—or so the Heralds say—
And lightning striking constantly transformed the night
    to day
The thunder roared the castle round—or thusly runs the
    tale—
And rising from the Northeast Tower there came a fear-
    ful wail.

It was no beast nor banshee that, the castle folk knew
    well,
Nor prisoner in agony, nor demon trapped by spell,
No ghost that moaned in penance, nor a soul in mortal
    fright—
'Twas just the Countess "singing"—for she practiced ev-
    ery night.

The Countess was convinced that she should have been
    born a Bard
And thus she made the lives of those within her power
    hard.
For they must listen to her sing, and smile at what they
    heard,
And swear she had a golden voice that rivaled any bird.

The Countess was convinced that she had wedded 'neath
    her state
And so the worst lot fell upon her meek and mild mate.

Not only must the Count each night endure her every
    song
But suffer silent her abuse, be blamed for every wrong.

It was a dark and stormy night—or so the Bards aver—
And so perhaps that was the reason why there was no stir
When suddenly the "music" ceased; so when dawn raised
    his head
Within the Tower servants found the Countess stiff and
    dead.

The Heralds came at once to judge if there had been
    foul play.
The questioned all most carefully to hear what they would
    say.
And one fact most astounding to them quickly came to
    light—
That *every* moment of the Count was vouched for on that
    night.

The castle folk by ones and twos came forward on their
    own
To swear the Count had never once that night been all
    alone.
So though the Tower had been locked tight, with two
    keys to the door,
One his, one hers; the Count of guilt was plain absolved
    for sure.

At length the Heralds then pronounced her death as
    "suicide."
And all within the district voiced themselves quite satisified.
It was a verdict, after all, that none wished to refute—
Though no one could imagine why she'd try to eat her
    lute.

MUSINGS

Lyrics: Mercedes Lackey   Music: Mercedes Lackey

(Selenay: *Arrows of the Queen*)

How did you grow so wise, so young?
Tell me Herald, tell me.
How did you grow so wise, so young, Queen's Own?
Where did you learn the words to say
That take my pain and guilt away
And give me strength again today
To sit upon my throne?

How could you be so brave, so young?
Tell me, Herald, tell me.
How could you be so brave, so young, Queen's Own?
How do you overcome your fear?
To know my path was never clear
While knowing Death walks ever near
Would chill me to the bone.

How can you be so kind, so young?
Tell me, Herald, tell me.
How can you be so kind, so young, Queen's Own?
To see the best, and not the worst—
To soothe an anger, pain, or thirst—
To always think of others first
And never self alone.

Where did you learn to love so young?
Tell me Herald, tell me.
Where did you learn to love so young, Queen's Own?
How did you teach your heart to care—
To touch in ways I would not dare?
Oh, where did you find the courage? Where?
Ah, Herald—how you've grown!

PHILOSOPHY

Lyrics: Mercedes Lackey   Music: Kristoph Klover

(Skif: *Arrows of the Queen*)

What's the use of living if you never learn to laugh?
Look at me, I grew up down among the riff and raff
But you won't catch me glooming 'round without a hint
of smile
And when I have to do a thing, I do it right, with style!

Chorus:
'Cause if you're gonna be the one to take that tightrope
walk,
And if you're gonna be the one to make the gossips
talk,
If it's your job to be the one who always takes the
chance,
And if you have to cross thin ice—then cross it in a
dance!

Now take the time when I was "borrowing" a thing or
two—
The owner of the house walked in—well, what was I
to do?
I bowed and said, "Don't stir yourself," before he
raised a shout,
"Thanks for your hospitality, I'll find my own way out!"

I'd just come up a chimney, I was black from head to
toe—
Climbed to the yard to find a watchman—wouldn't you
just know!
But in the dark he took me for a demon, I would bet,
'Cause when I howled and went for him—I think he's
running yet!

Take my Companion—did you know I thought to steal
her too?

This pretty horse out in the street, no owner in my
    view—
I grabbed her reins and hopped aboard, I thought I
    was home free,
Until I looked into her eyes—and now the joke's on
    me!

'Cause now *I've* got to be the one to take that tightrope
    walk
And now *I've* got to be the one who'll make the gossips
    talk,
And it's my job to be the one who always takes the
    chance—
But when I have to cross thin ice, I'll cross it in a
    dance!

LAWS

Lyrics: Mercedes Lackey   Music: Leslie Fish

(Skif: *Arrows of the Queen*)

The Law of the Streetwise is "grab all you can
For there's nothing that's true—nothing lasts."
The Law of the Dodger is "learn all the dirt—
The most pious of priests have their pasts."
The Law of the Grifter is "cheat the fool first
Or the one who'll be cheated is you."
But the Law of the Herald is "give all you can
For some day you will need a gift too."

The Law of the Liar is "there is no truth
It is all shades of meaning and greed."
The Law of the Hopeless is "never believe
For all faith is a hollowed-out reed."
The Law of the Empty is "there's nothing more,
Life is nothing but shadow and air."
But the Law of the Herald is "Seek out and find."
And the Law of the Heralds is "Care."

The Law of the Hunted is "guard your own back,
For the enemy strikes from behind."
The Law of the Greedy is "trust no one else,
Hide and hoard anything that you find."
The Law of the Hater is "crush and destroy,"
And the Law of the Bigot is "kill."
But the Law of the Herald is "faith, hope and trust,"
And the strength of the Herald is will.

All these Laws I have learned from the first to the
    last
From the ones who would teach me they're true—
And full many the ones who taught anger and fear,
But the ones who taught hope—they were few.
And I ask myself, "Which is the Law I must take,
Fitting truth as a hand fits a glove?"
Then I chose, and I never looked back from that day,
For the Law of the Heralds is "Love."

THE FACE WITHIN

Lyrics: Mercedes Lackey   Music: Kristoph Klover and
                                       Larry Warner

(Dirk and Kris: *Arrow's Flight*)

The Weaponsmaster has no heart; his hide is iron-cold
His soul within that hide is steel; or so I have been
    told.
His only care is for your skill, his only love, his own.
And where another has a heart, he has a marble stone.

That's what the common wisdom holds, but common
    is not true.
For there is often truth behind what's in the common
    view.
And so it is the Herald's task that hidden truth to win
To see behind the face without and find the face within.

He goads his students into rage, he drives them into
  pain;
He mocks them and he does not care that tears may
  fall like rain.
He works them when they're weary, and rebukes them
  when they fail—
Cuts them to ribbons with his tongue, as they stand
  meek and pale—

And will our enemies be fair, or come on us behind?
And will they stay their tongues or in their words a
  weapon find?
Or wait till we are rested before making their attacks?
Or will they rather beat us down and then go for our
  backs?

But he has no compassion, does not care for man nor
  beast—
And when a student's gone, he does not notice in the
  least—
And no one calls this man their love, and no one calls
  him friend
And none can judge him by his face, or what he may
  intend.

But I have seen him speak the word that brings hope
  from despair—
Or drop the one-word compliment that makes a student
  care—
And I have seen his sorrow when he hears the Death
  Bell cry—
His soul-deep agony of doubt that nothing can deny—

For on his shoulders rests the job of fitting us for war
With nothing to give him the clue of what to train us
  for.
And if he fails it is not he that pays, but you and I—
And so he dies a little when he hears the Death Bell
  cry.

And now you know the face within hid by the face
  without
The pain that he must harbor, all the guilt and all the
  doubt.
The Weaponsmaster has a heart; so grant his stony mask
For you and I aren't strong enough to bear that kind
  of task.

ARROW'S FLIGHT

Lyrics: Mercedes Lackey   Music: Paul Espinoza

(Talia: *Arrow's Flight*)

Finding your center—not hard for a child—
But I am a woman now, patterned and grown.
Thrown out of balance, my Gift has run wild;
Never have I felt so lost and alone.
Now all the questions that I did not ask
Come back to haunt me by day and by night.
Finding your center—so simple a task—
And one that I fear I shall never set right.

Chorus:
Where has my balance gone, what did I know
That I have forgotten in Time's ebb and flow?
Wrong or right, dark or light, I cannot see—
For I've lost the heart of the creature called "me."

Doubt shatters certainty, fosters despair;
Guilt harbors weakness and fear makes me blind—
Fear of the secrets that I dare not share—
Lost in the spiral maze of my own mind.
Knowing the cost to us all if I fail—
Feeling that failure breathe cold at my back—
All I thought strong now revealed as so frail
That I could not weather one spiteful attack.

An arrow in flight must be sent with control—

But all my control was illusion at best.
Instinct alone cannot captain a soul—
Direction must be learned and not merely guessed.
Seeking with purpose, not flailing about—
Trusting in others as they trust in me—
Starting again from the shadows of doubt
Gods, how I fear what I yet know must be!

Chorus 2:
Finding my center, and with it, control;
Disciplined knowledge must now be my goal.
Knowing my limits, but judging what's right—
Till nothing can hinder the arrow in flight.

FUNDAMENTALS

Lyrics: Mercedes Lackey   Music: Kristoph Klover

(Kris: *Arrow's Flight*)

Ground and center; we begin
Feel the shape inside your skin
Feel the earth and feel the air—
Ground and center; "how" and "where."

Ground and center—don't just frown,
Find the leaks and lock them down.
Baby-games you never learned
Bring you pain you never earned.

Ground and center; *do* it, child
If you'd tame that Talent wild—
Girl, you learned it in your youth—
Life's not fair, and that's the truth.

Ground and center, once again;
You're not finished—*I'll* say when.
Ground and center in your sleep
Ground and center 'till you weep.

Ground and center; that's the way—
You might get somewhere, someday.
Yes, I know I'm being cruel
And you're as stubborn as a mule!

Ground and center, feel the flow
Can you tell which way to go?
Instinct's not enough, my friend—
Make it *reflex* in the end.

Ground and center; hold it tight—
Dammit, greenie, *that's not right!*
(Every tear you shed hurts me,
But that's the way it has to be.)

Ground and center; good, at last!
Once again; grab hard, hold fast.
Half asleep or half awake—
Both of us know what's at stake.

Ground and center; now it's sure;
What you have *now* will endure.
Forgive me what I had to do—
Healing hurts—you know that's true.

Ground and center; lover, friend—
You won't break, but now you bend.
Costly lesson, high the price—
But you won't have to learn it twice!

OTHERLOVE

Lyrics: Mercedes Lackey   Music: Leslie Fish

(Talia: *Arrow's Flight*)

I need you as a friend, dear one,
I love you as a brother;
And my body lies beside you

While my heart yearns for another.
I wonder if you understand—
Beneath your careless guise
I seem to sense uneasiness
When looking in your eyes.

I need your help, my friend, and I
Had sworn to stand alone;
How foolish were the vows I made
My present plight has shown.
But don't mistake my need for love
However strong it seems—
For while I lie beside you
Someone else is in my dreams.

I wish that I could know your thoughts;
I only sense your pain—
Unease behind the smile you wear—
A haunted, sad refrain.
I would not be the cause of grief—
I've often told you so—
Yet there's a place within my heart
Where you, love, cannot go.

AFTER MIDNIGHT

Lyrics: Mercedes Lackey　　　　　　Music: Leslie Fish

(Kris: *Arrow's Flight*)

In the dead, dark hours after midnight
When the world seems to stop in its place,
You can see a little more clearly,
You can look your life in the face;
You can see the things that you have to—
Speak the words too true for the day.
In the dead, dark hours after midnight,
Little friend, will you listen—and stay?

In the time when I never knew you
I could view the world as my own—
I was God's own gift to his creatures,
And I wore an armor of stone.
I was wise and faithful and noble—
I was pompous, pious and cold.
I was cruel when I never meant it—
Far too cool to touch or to hold.

It was you who broke through my armor;
It was you who broke through the wall,
With your pain and your desperation—
How could I not answer your call?
How could I have guessed you would touch me,
And in ways I could not control?
How could I have known I would need you—
Or have guessed you'd see to my soul?

For as I taught you, so you taught me,
Taught me how to love and to care—
For your own love melted my armor,
Taught me how to feel and to dare.
When I looked tonight, I discovered
I could not again stand apart—
In the dead, dark hours after midnight,
I discovered I owe you my heart.

SUN AND SHADOW: MEETINGS

Lyrics: Mercedes Lackey   Music: Leslie Fish

(Kris: *Arrow's Flight*)

(When the "long version" of "Sun and Shadow" is sung,
this is sung as a kind of prologue)

She dances in the shadows; like a shadow is her hair.
Her eyes hold midnight captive, like a phantom, fell and
fair.

While the woodlarks sing the measures that her flying
     feet retrace
She dances in the shadows like a dream of darkling
     grace.

He sings in summer sunlight to the cloudless summer
     skies;
His head is crowned with sunlight and the heavens match
     his eyes.
All the wildwood seems to listen to the singer's gladsome
     voice
He sings in summer sunlight and all those who hear
     rejoice.

She dances in the shadows, for a doom upon her lies;
That if once the sunlight touches her the Shadowdancer
     dies.
And on his line is this curse laid—that once the day is
     sped
In sleep like death he lies until again the night has fled.

One evening in the twilight that is neither day nor
     night,
The time part bred of shadow, and partly born of light,
A trembling Shadowdancer heard the voice of love and
     doom
That sang a song of sunlight through the gathering eve-
     ning gloom.

A spell it cast upon her, and she followed in its wake
To where Sunsinger sang it, all unheeding, by her lake.
She saw the one that she must love until the day she
     died—
Bitter tears for bitter loving then Shadowdancer cried.

One evening in the twilight e'er his curse could work
     its will,
Sunsinger sang of sunlight by a lake serene and still—
When out among the shadow stepped a woman, fey and
     fair—
A woman sweet as twilight, with the shadows in her hair.

He saw her, and he loved her, and he knew his love
    was vain
For he was born of sunlight and must be the shadow's
    bane.
So e'er the curse could claim him, then, he shed one
    bitter tear
For he knew his only love must also be his only fear.

So now they meet at twilight, though they only meet to
    part.
Sad meetings, sadder partings, and the breaking of each
    heart.
Why blame them, if they pray for time or death to bring
    a cure?
For the sake of bitter loving, nonetheless they will endure.

*

SUN AND SHADOW

Lyrics: Mercedes Lackey   Music: Paul Espinoza

(Talia and Kris: *Arrow's Flight*)

"What has touched me, reaching deep
  Piercing my ensorceled sleep?
  Darkling lady, do you weep?
  Am I the cause of your grieving?
  Why do tears of balm and bane
  Bathe my heart with bitter rain?
  What is this longing? Why this pain?
  What is this spell you are weaving?"

"Sunlight Singer, Morning's peer—
  How I long for what I fear!
  Not by my will are you here
  How I wish I could free you!
  Gladly in your arms I'd lie
  But I dare not come you nigh
  For if you touch me I shall die—
  If I were wise I would flee you."

"Shadowdancer, dark and fell,
  Lady that I love too well—
  Won't you free me from this spell
  That you have cast around me?
  Star-eyed maid beyond compare,
  Mist of twilight in your hair—
  Why must you be so sweet and fair?
  How is it that you have bound me?"

"In your eyes your soul lies bare
  Hope is mingled with despair;
  Sunborn lover do I dare
  Trust my heart to your keeping?
  Sunrise means that I must flee—
  Moonrise steals your soul from me;
  Nothing behind but agony,
  Nothing before us but weeping."

"Sun and Shadow, dark and light;
  Child of day and child of night,
  Who can set our tale aright?
  Is there no future but sorrow?
  Will some power hear our plea—
  Take the curse from you and me—
  Great us death, or set us free?
  Dare we to hope for tomorrow?"

THE HEALER'S DILEMMA

Lyrics: Mercedes Lackey   Music: Bill Roper

(Devan: *Arrow's Fall*)

My child, the child of my heart, though never of my
    name,
Who shares my Gift; whose eyes, though young, are
    mine—the very same
Who shares my every thought, whose skillful hands I
    taught so well

Now hear the hardest lesson I shall ever have to tell.

Young Healer, I have taught you all I know of wounds
   and pain—
Of illnesses, and all the herbs of blessing and of bane—
Of all the usage of your Gift; all that I could impart—
And how you learned, young Healer, brought rejoicing
   to my heart.

But there is yet one lessoning I cannot give to you
For you must find your own way there—judge what is
   sound and true
This lesson is the cruelest ever Healer had to teach—
It is—what you must do when there are those you cannot
   reach.

However great your Gift there will be times when you
   will fail
There will be those you cannot help, your skill cannot
   prevail.
When you fight Death, and lose to Him, or what may yet
   be worse
You win—to find the wreck He left regards you with a
   curse.

And worst of all, and harder still, the times when it's a
   friend
Who looks to you to bring him peace and make his
   torment end—
What will you do, young Healer, when there's nothing
   you *can* do?
I can give only counsel, for the rest is up to you.

This only will I counsel you; that if you build a shell
Of armor close about you, then you close yourself in
   Hell.
And if your heart should harden, then your Gift will fade
   and die
And all that you have lived and learned will then become
   a lie.

My child, your Healing hands are guided by your Healing
  heart
And that is all the wisdom all my learning can impart.
You take this pain upon you as you challenge life
  unknown—
And there can be no answer here but one—and that's
  your own.

HERALD'S LAMENT

Lyrics: Mercedes Lackey   Music: C. J. Cherryh

(Dirk: *Arrow's Fall*)

A hand to aid along the road—
A laugh to lighten any load—
A place to bring a burdened heart
And heal the ache of sorrow's dart—
Who'd willing share in joy or tears
And help to ease the darkest fears
Or my soul like his own defend—
And all because he was my friend.

No grave could hold so free a soul.
I see him in the frisking foal—
I hear him laughing on the breeze
That stirs the very tops of trees.
He soars with falcons on the wing—
He is the song that nightbirds sing.
Death never dared him captive keep.
He lies not there. He does not sleep.

But—there is silence at my side
That haunts the place he used to ride.
And my Companion can't allay
The loss I have sustained this day.
How bleak the future now has grown
Since I must face it all alone.
My road is weary, dark and steep—
And it is for myself I weep.

FOR TALIA

Lyrics: Mercedes Lackey   Music: Larry Warner and
Kristoph Klover

(Dirk: *Arrow's Fall*)

The lady that I cherish is enamored of a fool—
A fool who lacks the wit to speak his mind,
A fool who often wears a mask indifferent and cool,
A fool who's often selfish, dense, and blind.

The lady that I cherish is enamored of a fool—
A fool too often wrapped in other cares,
Forgetting that his singlemindedness is wrong and cruel
To lock her out who gladly trouble shares.

The lady that I cherish is enamored of a fool
Who sometimes does not value what he holds
Until his loneliness confirms 'twere time his heart should
   rule
And the comfort of her love around him folds.

But though he must have hurt her without ever mean-
   ing to
Her temper never breaks and never frays,
And she forgives whatever careless thing that he may do
And loves him still despite his thoughtless ways.

She only smiles and says that there is nothing to
   forgive—
And I thank God she does so, for you see
I fear without her love and care this poor fool could not
   live—
The fool she loves and cherishes is me.

KEROWYN'S RIDE

Lyrics: Mercedes Lackey   Music: Leslie Fish

(This is a fairly common song in Valdemar, although it
originated several lands to the south.)

Kerowyn, Kerowyn, where are you going,
Dressed in men's clothing, a sword by your side,
Your face pale as death, and your eyes full of fury,
Kerowyn, Kerowyn, where do you ride?

Last night in the darkness foul raiders attacked us—
Our hall lies in ruins below—
They've stolen our treasure, and the bride of my brother
And to her side now I must go
To her aid now I must go.

Kerowyn, Kerowyn, where is your father?
Where is your brother? This fight should be theirs.
It is not seemly that maids should be warriors—
Your pride is your folly; go tend women's cares.

This is far more than a matter of honor
And more than a matter of pride—
She's only a child, all alone, all unaided
Though foolish and reckless beside,
Still now to her aid I must ride.

Grandmother, sorceress, I need a weapon—
I'm one against many—and I am afraid—
For the bastards have bought them a fell wizard's powers—
I can't hope to help her without magic aid.

Kerowyn, granddaughter, into your keeping
I now give the sword I once wore
"Need" is her name, yes, and great are her powers—
She'll serve you as many before—
Though her name be not found in men's lore.

Grandmother, grandmother, now you confuse me—

Was this a testing I got at your hand?
Whence comes this weapon of steel and of magic
And why do you put her now at my command?

Kerowyn, not for the weak or the coward
Is the path of the warrior maid.
Yes my child, you've been tested—now ride with my
    blessing
And trust in yourself and your blade.
Ride now, and go unafraid!

THREES

Lyrics: Mercedes Lackey   Music: Leslie Fish

(Again: a similar song from the same region as "Kerowyn's
Ride" that migrated northward.)

Deep into the stony hills, miles from town or hold
A troupe of guards comes riding, with a lady and her
    gold
She rides bemused among them, shrouded in her cloak of
    fur
Companioned by a maiden and a toothless, aged cur.
Three things see no end, a flower blighted ere it bloomed,
A message that miscarries and a journey that is doomed.

One among the guardsmen has a shifting, restless eye
And as they ride, he scans the hills that rise against the
    sky
He wears a sword and bracelet worth more than he can
    afford
And hidden in his baggage is a heavy, secret hoard.
Of three things be wary, of a feather on a cat
The shepherd eating mutton, and the guardsman that is
    fat.

Little does the lady care what all the guardsmen know—
That bandits ambush caravans that on these traderoads go.

In spite of tricks and clever traps and all that men can do
The brigands seem to always sense which trains are false
   or true.
Three things are most perilous—the shape that walks
   behind,
The ice that will not hold you and the spy you cannot
   find.

From ambush bandits screaming charge the packtrain
   and its prize
And all but four within the train are taken by surprise
And all but four are cut down as a woodsman fells a log
The guardsman and the lady and the maiden and the
   dog.
Three things hold a secret—lady riding in a dream,
The dog that sounds no warning, and the maid who does
   not scream.

Then off the lady pulls her cloak, in armor she is
   clad—
Her sword is out and ready, and her eyes are fierce and
   glad.
The maiden makes a gesture, and the dog's a cur no
   more—
A wolf, sword-maid and sorceress now face the bandit
   corps.
Three things never anger, or you will not live for long,
A wolf with cubs, a man with power, and a woman's
   sense of wrong.

The lady and her sister by a single trader lone
Were hired out to try to lay a trap all of their own
And no one knew their plan except the two who rode
   that day
For what you do not know you cannot ever give away!
Three things is it better, far, that only two should know—
Where treasure hides, who shares your bed, and how to
   catch your foe!

The bandits growl a challenge, and the lady only grins
The sorceress bows mockingly, and then the fight begins!

When it ends there are but four left standing from that
   horde—
The witch, the wolf, the traitor and the woman with the
   sword!
Three things never trust in; the maiden sworn as pure,
The vows a king has given, and the ambush that is "sure."

They strip the traitor naked and then whip him on his
   way
Into the barren hillsides, like the folk he used to slay—
And what of all the maidens that this filth despoiled,
   then slew?
Why, as revenge, the sorceress makes him a woman too!
Three things trust above all else—the horse on which you
   ride,
The beast that guards your sleeping, and your sister at
   your side.

(These songs can be heard on the tape *Heralds, Harpers, and Havoc* available from Off Centaur Publications, P.O. Box 424, El Cerrito CA 94530)

DAW
DAW Science-Fiction by
Hugo Award Winner
C. J. CHERRYH

The Chanur Series

THE PRIDE OF CHANUR
CHANUR'S VENTURE
THE KIF STRIKE BACK
CHANUR'S HOMECOMING

The Union-Alliance Novels

DOWNBELOW STATION
MERCHANTER'S LUCK
FORTY THOUSAND IN GEHENNA
VOYAGER IN NIGHT

The Morgaine Novels

GATE OF IVREL
WELL OF SHIUAN
FIRES OF AZEROTH

The Faded Sun Novels

THE FADED SUN: KESRITH
THE FADED SUN: SHON'JIR
THE FADED SUN: KUTATH

Other Novels

ANGEL WITH THE SWORD
BROTHERS OF EARTH
CUCKOO'S EGG
HESTIA
HUNTER OF WORLDS
SERPENT'S REACH
WAVE WITHOUT A SHORE

Anthologies

FESTIVAL MOON: MEROVINGEN NIGHTS #1
  (April 1987)
SUNFALL
VISIBLE LIGHT